I0590240

The Bonds of
STARLIGHT
AND
SHADOWS

The Bonds of
STARLIGHT
AND
SHADOWS

BY
CAMMY & ALY CRADY

Copyright © 2025 by Cameron Austin and Aly Crady. All rights reserved.

No part of this publication may be reproduced, distributed, or transmitted in any form or by any means, including photocopying, recording, or other electronic or mechanical methods, without the prior written permission of the publisher, except as permitted by U.S. copyright law.

For permission requests, contact twinninginfiction@gmail.com.

The story, all names, characters, and incidents portrayed in this production are fictitious. No identification with actual persons (living or deceased), places, buildings, and products is intended or should be inferred.

Book Cover by An-Nhien Nguyen
Editing by Bethany Dancel

ISBN: 979-8-9930528-2-3

CONTENTS

PREFACE

To the readers.

The star-chasers, the daydreamers, the ones who believe magic lives inside books.

We wrote this story for you.

For the late-night page-turners and the under-the-covers-with-a-flashlight romantics. For everyone who's ever wanted to ride a dragon, sneak through a fae-touched forest, or make a wish on a shooting star.

But before we could give it to you, a few other people helped us find the story.

To our children, Imani, Lily, and Tyler. Thank you for letting us spend countless hours hunched over our computers muttering to ourselves about character names and punctuation. You are our greatest adventures and our daily dose of *real-life magic*.

To our mother, Kim. You handed us the love of reading and the courage to go on wild adventures, even if they were sometimes in matching outfits. Your love of books, integrity, and curiosity are on every page.

To our incredible beta readers: Kristen, Amanda, Jill, Alex, Shelby, John, Ellie, and Samantha. *You legends.* You pointed out all the plot holes we tried to ignore, gave us your honest thoughts, and helped us turn this into something real.

To our editor, Bethany Dancel, and our cover artist, An-Nhien Nguyen, thank you for polishing our chaos into something beautiful.

To our partners, Alex and James. Thank you for cheering us on when we doubted ourselves, for bringing us snacks, and for listening to dramatic monologues about our characters like it was the most important thing in the world. Your belief in us carried us through.

And finally, to each other —

Growing up as twins meant sharing everything: a room, a birthday, a hundred inside jokes, and a mutual love of books.

We've always been two parts of a whole, same spark, same stubborn fire, yet beautifully, wildly different. Writing this book together made us laugh, cry, argue (just a little), and ultimately fall in love with storytelling.

So go on, step into the starlight, wander through the shadows, and may the magic stay with you long after the final page.

With all our hearts,
Cammy & Aly Crady

"Alright, my little stars," Dyaus murmured, voice rough with exhaustion as he tucked the thick woven blankets around his twin daughters. His eyes, the green of ferns after rain, gleamed with a familiar warmth as he leaned closer. "Close your eyes, and I'll tell you a tale, a tale of two fae sisters who once gazed at the night sky, just as you do."

Fadeya curled deeper into her blankets, a sleepy smile tugging at her lips. Seraphina, ever the curious one, sat up slightly, her green eyes, just like her father's, glittering like shards of emerald.

"A long time ago, there were two sisters, Aurora and Onyx, twins, just like you. They didn't have parents around to tell them bedtime stories, so they spent most nights exploring the woods near their village. They were curious, always chasing adventure."

Fadeya wiggled under the covers, tucking her toes beneath the blanket as she snuggled closer. Seraphina clutched a pillow to her chest, anticipation etched on her face.

"One evening, they found a mysterious altar hidden under leaves and vines. It was carved with pictures of stars and strange symbols. This magical place was called a Star Shrine. Aurora and Onyx were so excited to find the Star Shrine that they ran their hands over the glowing symbols embedded in the stone. Do you know what happened next?"

The girls giggled. "What happened, Daddy?" Seraphina asked eagerly, her fingers gripping the edge of the blanket.

"A burst of light!" Dyaus exclaimed, making a small explosion motion with his hands.

Fadeya gasped, drawing her knees up as if expecting magic to spark around them.

"Suddenly, the sky was ablaze, as bright as a million fireflies!" Dyaus hushed his voice as if the memory were sacred. "A shimmering spirit of starlight appeared and bonded with Aurora."

"MAGIC!" Seraphina squealed, bouncing slightly on the bed.

Dyaus chuckled, resting his hand gently on her shoulder to calm her excitement. "Yes, magic. Bonding with a magical creature is something truly rare, and only those with a pure heart and a great destiny can experience it. The creature grants its power, but in return, they must learn to understand and protect the world's magic."

He paused, drawing both girls deeper into the tale. "But magic, like the night sky, isn't all starlight. Where there are stars, there is also darkness. Neither Aurora nor Onyx had realized that lurking in the altar's shadows was a fearsome beast. A great black dragon with scales darker than night. When it emerged from the shadows, it chose Onyx, forging a bond as potent as Aurora's starlit one, but steeped in darkness."

Seraphina shivered, clutching her blanket tightly.

"At first, the sisters were thrilled with their newfound powers," Dyaus went on. "Aurora glowed like moonlight while Onyx commanded shadow and flame, but as time passed, the darkness within Onyx whispered, 'Enslave every magical creature, force them to bond with your council, then you will control all the magic in the realm.'"

"That's bad," Fadeya said, hugging her pillow tighter.

"Very bad," Dyaus agreed with a solemn nod. "The more Onyx listened to that darkness, the more she believed she had the right to control all magical creatures, even by force, if necessary. Greedy human kings and power-hungry fae flocked to her side, craving the dark bonds she offered. A war began, one that threatened both magical creatures and humans alike. The fae, magical creatures, and humans who stood on the side of celestial light tried to end the fighting. They gathered an assembly, and the leaders forged a treaty: separate the human realm from the magical one. At first, it looked like there would be peace." He paused a moment, fixing the pillow behind Fadeya's head, then continued. "But Onyx refused to accept the division. Her heart had darkened until it was cold and empty. Aurora tried to reason with her sister. 'Onyx, please, there must be another way. We can share magic without subjugating others.' But Onyx's ambition burned too fiercely."

"Why did she want so much power?" Fadeya asked, her brow furrowed in confusion. "Didn't she already have magic?"

Dyaus nodded thoughtfully. "She did, little star, but sometimes, when someone listens to the wrong voice for too long, they stop seeing what they have and only focus on what they want. The darkness inside her made her believe she didn't have enough, that she needed more, and that hunger for power can be dangerous."

Seraphina whispered, "I think she was just lonely."

Dyaus gave her a sad smile. "Maybe she was. And maybe, deep down, she thought power would make that loneliness go away."

He paused, letting the gravity of the moment settle. "Realizing the realms would be destroyed if she failed, Aurora made a desperate choice. She confronted the black dragon, begging it to break its bond with Onyx. The dragon roared in defiance. Yet Aurora's words carried conviction, sorrow for her sister, that made the beast waver."

Seraphina and Fadeya exchanged wide-eyed glances.

"In a single thunderous moment," Dyaus said, slamming his palm against the mattress to mimic the impact, "the dragon severed its bond with Onyx. Flames and shadows exploded around them as the link was shattered. Onyx screamed, and it seemed as though the darkness itself would devour her. Tears streaked Aurora's face as she cast one final, devastating spell, convinced she had no choice but to finish what the dragon had started. When the smoke finally cleared … Onyx was gone."

"That's so sad," Fadeya sniffed. Seraphina sat silent, tears pooling in her eyes.

Dyaus took a breath before continuing. "In the aftermath, Aurora founded Astral Unison University. A sanctuary where those with kind hearts could learn to forge magical bonds responsibly, never out of greed or hunger for power. She wanted to ensure that no one would suffer the same fate as Onyx."

The girls' glassy eyes widened with wonder. They'd heard rumors of the legendary university from travelers drifting through their village. Though the place lay far beyond mortal sight, both sisters clung to the hope that one day they might see it with their own eyes.

Dyaus smiled at the look of hope on their faces. He reached out, brushing a brown curl from Fadeya's forehead before taking Seraphina's hand in his. "Fate," he said, "doesn't always take us down the roads we expect. It leads us where it must, in its own time. When it does, remember this," he gave Seraphina's hand a small squeeze, "*who* you choose to be matters *more* than where you end up."

He paused, watching his daughters struggle to keep their eyes open. They'd had a long day, and the pull of sleep was growing too strong to resist. He leaned in and pressed a gentle kiss to each forehead. "Until morning, my little stars," he said, his voice calming. "Let your dreams carry you toward wonders only you can imagine."

Rising from their bedside, Dyaus stepped toward the doorway. Looking back, he could see the starlight spilling over his daughters like a protective veil. Their peaceful breaths steadied his heart, but the feeling of unease lingered in his chest.

"Starlight binds us all," he whispered, glancing at their tiny hands, "but even the brightest bonds can break under the shadow." As he closed the door, the stars above seemed to pulse faintly, their light carrying a silent reminder: *some bonds are destined to be tested, and some stories to be retold.*

"A bond with another life is like a star joining the constellation; together, we become part of something eternal, something greater than ourselves."

-Aurora

The Prophecy of the Fractured Realms
Born beneath the twilight's veil,
Twin fae sisters destined to fail.
Bound together, yet paths divide,
Light and shadow, side by side.
From their choices, the realms shall part,
A tear to break each sister's heart.
Through dragon's fire and starlight's divide,
Their bond shall waver, and love denied.
The realms each shall rend and break,
Humans & magic, two worlds they will make.
Yet, in the fracture, hope takes root,
As mortal stars tread fae's pursuit.
Human twins, flames mirrored true,
May heal the realms where sorrow grew.
Through dragon's bond and starlight's call
A test of will could bind us all.
Should they falter, shadow reigns,
Darkness binding, hope in chains.
But if the shadows are undone,
The sundered realms shall become one.
Twins of twilight, twins of man,
Fate shall rest within their hands.
To heal, to shatter, the tale unknown,
To forge anew or continue alone.

Chapter 1

DREAMS LIKE FALLING STARS

SERAPHINA

The Starlight Awakening is a sacred trial granted once yearly to those who have seen twenty-two winters. Only being able to test three times in a lifetime, it's more than a test of skill; it is a reckoning of the soul, a measure of one's worth in the eyes of the stars.

Seraphina's eyes traced the elegant, faded script etched into the pages of her book. Sitting at her desk, she sighed, the warm glow of the single candle casting long, wavering shadows across her bedroom. The light danced on the walls, reflecting dust motes in the air like tiny, sparkling stars caught in a waltz. Her dark hair fell around her face, slipping from the braid she had hastily tied that morning, now unraveling like her thoughts. The wool shawl draped around her shoulders slipped slightly as she hunched forward, and she tugged it back into place, fingers brushing the frayed edge.

The faint, lingering scent of stale coffee filled the air, a bitter reminder of the last few nights she spent trying to stay awake, searching for something to quiet the chaos inside her. She exhaled, pressing her fingers against her temples.

It's not enough, she thought, her heart aching in the stillness. *What am I even doing here?* No matter how long she studied, no matter how much she gave, it would never be enough.

Her mother's voice rose unbidden, twining with her own thoughts like a thorned vine. *You need to try harder, Seraphina. Your sister has so much drive. What do you have?*

The words settled deep in her bones, familiar and unshakable.

Fadeya, the perfect twin. The golden girl. Their mother's sunbeam, bright and unwavering, walking through life with the kind of confidence Seraphina had only ever admired from a distance. Where Fadeya stepped forward, Seraphina lingered behind. She had always been the quieter one, the watcher in the wings. A dreamer caught between thought and action, weighed down by questions that rarely had answers.

She drew a slow, sharp breath through her nose, trying to steady the ache that never quite went away.

Her eyes drifted to the framed photo on her desk.

The distance between them had become a chasm since their father's death, a loss that didn't just break Seraphina; it hollowed her out. He had been the only one who saw her, really saw her. Fadeya had always been more like their mother—brilliant, commanding, full of light, but Seraphina had belonged to her father's quieter world, where wonder lived in starlight and truth was often hidden beneath stillness. He had never minded that she lingered in thoughts longer than she should, or that she asked questions no one else had time to answer. Without him, the world felt skewed, off-axis. Each day scraped by like sandpaper on skin. His absence didn't fade. It calcified.

The photo stared back at her. His smile, still steady, felt like a cruelty she hadn't consented to.

"I just want to make you proud," she said, the words unraveling in her mouth. Her voice cracked, fragile and wrong, like a hymn sung off-key.

She exhaled through her teeth. Then, slowly—almost reverently—she reached forward and turned the photo face down.

The silence in the room was interrupted by a familiar voice. "Are you okay, Sera?"

Fadeya leaned casually against the doorframe, arms crossed, her deep brown hair cascading in perfect waves over one shoulder. The candlelight caught the delicate embroidery along the neckline of her dark yellow surcoat, its rich fabric draping effortlessly over a linen underdress.

"You've been in here all day." Her voice was quiet, but there was no mistaking the edge of concern beneath it. She stepped further into the dimly lit room, her attention pausing on the framed portrait lying face down on the desk.

"You know ... Dad would have been proud of you, Sera, no matter what happens next week."

Seraphina swallowed hard, her grip tightening around the fabric of her shawl. "It's not that simple," she said. The words came out frayed.

Fadeya huffed, shaking her head slightly as if she'd heard those words a thousand times before. She moved closer and placed a steady hand on Seraphina's shoulder.

"Maybe not, but you're not alone in this. Whether you want my help or not, I'm here." She squeezed her shoulder reassuringly before stepping back.

"I'll check on you later, okay?" Fadeya said, her voice soft but firm. "Just ... don't overdo it."

Seraphina nodded, not trusting herself to speak.

Fadeya lingered for a breath longer, then turned and left, the sound of her footsteps fading as she moved toward her room.

Seraphina's fingers hovered over the notepad, torn pages scattered like fallen hopes around her feet. A quiet sigh escaped her lips.

You're not supposed to feel this way, she thought, swallowing hard. You're supposed to be better than this.

She wasn't angry with Fadeya. Not truly. The bitterness that stirred inside her wasn't jagged—it was muted. A quiet weight pressed against her chest, born more of weariness than resentment.

With a slow, steadying breath, Seraphina picked up her pencil and forced her mind back to the task at hand. *The Starlight Awakening*. The one test that determined whether you were worthy enough to attend the university. A trial only offered once a year to college graduates, and only to those who had reached their twenty-second year.

Astral Unison University had been the center of her dreams for as long as she could remember. She closed her eyes, letting memories flood in. She and her best friend Cordelia had spent hours imagining the university, its libraries that whispered ancient secrets, its greenhouses where otherworldly plants thrived, and its laboratories where magic and science intertwined. The Starlight Awakening was her chance to break free from her mother's suffocating grip.

The hours passed unnoticed, her thoughts drowning in ink and parchment. It wasn't until the second knock at the door, lighter this time, almost hesitant, that Seraphina surfaced from her studies.

"Sera?" Fadeya voiced again, but softer. "It's almost midnight. Don't you think you should try to get some sleep?"

Seraphina stiffened, not turning around.

"I'm fine."

Fadeya sighed, stepping into the room. "Come on, Sera. You can't keep going like this."

Seraphina rubbed her face, exhaustion pressing behind her eyes. "I have too much to do."

"You always have too much to do."

Seraphina didn't respond. She stared down at the scattered papers and messy desk before her, the letters blurring together as fatigue tugged at her limbs.

Fadeya sat on the edge of the desk, nudging a crumpled piece of parchment with her fingertips. "You're going to burn yourself out before the Awakening even begins," she said, her voice calm but edged with concern. "It's not about how much you know. You don't need every answer to be worthy of the path."

Seraphina looked up, her mouth pressing into a thin line. "Everything comes so easy for you."

Fadeya flinched—just slightly—but Seraphina saw it.

Why did I say that? she thought, guilt already rising to her throat like a bitter taste. *She was only trying to help.* But it was too late. The sentence had already settled in the space between them, heavy and unfair.

"You think it's easy for me?" Fadeya's voice was tight, restrained. "You think I don't feel the pressure, too?" She let out a breath, somewhere between a sigh and a swallow of disappointment, and pushed away from the desk. "Come on," she said quietly. "Let's go."

Seraphina frowned. "What? Where?"

"Fresh air. Before you start growing roots into that chair."

She hesitated, but when Fadeya linked their arms, leading her toward the door, she didn't resist.

The night air was crisp, the scent of damp earth and night-blooming flowers curling through the darkness. The moon hung low, casting a silvery glow over the quiet forest beyond their cottage. They walked in silence for a while, their boots crunching softly against the path.

"You know," Fadeya finally said, glancing at her, "I always knew Astral Unison was your dream."

"I never told you that."

Fadeya gave her a smirk with a hint of knowing in her eyes. "You didn't have to. I found your drawings under your bed when we were kids."

Seraphina groaned, covering her face with her hands. "You weren't supposed to see those."

Fadeya laughed, the sound light and familiar. "I thought they were beautiful, and I didn't want to pressure you. Going to the university has always been my goal, too." Her expression softened. "You were always the dreamer, Sera. You see things no one else does."

Seraphina swallowed past the lump in her throat.

"Thank you," she murmured.

Fadeya just smiled and took her hand as they continued to walk. They turned toward the pond in the garden and paused to admire the moonlit water, its surface rippling gently from the breeze.

"Remember when Dad used to take us here as kids to make wishes on shooting stars?" Fadeya's eyes sparkled with the memory. "It always felt like the stars were speaking to us."

"Yeah, but my wishes were always too silly to come true," she admitted sheepishly.

"Well, maybe we should try again tonight." Fadeya looked up, eyes scanning the sky with hope. Seraphina followed her look, searching for a streak of light. Then, as if on cue, a bright flash darted across the night sky. Both girls gasped in awe and quickly closed their eyes, making their wishes, just like they did when they were little. For a moment, they both held their breath, the magic of the night lingering in the air around them. Seraphina felt something stir inside her, a moment of hope that had been buried deep for so long. *Starlight binds us all,* their father used to say—whenever they stood beneath the sky, shoulder to shoulder, dreaming of what might be. The memory wrapped around her now, steadying her. She opened her eyes and looked at Fadeya, who was still staring up at the stars, a smile on her lips.

"You know," Seraphina said quietly, "maybe my dreams aren't as silly as I thought."

"They are not silly at all," Fadeya said, nudging her shoulder against her sister's. "I think you're closer than you realize." She tilted her head back, gazing up at the stars once more. "Sometimes, they don't just grant wishes, they guide us, too."

Seraphina nodded in response. For the first time in a long while, she felt a sense of peace. Her path wasn't defined by her mother's expectations nor by her sister's achievements. It was hers to carve, one choice, one step at a time.

FADEYA

The next morning, Fadeya didn't waste any time with distractions. While Seraphina pored over her books on the other side of the house, desperate to cram in some mysterious last-minute knowledge, Fadeya had already refined her strategy. Her preparation to calm her mind was methodical, meticulous, flawless. She was ready.

This isn't about knowledge, she reminded herself. It's about presence. Control. Intention.

Sunlight poured through the tall windows of her study, revealing neat rows of floor-to-ceiling shelves and the constellation charts meticulously arranged on her desk. Not a single tome was out of place, nor a single page creased or smudged. The entire room reflected her exacting nature: each book pressed tight and unblemished on the shelves, and every star map spread out like an unfolding cosmos, edges perfectly aligned. She'd read every page and absorbed each line until it echoed in her mind.

In the heart of the room, Fadeya lowered herself onto a woven crimson rug, smoothing the fabric beneath her before adjusting the folds of her deep-blue tunic until they lay just right. The embroidered cuffs framed her slender wrists as she reached for the crystals, her fingers grazing each one with careful precision. Strands of her wavy brown hair slipped over her shoulder as she leaned in, eyes narrowed in quiet concentration. One by one, she inspected the stones, nudging them into a circle.

Fadeya straightened, biting her lip as she studied the circle one last time. Her green eyes moved over each placement, checking angles and distances out of habit rather than uncertainty. A small smile tugged at her lips, revealing the crooked tooth that set her apart from her twin. With a quiet exhale, she rested her hands on her knees, spine tall, breath steady.

Beside her, on a polished ebony stand, the replica orb gleamed, a miniature imitation of the legendary artifact that would determine her fate. The illusion of a galaxy swirled inside, stars spinning lazily around a luminous core. She studied it often, imagined what it would feel like when the real one responded to her touch when it flared to life beneath her fingertips and declared her worthy. She could already see it, feel it in her bones: the moment when she'd prove, beyond all doubt, that she belonged at Astral Unison University.

Her mother's entrance broke the hush of the room, the gentle rustle of silk the only warning before she appeared in the doorway.

Tall and graceful, she carried herself like a woman used to being obeyed. Her graying brown hair was swept into a bun, not a strand out of place, and the soft lines at the corners of her eyes spoke more of worry than age.

"How's it going, darling?" There was unyielding pride in her voice, as if Fadeya's success was already guaranteed.

Fadeya rose smoothly, standing to face her mother. "Progress is steady. The meditation has helped me focus."

Her mother's eyes shone with approval. "I expected nothing less. You've always been so composed, so … gifted." She set a hand on Fadeya's shoulder. "The orb will see it, too. You'll dazzle them."

Fadeya offered a small smile, which she hoped looked genuine. "Thank you, Mother." Something coiled tight in her chest because beneath the praise, she could hear it. The comparison, unspoken but ever-present.

Her mother returned the smile, oblivious to her conflicted thoughts. "You'll make the family proud," she said. With a last approving nod, she swept from the room, leaving an echo of perfume and lingering expectation behind.

Fadeya stared at the door long after it closed, her fingers brushing the cool surface of the replica orb. The energy within hummed faintly, a mere echo of the real thing. A reminder.

The Starlight Awakening wasn't just a test. It was a responsibility, one her mother had handed her years before she truly understood what it meant. Every lesson had been part of the preparation. Every correction, a reminder of who she was expected to become. Her mother had never yelled; a single glance was enough to convey disappointment more effectively than any lecture.

To her mother, destiny wasn't something to chase. It was certain, planned. She spoke of it like a finished road Fadeya merely had to walk, as if stumbling wasn't an option, as if failure wasn't even part of the equation.

Her grip tightened around the orb. It flared once as if sensing the conflict beneath her steady exterior. She exhaled slowly and let her hand fall away. There was no room for hesitation. Not now.

She closed her eyes again, steadying her breathing as she began another round of meditation. The orb wouldn't care about burdens. It wouldn't care about expectations, about the years of training. It would judge her for what she was in that moment, nothing more, nothing less. And that, more than anything, made her uneasy.

SERAPHINA

The library at the local college was vast and quiet. Shelves upon shelves of books stretched through the length of the room, each one a gateway to a different world of thought. Seraphina had practically lived here in the weeks leading up to the Starlight Awakening. Today, her mind was sluggish, her eyes burned from hours of poring over texts that offered more riddles than answers.

She tipped her head back, eyes shutting for a moment. The familiar hush of the library, usually a refuge, felt stifling now, each whisper, each turning page, a dull roar in her ears. *What if the orb saw through her—through all of this—as nothing more than desperation?* She clenched her fists against her lap, forcing herself to breathe, to push past the weight pressing in from all sides.

A loud thump jolted her from her thoughts.

Seraphina looked up just as her best friend Cordelia slammed a heavy book onto the table with little regard for the sacred hush of the library. A few students shot irritated glances their way, but Cordelia only grinned, utterly unbothered.

Cordelia was, in many ways, Seraphina's opposite, a vibrant force in a world that often felt muted. Tall and effortlessly regal, she moved with a confidence that demanded attention, her deep brown skin radiant in the soft light of the library. Her black braids cascaded around her face, untamed and beautiful, framing dark eyes that sparkled with mischief. Everything about her—from the way she carried herself to the way she spoke—was bold and unapologetic.

And, as always, she was impeccably dressed.

Today, she wore a coral gown that shimmered like reef fire beneath the waves, cinched at the waist with a sash of gold brocade. The long sleeves tapered to her wrists, paired with leather boots that made her every step echo like a declaration.

With a smirk, Cordelia surveyed the chaotic mess of books and papers surrounding Seraphina.

"Still at it, I see," she teased, sliding into the chair across from her. "You look like you've been swallowed whole by the library."

Seraphina groaned, stretching her aching neck. "It feels that way. These books offer more questions than answers, and I'm running out of time to make sense of them all."

Cordelia propped her chin on her hand, tapping her fingers against her cheek in mock contemplation. "Let me guess; cosmology?"

"And philosophy. And arcane theory. And geometry," Seraphina muttered, gesturing at the scattered texts. "You name it, I've tried it. At this point, I think the Starlight Awakening is just some elaborate trick designed to make us all go mad."

Cordelia snorted. "If that's the case, you're certainly leading the charge." She leaned forward conspiratorially. "You know what they say about all work and no play, right?"

"And what exactly do they say?"

"That it makes Seraphina a very dull girl," Cordelia quipped, grinning. "Come on, Sera. Just one break. Five minutes outside, let the sun hit your face, maybe even …" she gasped theatrically, "breathe fresh air."

Seraphina hesitated, fingers drumming against the edge of her notebook. "I don't know, Cordelia. There's too much left to research, and every minute counts."

Cordelia rolled her eyes, crossing her arms. "And what good will all this studying do if you collapse into a coma before the Starlight Awakening even begins?" She nudged Seraphina's arm. "One hour. That's all I'm asking. Plus, I'm starving."

Seraphina exhaled, shaking her head. "I'll take a break soon. I promise." She paused, her attention drifting back to the book in front of her. "I feel like I'm on the edge of something. Something big."

Cordelia studied her for a long moment, then sighed. "Fine, fine. Stay here and work yourself into an early grave, but listen to me, Sera." Her voice softened, losing its usual teasing lilt. "You're overthinking this. The Awakening isn't about how many facts you can cram into your brain; it's about being worthy. Trust your instincts. Stop trying to out-think the universe and start believing in yourself."

She reached out, placing a hand over Seraphina's. "And don't let Fadeya's presence at the Awakening mess with your head. She's got her path, and you have yours. You're not here to compete. You're here to show the world who *you* are. Trust me." She smirked, squeezing Seraphina's hand. "The world isn't ready for you."

Seraphina met Cordelia's gaze, something in her chest loosening at her friend's unwavering confidence. *She always knew the right things to say.*

"Plus, you're not the only one facing this," Cordelia continued. "I've got my own Awakening to prepare for. We're in this together, okay?"

Seraphina huffed a quiet laugh. "Thanks, Cor. You're the best."

Cordelia grinned. "I *am* pretty spectacular."

Seraphina rolled her eyes as she pushed back from the desk. "Alright. Let's get coffee, but if I fail because of this, I'm blaming you."

Cordelia gasped. "How dare you! *I* am your savior, dragging you from the brink of self-destruction!" She tossed her braids dramatically. "And *you're welcome.*"

Laughing, Seraphina followed Cordelia out of the library and into the cool evening air. The city streets were dusted with snow, and the cold nipped playfully at her cheeks.

"It feels like the world slows down when it snows," she said, spinning in place with her arms outstretched like a child.

Cordelia tucked her hands into the pockets of her coat, her voice softer than usual. "It does. Like it's holding its breath."

They walked in comfortable silence, their boots crunching over the fresh snow as they followed the winding path behind the library.

"Do you remember how many made it through the Awakening last year?" Cordelia asked.

Seraphina slowed. "From our district?"

Cordelia nodded.

"Four," Seraphina said, glancing over before looking away. "Out of nearly two hundred."

Cordelia let out a low whistle, her breath puffing into the air. "Four. That's brutal."

Seraphina shrugged. "Chefridge had twelve."

Cordelia rolled her eyes. "Of course they did. The orb probably lights up as soon as it smells expensive cologne and generational wealth."

Seraphina laughed, catching a snowflake in her hand and watching it melt. "Most people there are struggling too, you know. I visited once a few years ago and was shocked at how normal everything felt. Kind of boring, honestly."

They crossed the street carefully, stepping over a slush-covered curb. A small café on the corner glowed invitingly. Cordelia nudged Seraphina with her elbow. "Come on. If I'm going to freeze to death, I'd rather do it with caffeine in my system."

The warmth of the café was a welcome relief, light spilling through the windows as they stepped inside and stamped the snow from their boots. The scent of roasted coffee beans and fresh pastries wrapped around them. They ordered their drinks, Seraphina opting for a cappuccino while Cordelia chose black coffee *and* a slice of chocolate cake.

Seraphina raised a brow. "Cake? Before dinner?"

Cordelia gave her an incredulous look. "Excuse me, cake is appropriate at all hours."

As they settled into a booth near the window, watching the snow drift outside, Cordelia gave her a reassuring smile, though a glimmer of anticipation danced in her eyes. "We've come this far, haven't we? Tomorrow's the Starlight Awakening. The moment we have dreamed of all these years."

"Tomorrow," Seraphina repeated, a mixture of nerves and excitement swirling inside her. *One way or another, everything changes tomorrow.*

Chapter 2

THE STARLIGHT AWAKENING

SERAPHINA

The night of the Starlight Awakening had finally arrived. The air in the small library meeting hall hummed with anticipation, thick with the scent of candle wax.

Despite the gentle lights and hushed chatter, Seraphina couldn't shake the tightness in her chest. She remembered the nights she and Fadeya used to sneak out of bed when they were younger, poring over the same worn, faded books about Astral Unison University. Even then, Fadeya was always the composed one, devouring books while Seraphina watched the night sky and dreamed about the day they'd both stand exactly where they were now, on the brink of something new, something great.

Tonight, her heart thundered with the realization that the dreams of two little girls might not unfold the way they'd imagined.

Near the back of the room, Seraphina and Fadeya sat side by side, their identical features marked by the same high cheekbones, brown hair, and green eyes. On the surface, they were the same, but they could not have felt more different.

Fadeya was poised, her silver gown cascading over her frame in smooth, shimmering folds, each breath setting the glittering fabric gently in motion. Her brown hair was coiled into a flawless twist, not a single strand out of place. She inspected the stage area with a glance, focused and in control.

Seraphina shifted uncomfortably, the weight of her sapphire dress pressing against her like a tide she couldn't hold back. A few strands of hair had slipped from their pins, falling around her face in quiet defiance. Her fingers drifted to the embroidery at her waist, tracing the pattern with practiced familiarity, habit, distraction, anything to keep her grounded. *Just breathe,* she told herself, glancing around the room for the third time in less than a minute.

Her gaze caught on a tall, broad-shouldered man loitering near the library wall. He moved to lean against it—missed by a fraction—and stumbled slightly. Just enough to throw him off-balance, but instead of bristling or pretending it hadn't happened, he righted himself with a low, unbothered chuckle.

Aleron.

Seraphina's hand flew to her cheek, fingers grazing heated skin. *Stars, he looked good.* Better than she remembered.

The candlelight brushed against the brown of his skin, highlighting the sharp cut of his jaw, the easy curve of his mouth. And those eyes, golden-brown, lit with mischief and a depth that had haunted more than a few of her daydreams.

A year. One full cycle of seasons since she'd last seen him. And yet her heart betrayed her the same way it always had, fluttering, tripping over itself at the sound of his laugh, at the way he filled a room with that impossible mix of warmth and chaos.

Fadeya's grin was positively wicked, like she could read every thought blazing behind Seraphina's carefully composed face. "Look who finally decided to stop gallivanting across the continent."

Aleron pushed off the wall and approached them, his gaze locking onto hers. "Seraphina." He squeezed into the row and took a seat next to her. "It's been a while."

She nodded, trying, failing, to ignore the heat unfurling in her chest. "Over a year. I almost didn't recognize you without a stack of books and a half-empty coffee cup."

"I've upgraded to tea. More mysterious. Less predictable."

"Well, hello to you too, old friend," Fadeya cut in, reaching over her sister to give Aleron a playful shove. "Glad you made it on time."

Aleron smirked, not missing a beat. "You know me, Dey, always showing up just in time to steal the spotlight."

Fadeya sighed. "You're lucky you're funny."

"And devastatingly handsome," he added, winking at Seraphina.

Fadeya leaned closer, her lips curving in amusement as she whispered in Seraphina's ear. "There's a five-minute limit on Aleron-related swooning. You've got three left."

Aleron raised an eyebrow and tucked his hands casually behind his back. "Should I be concerned that you're whispering and then looking at me like that?" he asked.

Fadeya waved him off. "Not everything is about you."

Seraphina tried to return his smile, but it faltered before it reached her eyes.

Aleron's expression shifted, just slightly. The teasing fell from his features as his posture eased, and his voice quieted. "Hey," he said, "You all right?"

Seraphina glanced up at him, then quickly looked away, her fingers fidgeting with the edge of her sleeve. "Just ... nervous," she admitted, her voice nearly lost beneath the quiet hum of conversation around them.

He exhaled, his gaze distant. "Funny how we spend years shaping ourselves for a moment that lasts only seconds. As if one flicker of light can measure everything we are, everything we could be."

Seraphina snorted. "Great. No pressure or anything."

He studied her for a moment, then gently reached out, stilling her hand before she could pick at her dress again. "Relax," he said with a small smile. "It's just a glowing orb, right?"

Seraphina let out a dry laugh, one corner of her mouth twitching upward. She met his eyes. "Guess we'll see how *you* do under the orb's judgment."

"I'm sure you'll light up the room," he said teasingly. "But if you don't, I'll buy you ice cream to make up for it."

She tilted her head. "Ice cream? That's your grand gesture?"

He shrugged and shifted forward, his knee knocking into the back of the chair in front of him with a dull thud. He winced, rubbing his leg with an exaggerated scowl. "I could throw in a pastry if you're feeling dramatic,"

Beside them, Fadeya let out a long-suffering sigh. "Some things never change. You should've seen him during finals week. He practically bribed half our study group with sweets just to keep us motivated."

He grinned, entirely unrepentant. "And it worked, didn't it? You passed, top of the class."

Fadeya crossed her arms. "I would've passed anyway."

"Sure," Aleron said. "But I maintain that pastries helped."

From across the room, Cordelia's voice rang out. "Did someone say pastries?"

Seraphina turned just in time to see her best friend stride toward them, her hair styled in dozens of tiny braids threaded with gold beads. They swung against her shoulders, wild and glittering. She wore a deep crimson surcoat cinched at the waist with a gold belt, the rich velvet of her gown pooling elegantly around her boots.

"I'm definitely in on that deal," Cordelia declared, sitting in the chair directly behind her and leaning over her shoulder to give her a squeeze. "Whether the orb glows or not, I still expect dessert."

Before Seraphina could respond, a hush fell over the room.

Professor Shay moved to the front of the room and rang a small bell to get everyone's attention. The murmurs died down at once. They were draped in layered robes etched with fading sigils, with a constellation-shaped pin at their collar. Their dark eyes scanned the room, thoughtful and discerning, as if measuring not only posture and attentiveness, but also purpose. Their hair, peppered with silver, curled slightly at the temples, and their expression, though solemn, held a thread of compassion. A hush fell over the room as the professor began to speak.

"Welcome, everyone, to the Starlight Awakening." Their gaze swept over the faces before them. "Tonight, you will take part in a tradition that has shaped this community for over three hundred years. This ceremony is more than just a reflection of your potential, it is the key that determines whether you are worthy to learn the magic that Astral Unison University has to offer."

They gestured toward the pedestal at the center of the room, where the orb rested, glowing faintly. "Magic is not something earned through effort alone. It is not a reward for ambition, nor a tool to be mastered by will. It is a gift, one that flows from the bond between a soul and the creature willing to share its power."

They stepped forward, the rustle of their robes the only sound as they approached the orb, pausing just short of the pedestal.

"This orb is not a relic for show. It was crafted long ago, when the stars still guided the fates of men and beasts alike. Their light still lingers within it. When you place your hand upon it, the stars will search your heart, not for strength or skill, but for truth. They seek the spark of harmony, the readiness to be chosen."

The professor's expression was reassuring. "If the orb responds to you, it means the celestial spirits have acknowledged your soul's connection to magic, granting you the opportunity to learn and potentially form a bond at Astral Unison University. If it does not respond, it does not mean you lack purpose or value; it simply means that your destiny lies elsewhere, on a path the stars have yet to reveal. Each of you has a role to play in the balance of this world, whether it is within this realm or beyond."

Seraphina's stomach twisted as she listened, her fingers tightening against the folds of her dress again. Beside her, Fadeya sat perfectly still, her expression unreadable.

Professor Shay continued. "No matter the outcome, know that stepping forward takes courage. Tonight, you take your first step into something greater."

"Come on," Seraphina whispered. "The waiting is unbearable. I feel like my heart is trying to claw its way out of my ribs."

"You'll be fine," Cordelia said under her breath, rubbing tiny circles on her back.

Professor Shay scanned the clipboard in their hands. "Let's begin. First up, Alarim Hillston."

Alarim shuffled forward, each step stiff with nerves. The room had fallen quiet as he placed his trembling hands on the orb. The swirling light within remained still, mute and unyielding. He stepped back, jaw tight, face pale.

"Jacob Albright," Professor Shay called next, their voice carrying through the hushed chamber as they scanned the sea of students.

A man Seraphina vaguely recognized from her college physics class stood slowly, his foot tapping a quiet, restless rhythm against the floor before he moved. As he approached the pedestal, he rolled his shoulders once, as if trying to shake off the tension clinging to him. Then, with a steadying breath, he placed his hand on the orb.

Still, nothing. Not even a glimmer of light.

One by one, each person called to the pedestal pressed their hands to the orb. And one by one, they stepped away, their shoulders sagging, their faces drawn. Some looked dazed, blinking against the weight of disappointment.

Then Professor Shay called out, "Liora Vale."

A murmur swept through the crowd. Liora, top of their class, sharp-minded, confident, and already whispered about as a prodigy, rose gracefully from her seat and strode toward the pedestal.

Liora placed her hand on the orb.

Nothing.

After a long moment, she stepped back, her face unreadable, but her uneven breaths gave her away. She returned to her seat without meeting anyone's eyes.

A bead of sweat slid down Seraphina's spine. *If Liora couldn't make it glow ...*

"Seraphina Elaris."

Her name struck like a bolt of lightning, echoing through the chamber. For a moment, she forgot to breathe. She swallowed hard, forcing her feet to move. Step by step, she approached the pedestal, the orb waiting at its center, glowing faintly in the dim light. It looked no different than it had for the others—silent, unreadable. Watching.

Her ears rang as she reached out, her fingertips hovering just above the cool, glass-like surface. *What if nothing happened? What if it rejected her like the others?*

She pressed her hands to the orb. For a single, agonizing heartbeat, nothing.

Then, light.

Warmth bloomed beneath her fingers, a soft golden glow unfurling like the first light of dawn. It pulsed once, then again, spreading outward in slow, steady waves. Gasps rippled through the room, a murmur of awe and disbelief.

A sharp inhale shuddered through her as the light wrapped around her tingling fingers, seeping into her skin, electric and alive. It surged through her, racing along her veins, filling every inch of her being, as though it had been waiting for her all this time.

She took a shaky step back, heart pounding so loudly she could barely hear.

"A lovely reflection of your potential," Professor Shay remarked, their eyes filled with quiet approval.

She barely heard the crowd cheering as she returned to her seat. Cordelia reached over and squeezed her hand. "Told you," she whispered. "Your spark's too bright to hide."

Seraphina exhaled shakily, allowing the warmth still buzzing in her fingertips to anchor her. She felt as if a gust of wind had ripped through her chest, mixing relief with elation. She glanced toward Fadeya, who didn't say a word but gave her a single nod.

Aleron turned slightly in his seat, resting his arm across the back of her chair. "I'd still like to take you for ice cream," he said, his voice low and genuine.

Seraphina couldn't help the smile that tugged at her lips.

Fadeya sat motionless, the fabric of her dress pressed smooth beneath her palms. Her breath came slow and even. A practiced calm.

"Fadeya Elaris."

Her name reverberated through the library like a stone dropped in water. Every ripple of conversation faded. The orb, placed on the pedestal at the front of the room, waited, mute, indifferent.

She rose and stepped forward, each footfall measured, deliberate, like she was tracing a line only she could see.

Fadeya inhaled deeply, then stretched out her fingers, pressing them against the smooth surface. Cool glass met warm skin.

And nothing happened.

Her fingers pressed firmer, as if will alone could awaken it, but the orb remained still, silent and cold, as if she were not there at all.

The shift in the room was small, but she felt it. The air had changed. The curiosity that had stirred moments ago was thinning.

Why isn't it responding?

Her jaw tightened. She held her stance, face stoic, posture poised, but her fingers twitched, barely. A betraying flicker.

And still, the orb gave her nothing. Disappointment twisted into quiet irritation, and though she kept her composure, there was no mistaking the glint of frustration in her eyes as she walked back to her place.

"Thank you, Fadeya," Professor Shay said, their tone carrying no judgment.

She inclined her head, then sat slowly.

Aleron leaned in, his tone soft. "Hey, don't let it get to you. You're still one of the smartest people I know, glow or no glow."

Fadeya forced a smile. "Thanks, Aleron," she said, her voice quieter than she meant it to be. "I just didn't expect *nothing*."

Not even a flicker. No hum, no shimmer—just silence. Like it hadn't seen me at all. Like I wasn't even there.

He lifted a brow, offering that easy grin. "Maybe it's intimidated by you. I would be."

She forced a laugh, thin and weightless. It vanished before it reached her eyes.

Then Seraphina shifted beside her, sliding closer without a word. Fadeya felt the warmth of her sister's hand slip into hers. She didn't look up. Didn't speak.

More names. One by one, they stepped forward, pressing their hands to the orb, only to step back moments later, their faces worn, their shoulders stiff with the weight of rejection. Fadeya sat with her hands clasped tightly in her lap, fingers twined so tightly her knuckles ached. She kept her expression calm and composed, but inside, the tension coiled tighter with every name called.

"Cordelia Hallowmere."

The name rang out, bringing Fadeya back to the present.

Cordelia strode confidently to the pedestal, her posture upright and her steps purposeful, a determined glint in her dark brown eyes. Her hand hovered over the orb for a heartbeat, then two.

And then she touched it.

Light erupted from beneath her fingers, *silver*, blinding, radiant, alive. It flared through the chamber like lightning, bouncing off shelves and walls, casting long, distorted shadows across astonished faces.

A collective gasp burst from the crowd.

Fadeya squinted against the glow, shielding her eyes with a hand as the energy surged, *not fading*, but building, as if the orb were pouring itself into Cordelia.

The room was silent, reverent. Awed. Even Professor Shay's lips parted, eyes wide. Then the crowd erupted.

"That's my girl," Seraphina whispered, clapping for her friend.

As Cordelia's dazzling light flooded the room, Fadeya's grip on her chair tightened. She hated the bitterness creeping into her thoughts, but she couldn't stop it.

What had she done wrong?

Her mother's disappointment was on her mind, her voice echoing in the back of her thoughts. She glanced sideways at Seraphina, whose attention was now on Cordelia's triumph, and for a brief moment, Fadeya felt utterly alone. She wished the orb had given her a chance, just one spark, something to reassure her that she wasn't invisible. That she wasn't a failure.

Cordelia returned with a triumphant grin and leaned over to whisper to Seraphina, "Guess we're both shining stars, huh?"

"Always," Seraphina whispered back, giving her a quick hug.

A flush crept up the back of Fadeya's neck, hot and sharp. Not anger. Not envy.

Shame.

"Emeric Vexley."

The name tore through the room like a slow-moving storm, drawing all attention toward him. Fadeya swallowed hard, turning her attention back to the front of the room as a man strode forward. He didn't just move, he prowled. A predator entering a space he already owned. His white-blond hair gleamed in the candlelight, every perfectly placed strand like spun silver, but it was his eyes, piercing gray, that made the air feel thinner. They swept across the crowd with the ease of someone who already knew how this night would end. As he approached the orb, an unnatural stillness crept into the room, wrapping itself around the space like an invisible shroud.

The air felt dense, almost suffocating, charged with tension that prickled against her skin. When his fingers finally brushed the surface, the orb ignited with energy, its reaction instantaneous and overwhelming. A piercing, cold blue light exploded outward, so intense that Fadeya had to remind herself to breathe. The light lingered in the air like frost clinging to a windowpane, its icy presence pressing against them, leaving the room suspended in a moment of frozen awe.

"Seriously?" Fadeya muttered, her voice dripping with disdain as she watched Emeric's theatrics.

Seraphina glanced over at her sister, brow raised. "What's his deal?" she asked quietly, watching Emeric bask in the attention, his smug grin widening.

Cordelia, who had been silently observing, leaned in with a shrug. "Typical Emeric," she replied. "He was in a couple of my college classes last year. He was always playing the part of the mysterious, untouchable guy. He thrives on making everyone uneasy, some sort of game for him, I think. Just wait, though. That kind of arrogance won't get him very far at Astral Unison."

Seraphina raised an eyebrow. "Is he always so ... self-important?"

Cordelia nodded. "He's living in his brother Rian's shadow. He was famous around town for getting into Astral Unison University a few years back. Everyone expects Emeric to follow in his footsteps, but I don't think he's doing it for the right reasons. He doesn't care about the awakening. It's all about proving something ... to himself, maybe."

As Emeric walked past Fadeya on his way back to his seat, he cast her a sidelong glance, lips curling into a smirk.

"I suppose *some* of us were just born to shine brighter," he said, his voice laced with condescension.

His gaze lingered a moment too long, sizing her up like she was nothing more than another obstacle in his way. Fadeya's stomach tightened with irritation, but she refused to give him the satisfaction of a reaction. She kept her head fixed straight ahead, feeling a strange, unwelcome surge of distaste for the young man.

An hour slipped by, marked only by subtle movements as names were called one by one. The orb remained stubbornly dim, refusing to light up. Then came the final name.

"Aleron Falcrest." All eyes turned to him, the last hope for the night.

Aleron stepped toward the pedestal, and in true Aleron fashion, his boot caught the edge of a rug. He lurched forward, barely managing to right himself before disaster struck. A hushed chuckle rippled through the crowd. Undeterred, he flashed a grin back at them before rolling his shoulders and walking up the rest of the way to the stage. He shook Professor Shay's hand, then reached for the orb. The moment his fingers met its surface, a faint hum resonated, so soft it was almost missed before the orb began to stir.

A golden light unfurled from the orb's core, spreading outward like sunlight at dawn. It wrapped around Aleron in an embrace, not blinding or overpowering, but quietly powerful. The light filled the room with a profound sense of peace, trust, and something deeper that stirred every soul present. As the glow reached the crowd, they rose to their feet, erupting into cheers.

Every eye was on Aleron, every eye except Fadeya's. She was watching Seraphina. Her sister stood frozen, her breath caught in her throat, eyes wide with something that looked like wonder. Or longing.

They're all moving forward. Together. Without me.

As Aleron settled back into his seat, Seraphina glanced at him again. Cordelia whispered from behind them, "You're staring."

Seraphina quickly turned her gaze away, flushing slightly. "No, I wasn't."

Fadeya didn't miss the way her sister's fingers curled slightly, like she was trying to ground herself.

Professor Shay stood before the crowd. The room, still echoing with the energy of the evening, quieted once more as all eyes turned toward them.

"Students," they began, looking over the group with an air of gravitas, "you have all shown your potential, your dedication, and your worth. However, only those whom the orb has recognized as truly ready for the path ahead will remain here for the next steps. To those of you chosen, congratulations." They paused, letting the room take it in.

Fadeya, who had been forlorn since the orb's reaction, was visibly tense. She noticed her sister's stare and whispered, barely audible, "I didn't even get a soft glow, Sera."

Seraphina responded, voice low, "It's not the end. You know that. You can try again."

Fadeya shook her head, her voice trembling with doubt. "You don't get it. Mother … She always believed in me. She always said I'd make it. What will she think? I failed her. I failed myself."

Seraphina placed a hand on her arm. "You haven't failed anyone. You are so much more than what the orb shows. Your worth doesn't depend on it."

Fadeya's attention slid from Seraphina to the pedestal, that dull orb still haunting her. She'd done everything right. Everything. Yet this was her reality. She could almost hear her mother's voice echoing through her thoughts. The sense of betrayal, of emptiness, unraveling the confidence she'd once worn so comfortably.

Her face flushed, frustration turning into quiet anger. She looked away, trying to hide the tears threatening to well up in her eyes. "It's not about that. It's about what comes next. I was supposed to make it."

Seraphina opened her mouth to respond, but the professor's voice cut through the air once again.

"To those who have been chosen, stay behind. I will provide you with all the necessary information. The rest of you may leave and continue on your paths, but know that your journey is far from over. The trials of this world are only just beginning."

Fadeya swallowed hard, her mother's voice ringing in her mind: *You're destined for greatness, darling.*

Her hand gripped the edge of her seat, fingers digging into the wood as if she could anchor herself against the rising tide inside her.

Expectations. Pressure. All of it pressed against her chest like a stone. Without a word to her sister, Fadeya rose.

She caught it—the concern in Aleron's eyes, the sympathy shining in Seraphina's, but she didn't stop. Didn't flinch. She moved forward toward the exit, each step wrapped in quiet resolve, a wall of determination shielding the rawness beneath.

Chapter 3

A FUTURE NOT YET WRITTEN

SERAPHINA

The carriage ride home was silent. The city lights blurred past the frost-kissed windows, the rhythm of the horses' hooves a steady rhythm against the tension between them. Fadeya sat rigid, her arms crossed, staring out into the darkness as if willing herself to disappear into it.

Seraphina, hands clenched in her lap, stole glances at her sister, unsure of whether to speak or let the silence devour them both. Her mind spiraled with thoughts of the father they'd lost, a man who once filled this same carriage with laughter, who believed in both Seraphina's and Fadeya's potential with unwavering faith. She remembered how his gentle voice could soothe even Fadeya's worst moods, turning stubborn silence into reluctant laughter. Now, that seat across from them felt emptier than ever, a void that made every second of quiet ache with unspoken grief.

By the time they reached home, the disdain that lay ahead settled fully upon them.

Their mother was waiting.

Maris stood in the grand foyer, draped in red silk, her dark curls swept into a regal updo. The firelight flickered against the sharp angles of her face, making her look like something carved from marble—cold, unyielding. She barely spared a glance at Seraphina. Her gaze went straight to Fadeya.

"Well?" she asked, the single word slicing through the air like a blade.

Fadeya didn't answer. She didn't have to. The silence spoke for her. Seraphina watched as their mother's expression shifted, so subtle, yet devastating. The ever-present pride in her eyes dulled, replaced by something unfamiliar. *Disappointment.* For the first time in her life, Fadeya was the one who had failed.

Maris exhaled slowly. "I don't understand," she said at last, her voice devoid of affection. "You've been preparing for this for years."

Fadeya lifted her chin, but her posture was too stiff, too controlled. "I know."

A beat of silence.

Then, Maris turned to Seraphina, and the pressure of her scrutiny settled upon her like a cloak. *Here it comes,* Seraphina thought, steadying her breath.

"And you?"

Seraphina forced herself to stand taller to meet her mother's attention head-on. "The orb glowed for me."

Something unreadable passed over Maris's face. Approval, perhaps, but there was something else beneath it. *Doubt.*

"Are you strong enough for what lies ahead?" her mother asked, her voice sharp as if to carve away any illusions Seraphina might have held. "You've always been the dreamer, Seraphina. Always getting lost in your stories, in your thoughts. This will not be a game. You will be tested, torn down, broken."

Seraphina swallowed hard. "Yes."

Maris studied her for a long moment. Then, without another word, she turned and strode out of the room, leaving behind an emptiness colder than the night outside. The moment she was gone, Fadeya let out a breath and stormed toward the stairs.

"Fadeya, wait!" Seraphina called, quickening her steps to catch up.

The heavy door groaned as it swung open, nearly slamming against the frame. Seraphina caught it just in time and stepped inside after her sister, heart pounding.

"You don't have to do this alone," Seraphina said quietly.

Fadeya scoffed, unfastening the delicate silver pins from her hair one by one, lining them up in a neat row, each perfectly spaced. "I didn't make it, Seraphina. It's over."

"No, it's not," she insisted, stepping closer. "You can try again next year."

Fadeya's laugh was sharp. "And what? Spend an entire year waiting while you live our dream?"

Seraphina stiffened, standing a little taller than she used to, fists clenching at her sides. "That's not fair."

"Isn't it?" She whirled to face her sister, eyes burning viciously. The candlelight cast jagged shadows across her face, the flickering glow barely masking the storm brewing beneath.

Seraphina held her ground, though every instinct screamed at her to step back. "I know this hurts," she said, quieter now. "But I will help you." She reached out, fingers trembling, but Fadeya jerked away.

Her throat tightened. "I'll write to you every week," she pressed on. "I'll tell you everything I learn. Every lesson, every challenge, every strategy. You'll know exactly what to prepare for so that when the next Starlight Awakening comes, you'll be ready."

Fadeya's breath hitched. Just barely, but Seraphina caught it.

She took a step closer. Slowly, cautiously, as if approaching a wounded animal. "Please, Fadeya," she murmured, reaching for her hand again. "Don't shut me out. You're my sister, and I will do everything I can to make sure you get there."

Fedaya's lips parted, something unspoken, trembling on the edge. Then she stepped back, deeper into the shifting candlelight. "Go to bed, Seraphina."

Seraphina didn't move. "Fadeya, "

"I said *go*." The words cracked like thunder.

Seraphina lingered for only a second before she sighed and backed toward the door. "Goodnight." She closed the door softly behind her and retreated to her bedroom.

She sat on the edge of her bed, gazing out the window, the stars above twinkling like scattered diamonds. Somewhere out there, her future was waiting. The university. The magic. The unknown.

Excitement curled in her chest, even as guilt gnawed at the edges.

Am I strong enough to make it? The question haunted her. She had to be. As she traced constellations with her eyes, a quiet determination settled in her bones.

FADEYA

Fadeya stood at her window, the cold glass pressing against her fingertips as she stared past the stars. They were too bright tonight. Too distant. Too cruel. She squeezed her eyes shut, pressing a hand to her temple, but the memories broke through anyway— her father's voice, low and steady, filled with certainty.

He had believed in them, in her. And she had failed him. The stars did not care. They glowed above, sharp as shattered glass, whispering of futures that would never be hers. Once, she had looked up and seen endless possibilities. Now, all she saw was everything she had lost. Fadeya exhaled sharply and turned away. She didn't spare the stars another glance. Let them shine for someone else. Stepping back into the shadows, she let the darkness take her.

SERAPHINA

The next morning, Seraphina sat cross-legged on Cordelia's bed, watching in amusement as her best friend riffled through her wardrobe like a woman on the verge of catastrophe. Silk dresses, embroidered jackets, high-collared tunics, each piece was considered, rejected, and tossed onto the ever-growing pile beside Seraphina.

"I swear to the stars," Cordelia muttered, flinging a deep green dress onto the heap, "packing should not be this stressful. What's the point of owning so many beautiful things if I can't bring *all* of them?"

Seraphina smirked, propping her chin on her hand. "I don't know, Cor. Maybe because you have a *problem*?"

Cordelia whirled on her, braids bouncing. "Excuse me, but fashion is an *art* form, and I refuse to look anything less than stunning when I step foot on that ship. First impressions matter, Sera."

Seraphina rolled her eyes. "Right. Because clearly, the professors will determine our worth by the elegance of our wardrobe."

"Not just the professors," Cordelia said, waggling her eyebrows. "There will be beautiful fae at the university, too, and if I have to suffer through months of training and magical classes, I should at *least* get some entertainment out of it."

Seraphina snorted. "Priorities."

"Always." Cordelia huffed, then dramatically collapsed onto the pile of discarded clothes. "Ugh. I can't decide. What if I bring too much? What if I bring too little? What if—"

"Cordelia," Seraphina interrupted, "two days. You have two days to figure this out. Maybe focus less on your wardrobe and more on going to the university?"

Cordelia groaned into a velvet shawl. "Boring. Besides, I have you for that. You'll make sure I learn what I need to."

Seraphina's thoughts drifted back to her sister. She hadn't spoken to Fadeya at breakfast. Not for lack of trying, but her sister had barely looked at her.

We used to share everything. Now I can't even get her to look me in the eye. Everything had changed, and Seraphina had no idea how to fix it.

"Alright, what's wrong?" Cordelia's voice cut through her thoughts.

Seraphina blinked. "What?"

Cordelia sat up, crossing her arms. "You've been staring at the floor like it's about to reveal the secrets of the universe. What's going on?"

Seraphina hesitated. "It's Fadeya."

"Is she still not talking to you?"

"She's *talking*," Seraphina admitted. "But it's … *off*. I don't know how to reach her."

Cordelia made a sound between a groan and a sigh. "Twin angst. My favorite genre."

"I'm serious." Seraphina turned her head. "It's like there's a wall between us, and I don't know how to tear it down."

"She's hurting," Cordelia said simply. "And unfortunately for you, you're the easiest target. Classic emotional projection. Honestly, I'd be more concerned if she weren't acting weird."

Seraphina let out a humorless laugh. "Great. So her cold shoulder is actually healthy emotional processing. That makes me feel *so* much better."

Cordelia flopped dramatically onto her back. "Look, Sera. You got in. She didn't. That's not something even the best sisters get over overnight."

Seraphina stared out the window above Cordelia's bed, her voice quiet. "She deserved it just as much as I did."

"I know," Cordelia said softly. She set down the half-folded dress in her lap and moved to sit beside her. "And so does she. That's what makes it so damn hard."

A beat passed before Cordelia spoke again, more lightly this time. "You know, twins are ridiculously rare. I read in one of Professor Elandra's books that they're considered celestial omens."

Seraphina frowned slightly. "I guess I've never actually met another pair of twins."

She leaned back against the bedpost, eyes fluttering shut. "Two days. That's all I have left before we leave."

"Then use them," Cordelia said, nudging her elbow against Seraphina's. "Be obnoxious. Be loud. Be the annoying twin who refuses to stop knocking until the door opens again."

Seraphina opened her eyes and let out a small laugh. "You're a surprisingly good listener, you know."

Cordelia gave her a wink. "And I don't even charge." Then, after a pause, her tone shifted. "You were born together. That means your story's not meant to end apart."

Seraphina nodded, but the knot in her chest didn't loosen. *Two days.* That was all the time she had left to fix what was broken.

FADEYA

The book in Fadeya's hands was interesting. At least, it *should* have been. She had chosen her favorite spot in the park: a secluded bench beneath a sprawling willow, away from the bustling streets and prying eyes. It was peaceful, a quiet sanctuary from the disappointment hanging in the air since the Starlight Awakening. And yet, she had read the same sentence five times.

She sighed, snapping the book shut. The disappointment in her mother's eyes. The way Seraphina looked at her like she wanted to fix something that couldn't be fixed. Fadeya scowled and shoved the book into her bag. Lost in thought, she stood and turned, only to collide with something solid. *Someone solid.*

A firm grip caught her wrist before she could stumble, steadying her. Fadeya's head snapped up, and she was met with cool, piercing gray eyes. Emeric. *Of course, it was Emeric.*

"Well, hello," he mused, tilting his head. "Which twin are you? The one who got in, or the one who failed?"

Fadeya's fingers curled into fists at her sides, heat flashing through her veins. She forced herself to take a step back. "Get out of my way, Emeric."

He didn't move. Instead, he arched a brow. "Touchy subject?"

Her jaw locked. She turned on her heel, ready to walk away.

"Well, I guess that answers that question," he called after her. "Interesting."

Something inside her snapped. Fadeya whirled. "You want to know what's interesting?" she hissed, stepping right into his space, close enough to see the surprise in his eyes. "I spent years preparing for this. Years doing everything right, and it didn't matter. I still wasn't enough."

Emeric blinked, clearly not expecting the outburst.

She let out a bitter laugh. "So, congratulations, Emeric. You get to go to the university with all your smug, over-privileged brilliance, and I get to sit here and be reminded every damn day that I failed." She braced herself for a smirk. For some cruel, razor-edged remark, but his expression didn't shift into mockery. Instead, something flashed across his face, something almost ... human.

Then, he exhaled and said, voice flat, "Well, that's just pathetic."

Fadeya recoiled. "Excuse me?"

Emeric shrugged. "You think you're the first person to fail? The first person to fall short? Get over it."

She gaped at him. "Wow. Truly inspiring words."

"Hey, I don't do soft." He leaned against the tree, hands tucked into his pockets, but there was something playful in the tilt of his mouth now.

She narrowed her eyes. "You are *trouble*, you know that?"

Emeric's grin widened. "Trouble suits me."

She stared at him, incredulous. "Do you *ever* take anything seriously?"

"Only when I'm dueling or dying. Everything else is just ... recreational suffering."

Fadeya made a frustrated sound and turned to walk away.

"Hey," he called, and she stopped. "You do realize you're not actually made of glass, right?"

She turned back slowly. "What is *wrong* with you?"

Emeric grinned, pushing off the tree and strolling toward her with maddening ease. "I think you're spiraling, and I find that mildly entertaining, mostly because you're being wildly unfair to yourself. Let me guess, when you were five, you cried because you colored outside the lines?"

Her lips twitched. "Once. And I redid the entire page."

"Of course, you did." He nudged her shoulder. "Come on. I promise the world isn't going to implode."

She rolled her eyes, but the corner of her mouth curved—barely.

Emeric caught it instantly, his grin widening. "See? I knew you liked me."

"I *don't* like you."

"You *kind of* like me."

"I *actively* dislike you."

"You say that now."

Fadeya huffed, pulling away from him. "Shouldn't you be off reveling in your genius instead of bothering me?"

He closed the space between them in a single lazy step. The warmth of him brushed against her skin, a stark contrast to the cooling evening air. "I don't know," he murmured, gaze dropping just briefly to her lips. "Maybe I just like getting under your skin."

Fadeya refused to step back again. "You must be very bored, then."

His eyes glinted. "Not at all."

Her breath hitched, just a little, and she hated herself for it. His smile deepened. Fadeya shoved past him, heart hammering. "Goodbye, Emeric."

He gave a lazy salute. "Until next time, *failure*."

Fadeya rolled her eyes; the nickname hit a little too close to home. Still, she refused to give him the satisfaction of a reaction. Instead, she turned away, adjusting the strap of her bag as she walked back toward the cobbled path.

Maybe Emeric was right. Maybe she should be plotting her comeback. She exhaled slowly, letting the cool evening air push some of the tension from her shoulders. The past few days had been nothing but disappointment, shame, and anger. She had let it consume her, but now, standing at the edge of the park, her pulse finally steady, she could hear her father's voice in the back of her mind.

Never let failure define you, my little star. Rise, even when it hurts.

Her father had believed in her. Not because of her achievements, not because of the expectations placed on her, but because of who she was. He had believed in her because she stood back up *every time*. Because she looked at a closed door and searched for another way in.

He would not have wanted her to abandon the path. He would not have wanted bitterness to shape her future.

The stars overhead were faint, barely cutting through the clouds gathering over the city rooftops. Snow began to fall, soft, patient, inevitable. It clung to her shoulders, her hair, her lashes.

They had never had much, even before. Their father's income had kept them steady, just enough to get by, but when he died, things shifted overnight. Warm meals became simpler. Books were borrowed, not bought. Luxuries disappeared one by one, until even dreams felt like something they had to ration.

Seraphina had never stopped dreaming, though. That had always been her gift. Her curse, maybe. The kind of hope that could make something from nothing, just by believing hard enough. Seraphina always looked for the good, always chose what was right.

Fadeya … she had learned to be practical.

Still, it hadn't been enough this time.

She gritted her teeth as she turned onto the street leading home. She would not let this defeat be the end of her story.

Emeric, despite his irritating commentary and relentless smirking, had reminded her of something she had nearly forgotten: failure was a teacher.

Her boots crunched against the cobblestones, and with each step, her resolve deepened.

She didn't know when or how, but she would find another way in. And when she did make it to Astral Unison University, she'd make damn sure Emeric regretted ever calling her a failure.

Chapter 4

WALKING ALONE

SERAPHINA

Seraphina stepped into the biting morning air, the world around her muffled by fresh snow. It clung to everything—branches, rooftops, fence posts—turning even the mundane into something strangely beautiful. She shivered slightly, adjusting her cloak hastily. Its clasp was, predictably, crooked again.

Their mother had been insistent, a note of finality in her voice that brooked no argument. Life must continue as usual, even though Seraphina's entire world would shift tomorrow when she left. So, routine it was. Sword practice at dawn, in the freezing cold, like they had done every Tuesday since their father's passing.

Across the training yard, Fadeya stood ready, her presence steady as a stone. Her hair was braided tightly, tucked beneath the fur lining of her cloak. Her leathers gleamed where the sunlight touched them—clean and mended.

Seraphina caught her sister's eye and gave a sheepish smile. "I overslept."

Fadeya arched an eyebrow. "I can tell." Her eyes swept over Seraphina's mismatched gloves and hastily tied boots. "Ready?"

"As ready as I'll be," Seraphina responded, raising her practice sword awkwardly. The sword felt cumbersome and unnatural, making her miss the slender knife tucked beneath her mattress.

At first, it was the same pattern they had done every week. Strike. Parry. Shift. Counter. Seraphina moved a beat behind her sister, always just a little too slow, a little too unbalanced. Her blade slipped from the optimal angle. Her footing was cautious, hesitant.

"You're gripping too tight," Fadeya murmured after a few passes. "Loosen your hands. Let the sword move with you."

Seraphina adjusted. "I always feel like it's going to fly out of my hands."

"Then you're not breathing right. Again." Fadeya moved forward, measured, and controlled. "Remember your footwork."

Seraphina nodded, immediately stumbling as she tried to match her sister's smooth movements. Her cheeks flushed hotter with embarrassment. "Sorry."

"Don't apologize," Fadeya corrected, stepping back again, patient today rather than frustrated. "Adjust your stance. Try again."

They continued in silence for a few moments, the quiet punctuated only by the clash of wooden blades and their measured breaths. Finally, Fadeya paused, watching Seraphina closely.

"You're distracted," she noted. "Worried about tomorrow?"

Seraphina lowered her sword slightly, meeting her sister's eyes. "Not about leaving," she confessed. "About leaving you."

Fadeya studied her closely, a faint, almost reluctant smile crossing her lips. "Do you remember when we were younger, the spring the river flooded?"

Seraphina squinted, caught off guard by the memory. "We were supposed to stay inside, but you convinced me to go out anyway."

Fadeya nodded, eyes brighter. "I still can't believe you let me drag you outside. We built a raft out of old wood from the shed. Mother was furious when she found us drifting halfway downstream."

Seraphina laughed softly. "I told her we were explorers. That we were going to discover a new land."

Fadeya's smile widened. "You always believed it. You saw adventure where I just saw trouble."

Seraphina stepped closer, lowering her sword fully. "Things seemed so much simpler then."

"Simpler?" Fadeya chuckled. "We nearly drowned."

"True," Seraphina admitted. "But at least we did it together."

Fadeya sighed, looking away for a moment before meeting Seraphina's gaze again. "I envy that about you. Your ability to always see the best in everything."

She opened her mouth to say something else, but a voice interrupted.

"Seraphina." Their mother stood at the edge of the yard, arms wrapped tightly around her cloak. Her hair was swept up neatly, as always, but there were new creases beside her eyes this morning, more than there had been last week.

Seraphina turned, still flushed. "Yes?"

Her mother's expression wasn't angry. Just tired. "Did you bake last night?"

Seraphina blinked. "I … yes. I made honey bread."

"I found flour in the butter dish. Jam on the floor. Two knives in the sink and one in the fireplace. How does that happen, Seraphina?"

Seraphina opened her mouth, then shut it again. "I just … I wanted to leave something behind," Seraphina said, her voice small. "Something sweet."

Their mother's expression softened minutely, but she said nothing more. She only looked between the two of them. Then she turned and went back inside, the door closing behind her with a *click*.

Seraphina stared at the spot where she'd stood, shoulders sagging. "She's right. I'm such a mess."

"You're not a mess," Fadeya said immediately. "She just doesn't know how to say what she's feeling."

Seraphina gave a hollow laugh. "Guess that runs in the family."

Fadeya didn't smile. "She's scared."

Seraphina looked over. "Of what?"

"Of losing you." Fadeya's voice was so quiet, it was almost a breath. "Of what it means when you leave."

The words settled between them, painful and true. Seraphina swallowed hard.

Fadeya squeezed her shoulder gently, then she took a deep breath, stepping back, sword raised once more. "Come on, let's go again. And this time, keep your eyes on me, not your feet."

FADEYA

The next morning, the smell of brewing coffee hung in the air, a comforting scent that usually signified calm, but that day it felt suffocating, heavy with unspoken words. Fadeya stood by the window, watching the morning mist dissipate, as she mentally steeled herself. Her mother was sitting at the oak table, a mug cradled between her hands, her gaze distant. She hadn't said much that morning, a quietness that only deepened the tension.

Fadeya exhaled sharply before turning to face her. "Mother," she began, her voice calm but firm, "why are you not going to see Seraphina off?"

Maris didn't flinch. She took a long sip from her cup, her eyes avoiding Fadeya's, her lips pressed into a thin line. "Ah. This again," she replied after a long pause.

Fadeya's muscle quivered in her cheek as she fought to keep her expression neutral. "I just don't understand it. Seraphina's your daughter. Don't you think you owe it to her to at least tell her goodbye?"

Maris set the mug down, her fingers lingering on the rim as she gathered her thoughts. "She's reckless, just like Dyaus. She doesn't think before she acts. Your father was that way, always off chasing some adventure, never thinking about the consequences, and look where that got us. He left me to raise you both alone, without a second thought." Her voice softened for a moment, but the edge was still there. "She has to learn how to survive on her own. If I shield her, she'll never make it in that world."

The words struck harder than they should have. Fadeya folded her arms, grounding herself against the familiar ache in her chest. This wasn't about Seraphina. It never had been. It was about him. Their father's ghost lived in every bitter syllable Maris spoke. In the sharp edges of her posture. In the wall of steel she had built around herself long ago, one Fadeya had spent years trying to scale.

Maris sighed, rubbing a hand over her face before looking back at her. "Sometimes love means giving tough lessons."

Fadeya swallowed, feeling a bit uncomfortable with the conversation, but wanting more information; her mother never spoke of their father.

Leaning forward, Maris rested her forearms on the table. "The world doesn't care about your feelings. If I show her affection, it'll only make her weak. And that's not what she needs." Her voice softened, but the steel remained. "She needs to learn what it takes to stand on her own."

Fadeya forced herself to meet her gaze, even as a weight twisted deep in her gut. Because beneath the surface, she knew her mother meant every word. And worse, some part of Fadeya believed it, too.

Before she could respond, the door creaked open, and Seraphina stepped into the room, her bags slung over one shoulder, looking every bit the excited young woman on the brink of a grand adventure. Her bright eyes snapped between them, sensing the unease.

"What's going on?" she asked, her voice light, trying to bridge the gap between their unspoken words.

Fadeya opened her mouth to respond, but Maris spoke first, her voice quieter now. "You remind me of him, you know."

Seraphina blinked. She hadn't expected that.

Maris traced a line that ran along the oak table Dyaus had built, her stare distant. "Your father had the same way of looking at the world, like it would all fall into place if he just reached for it." A bitter smile passed across her lips. "He always thought things would work out in the end. That life would bend to his will if he wanted it badly enough." She exhaled sharply, shaking her head. "And look where that got him."

Seraphina's fingers twitched at her sides. She didn't speak. Didn't dare interrupt whatever storm was brewing beneath their mother's carefully measured words.

Maris finally looked at her, studying her with those unreadable eyes. Then, she sighed. "I suppose we'll see if you're any different."

The words were soft, barely more than a murmur, but they cut deep.

Fadeya watched as Seraphina's shoulders tensed, as that glimmer of hope died before it could fully take root. Blinking, taking in the strange mix of encouragement and harshness, she said nothing in return. Fadeya glanced at her mother, who was already rising from the table, as if dismissing the conversation altogether.

"I'll help you with your bags," she offered, a small apologetic smile on her lips as she grabbed Seraphina's larger pack from her. Her sister hesitated for only a moment before following her toward the door.

Outside, the air was crisp, the road leading to the port glimmering in the light. Fadeya fell into step beside her sister, the weight of the bags surprisingly light in her hands.

"I'm sorry," Seraphina murmured as they walked, her voice barely above the crunch of gravel beneath their boots. "I know how much going to the university meant to you. I wish …" Her throat bobbed. "I wish with all my heart that we were going there together."

Fadeya exhaled slowly, turning her head toward the sky. "It's not your fault." Her voice was shaking. "You can't control the path your life takes. And neither can I."

She slowed her steps, glancing at Seraphina. "You've got so much ahead of you," she said, her tone quieter now. "Don't let anyone or anything change who you are."

Seraphina nodded, kicking at rocks as they walked.

"You know," Fadeya said, voice softer, "you *do* remind me of him."

Seraphina's head snapped up. "Of Father?"

Fadeya gave her a small, wry smile. "Yeah. The way you look at the world, like it's something meant to be unraveled. He had that too."

Seraphina hesitated, then reached out, her fingers brushing against Fadeya's. "I'll write," she promised. "I'll send letters, everything I learn, anything I can to help you next year. I swear it."

Fadeya met her sister's gaze. "You better," she teased. "And when you get there, make sure you don't get eaten by a dragon or something crazy."

Seraphina laughed, the sound a balm for Fadeya's nerves. "No promises," she grinned.

By the time they reached the ship, the mood and sun had shifted, but a quiet unease lingered. The ship loomed before them, a massive vessel with ancient runes etched into its sides. *Eclipsion.*

As Seraphina stepped away to check in, Fadeya spotted Aleron standing off to the side, quietly saying goodbye to his family. When she approached, his eyes found hers, and a faint, bittersweet smile tugged at the corners of his mouth.

"I guess this is it, huh?" he said, his voice low.

Fadeya nodded, her heart heavy, though her voice stayed steady despite the storm of emotion within her. "Hello, my friend."

He paused, a quiet warmth settling over his features. "And I suppose … goodbye."

Before she could respond, Aleron stepped forward and wrapped her in a hug. It was firm, comforting—one of those rare moments that said everything words couldn't. When he pulled back, his hand lingered for a moment on her shoulder, giving it a gentle, reassuring squeeze.

She lowered her voice so no one else could hear. "Aleron, listen to me. Watch over her. She's just so free-spirited. She doesn't realize how cruel the world can be." There was a vulnerability in her eyes that she rarely showed.

Aleron's expression changed as the weight of her words sank in. Determination set in his eyes. "I will," he said, "I promise." He gave her shoulder one last reassuring squeeze. "I'll be seeing you," he said.

Fadeya nodded and took a step back. "Thank you," she whispered as she watched him walk toward the ship.

She barely had a chance to breathe before a voice drifted in—smooth, familiar, and irritatingly smug.

"Well, hello, failure," Emeric drawled, strolling into view with that infuriatingly casual gait. "Look at you. Upright. Awake. Hair brushed. Did someone finally decide to stop wallowing?"

Fadeya didn't turn right away. She took her time, rolled her eyes, and let the smallest smirk tug at her mouth. *Damn him.*

"Actually," she said, finally facing him with a tilt of her chin, "I thought I'd try this new thing where I function like a semi-competent human being. Revolutionary, really."

Emeric stepped closer, just a breath inside her space—close enough to make her spine straighten out of sheer reflex. "That's my girl," he murmured, voice low and far too amused. "Knew you had it in you." He leaned in, breath brushing the curve of her ear, and goosebumps prickled along her arms before she could will them away. "So," he murmured, "you'll miss me when I'm gone, won't you?"

Fadeya stifled a laugh, biting the inside of her cheek. "I think I'll survive."

He grinned, reaching up as if to tuck a strand of hair behind her ear, but stopped just short. His fingers hovered there a moment before dropping. "Shame," he said softly. "I was hoping for a tearful goodbye."

She stepped around him, her shoulder brushing against his chest as she passed. "Keep dreaming, Emeric."

For once, he didn't fire back right away. Instead, he watched her with a quietness that tugged at her ribs.

"You know," he said after a beat, tone gentler now, "I get it. The sibling thing. Always trying to be seen, to be enough. It's … exhausting."

Fadeya turned. "It is what it is," she said, though the words rang hollow in her mouth. This must be what Seraphina felt all those years—living in my shadow, even when I didn't mean to cast it.

Emeric's expression shifted. Gone was the smirk. "I don't have the answers," he said, "But you're not the only one fighting that feeling. And you don't have to prove yourself to people who already see you."

She met his eyes. There was no challenge there. No mockery. Just surprising honesty that made the space between them hum with a different kind of tension.

"Don't worry," he said, stepping back, the old grin creeping back into place. "I'm sure I'll see you next year. I'm looking forward to it." And with a final wink, he turned to walk away, tossing one last parting shot over his shoulder.

"Try not to miss me too much, Failure."

Fadeya let out a soft laugh, shaking her head. "Arrogant bastard," she muttered under her breath, but there was a warmth in her chest she didn't bother to suppress.

With a sigh, Fadeya let her gaze sweep across the bustling dock, through the chaos of shouted farewells and the low groan of ropes tightening on wood. And then she spotted her—Seraphina—standing by the gangplank, her cloak clutched tightly around her shoulders, eyes wide as she stared up at the ship.

Watching her sister felt like watching a version of herself she'd forgotten—hopeful, nervous, brave. She crossed the dock in long, purposeful strides, weaving through the crowd until she was beside her.

Seraphina looked up, eyes bright with excitement, but behind it, just barely, Fadeya saw the flicker of nerves. Of doubt.

"You'll do great," Fadeya said, pulling her into a hug.

"I love you, Fadeya. I'll miss you," Seraphina breathed against her shoulder, the words muffled by fabric and emotion.

Fadeya swallowed hard. "Starlight binds us," she whispered, the old phrase catching in her throat like a prayer.

When they finally pulled apart, Seraphina nodded, blinking back tears. Then she turned toward the ship, her back straightening with every step.

SERAPHINA

As the sun began to set, Seraphina stood at the rail of the ship, gazing down at the dock below, and a rush of emotions swelled in her chest—excitement, nervousness, and something quieter, harder to name. The ship beneath her feet creaked gently, sails fluttering like wings ready to carry her toward everything she had dreamed of—and everything she wasn't sure she was ready for. Before she could sort through them, a familiar voice pierced through the air, and Cordelia appeared like a burst of color.

She was wrapped in a deep crimson coat that cinched at the waist with brass clasps, the velvet fabric lined with fur at the collar and cuffs. Beneath it, a high-necked dress peeked out—dark plum with embroidered constellations that shimmered faintly in the pale sunlight. Her tall leather boots clicked smartly against the deck as she approached, and her gloved hands carried far more rings than seemed necessary for a sea voyage.

Without missing a beat, Cordelia rushed forward, throwing her arms around Seraphina in a tight, exuberant hug. "Oh, my stars, I can't believe this is actually happening! The university, magic, adventure, we're going, Seraphina! This is *it*!" She pulled away, her eyes scanning Seraphina's face before giving her an approving nod. "And you, my friend, look stunning, as always."

Seraphina glanced down at herself with a wry smile. She wore a thick, slate-blue wool coat fastened with a cord, the hem brushing just below her knees. Beneath it, a simple tunic and fitted trousers. Practical, warm, nothing like Cordelia's theatrical ensemble. Her hair, braided hastily that morning, had already begun to rebel. Strands had escaped, whipping across her face in the wind, though the ship hadn't even left the dock yet.

"Me? Look at *you*," Seraphina sighed, brushing a tangle of hair from her cheek.

Cordelia grinned and twirled, the heavy fabric of her coat flaring out around her like a crimson flame. "I know it's not exactly ship-appropriate," she said, gesturing at her ensemble with a flourish, "but a girl's gotta make an entrance, right?"

Seraphina smiled, shaking her head at Cordelia's relentless confidence. "You're something else, Cordelia."

"And don't you forget it!" Cordelia grinned, giving her another exaggerated wink. She dropped her bags for a moment and swept her into a hug. "But seriously, this is going to be amazing. I'm so proud of us."

Seraphina's heart swelled with affection as she hugged her best friend back. "I'm so glad you're coming with me, Cordelia. I don't know how I'd do this without you."

As the ship lurched gently beneath her feet, Seraphina's heart raced with equal parts excitement and terror. The ropes were pulled in, and the sails caught the wind with a snap as the vessel began to drift from the dock. She hurried to the rail, fingers gripping the wood as she looked back one last time.

There, among the thinning crowd, stood Fadeya.

Their eyes met, and for a moment, everything else faded. The bustling deck, the shouting sailors, even the ache in her chest. Just the two of them, caught in the space between what had been and what was to come.

Seraphina lifted a hand in farewell, her breath catching as Fadeya nodded once, strong, proud, and heartbreakingly still.

FADEYA

The space between them stretched wider with every breath. The stars above glimmered coldly, too bright, as if mocking her, reminding Fadeya that her sister was sailing toward a future that no longer included her. The ship slipped into the darkness, swallowed by the vast, uncharted sea of possibility.

The road home felt endless as Fadeya turned away from the dock. The weight of an unfamiliar loneliness settled on her shoulders. With each step, the gap between them widened, and with it, the existence she had once envisioned for herself began to fade. Fadeya realized, with a sudden, overwhelming clarity, that she was no longer walking as a twin. She was walking alone, into a life that no longer mirrored the one she had known, one that seemed uncertain and boundless, stretching far ahead, with no one beside her to help guide the way.

Chapter 5

TWO SOULS ADRIFT

SERAPHINA

Seraphina awoke to the gentle roll of the ocean, sunlight slicing through the porthole in her cabin and dancing across the polished brass fittings inside. She blinked away the last remnants of sleep, her heart skipping in excitement for the day ahead. After weeks of anticipation, the reality of stepping foot on the Eclipsion still felt surreal.

Outside, gulls wheeled and cried overhead, their calls sharp against the salty breeze. She stepped onto the deck and spun around with a laugh, the wind catching her hair as she twirled.

"This is … astonishing," Seraphina breathed, hardly aware that Cordelia had come up beside her.

Cordelia let out a laugh, stepping closer as she ran her fingers over the railing. "Astonishing?" she replied, flashing Seraphina a grin. "It's a dream come true." She leaned in, tracing the swirling forms of dragons and phoenixes locked in battle, their wings spread wide, their jaws open in silent war. "Look at this," she murmured, knocking her knuckles against the wood. "The detail, every scale, every feather. I swear, if I stare long enough, they will start moving."

Every inch of the ship radiated a blend of luxury and enchantment. The figurehead at the bow was no mere ornament; it was a masterpiece. A massive griffin, carved from deep ebony wood, reared up as if ready to take flight. Gold filigree traced the curve of its wings and talons, catching the sunlight in dazzling flashes. Its eyes, two gleaming emeralds, burned with an eerie intensity, so lifelike that Seraphina half expected them to blink. It was worlds away from the human realm, where life was all peeling paint, patched boots, and magic only existed in stories.

A polite cough made them both turn. A young steward in crisp navy uniform stood near the entrance to the lower decks, bowing graciously.

"Ladies, welcome aboard Eclipsion. If you're ready, breakfast is being served in the dining room. We also offer refreshments on the promenade deck and activities for your leisure, should you wish to explore."

Cordelia turned to Seraphina, one brow raised in delight. "Activities? What kind of activities?"

The steward's smile widened as he listed them off. "Archery on the aft deck, a library of rare and enchanted volumes in our study, a lounge for games, and, of course, the observation deck for stargazing later tonight."

With a hand pressed to her chest, Cordelia let out a dreamy sigh. "I think I'm in love," she declared.

Seraphina chuckled at her friend's enthusiasm. Despite Cordelia's dramatic tendencies, Seraphina felt much the same.

"Let's start with the dining room," she suggested with a more practical tone. "We'll need our strength if we plan to try out every activity."

Cordelia slipped her arm through Seraphina's, a wicked grin tugging at her lips. "Now, that's the best idea you've had today."

The dining room was a marvel unto itself. Massive chandeliers hung from the vaulted ceiling, their crystals enchanted to refract light into a kaleidoscope of colors. Long tables, covered in white linens, were laden with a spread that looked almost too good to eat. Platters of eggs and bread, bowls of fruits, and a variety of pastries were laid out in perfect symmetry.

Cordelia let out an appreciative whistle. "Now this … *this* is my kind of buffet." She grabbed a plate and began selecting from the bounty, her enthusiasm contagious. Seraphina followed suit but with a more measured approach. "You're going to fill your plate before we even see the dessert table."

"Don't underestimate me," Cordelia replied, balancing her plate expertly while reaching for a small cake topped with spun sugar. "I'm just getting started."

As they found a table by a wide window, the view offering a sweeping panorama of the endless ocean, a voice called out behind them.

"Seraphina. Cordelia."

Both women turned as Aleron strode toward them, his dark curls tousled by the morning breeze, his sharp features carved with amusement. Sunlight kissed the sharp angle of his jaw, and that damnable smirk of his was already in place.

"I had a feeling you two would be here," he said, his voice threaded with easy familiarity.

Seraphina forced herself to stay relaxed, though her fingers curled slightly against the table. She ignored the way her pulse kicked up. "Awake so early, Aleron? I figured you'd still be draped over your bed, recovering from yesterday's ... excitement."

He gave a low chuckle. "And let you have all the fun without me? I'd never forgive myself." He dropped into the seat across from her, his eyes flicking toward Cordelia's plate, which was practically overflowing. His brows lifted. "Either you've acquired a second stomach overnight, or you're planning for battle."

Grinning shamelessly, Cordelia replied, "If you don't get your share now, you might not get any by the time I'm finished."

He chuckled. "Noted." Then, turning to Seraphina with a spark in his brown eyes, he asked, "So, how are you finding the Eclipsion? Living up to the hype?"

Seraphina let her gaze sweep the dining room. "It's ... beyond anything I imagined. Feels like stepping into a fairy tale." Her voice softened as her eyes landed back on him. "Almost too perfect." He looked ... good. Of course, he did. He carried himself differently than he had a year ago. More grounded. The usual mischief was still there, tucked in the corner of his smile, but there was something quieter beneath it. Measured. Older.

What happened to you this past year? She wondered, catching the small crease between his brows that he hadn't had before.

Aleron leaned in slightly, breaking her thoughts. "What would make it perfect?"

Seraphina hesitated, his look pinning her in place. "I don't know ... maybe good company?" she mused, keeping her tone light, though her cheeks betrayed her with the slightest flush.

"Well, I'd say you're in luck," Aleron replied smoothly, his lips curling into a playful smile. He leaned in closer, his voice lowering. "If there's anything else you need, you only have to ask."

Cordelia let out a dramatic sigh, drumming her fingers against the table. "Right, well, since you two are clearly in your own little world, I'll be helping myself to the dessert table." She tossed Seraphina a wink before sauntering off, already zeroing in on a tower of éclairs.

She studied him for a long moment, the teasing in her smile slowly fading into something quieter, more serious. "You seem different, Aleron." Her voice dipped, barely above a whisper. "What happened out there while you were gone? Why did you really leave?"

He didn't answer right away. His gaze shifted toward the window, his posture still, as if the question had unlocked a memory he wasn't sure he was ready to share. Then he exhaled slowly and leaned back in his chair.

"After Liora died," he said, his voice rough around the edges, "everything stopped making sense. My parents, stars, they didn't know how to move forward. None of us did. She was the heart of our family. The youngest, the brightest. And when we lost her ... something in them broke."

He paused, swallowing hard. "They started holding on too tightly. If I was gone too long, they panicked. If I mentioned traveling, they would shut it down before I finished the sentence. They meant well, I know that now, but the grief ... it twisted into fear. And that fear—it started to wrap around me, like vines."

Seraphina felt her chest ache. She remembered Liora, always laughing, always asking too many questions, tagging along at Aleron's heels.

"I got this job offer, nothing grand, just hauling supplies between a few coastal ports, but it was enough. A reason to go. A chance to get out and … see something else. Anything else."

"There have been many times over this past year I've wanted to escape my family," Seraphina whispered. "To just leave and go on an adventure."

"That's just it," he continued. "I thought it would be the kind of adventure people romanticize. Foreign lands, vibrant markets, sunsets that burn the sky. And there was some of that, yes, but what stayed with me … were the parts no one writes about. The hunger. The sickness. Entire villages forgotten by the world."

He paused, staring at the grain of the table as if it might steady him.

"I started out with this excitement, like I was finally claiming the life I'd been waiting for, but what I found was pain. Not just mine. Everyone's. It's everywhere, Seraphina. Quiet. Constant. And it changes you."

He looked at her again, and this time, there was no trace of charm or confidence, just honesty.

"I left thinking I would find myself, but now I think … it's not about finding anything. It's about seeing what's real. And choosing—deliberately, painfully—who you want to be in the face of it."

He shook his head as if trying to erase the memory, then reached for his glass and knocked it clean over. Water spilled across the table in a swift, gliding sheet.

"Ah, damn it," he muttered, snatching a napkin and scrambling to mop it up.

Seraphina blinked, then let out a short laugh, the tension in her chest breaking like a cracked shell. "Well," she said, passing him another napkin, "you may have gained all this perspective, but your coordination clearly hasn't improved."

Aleron looked up, sheepish, and chuckled. "Some things never change."

"No," she said, a smile tugging at her lips. "I think that's a good thing—" But the chime of a bell echoed through the dining hall, cutting her off and sending a ripple of movement through the room.

"That's our call for orientation," Aleron observed, rising to stand. He offered his hand to Seraphina. "Shall we?"

She hesitated only for a heartbeat before placing her hand in his. His skin felt warm against hers, and that same strange flutter returned to the pit of her stomach as they made their way to the reception hall.

Cordelia, arms precariously full of desserts, spotted them and beamed. She took a bite of a chocolate-drenched fruit tart, then leaned in with a smirk and whispered, "Looks like someone's already making the most of this trip."

Seraphina nudged her friend lightly, a small smile playing on her lips. "Maybe."

Rows of plush chairs faced a raised stage, upon which a map of the Eclipsion was displayed. Runes glowed along the edges of the map, marking crucial points, emergency wards, storerooms, and crew quarters. Sounds of excitement filled the hall as new arrivals searched for seats. Seraphina and Aleron found two near the center, Cordelia close behind with her plate of sweets.

"Are you planning to eat that entire plate by yourself?" Aleron teased, eyeing the stack of pastries in Cordelia's hands.

She scrunched her nose. "If I share, it's only because I like you two. I get first dibs."

A hush fell over the room as Professor Shay stepped onto the raised stage. They moved with quiet authority, dark cropped hair and thick eyebrows giving them a striking presence. Their navy robes shimmered with silver trim, a scabbard resting at their waist. With hands outstretched in welcome, their voice rang clear above the murmurs. "Greetings, everyone. My name is Professor Shay, and I'd like to formally welcome you aboard Eclipsion and, more broadly, into the magical realm."

Seraphina dared a glance at Aleron once more, finding him watching her with that same knowing smile. Her pulse jumped, and she looked away, feigning rapt attention to the stage.

Professor Shay continued. "Most of you come from ordinary lives, the human realm, where magic is nothing more than a story whispered around the fire." They let the words settle, the gentle lurch of the ship punctuating the silence. "As we journey to Astral Unison University, this is your time to prepare for what lies ahead. If you are deemed worthy by a creature of the realm, you will form a bond with them. That bond will tether your soul to that creature—and in turn, allow you to channel the magic they hold."

A ripple passed through the students: excitement, fear, awe. Seraphina barely breathed.

"Forging a bond is sacred," the professor continued. "It is the heartbeat of our realm. Without these connections, there would not be enough magic to heal the sick, nourish the land, or guard against the darkness that lies beyond our borders. You will come to know the creatures who walk beside us, not as familiars or servants, but as equals, bound to you by something greater than fate."

From beneath the stage's high table, a rumble echoed. It was almost musical, a low, thrumming hum. Moments later, a creature emerged, slender and regal, with midnight-blue scales gleaming in the chandelier light. Tall ears framed a serpentine face, and fins ran down its spine, shimmering every time it moved.

"This," Professor Shay announced, resting a hand on the creature's scaly neck, "is Kymaris. A tide-wyrm known for her skill in manipulating water currents. Kymaris and I are bonded." The creature curled protectively around the professor's arm, meeting the audience with wise, golden eyes. A hushed awe settled over the students.

Professor Shay stroked Kymaris's neck affectionately, a faint glow emanating from where their hand made contact. "In our world, magical creatures choose humans as much as humans choose them. It's a twofold process of mutual recognition of potential. I chose Kymaris because I saw in her a fierce loyalty and unwavering curiosity that echoed my own."

They stepped forward, eyes sweeping over the gathered faces. "When that bond forms, when trust and respect flow in both directions, magic awakens in you. It becomes part of you, drawn from the heart of your companion and infused into your own spirit."

From her side, Aleron leaned toward Seraphina. "I've heard stories of tide-wyrms, but I never thought I'd see one. Look at how graceful she is."

Cordelia leaned in, eyes wide with awe. "Graceful?" she whispered. "She's absolutely stunning." Her gaze lingered on the shimmer of Kymaris's fins, wonder softening her voice. "I wonder if there are any like her ... in shades of pink."

A smug snort cut Cordelia off. Seraphina stiffened at the sound, already knowing who it belonged to before she even turned.

Emeric lounged in his chair, legs kicked up on the empty seat in front of him. He toyed with a silver ring on his finger, the smirk on his lips lazy, practiced.

"If I'm going to bother bonding at all, it's going to be with something worth my time," he drawled, inspecting his nails as if the conversation barely deserved his attention. "Something ... legendary."

Seraphina rolled her eyes and whispered to him, "Maybe bond with a mirror instead; you're clearly captivated by your own reflection."

"You may be wondering," Professor Shay explained, "why a creature would choose to bond with a human—or a fae—at all."

They paused, letting the question hang in the air for a moment.

"The truth is, magical creatures cannot reach their full potential alone. Without a bond, their magic remains ... incomplete. When a bond is formed, it strengthens both sides. The creature gains greater power, sharper clarity of thought, deeper access to magic, and in many cases, a longer life. Communication becomes easier."

Kymaris gave a small chirp, rubbing its scaled cheek against the professor's shoulder as though in agreement.

"If you have questions, I will do my best to counsel you, for the bond with a magical companion is a gift unlike any other. It brings responsibility, too. A connection forged in honesty and respect, or else not at all."

A thoughtful silence enveloped the orientation hall. Seraphina's heart thundered in her chest. Could she earn a bond as profound as she saw between Professor Shay and Kymaris?

The professor raised their hands in a final, welcoming gesture. "On behalf of Eclipsion's crew, and every creature that calls this realm home, I bid you welcome. May you find exactly what you seek on this journey … and perhaps a bit more."

Applause broke out then, hesitant at first but quickly building. Seraphina joined in, her hands tingling with excitement. She exchanged a glance with Cordelia and then with Aleron, who looked quietly determined. Something in his expression told her he'd been waiting for this moment for a long time.

Kymaris emitted a soft purring trill, and Professor Shay bowed gracefully before stepping off the stage with their bonded companion in tow.

The room slowly began to fill with chatter again as small groups formed to exchange hushed words of wonder and speculation. Seraphina's mind whirled with possibility. The world had just become infinitely larger, and if she closed her eyes, she could almost imagine the gentle brush of magic waiting, just beyond her grasp, hoping she would reach for it.

As she opened her eyes, she caught sight of Aleron watching her. Cordelia threw an arm around her shoulders, drawing her close, chocolate éclair forgotten in her other hand.

"Well," Cordelia said, her voice filled with awe, "it seems this might be more exhilarating than even I anticipated."

Seraphina's lips curved into a smile. "I guess we'll find out." The thrill of possibility hung in the air as the three of them followed the crowd.

Days stretched into a cruel, lingering ache in her chest, each dawn a stark reminder that she was still here, alone, while her sister was somewhere else entirely.

No one had ever described Fadeya as anything but confident and headstrong, yet now an unfamiliar hollowness gnawed at her, an unnameable fear that she wasn't good enough, hadn't been chosen, and perhaps never would be.

She tried to busy her hands to quiet the storm inside her—scrubbing linens until her fingers went raw, rearranging the shelves until everything was perfect, and then undoing it again. The garden was little more than brittle stalks and cold soil this time of year, but she forced herself to tend it anyway—just for something to do, but nothing settled her. Her hands trembled from the weight of her own doubt, each task unraveling into a reminder that she had been left behind.

Now, she hovered near the kitchen's wide hearth, watching embers glow in the grate as if they might offer answers she didn't know how to ask for. The scent of woodsmoke and herbs hung in the air. She didn't register the scuff of her mother's footsteps until a warm hand settled firmly on her shoulder.

"Still sulking?" Maris asked, giving the pot on the stove a stir, her voice as dry as kindling.

Fadeya didn't flinch. She turned her head slightly, just enough to meet her mother's eyes over her shoulder. "I'm not sulking," she murmured, but even to her own ears, the words felt flimsy.

"Oh? Then what do you call all this pacing and brooding?" Maris arched an eyebrow and turned to face her fully.

"I just ..." Fadeya exhaled, her gaze falling to the worn wooden floorboards. "I thought I knew who I was and what I wanted. Now everything feels ... wrong."

Maris placed the spoon down with a deliberate clatter and folded her arms. "Your sister is gone, yes. She's walking a path you dreamed of. And I know it hurts, stars know I do, but sitting here wrapped in self-pity like a second blanket isn't going to fix what feels broken inside you."

Fadeya bristled, but it wasn't anger—it was shame, and confusion, and a hundred other things she didn't know how to say. "I don't know what to do," she admitted, voice small.

Maris didn't answer right away. She reached across the table and grabbed a knife, the metal gleaming in the firelight. Then, she turned and pressed the hilt firmly into Fadeya's hand.

"Just do *something*," she said.

Fadeya stared down at the knife, her fingers slowly curling around the handle.

Maris stepped closer, voice softer now. "You keep waiting for someone to name your path, but that's not how life works. You think I wanted to raise two daughters alone? You think I got to stop and ask the stars what I was meant for?" She laughed quietly, without mirth. "No, girl. Life handed me ashes, and I learned to make bread."

Fadeya's mouth twitched, almost a smile—but it didn't quite make it there. She looked up.

"I've always believed in you," Maris said, quieter now. "Not just because you're clever, though you are. Not because you're strong, though you've always had more fight in you than sense. I believe in you because you remind me of myself—but braver. You stand up faster. You hold your ground longer. You've never faced a challenge and turned away from it. Not once."

Fadeya blinked. "Then why does it feel like I failed?"

Maris reached up, brushing a loose strand of hair from Fadeya's cheek. "Because you care. Because you *wanted* it badly enough to feel this way. That doesn't make you weak, my girl. That makes you human." Her thumb rested gently on her daughter's chin. "The world isn't fair, but you are still *you* in it. And that has always been enough."

Fadeya looked back down at the knife, then to the cutting board on the table.

Maris stepped back toward the stove. "You don't need some grand prophecy or chosen path to matter. Sometimes, it's enough to just take the next step." She turned back to the hearth, lifting the lid from the stew pot. "And today, that step looks a lot like chopping onions."

Chapter 6

BENEATH THE SURFACE

SERAPHINA

"I don't like this." Cordelia glowered, her gaze darting to Seraphina. The sea loomed around them like a vast, inky void beneath a starless sky, its waves slapping against the hull in an ominous rhythm.

It had been a lovely week at sea—clear skies, warm sun, and calm waters that shimmered like glass. They'd laughed over shared meals, marveled at schools of flying fish, and watched the stars bloom overhead each night like lanterns guiding them forward.

But now, something had shifted.

"The sea feels ... wrong," Cordelia muttered uneasily, glancing over the dark waters that seemed to stretch forever.

"You're not imagining it," Seraphina replied in a hushed tone. She braced against the rolling ship, eyes roving over the horizon. "There's something out there." She was suddenly grateful she'd chosen a more practical outfit that morning—sturdy boots, a belted tunic, and a thick cloak she hadn't needed until now.

Above them, the sails thrashed in the gusting wind as another grumble of thunder rolled across the sea.

At the prow, Professor Shay held their ground, the glow of their bondmark casting flickering light across salt-worn timbers. They turned, moving closer to the group with a grim set to their jaw. "Sirens."

Seraphina stiffened. "Sirens? Aren't they just—"

"Stories? No," Shay cut in, voice low. "They're very real." They began adjusting the string on their bow with practiced precision. "I was hoping we'd avoid them entirely on this route," they muttered, eyes narrowing toward the darkening sky.

Around them, the deck had erupted into motion. Crew members shouted to one another as they dashed to secure lines and ready weapons. The once-calm evening had shifted into barely contained chaos—barrels clattered, sails groaned, and steel was drawn from scabbards with hissing finality.

Aleron fastened his sword to his belt with a sharp click, jaw tense. "How many do you think are out there?"

Professor Shay flexed the bowstring and let it snap with a soft *thrum*. "Last time I saw them, a decade ago, they moved in a pack of around twenty."

Seraphina's stomach turned. *Twenty.*

Emeric appeared behind them, rolling his shoulders as if preparing for a sparring match instead of a life-or-death encounter. "Well," he said dryly, "I was starting to get bored with all the sunshine and pleasant conversation. Screaming sea monsters sound like a lovely change of pace."

Seraphina shot him a glare. "Do you ever take *anything* seriously?"

He shrugged, entirely too relaxed. "You sound like your sister."

She opened her mouth to fire back, but her thoughts snagged instead—*How would he even know what Fadeya sounds like?*

Cordelia muttered, "It's a miracle you've lived this long."

And then the wind shifted.

It came suddenly, a sharp howl cutting through the air, and with it, a song.

Faint at first. A hum wrapped in wind, nearly drowned beneath the creaking of the ship, but it grew. And grew.

The melody was cold and beautiful, and wrong in a way that prickled her skin. It didn't come from above or below. It came from *everywhere.*

Seraphina felt it in her chest, an irresistible tug, as though the sea itself was calling to her.

A large ripple disturbed the water, subtle at first, but then it shimmered, unnatural, drawing closer with every passing second. A figure began to rise from the depths, slow and fluid. When it broke the surface, the siren's silver hair fanned out around its body, clinging like wet silk to its sharp, gleaming form. Another siren appeared beside it, then another, their forms like ghostly apparitions rising from the deep. They moved as one, their voices joining in perfect harmony, weaving a deadly lullaby that threatened to steal away their wills.

Seraphina could see the sirens' eyes now, deep pools of black that seemed to draw her soul in, urging her closer to the edge of the ship.

"Stay focused," Professor Shay's voice cut through the fog of temptation. "Do not listen to them. They will drag you into the sea." Kymaris, Professor Shay's bondmate, wrapped around their arm as Professor Shay directed her to guide the ocean's current away from the sirens.

The sirens' melody grew louder, the sound becoming maddening as it engulfed them like an invisible fog. Cordelia clutched the railing tightly, her eyes wide with fear. "Why does it feel like they're inside my head?" she whimpered, her voice trembling. "I can't … I can't think straight."

"Don't listen to them!" Emeric shouted, covering his ears with his hands.

Seraphina could feel it pulling her. The weight of the song moved her feet slowly toward the railing.

"We need to block it out," she muttered, her hands trembling. "It's too strong." Another boom of thunder shook the deck as the storm grew nearer.

Aleron's eyes darted to the sails, then back to the others. Without a word, he ripped a strip of cloth from his cloak. "We don't have much time," he said, tearing more fabric. "This will work, just make sure it's tight."

Professor Shay bellowed, "Everyone, rip something from your clothes and plug your ears. Quickly!"

Seraphina followed suit. She tore a piece from her sleeve, feeling the fabric bite as she yanked it free. The sound was unbearable now, gnawing at her thoughts, but she pushed the torn fabric into her ears with shaking hands. The sound softened to a distant, barely there hum, still powerful but no longer overwhelming.

"Better?" Aleron shouted. His cloth plugs were securely in place.

"Much better," Seraphina said to herself, relief flooding through her.

Professor Shay nodded grimly as they scanned the horizon. "It'll give us some protection, but it won't last long. The sirens won't give up easily." Kymaris' blue scales started to shimmer as she silently guided the wind into the sails.

"I thought we were supposed to bond with magical creatures," Cordelia shouted, her voice a mix of panic and frustration. "Not be hunted by sea monsters!"

Emeric shot her a sharp glance, tightening his grip on his sword. "Survival lesson number one," he replied, his tone cool and composed. "Fight first, ask questions later."

Another ripple of motion in the water on the other side of the ship sent a jolt of terror through Seraphina, tearing a scream from her throat. Then the sirens surfaced again, closing in around the ship in a tightening circle, their once-melodious voices now raw, guttural shrieks.

And just as suddenly, they vanished. The wind stilled, as though banished by an unseen hand, and the sea fell silent. Everyone stood transfixed, braced for a threat they knew lurked just out of sight.

A haunting melody rose from the depths, faint yet insistent. Most of the people on deck froze where they stood, eyes glazing over as the alien song coiled into their minds. For an instant, Cordelia's face flickered with panic before slackening under the pull of the siren lure.

"Cordelia!" Seraphina shouted, her voice slicing through the suffocating hush. "Focus! Don't let them get in your head!"

Cordelia jolted awake as if from a dream, her features set in grim determination.

Professor Shay, knuckles white around their bow, murmured, "You are stronger than they are," an almost prayerful conviction in each syllable. Then they loosed an arrow into the water, piercing a flash of scales before it vanished.

With a keening, earsplitting shriek, the sirens exploded onto the deck, their forms grotesquely beautiful. Webbed fingers clawed at the railings; their mouths yawned wide in unearthly cries.

Chaos engulfed the ship. It heaved under the punishing waves, the deck slick with saltwater and the first streaks of blood. Crew and students fought back in a whirlwind of flashing steel and desperate shouts. The sirens' shrieks reverberated with a savage hunger, raking across the defenders' senses like jagged shards of glass.

Aleron stumbled forward, nearly tripping over a loose rigging as he raised his blade. A siren lunged, its clawed hand snatching at his cloak. He wobbled, barely keeping his footing, and let out a startled curse.

Desperation took over, and he lashed out in a wild thrust that found its mark. With a shriek, the siren collapsed to the deck, Aleron's sword lodged deep in its chest.

Cordelia's scream cut through the maelstrom, sharp and desperate. She staggered backward, boots skidding across the slick planks of the ship. She threw herself behind Emeric, who stood like an unyielding fortress against the onslaught. Twin blades gleamed in his fists, catching the lurid flare of the lanterns swinging above the deck.

As a siren lunged from the shadows, its clawed hands outstretched, Emeric moved. He pivoted smoothly, one sword sweeping low to catch the creature off-balance while the other struck true, driving forward in a clean, brutal thrust. The siren's shriek cut off in a spray of brine and blood, its body crumpling at his feet.

He's arrogant, reckless, and absolutely insufferable, Seraphina thought, eyes narrowing on Emeric as he adjusted his stance. But he is damn good with a sword. He might even be better than Fadeya.

Another siren leapt onto the railing, eyes glinting, teeth bared in a vicious grin. Emeric surged forward in a single, fluid step. His swords whirled like twin vipers. His breath hissed between clenched teeth, each strike precise, brutal, unrelenting.

Seraphina's heart thundered the moment she saw Cordelia pinned against the splintered railing, a siren's claws buried in her shoulder. Seraphina shoved forward, desperate to reach her friend, but a writhing tangle of sirens and sailors blocked her path.

She watched, helpless, as her best friend staggered forward and swung a shattered plank with everything she had. The crack of wood against bone echoed over the crashing waves, and the siren crumpled at her feet.

Cordelia's chest heaved. Her hair clung to her face, eyes burning with desperation. Seraphina's heart clenched.

Then she saw it, a flash of silver across the slick deck. A knife, spinning toward the edge. Cordelia dove. Seraphina's breath caught as her friend's fingers closed around the hilt, but before she could rise, another siren launched from the deck, colliding with her mid-stride.

They went over the rail in a tangled blur. A cry tore from Seraphina's throat as she surged forward, but the sea had already swallowed them.

Then, a voice rose.

Professor Shay moved across the deck, their dark robes soaked and clinging to their frame as they mouthed words in a language older than wind. They raised their arms.

The storm obeyed.

Sirens screeched as the wind slammed into them like a wave. Professor Shay's hands carved through the air, summoning twin gusts that hurled two of the creatures off the ship, their screams lost in the sea spray.

"Enough!" their voice cracked. Electric energy arced between their fingers, then shot skyward before raining down in spears of golden lightning. Each bolt found its mark, sirens bursting into steam and ash, their unnatural howls cut short.

Seraphina tore through the stunned crowd, parting in the wake of Professor Shay's magic.

"Cordelia!" Seraphina's scream tore from her throat. She flung a single, agonized look at Aleron, whose eyes were wide with horror, then she vaulted over the side without a second thought.

Seraphina plunged into the sea, the water's icy bite knocking the breath from her lungs as if she'd slammed into a wall of glacial stone. In a single instant, the tumultuous world above dissolved into churning darkness. The distant flashes of lightning lit the underwater gloom in sporadic bursts, revealing flashes of the ocean surrounding her.

She forced her body deeper, each stroke a struggle against the powerful current that threatened to drag her away. Salt stung her eyes, but that pain was nothing compared to the shock she felt when she saw Cordelia below.

A siren raked its claws across her friend's arm, sending ribbons of red spiraling through the water. Cordelia's eyes were wild and terrified. Seraphina kicked harder, though it felt as if she were wading through syrup.

This can't be the end, she thought, furiously pushing past her exhaustion. Then Cordelia's expression hardened, and resolve settled over her features like a battle hymn. She slammed the knife she'd snatched from the ship into the siren's chest. The creature jerked once, then vanished into the dark in a cloud of inky blood. Relief flared hot in Seraphina's veins, only to turn to horror as she realized Cordelia wasn't moving. Her body drifted, lifeless as a rag doll.

No. Not like this. Seraphina's mind roared, her lungs burning as she pushed herself to the limit. She struggled back to the surface for one frantic gulp of air, gasped Cordelia's name into the storm, then dove again, ignoring the savage wind and rain thrashing above. A glow caught her eye, faint against the swirling darkness. For a moment, Seraphina thought it might be moonlight cutting through the storm-tossed waves, but it was far too bright, too steady. She twisted, following the strange luminescence.

Shock filled her at the sight of a hippocampus emerging from the gloom. Even through the chaos, Seraphina could discern its powerful equine torso and shimmering scales, each one awash in emerald and silver. Its mane flowed around its head, radiant as strands of starlight caught in the current. Those luminous eyes seemed to pierce the darkness, assessing, otherworldly, as if the ocean had birthed a guardian spirit.

Cordelia lay still on the seafloor, her hair drifting like tendrils of seaweed. The hippocampus glided toward her, moving with grace. The creature bowed its head, meeting Cordelia's half-lidded gaze. A swirl of magic rippled through the water, and light wrapped around Cordelia's wounded arm. Seraphina watched, both terrified and awed, as a sigil of blazing gold took shape on Cordelia's skin, a reflection of the hippocampus's own majestic form.

Her lungs screamed for oxygen. She should have surfaced again, but something about the hippocampus's presence held her transfixed. It radiated power—vast, serene, and yet undeniably fierce. The creature coiled around Cordelia's motionless body, and with a single mighty surge of its tail, launched them both upward.

Seraphina kicked in desperation, following the glowing trail. When her head broke the surface, the storm's wrath struck her all at once, rain pelted her face, and wind howled in her ears. Cordelia bobbed near the ship, the hippocampus nudging her gently, guiding her toward the rope ladder dangling from the hull. Teeth chattering, Seraphina fought her way over. Her arms nearly gave out when she finally found Cordelia's hand, but she poured every scrap of strength into hauling them both up.

Lightning crackled again, revealing a battlefield of carnage on the deck: sirens, steel, and the shrieking crew. With a grunt, Seraphina hauled Cordelia onto the deck, collapsing beside her in a trembling heap. Their lungs rasped in unison. Gasp after gasping breath mingled with the sharp tang of blood and salt.

The hippocampus let loose a thunderous roar from below, a sound so deep, so primal, that it vibrated through the very marrow of the sea. The storm seemed to shudder at its call, the waters thrashing in response. Even above the shrieking winds, the cry resonated, a challenge, a warning, a fury unleashed.

Then it charged.

The sirens balked when the hippocampus surged upward in a blur of silver and emerald. Its powerful, muscular frame cleaved through the water like a spear, hooves pounding through the surf with impossible power. The first siren didn't have time to react before the creature reared, striking with its forelegs. A sickening crunch echoed through the waves as bone met force.

It spun mid-current, tail coiling with whip-like precision, slamming another siren against the reef below. Teeth flashed, sharp and gleaming, sinking into scaled flesh. The sea frothed with blood.

Another tried to escape, darting toward the depths, but with a flick of its mighty tail, the hippocampus surged forward and slammed into its flank, sending it spinning into the gloom.

The remaining sirens faltered and scattered, screams swallowed by the deep.

And then, it was over.

The hippocampus turned. Water cascaded down its shimmering hide, each scale dripping with moonlight.

Seraphina, trembling, closed her eyes. Her tears mingled with the rain, their warmth indistinguishable from the cold. Her breath came in shudders, but she felt a presence beside her.

They were alive.

Cordelia whispered a quiet promise, "*Together, then.*"

The hippocampus, as if understanding her silent vow, let out a low, melodic cry, affirming that the bond between them had now been sealed.

Seraphina reached out to grasp her hand. "Cordelia," she managed, swallowing the lump in her throat, "what ... what happened down there?"

Cordelia's gaze drifted to the glowing mark etched on her arm. "I'm not sure," she whispered, voice trembling as she tried to stand. A tremor of emotion flashed across Cordelia's face. "She didn't just save me," she went on. "She chose me."

Emeric approached, his swords still in hand as he scanned the waters. His gray eyes narrowed when he saw the creature's radiant form gliding beside the ship. "Well, shit. That was an unexpected turn of events."

The hippocampus let out another cry, and Cordelia's bond-mark glowed in response. She exchanged a look with Seraphina, who smiled back at her through her tears.

"Boyde," Cordelia whispered, the name escaping her like a prayer.

A voice quivering with concern cut through the roar of the waves. "G-guys, are you okay?" Aleron approached from the far side of the deck, nearly stumbling over the body of a siren. Gone was any bravado; he looked utterly rattled, a smear of blood across his face.

Seraphina met his eyes. "We'll be alright," she whispered, forcing more strength into the words than she felt.

He ran a shaking hand through his soaked hair. "You're alive. Thank every star in the sky."

Seraphina and Aleron helped Cordelia to her feet and together led her across the bloodstained deck, the loop of their arms around her waist the only thing holding her upright. The three of them were soaked through, bruised, and shaken to their cores.

On their way below, Seraphina's breath caught. Strewn across the deck lay the twisted shapes of both man and siren, blood-darkened bodies half hidden by tattered sails and shattered barrels.

Professor Shay knelt among them, methodically dragging the fallen aside to clear a path, their shoulders tense with the weight of too many dead. A sheen of sweat mixed with sea spray glistened on their brow. They offered Seraphina a grim nod, but their eyes burned with unshed grief, their knuckles white as they hauled a lifeless siren to the far edge of the deck.

When they reached the cabin, Seraphina helped lower Cordelia onto a rickety chair.

Aleron cleared his throat. He hovered as if he didn't quite know what to do with his hands, shifting his weight from foot to foot. At last, he ventured, "I should go up top and help." The words tumbled out in a rush.

Seraphina managed a tight smile. "Thank you, Aleron." She watched him disappear down the corridor, his cloak trailing behind him, shoulders still tight with grief and urgency.

Despite the sharp ache coiled in her muscles and the ringing still echoing in her ears, Seraphina turned her attention to Cordelia. She reached for a dry cloth and knelt beside her, gently pressing it to the bleeding scrapes along Cordelia's arms. The blood had already started to dry in jagged trails.

"You'll be okay," she said softly. "Just breathe."

Cordelia let out a groan. "People died, Seraphina."

"I know," Seraphina murmured, voice cracking at the edges. "I know."

The two of them sat on the floor of the cabin, seawater dripping from their clothes, leaving dark puddles across the wooden boards. Seraphina stripped off her soaked tunic with trembling fingers, her body shaking from more than cold.

Cordelia followed suit, tossing her cloak aside and pulling on clean clothes before wrapping herself in a rough wool blanket.

For a moment, they just sat there, silent, the air between them thick with salt and sorrow.

"I can't believe you just bonded," Seraphina whispered.

Cordelia blinked, looking down at the bondmark on her arm. "Yeah," she said, voice tight. "Neither can I."

The ship lurched once more, then abruptly steadied. The storm's violent pitch and sway seemed to have calmed. Footsteps echoed from the corridor. Seraphina glanced up to find a tall woman stepping into the cramped space. Her hair, the color of moonlight, fell past her shoulders in a shimmering curtain, and her indigo robe was embroidered with swirling patterns reminiscent of ocean currents, but it was the scar running from her neck to her cheek that caught Seraphina's attention.

"There you are," the woman said, her voice carrying both authority and reassurance. Her turquoise eyes scanned them. "Cordelia, correct?" She stepped closer, the train of her robe whispering against the floor. "I'm Professor Hera, your bonding instructor. Word reached me that something unusual happened tonight."

Seraphina felt Cordelia tense under her hand. She squeezed Cordelia's shoulder. "She's been through a lot," Seraphina ventured, though her throat felt oddly tight. "Professor, she—"

"I understand," Professor Hera said, her gaze lingering on the glow of the mark still visible on Cordelia's arm. "May I?"

Cordelia swallowed hard, looking to Seraphina for reassurance. With a slow, shaky nod, she extended her arm, the radiant sigil visible even in the dimly lit cabin.

Professor Hera moved closer, her glowing silver hair catching the faint lantern light, and Seraphina's eyes narrowed. There was something … otherworldly about the woman, the fluid way she moved, the almost musical quality of her voice, and the faint shimmer around her figure. And then Seraphina saw them—ears, delicately pointed and partially hidden beneath that silver fall of hair.

She's fae.

The stories she had read growing up rushed back to her.

Hera leaned in, her fingers hovering near the glowing bond-mark on Cordelia's arm without touching it. "A hippocampus," she murmured, her tone reverent. "Extraordinary. And under such dire circumstances … quite the feat." She examined Cordelia's face, her expression kind but probing. "Did you feel anything unusual during the bond? A surge of energy or … something more?"

Cordelia hesitated. "It wasn't just energy. It felt … like a connection beyond words. Like we became something together. She said, 'We are one.'"

For a moment, silence hung between them. Then Hera's lips curved into a smile, though the scar on her cheek made it seem slightly forced. "A fusion bond," she said quietly as if savoring the term. "A true fusion bond. Incredibly rare, especially with a creature as ancient as a hippocampus. Did anything linger afterward?" Hera continued, tilting her head slightly. "A tether, perhaps? An awareness of the creature?"

Cordelia bit her lip. "I can still feel her," she admitted. "She's ... nearby."

Hera looked toward the porthole, where the hippocampus's shimmering form glided alongside the ship, its glowing mane lighting the dark water. "Fascinating," she murmured, more to herself than anyone else.

Straightening, she clasped her hands in front of her, her expression once again composed. "You may be experiencing a magical tether, a bond that persists beyond the initial connection. Such bonds are exceedingly rare, but when they do occur, they can yield great power. I'll need to test the strength of the bond," Hera added after a moment, her voice carrying a note of urgency. "The first twenty-four hours after a bond is formed are critical. Without proper inspection, instability can occur, and that can be dangerous for both you and the creature. Only someone with the right knowledge can ensure it remains stable."

Cordelia glanced at Seraphina, who sat nearby with a wary expression, but before either could speak, Hera extended her hand toward Cordelia's arm, her fingers glowing faintly with a pale blue light.

Seraphina's breath hitched as she saw Cordelia stiffen, her jaw tightening.

Cordelia frowned. "What ... what did you do? It feels different."

Hera withdrew her hand, her expression serene. "Good. The bond is stabilizing now. It was strong, but that strength can cause volatility without guidance. You should feel more balanced. The tether may seem weaker, but it's safer this way."

Cordelia gave a hesitant nod, reassured by Hera's calm tone.

"You'll need to rest," Hera said, clasping her hands in front of her. "Bonding, especially one so profound, can be taxing. I'll want to speak with you again soon, once the bond has fully integrated. Until then, stay close to your friends, and inform me of any changes you notice."

Seraphina crossed her arms, clearly still skeptical. "Is this something that happens with every bond?"

Hera's lips twitched, a flicker of annoyance in her turquoise eyes, subtle, sharp, and gone almost as quickly as it appeared. "Every bond is unique, but the early hours are always crucial. It's best not to take chances with magic as ancient as this."

Hera gave one final glance toward Cordelia, her silver hair shimmering in the dim lamplight. "Rest well, Cordelia. Remember, if anything changes, seek me immediately." Without waiting for a response, Hera turned and glided out of the room, her robes trailing behind her as she disappeared down the corridor.

Cordelia sat slumped in silence, the weight of exhaustion draped over her. Seraphina watched her for a moment, heart tugging at the sight of her friend so drained, her usual spark dulled. She stepped closer and laid another blanket around Cordelia's shoulders.

"You okay?" Seraphina asked, her voice threading through the quiet.

"I think so," Cordelia replied, but Seraphina caught the subtle tremble in her voice. "Just tired."

Seraphina gave a reassuring smile. "Get some sleep. You've had enough excitement for one night."

Cordelia nodded again. She leaned back against the cushions, her eyes fluttering closed as the events of the night caught up with her.

Seraphina couldn't sleep. The night's horrors pressed in on her, as suffocating as the damp air clinging to the ship's timbers. She slipped away from Cordelia's bedside, making sure her friend still breathed evenly, then moved to the small porthole set in the cabin's curved wall. She pressed her palm against the chilled glass; the water stretched into an endless black void.

She swallowed hard, remembering that somewhere down there, a hippocampus—the very one now bound to Cordelia—lurked among the waves. The thought should have been a marvel, but in the wake of everything else, it felt more like a reminder of how little she understood this new world she'd stumbled into.

A tremor ran through her as her mind replayed the siren attack: the shrieking wind, the splatter of blood on the deck, the limp forms of those who hadn't risen again. Seraphina had never seen such finality. Even now, she could envision the vacant stare of a fallen crewmate, frozen, as though still grappling with the impossibility of death. The image twisted her stomach, forcing her to clamp a hand over her mouth.

She took a deep breath, drawing in air slowly. The hippocampus, the sirens, the very real possibility that none of them might have lived to see the dawn, crashed over her like a rogue wave. Yet her thoughts refused to stay on the night's terror. Instead, they drifted across the ocean to the memory of Fadeya, her sister.

Fadeya had stood on the dock, chin high and eyes bright with an emotion somewhere between pride and envy. Her final words echoed in Seraphina's mind.

"I'm happy for you both. Just … write to me, okay? Tell me everything."

The memory of Fadeya's forced smile clung to Seraphina's mind, a stubborn ache that refused to fade. She could still see the hurt her sister tried to hide as she said goodbye. Pressing her forehead against the cold window, Seraphina blinked back the tears prickling at the corners of her eyes. In the excitement and chaos, she'd let her simple promise to write a letter slip away.

She drew in a trembling breath and let it out until the window blurred. *Tomorrow,* she vowed, *I'll fill the page with every moment of this voyage for Fadeya.* She couldn't send the letter until they reached the university, but nothing was stopping her from putting pen to paper.

Stepping back from the porthole, Seraphina spared a glance at Cordelia, whose chest rose and fell in steady sleep. With a sigh, Seraphina made her way to the other bed and let herself sink into its thin mattress. She closed her eyes, focusing on the promise she'd made, and let the steady roll of the ship lull her to sleep.

Chapter 7

ASTRAL UNISON
UNIVERSITY

SERAPHINA

Professor Shay and their bondmate, Kymaris, commanded the wheelhouse, shimmering threads of magic swirling through the wind as they guided the battered ship into the harbor. As the lines were tied to the pier, the gilded sails folded in compliance, like a mighty beast settling into uneasy slumber.

Beyond the docks, a winding road led up toward the university, where carriages waited, their steeds stamping the ground with restless energy. Seraphina stepped onto the dock and felt it immediately. Her legs wobbled, unsure, like part of her still expected the deck to sway beneath her. She grabbed the railing, steadied herself, and exhaled. She tried to focus on the excitement she had felt earlier on in the voyage, yet the sirens' attack haunted her. Only a week had passed since those deadly creatures rose from black waters, ending eight lives and shattering her innocence in a breath. Each time she blinked, she saw it all again.

Cordelia moved beside her. The bondmark on her arm shimmered, an iridescent curl of magic bound to her skin. It was still so new, so impossible, that Seraphina had to resist the urge to reach out and touch it.

A voice, smooth as silk, cut through the morning air. "Cordelia."

Professor Hera's presence was overwhelming as she swept down the path to meet them. Her sharp gaze examined Cordelia's arm, and for a moment, her impassive expression softened.

"How have you been adjusting to the bond?" she asked, her voice carrying an undertone of curiosity. "Have you sensed the creature's presence since the other night?"

Cordelia's face lit up. "Yes! She's incredible. I feel …" She hesitated, searching for the right words. "I feel like she understands me. Without words. Without effort. Like she's always been part of me."

Professor Hera nodded approvingly, though her expression remained neutral. "A rare connection indeed. Does she have a name?"

"Boyde," Cordelia said, pride swelling in her voice. "I wish I knew more about Hippocampi. I've tried scouring the ship's library, but it's mostly half legends and scribbled notes."

She hesitated a moment, then said to Seraphina, "Fadeya would have known exactly where to look. I swear she had a knack for finding obscure tomes even the librarians forgot existed."

A shift of emotions clouded Seraphina's face, remorse and pride woven together. "Yes," she said, eyes lingering on the waters beyond the dock. "My twin has a way of knowing things."

Cordelia reached out, her fingers brushing Seraphina's hand in comfort. "I have no doubt she will be here next year with you. She can try again at the next Starlight Awakening."

Professor Hera stilled. "Twin?" she repeated, her head tilting slightly. "That's … unusual. Twins are unheard of in the human realm."

Seraphina tucked a loose strand of hair behind her ear, her fingers lingering there a moment too long. "So I've been told," she said, voice measured, though the faintest tremor of vulnerability slipped beneath the surface.

"A twin," Hera murmured again, more to herself than anyone else.

She studied Seraphina like a puzzle she suddenly needed to solve. Then, almost absently, she murmured, "Strange, how the universe does that. Make two of something. A perfect reflection … until it isn't."

Something in Hera's tone unsettled Seraphina, not curiosity, but recognition, as if she were recalling a truth she'd once known too well. Cordelia cleared her throat beside her, and Hera blinked, the moment breaking.

"You should be on your way," the professor said, stepping back, already retreating into the sea of students. Just before she vanished, her voice reached them once more. "Reflections are fickle things, Seraphina. Best to remember that."

Then she was gone.

Cordelia exhaled only when the professor was out of earshot. "I didn't mean to stir anything up," she murmured.

Seraphina's smile was tight, almost convincing. "You didn't." Then she squared her shoulders. "Come on. The carriages are waiting."

Cordelia hesitated, but then nodded, falling into step beside her friend. They made it to a carriage, and Cordelia took both bags to put into the back.

As Seraphina settled into the cushioned interior, the scent of leather wrapped around her. The carriage jolted as Aleron climbed in, his tall frame folding into the space.

"Smooth." Seraphina chuckled as Aleron sat down a little too hard on the seat across from her. Undeterred, he grinned, his warm brown eyes gleaming as he lounged back, one arm draped carelessly over the seat. His cloak was slightly rumpled, as if he hadn't quite managed to keep himself together since the siren attack.

"You look like you're bracing for battle," he mused, tilting his head at her.

Seraphina arched a brow. "Maybe I am."

His smile widened. "Against what, exactly?"

She hesitated. The truth curled at the back of her throat, fragile, uncertain. Instead, she let her lips curve into something teasing. "The unknown."

Aleron chuckled, but there was a glint in his eyes, like he was two steps ahead in a game she didn't know they were playing. Before she could push further, the carriage door banged open again, and Cordelia all but flung herself inside.

"Move, move, move," she huffed, her elaborate skirts billowing as she squeezed in beside Seraphina, nearly knocking her off the seat.

Seraphina had barely caught her breath before Cordelia leaned in, eyes flashing with playful exasperation. "Are we writing our own epic now, or can we acknowledge the actual miracle here?"

With a flourish, she tossed her long black braids over her shoulder, her brown skin practically glowing. "We survived. The sirens, the storm, the ship nearly splitting in half, and let's not forget my completely unplanned but obviously destined bonding with a hippocampus." She waved a hand as if this were a minor detail. "Which, by the way, was the best part of the whole voyage."

Seraphina scoffed, leaning back against the cushioned seat. "Survived is a strong word."

Cordelia gasped, clutching her chest like she'd been mortally wounded. "I think we should all be impressed with ourselves. Flesh-eating sea demons are a pretty huge thing to overcome."

Aleron stifled a laugh, his long legs knocking against Seraphina's. "She's got a point."

Seraphina rolled her eyes, but a smile tugged at her lips. "Both of you are wicked."

Cordelia gasped again, this time with theatrical devastation. "And yet, here we are. Bound together by fate, tragedy, and the ever-shifting fabric of destiny."

Seraphina glanced between them, the weight of it all settling in her chest. "It was terrifying," she admitted. "For a moment, I thought ..." She trailed off, shaking her head.

Cordelia nudged her gently, her voice softer now. "We made it. We're here."

Outside, the world blurred past in streaks of gold and green. The carriages crested the final hill, and her jaw dropped as she gazed out of the window.

Astral Unison University loomed ahead, carved from pale opalescent stone that caught the light like ice kissed by morning sun. Its spires soared into the sky, tall and slender, each crowned with a golden sculpture of a magical creature, wings outstretched, claws poised, horns gleaming. Along the tallest tower, constellations rippled across the surface, shifting gently as if stirred by some unseen current.

Seraphina couldn't tear her eyes away. Her chest tightened, breath catching with awe. This place didn't just look magical, it felt *alive*. Vibrant. Whole. Everything shimmered with a quiet energy, like the land itself was humming. Back home, the human realm felt muted by comparison, dusty streets, crumbling stone, buildings worn thin by time and weather. Nothing like *this*.

She shifted in her seat, overwhelmed. She had never seen such beauty… or such wealth. The richness of color, the clean air…

The gardens unfurled in paths winding like ribbons through beds overflowing with blooms. Morning light streamed through the mist, catching on dew-draped petals that shimmered. At the center, a wide, still pond reflected the awakening sky—blues and pale pinks mirrored perfectly across its surface. It was spring here in the fae realm—undeniably, breathtakingly so.

"Wow," Cordelia breathed beside her as they stepped out of the carriage, eyes wide with wonder. "It's like something out of a storybook. Look at the architecture, Sera. You can practically feel the magic."

Seraphina nodded, her fingers grazing the cool stone of a nearby pillar.

Aleron walked beside them, his voice low, reverent. "It almost feels like the stars themselves are watching us."

She glanced up at him. "Do you think they are judging whether or not we are worthy?"

His eyes landed on hers. "I think they already know what we'll become."

A shiver trailed down her spine, though she wasn't sure if it was from the cool air or the depth of his words.

Professor Shay stood at the entrance, their sharp gaze sweeping over the group. "Please proceed to the main hall for your welcoming ceremony."

The group moved as one, stepping toward the property threshold. The enormous university archway loomed before them, humming with an energy that vibrated through Seraphina's bones. The arch was carved from moonstone, its pale surface gleaming in the light. Twisting up its towering frame were runes etched in sapphire, their shapes alive with motion. The etchings twisted and shifted, light flowing through ancient symbols.

And then they stepped through.

The cold hit her like a wave breaking on the beach. It sank straight through her clothes, clinging to her like wet linen. Her breath hitched, her body stiffened, and for a moment, it felt as though her muscles forgot how to move.

Seraphina braced her feet against the ground, but the stone beneath her boots felt unsteady, as if the world had tilted. The chill gripped her spine and climbed, wrapping around her ribs like iron bands. Her hands curled reflexively, fingertips aching with the sudden shift in temperature. A sharp tremor ran through her legs, and she had to fight the urge to fall to her knees. Her vision blurred, and her breathing turned shallow. Sweat beaded at her temples despite the cold. Every limb screamed for motion, to run, to shake this feeling off, but she stood still, jaw clenched, her entire frame locked in place.

A hand brushed her elbow, grounding her.

She blinked, and Aleron was there, his brow furrowed, his grip light but steady. "You okay?"

Seraphina forced a breath, shaking off the sensation like water from her skin. "Yeah. Just … a lot of magic at once."

His fingers lingered for a second longer than necessary before he let go. "Careful, Sera. If the magic's already making you swoon, I'm not sure how you'll handle the rest of the year."

She blinked once, trying to reorient herself. The ground still felt a little too far away, like her feet weren't quite anchored, and her pulse hadn't returned to normal. She forced herself to stand straighter, to lift her chin like she hadn't just come apart moments before. "I think I'll manage."

He examined her for a moment longer, concern on his face, before nodding toward the entrance. "After you."

Seraphina rolled her shoulders back and, with one final exhale, she stepped forward toward the towering doors.

The floors gleamed, inlaid with specks that glowed faintly beneath each step. Above, the domed ceiling stretched impossibly high, a perfect rendering of the cosmos in motion. Stars drifted and realigned in real time, their silver glow mirrored in the black glassy stone beneath, creating the illusion of walking between two skies.

Cordelia tilted her head back to gawk. "Is that a celestial map?" Seraphina barely heard her. The constellations shifted, their pull unmistakable. It wasn't just a map.

It was *leading* them.

"To our purpose," she whispered under her breath, more to herself than anyone else.

Aleron leaned in, his breath warm against her ear. "And what's yours?"

She turned to him, pulse hammering against her ribs. For a moment, she wasn't sure. For a moment, she couldn't quite remember.

At the front of the hall, an elevated dais stretched wide. At its center stood a towering statue carved from stone: Aurora, the university's fae founder.

Her face was serene, a mixture of wisdom and defiance. One hand rested on the hilt of a sword embedded in the ground before her, the blade wrapped in coiling vines of carved silver. Her other hand was outstretched, fingers splayed, palm upward, as though offering something unseen to the heavens. Around her neck, resting against the sculpted folds of her robes, hung an amulet, not carved from the same material as the rest of the statue, but real metal, dark and worn with age. A gemstone glimmered at its center, catching the torchlight with an eerie glow, as if the magic within it was alive.

The room filled slowly as students found their places on the long, curved benches arranged in a half circle around the dais. A low murmur of voices swept through the hall, whispers echoing against the high stone walls.

Cordelia nudged Seraphina. "Look at her. She almost looks alive."

Seraphina, who had been quiet since they stepped through the archway, blinked as if startled. She studied the statue, then shook her head. "She *is* alive. Not physically, but in every other way that matters."

Before Cordelia could press further, a hush fell over the hall as an older fae female stepped onto the dais, her presence commanding instant silence. Her brown skin bore the lines of a life well-lived, each crease etched with wisdom. Silver streaked through her thick, coiled hair, woven into an intricate crown of braids that framed her strong face. Perched on her shoulder was a magnificent bird, its purple feathers hanging down to the floor.

"Good afternoon," she said, her voice rich and resonant, reaching every corner of the great hall. "To those who are new, and to those returning, welcome to Astral Unison University. I am Headmistress Fallyn."

She moved along the platform, her long robes whispering across the stone. The bird on her shoulder released a trill, its song twining with the faint thrum of ambient magic that seemed to breathe from the very walls.

"Tonight marks the beginning of your journey within these sacred halls. A journey that, should you prove yourselves worthy, will bind you to magic in ways few can comprehend.

"Our founder, Aurora, built this university during an age when the world was fractured," Fallyn said, her tone deepening. "It was an age when humans could bond with the great magical creatures, when trust and respect ran both ways, but over time, and with evil influence, that began to change. Selfishness took root. Greed, fear, and cruelty spread through the human realm, and with it, the bonds began to be manipulated. What was once sacred was slowly corrupted."

She stepped forward, eyes filling with tears. "Some sought to force bonds, creating an imbalance that corrupted magic. The creatures, who had once given their trust freely, withdrew, retreating into the wilds."

She paused at the edge of the dais as she looked out over the students and tried to compose herself. "Many believed the connection was lost forever, but Aurora refused to accept that. She believed that among humanity, there were still those who carried the spark, the capacity to forge bonds through trust, not coercion. She created this place not just as a sanctuary, but as a challenge. A beacon. She studied the old ways, learned from the fae and celestial spirits, and in time, she discovered the Celestial Orb, a relic of immense power and judgment."

Fallyn rested one hand over her chest, her voice steady now. "It became the key. Through it, the first students were chosen, human and fae, whose hearts resonated with harmony rather than hunger, those capable of rebuilding what had been broken."

She took a slow breath. "Aurora prevailed. Her vision endured. And because of her, we stand here today, the inheritors of her legacy."

The bird on her shoulder gave a softer trill, almost wistful. Fallyn reached up and stroked the feathers behind its neck. "This is Serenith," she said. "She has been my bonded companion for many decades."

Her hand dropped to her side, and she turned again toward the assembly. Her eyes swept across the students, halting on something, or someone, at the far end of the hall.

Seraphina turned her head to follow the direction. Two fae stood at the far side of the room, their presence impossible to ignore.

The male fae stood with unnerving stillness, his presence like the deep, endless stretch of a midnight sky, vast, unknowable, and quietly consuming. His tall frame was built not with the overbearing weight of strength, but with the lethal ease of something perfectly designed to move through the world as it pleased. His hair, dark as ink, fell just past his shoulders, catching the torchlight with hints of deep blue. His face was all sharp lines and striking symmetry, a sculptor's impossible vision made real; cheekbones carved like the edges of a blade, and a mouth that looked neither cruel nor kind, but capable of being both. His eyes, a rich, bottomless brown, were unreadable and unbothered, as if everything before him was already decided.

Beside him, the female fae was something else entirely. Where he was shadow, she was the whisper of starlight. Her skin carried a faint iridescence, not obvious but present. Her dark hair cascaded down her back in loose waves, but it was her eyes that held the most weight—dark, endless pools with flecks of gold, like distant galaxies were caught within them.

They did not simply stand apart from the others. They existed differently, like beings who had stepped out of another world, still carrying its echoes in their bones.

Cordelia exhaled slowly, her attention fixed on the fae woman. "She's … breathtaking," she murmured, almost to herself. "Not just beautiful, unnerving. The kind of gorgeousness that makes you forget how to think."

Seraphina smirked. "Don't fall too hard, Cor. The way humans and fae age differently makes romance complicated."

Cordelia scoffed, tilting her head as she studied the fae. "Falling? Please. I don't fall, I observe." A slow, interested smile curled at her lips. "And they are worth observing. I wondered if they're students."

"They are," came a voice from behind, low and soaked in self-satisfaction.

Seraphina and Cordelia turned. Emeric stood just behind them, arms loosely crossed. The glint in his eye said he'd been listening longer than he should have

"That's Evander and Isadora," he continued, nodding toward the two fae.

Cordelia barely glanced at him, her attention still fixed on the pair across the hall. "How do *you* know them?"

Emeric gave a casual shrug. "I overheard someone talking earlier about them. They're the Prince and Princess of Aranroth."

Seraphina's stomach tightened. *Aranroth. The fae kingdom.*

A place where humans were nothing more than a passing thought.

Of course, they are royalty, she thought. Everything about them screamed nobility. They even stood with the kind of certainty that came from generations of power.

Cordelia's eyes roamed over Princess Isadora with keen interest. "A fae princess," she mused. "How delightful."

Aleron arched his brow. "You sound like you're planning something."

Cordelia grinned. "Maybe I am."

The Headmistress's voice called them back to attention. "In the coming days, you will attend classes, make friends, and learn the ways of the university. By the end of your first month here, many of you will begin bonding."

A ripple of murmurs spread through the students, but Fallyn silenced them with a raised hand. "For now, rest. Explore. Learn. And if you have the ambition, prove yourselves worthy of what this place has to offer."

With that, the ceremony ended.

As students began to disperse, Seraphina caught sight of Prince Evander making his way toward the exit, already flanked by a small group of students. He was pointing out features in the room. With that easy confidence, that smooth, assured way he spoke as he gestured to the grand architectural details around them, it was clear he was used to people hanging onto his every word. Princess Isadora walked beside her brother, poised and radiant.

Seraphina wasn't the only one who noticed.

"I'm going on that tour," Cordelia said suddenly, her voice steady, determined.

Seraphina turned to her, brows lifting. "With them?"

Cordelia's focus remained locked on the princess, something unreadable flashing behind her eyes. "It's practical."

Aleron scoffed, crossing his arms. "Practical. Sure."

Seraphina knew that look. Before she could say anything, Cordelia was already moving, weaving through the dispersing students with quick, confident strides, her braids bouncing with each step. Seraphina sighed, sharing a knowing glance with Aleron before following.

Chapter 8

WHAT HE LEFT BEHIND

FADEYA

Knees hugged to her chest, Fadeya sat atop her bed, meticulously threading beads onto a thin silver wire. The pattern had to be perfect: three amethysts, two pearls, one jade, then repeat. She'd already restarted it twice when a bead hadn't aligned just right. The rhythm of the work usually soothed her, the click of beads sliding into place like a quiet metronome for her thoughts, but today, her focus kept splintering. A misplaced knot in the cord made her pause, lips tightening as she stared it down. She unwound the entire row and started again.

Outside, the old oak tree swayed, its leaves rustling in the breeze. Spring had finally arrived, painting the world in soft color and warmth, but the ache inside her hadn't thawed. It had been a month since Seraphina left, yet the absence still pressed against her ribs like a bruise that refused to fade. The sound of the leaves, once a comfort, now only reminded her of how much had changed.

She looked up at the faint creak of the floorboards, and there her mother was. She stood in the threshold, silhouetted against the dim hallway light. A practical yet elegant traveling cloak draped over her shoulders, her sturdy boots dusted from an early morning errand. A packed leather satchel hung over one arm, the strap digging slightly into the fabric of her sleeve. Her dark hair, always so neatly pinned, had begun to show streaks of silver, but it was the set of her jaw that caught Fadeya's attention—that unyielding, determined expression she had come to know too well.

"It's time I went to visit your grandmother in Chefridge," Maris announced without preamble, her voice clipped. Her mother didn't step inside, didn't soften the words with even a hint of hesitation. One hand still rested on the doorknob, as if she were ready to leave before the conversation had even begun. "I've told the housekeeper to look after you and make sure you have meals. The carriage will be here any moment."

Fadeya's stomach sank. "So soon?" she asked, unable to keep the bitterness from her voice. "Seraphina is gone, and now you're leaving too?"

Exhaustion covered her mother's face, but she gathered herself quickly. "You know this trip is necessary," Maris said, adjusting the strap of her satchel. "We rely on your grandmother's money to keep this household running, to keep you fed, to pay for those lovely books and all the training you'll need if you actually plan on getting into the university next year."

Fadeya's face burned. She wanted to lash out, to hurl some scathing remark about how her mother never stuck around long enough to show she truly cared.

Her hands clenched into fists. "I'm not sure if I even want ..."

"Stop." Maris cut her off as she stepped farther into the room. "You can't afford to 'not be sure.' Sitting around moping, reading the same storybook pages over and over again, won't earn your acceptance." She exhaled, eyes flicking over the beads scattered on the bed. "This is the real world, Fadeya. Opportunities don't come knocking. You have to seize them. Now, I'm sorry I'm leaving, but you're old enough to understand priorities."

Fadeya clenched her jaw, wishing she could sink into the bed and disappear.

"I *do* understand," she managed, her voice tight. "Go. Do what you have to do."

Her mother's expression wavered with something akin to regret, but it was gone before Fadeya could define it. "I've left some coins in the kitchen. Don't be careless with them." She hesitated, reaching out a hand as though she might rest it on Fadeya's arm. Instead, she let it drop. "Good luck, my dear. Write to me if anything urgent happens."

She turned toward the door, her movements brisk, decisive, already halfway gone before Fadeya could process the weight of it all. Her gaze followed her mother, a tight, burning knot forming in her stomach. The hallway beyond gaped wide and empty. Once, their home had been filled with warmth, with laughter that clung to the walls. Now, it felt like a shell, hollowed out, piece by piece.

Her mother's footsteps faded down the corridor, steady, unhurried. No pause. No hesitation.

"Safe travels." The words felt small, swallowed by the vastness her mother left behind.

Moments later, she heard the muffled clatter of carriage wheels on the gravel drive. Then silence. It was the worst kind of hush—heavy, accusing, as if the entire house bristled with the knowledge that Fadeya was alone, *again*.

The lonely hush pressed in until she could bear it no more. She slid off the bed and padded out of her room. The attic door groaned in protest as she pulled it open. A stale, dusty scent drifted down the narrow staircase. She lit a small lantern hanging from a peg, watching the glow spill across old trunks and forgotten luggage. She made her way through the clutter, carefully navigating around ancient furniture draped in moth-eaten sheets.

Her heart ached as she remembered how Seraphina had promised to write every week from the university. It had been over a month. Not a single letter. What was she doing that was so important she couldn't take five minutes to scribble a quick note? Her thoughts betrayed her, unbidden and cruel, conjuring Seraphina; radiant, happy, thriving within the hallowed halls of Astral Unison University. No doubt she was surrounded by new friends, lost in lectures, basking in the glow of a life Fadeya could only imagine. *A life that didn't include her.*

The jealousy that surged wasn't sharp, it was molten, slow and heavy, pooling in her chest like a weight she couldn't set down. Worse than the jealousy was the whisper of fear threading through her. *What if Seraphina no longer needed her? What if her sister had already forgotten the bonds that tied them?*

Fadeya forced the thought down and looked to the cracked leather trunk resting at her feet. Its surface bore the marks of countless journeys, the family crest scuffed and faded with time. She crouched, brushing a hand over the worn lid. The feel of it sent a pang of nostalgia through her, stirring a memory. Her fingers lingered over the rusted latch, and she could almost hear his voice, her father, always evading her questions. *What's inside?* She'd once asked, and he'd only laughed.

Things meant for another day, Fadeya.

With a sharp twist, the latch gave, and the trunk creaked open. Dust spiraled upward, catching in the weak light, as if the trunk itself exhaled after years of silence. Fadeya's breath quickened as she stared down at the contents: a collection of old garments folded with care, brittle notes tied together in bundles, and at the very center, a tarnished silver ring. A simple pearl gleamed faintly from its setting. Her father's ring. She reached for it with trembling fingers. The cool metal pressed against her palm, and the weight of it felt unbearably heavy, as if the years since her father's death had settled into that one small object. Her throat tightened, the ache in her chest almost too much to bear.

Something beneath the ring caught her eye. A journal with a worn spine and a star-shaped clasp. She didn't recognize it, and she thought she'd gone through every one of her father's notes after he'd passed.

Fadeya carefully pulled the journal free, cradling it as though it might crumble under her touch. She glanced around the dim room before settling herself on an old chair nearby. Her pulse quickened as she undid the clasp, the *click* loud in the still air.

Inside, in ink that had faded with time, was his name. *Dyaus Elaris.*

She froze as she stared at the familiar loops of his elegant handwriting. Fadeya let her fingers trail down the edge of the first page. And then, slowly, she began to read. As she scanned the words, the bitterness and jealousy that had festered within her moments before ebbed away, replaced by something far more dangerous.

A spark. Her father had left her more than memories.

"I have never felt so inspired, so challenged, as I have these last few weeks at Astral Unison University ..."

The journal trembled in her hands. *He went to Astral Unison University?*

The idea was as foreign as it was thrilling. Her mother had never spoken of it. And her father? He'd never so much as hinted at academic accolades or time spent in a magical place. Yet there it was, written plainly in his own hand. She turned the page with care, the paper thin and delicate beneath her fingers. Her heart thudded as her eyes raced over his words.

"The sky here is breathtaking at night; it makes me wonder about the ancient starlight that guides each bonding."

Bonding. The word struck like a lightning bolt, her mind reeling. She pictured her sister among the sprawling university grounds, connecting with magical creatures she'd only dreamed about. Fadeya swallowed hard, pushing away the pang of jealousy, forcing herself to read on.

"Hidden chambers, cloaked in enchantments older than any we've ever studied, rumored to hold relics from Aurora, the founder herself. Few believe the tales, but I've seen the corridors etched with runes, ones that pulse with light under the right conditions. Accessible only to those who know where to look."

The words blurred for a moment as her mind caught on the images his writing conjured. Clandestine rooms, relics of the university's founder, secret corridors glowing with starlight. Her father, her quiet, reserved father, had *walked* those halls. He'd stood where Seraphina stood now, learning, exploring, uncovering secrets.

Fadeya's fingers tightened on the journal. If he had known so much about the university, why had he never spoken of it? Why had he kept it all locked away? Had he intended to tell them? One day, when they were older, perhaps when she and Seraphina were capable enough to understand? Or had he been waiting for something else entirely, something he hadn't lived long enough to see?

She turned another page, breathless now, driven by the burning need to know more. His words unraveled a vision of Astral Unison University unlike anything she'd imagined, a place alive with ancient magic and creatures. In the growing shadows of her father's secrets, she felt the first stirrings of something wild and reckless deep within her. She closed her eyes, exhaling shakily.

If only her sister had written, maybe they could have shared these revelations, but Seraphina was gone, lost in a new world, and apparently, she no longer cared enough to keep her promise of writing home.

She shut the journal gently, running her fingers over the star-shaped clasp. The dust-laden air of the attic felt a little less stifling now, as though a window had cracked open to allow a hint of fresh possibility. Every breath felt electric with the promise of secrets waiting to be uncovered. Rising with renewed purpose, she tucked the journal under her arm.

Let her mother travel, let her sister forget about home. She would learn all she could because maybe, just maybe, the stars were watching. And perhaps her father's words, etched in the pages of his journal, would guide her toward a destiny beyond what anyone had imagined.

SERAPHINA

Prince Evander dipped his head in a greeting. "Welcome. I trust your morning has been exciting." His voice carried a soft lilt of mischief.

Cordelia's eyes roamed over the group, lingering momentarily on Isadora, who flushed a deep crimson before managing a respectful nod.

Seraphina cleared her throat, forcing her attention back to Evander. "We're grateful for the tour," she said, voice echoing in the hush that had fallen over the courtyard. "It is unbelievable to see Astral Unison in person."

Evander's lips curved into the barest hint of a smile as he gestured for the group to follow. "Then come. Let us show you the heart of the university."

They moved in his wake, the hush of late afternoon wrapping around them like a well-worn cloak. Sunlight filtered through the canopy overhead, dappling the stone walkway. The trees flanking the path were old, their limbs swaying gently as if whispering secrets to the wind. Lanterns of etched crystal hung from wrought iron posts, each one glowing faintly, not from flame but from magic.

Cordelia walked confidently, her gaze sweeping over their surroundings, cataloging details with keen interest. Seraphina, on the other hand, hesitated, keeping a step behind, her fingers grazing the sleeve of her cloak. The air here felt different, charged, humming with a magic she hadn't quite grasped yet.

"Look at that," Cordelia murmured, nudging Seraphina's elbow and pointing toward a cluster of deep midnight-blue flowers sprouting from the edge of a shimmering mosaic. The petals glowed whenever a student neared. "It's like the plants are alive with magic."

"They are," a soft voice chimed in. They turned to see Princess Isadora, who had drawn closer.

"They're called Astro-Blooms," Isadora explained, kneeling gracefully to brush a fingertip along one of the petals. The flower brightened at her touch, flaring to life. "They respond to the energy of anyone who walks by, fae or mortal." A wistful note entered her voice as she added, "They remind me of home."

Cordelia's eyes lingered on Isadora. There was a tenderness in the way she looked at her, as though compelled by the princess's quiet grace. "They're beautiful," she said, her voice hardly above a whisper.

A small smile grew across Isadora's lips before she stood once more.

They continued on, the path opening onto a broad plaza where the dormitories loomed before them in a crescent of pale marble. Golden filigree scrolled across the exterior walls, shifting almost imperceptibly as the sun sank lower in the sky.

"These are the student dormitories," Evander announced, sweeping an arm toward the nearest set of doors. "You'll be assigned your rooms by the end of the day."

Aleron let out a low whistle as they stepped inside. The room was all polished floors and arched ceilings, frescoes of celestial beasts dancing across the high walls. He let out a quiet breath. "Isn't it strange," he said, eyes lifted, "how beauty like this is built for the in-between moments? Just a place to sleep, to pass through, and yet someone carved eternity into the ceiling."

Before the words had fully left his mouth, he turned to Seraphina, launching into a story with animated gestures. So caught up in his own excitement, he didn't notice the low-hanging lantern until it clocked him squarely in the forehead with a dull *thunk*. He stumbled back with a sharp curse, hands flying up a beat too late. The enchanted light bobbed away, wobbling like it had taken offense.

Seraphina clapped a hand over her mouth, shoulders shaking with barely contained laughter.

Aleron, ever the picture of dignity, straightened, rubbing his forehead with an exaggerated wince. "That lantern came out of nowhere," he muttered, shooting it a betrayed look before sidling up beside Seraphina.

Undeterred, he leaned in, voice pitched low.

"So," he murmured, as if nothing had happened. "Have you decided which creature you'd like to bond with?"

She swallowed, trying to steady her nerves. "Maybe a moonlight griffin," she said, cheeks warming the instant the words left her lips. "I've always loved the night sky."

He looked over at her with clear admiration. "That doesn't surprise me. You radiate a certain essence … as though you've been touched by starlight."

"Starlight binds us all," Seraphina whispered, the words escaping before she could stop them.

Cordelia, watching them from a few steps away, let out an exaggerated sigh. "You two! If you're going to make moon-eyes at each other, warn me so I can find a less nauseating spot."

Aleron chuckled, stepping back, but not before casting Seraphina one more lingering glance that set her heart racing. "We can't help it if bonding is on our minds," he said, offering Cordelia a playful shrug.

Prince Evander ushered them through a side passage where they emerged in front of a sprawling building shaped like a crescent moon. Made of pale limestone and dark timber beams, it had the stately presence of something built to last.

Inside, the space opened into a grand dining hall. Long wooden tables stretched from end to end, their surfaces smooth from years of use. The air smelled faintly of baked bread and roasted herbs, the lingering echo of a recent feast.

"Welcome to the commons," he announced. "Fae influences run strong in the cuisine here. Be prepared for some … exotic flavors."

A laugh bubbled up from Cordelia. "I can't wait to try something new." She glanced meaningfully at Isadora, who raised a brow in challenge.

"You may regret those words," Isadora teased. She leaned in slightly, her voice dropping to a conspiratorial murmur. "Some dishes tend to … sprout wings halfway through a meal."

Cordelia's eyes widened. "You're serious?"

Isadora's only answer was a mysterious smile.

Seraphina shot Aleron a sideways glance, her expression wry as they moved farther into the room. He matched her stride easily, hands tucked in his pockets, that familiar spark dancing in his eyes. "Are you as bold with your food choices as you are with your words?"

She tipped her chin up with a smirk. "I'd try anything once."

Aleron's expression was wolfish. "Then I'll make sure to sit next to you," he murmured, close enough that his words sent a warm shiver down her spine.

Their footsteps echoed as Evander led them deeper into the university. Other students drifted past, some watching curiously, others lost in their own worlds. Hallways splintered off in all directions, vanishing into the grandeur of the place.

Seraphina's gaze flicked from face to face—horns, wings, silvered eyes, skin that shimmered like stone or shadow. There were humans, yes, but far fewer than she expected. Here, they seemed like the exception rather than the rule. The realization settled over her like a mist.

Finally, they halted in front of two towering doors fashioned from glass and silver. Moon-and-star motifs were etched in intricate patterns across the surface, and as Evander drew near, the doors swung open of their own accord. Instantly, the hush of the library enveloped them like a protective cocoon.

Seraphina stood frozen for a moment, wonder blooming in her chest at the sight that unfolded. Shelves of well-worn oak curved along the walls, climbing steadily toward the high, timber-framed ceiling. The wood bore the weight of centuries, its grain darkened by age, its edges softened by touch. Leather-bound volumes and brittle scrolls filled every space. Beneath their feet, the stone floor was mottled and uneven, its surface dulled by the passage of countless footsteps. Carved archways framed the room, each one traced with slender threads of silver and gold in the shape of flowering vines. Suspended in the air were wisps of light, translucent and ever-shifting in form. They floated like fireflies, humming gently as they passed, their sounds resembling distant melodies or whispered incantations.

Isadora's voice was hushed as she stepped forward, fingers trailing lightly along the edge of a nearby shelf. "The Library of Astral Unison University. A sentient haven that rearranges itself according to one's intentions and needs."

Cordelia let out a soft gasp as one of the shelves slid closer, offering her a tome whose spine shimmered faintly with silver glyphs. "This is … incredible," she murmured, already reaching out. Her fingers closed around the book's worn leather binding.

She brushed her thumb along the cover and read aloud, "Tides Entwined: Bonding with the Hippocampus and Other Aquatic Creatures." Her eyes widened, and she turned to Isadora, her voice hushed with awe. "It sensed exactly what I needed."

Isadora met that gaze, a flash of something deeper passing between them. "That's precisely how it works," she said. "Believe me, once you learn to listen, the library will guide you to answers you never knew you needed."

Seraphina was only half listening, her attention stolen by the moonstone table at the center of the library. Its surface emanated a pearlescent glow. She approached it, mesmerized by the swirling patterns that seemed to shift beneath its surface. She extended a hand, brushing the cool stone with her fingertips. A subtle warmth bloomed in response, a whispered recognition that prickled along her skin.

Evander cleared his throat, drawing everyone's attention back to him. "We've come to the end of our tour, though there is much left to discover on your own. The library is yours to explore. All I ask is that you treat it, and one another, with the respect and wonder this place deserves."

Isadora nodded, though her attention still drifted to Cordelia's with a curious, almost tender gravity.

Aleron crossed the room and came to stand beside Seraphina, who still examined the table in the center. "I'll have you know," he said, flashing her a grin, "I have an excellent track record with libraries."

Seraphina arched her brow. "Oh?"

He leaned in, voice dropping just slightly, like a secret meant only for her.

"I've only been thrown out of three."

She snorted, unable to stop the laugh that escaped her, and Aleron's smile changed, just for a second. Softer. Less like a smirk, more like a moment. She'd forgotten how effortlessly he could make her laugh. Forgotten how good it felt to have him near. Stars, she had missed him.

Before she could react, he was already stepping away, hands in his pockets

"Come on, starlight," he called over his shoulder, throwing her one last glance. "Try to keep up."

She exhaled with a huff, head shaking in mock exasperation, yet her grin lingered as she followed after him.

Chapter 9

NOT ALL DOORS ARE MADE OF WOOD

FADEYA

adeya sat beneath the gnarled arms of the oak tree in her backyard, its twisted limbs stretching wide as if to cradle the fading remnants of daylight. The grass beneath her was still warm, steeped in the sun's lingering kiss, but the encroaching twilight carried a whisper of cold, curling around her bare arms like phantom fingers. Yet she barely noticed. Her world had narrowed to the worn leather journal in her lap, the scent of aged parchment and a trace of his cologne rising from its pages, ghosts of a life stolen too soon.

"There is no word for 'ownership' in the fae tongue. Not when it comes to creatures, or magic, or even love. Everything is shared or borrowed. That is why a bond must be mutual. Anything else would shatter the bond before it ever takes root."

She ran a reverent finger over the inked words, faded but still etched with purpose as if they might tether her to him, as if they might summon his voice from the spaces between each letter. Stars, how she longed to hear it again.

The day her father had vanished was a day she would never forget. Dyaus Elaris had kissed her mother's forehead, drawn both Fadeya and Seraphina into one of his steady, reassuring embraces, and offered that crooked smile he always wore when he wanted to ease their worries. "I'll be home before the next full moon," he'd said, voice calm, certain, but he hadn't come home.

She remembered her mother pacing the length of their sitting room, hands wringing in her apron, while Fadeya sat by the door, staring into the dark, willing him to step through it.

Weeks passed. Then a month.

Then the letter arrived. The cold, impersonal words, scrawled in a stranger's hand. He had perished on the journey. No explanation. No details. Just gone. As if life could be reduced to ink and paper.

His untimely passing left a hole in their lives that felt immeasurable. The journal was one of the few pieces of him she had left: his thoughts, aspirations, and the humor with which he viewed the world. Now, so close to nightfall, reading his recollections offered a semblance of comfort.

A tear slipped down her cheek. "I wish I could talk to you, Papa," she whimpered. "I wish you could tell me what to do, how to make sense of all of this."

She closed the journal with a snap; a shaky breath escaped her as she wiped at her cheeks, the tears already cooling in the night air.

Tilting her head back, she let the stars fill her vision, sharp and endless, like shards of broken light scattered across the sky. Without a word, she sent her plea into the void.

Just as she pushed herself up from the grass, the air in front of her rippled. A shimmer, subtle at first, like heat warping the horizon. Then, all at once, a rift tore through the night, silver light spiraling in delicate, curling tendrils that wove into the shape of a doorway. It vibrated, alive and humming with raw power.

Fadeya froze. What in the stars …?

A gust of energy rushed outward, pressing against her skin as the world around her dimmed.

Then, from within the glowing threshold, a figure stepped forward.

Fadeya stumbled back, her foot snagging in the thick grass as her pulse thundered in her ears. She barely managed to keep her balance as she scrambled away, breath shallow, chest tight.

The woman before her radiated power. Her silver hair flowed loose down her back, catching the moonlight in soft waves that shimmered with each movement. Her eyes, cold turquoise, sharp and unwavering, locked Fadeya in place. They weren't cruel, but they offered no refuge, as if they could strip away every mask she wore and lay bare the truth beneath. A single scar ran down her cheek, clean and precise, a mark not of weakness, but of survival, of stories left untold. It didn't diminish her beauty. It defined it. *Who is she? What is she?*

Fadeya swallowed hard, her mind screaming at her to move, to run, to do anything but sit frozen beneath the weight of that gaze, but she could only stare, transfixed, as the stranger took another step forward.

"I'm so sorry to startle you," the woman said, her voice like distant thunder rolling across an empty plain, dipping her head in a courteous bow. "You must be Fadeya. I am a Professor at Astral Unison University. My name is Hera."

Fadeya's fingers tightened around the leather-bound journal. "P-Professor?" The word barely made it past her lips.

Hera inclined her head. "Yes. I teach the Principles of Magical Bonding," she said. "Although lately, my teaching has been over-shadowed by troubling developments. And yes, I know your sister Seraphina. Forgive me for appearing so … dramatically." She offered a wry smile. "But time is of the essence, as they say."

Seraphina … The sound of her sister's name cracked something open inside her. Fadeya slowly steadied herself as she stepped closer. "What is going on?"

"There's a danger at the university. Someone I have yet to identify is interfering with the bondings between students and creatures. I fear the consequences if this saboteur continues unchecked. Bondings require delicate timing and guidance, and if these interruptions persist, many lives could be irreversibly harmed." She paused, folding her hands before her. "Your sister could be at risk, too."

At the mention of Seraphina, Fadeya's chest heaved. Thoughts of her sister conjured a swirl of emotions.

"Is she okay?" she whispered.

"For now, ..." Hera replied as she walked toward her and gestured toward the grass to sit.

Fadeya hesitated, her legs still tense, ready to bolt. This could be a trap, but if it's real, if there's even a chance Seraphina's in danger, I have to know more.

"What ... what does this have to do with me?" Fadeya asked, before sinking down to the ground.

Hera knelt gracefully as she met Fadeya's gaze at eye level.

"I need someone I can trust at the university," Hera said, folding her arms and watching Fadeya with the keen patience of a hunter. Not eager, not desperate, but *strategic*. As if she'd already run through every possible scenario in her head and had settled on this one: *Fadeya Elaris was the best option.*

Fadeya frowned. "You don't know me."

"I know enough," Hera said. "And most importantly,"—she gestured toward Fadeya's face, her turquoise stare unwavering—"you look exactly like your sister."

Fadeya stiffened.

Hera nodded as if confirming something to herself. "That's the real reason I sought you out. If anyone sees you, they won't stop to question your presence. They'll assume you're Seraphina. That alone makes you more valuable than anyone else I could recruit."

She shook her head in disagreement. "That's a terrible plan."

Hera's face shifted slightly in disappointment. "Is it?"

"Yes," Fadeya said. "Because the moment I open my mouth, the moment someone *actually* interacts with me, they'll realize I'm not her."

Hera rubbed her chin, considering. "Perhaps, but you won't be speaking to anyone."

Fadeya blinked. "You want me to sneak into Astral Unison *without talking to anyone?*"

"That's the idea," Hera said, her voice calm but edged with urgency. "Your job isn't to interact, it's to watch. Listen. Find out who is interfering with the bondings and how they're doing it."

She turned, eyes scanning the woods. "I'm stretched thin," she admitted. "Between teaching, research, and overseeing the bonding rituals, I barely have time to sleep, let alone keep track of every student forming a bond. Things are shifting faster than I can follow, and I need someone who can be where I can't."

Hera looked back at her. "I need an extra pair of eyes. Someone discreet."

Her thoughts drifted to her mother, unbidden. How long until she came back home and noticed she had disappeared? Would she even care?

A bitter answer rose in her chest. She left. Packed a bag, gave a list to the housekeeper, and vanished like it meant nothing. The ache in her ribs deepened, but she forced herself to swallow it. If she can walk away so easily ... Fadeya clenched her jaw. *Then maybe I can, too.*

Something flickered at the edges of her fear: curiosity. Possibility. A reckless, glinting thread of *what if.* Here was a way in, an opportunity.

Hera's words hung in the air, heavy with the gravity of the task. "This won't be easy," she continued, "but I believe you're the one who can do it."

Fadeya frowned, anxiety creeping into her stomach. "So ... you want me to spy? You want me to walk the halls of the university, eavesdrop on any new bondings, and summon you in secret?"

"Spy is such a harsh word," Hera replied. "I need your keen eyes and your discretion. Let's say I need a *shadow.* Someone invisible. Someone who can slip through the cracks without anyone noticing." She let the silence stretch, then added, "And no one, *especially* not your sister, can know."

Fadeya tightened her grip on her father's journal. A part of her burned with resentment; she'd dreamed of attending the university, but not like this, not in the shadows and subterfuge. Yet the other part of her ached with the desire to matter, to do something significant. Her father's words echoed through her, drawn from the pages she'd just read:

It's easy to wait for certainty, but if I have learned anything in this place, it's that certainty rarely comes. We act anyway. We choose, knowing we might fail. There is dignity in trying. There is honor in showing up for what matters.

Fadeya's breath caught in her throat. He would've gone. He would've said yes, not because it was easy, but because someone needed to. Because it was right.

"I ..." She hesitated, words tangled at the edge of her throat. She rose slowly, almost reluctantly, brushing stray grass from her skirt with a shaky hand. "I don't know. This isn't how I imagined finding my way there."

Hera stood. "I understand," she said, placing a hand on Fadeya's shoulder. "I truly do, but this isn't just about the university. It's about protecting students, protecting your sister, and ensuring that the sacred bonds that form between students and magical creatures aren't destroyed before they can blossom. If you agree to help me, you will be saving lives. And," she added, "I'll happily help you prepare for the Starlight Awakening next year."

Fadeya's thoughts tumbled in her mind. This was a chance to have a purpose, and it would help her attend the university next year. She inhaled slowly, gazing up at the distant stars flickering like silent witnesses to this momentous choice.

"All right," she said, at last, her voice trembling but determined. "I'll do it."

Hera's face brightened, and with a snap of her fingers, the swirling portal came back to life, bathing the yard in its soft, silver light.

"Come," Hera said, offering a reassuring smile. "We can't waste another moment."

With a shaky breath, Fadeya cast one last glance at the familiar shapes of her backyard: the oak tree, the low stone wall, and the garden overrun with wildflowers. She etched each detail into memory. Her fingers found Hera's outstretched hand, and she hesitated for only a heartbeat before slipping her own into her firm grasp. The strength of Hera's hand was reassuring. As their fingers entwined, a tingling rush of magic surged through Fadeya, sweeping over her like a sudden gust of wind. She took a steadying breath, then, together, they stepped forward. The world around her dissolved in a cascade of light, folding in on itself in dazzling waves. Fadeya felt weightless and grounded all at once, as though she were caught in a dream she couldn't wake from.

The weight of the portal's magic still clung to her skin, static, tingling, as if reality itself had momentarily unraveled to let her through. She clutched her father's journal, blinking as her surroundings sharpened into focus. Gone was the sprawling oak, the familiar garden she had known. In its place, a courtyard stretched before her, a sanctuary of tangled beauty hidden within the heart of the university. A stone path wound through beds of flowers, their petals curled in sleep, their fragrance thick in the damp night air.

She could hear the distant trickle of water, a fountain hidden somewhere beyond the hedges. And beneath it all, a quiet energy buzzed in the air, subtle but unmistakable.

Magic.

She spun slowly, pressing a hand against her chest as if to steady herself. Anxiety flickered, sharp and insistent, but beneath the uncertainty, the unknown, a spark of something else stirred.

Anticipation. She was here.

Behind her, Hera stepped forward, her silver hair catching in the soft light.

"Welcome to Astral Unison University."

Seraphina ran a hand through her hair as she followed Aleron out of the lecture hall, trying not to focus on the way his broad shoulders moved beneath his jacket. The late-day sunlight that had spilled through the arched windows was gone now, leaving the corridors draped in a dusky violet hue. The university's stone walls echoed with the shuffle of students eager to escape to their dormitories or into the city for a night of mischief.

Aleron cast her a glance, the corner of his mouth curling in amusement as if he could hear her thoughts. "You're staring."

She snapped her gaze forward. "I was not."

"You totally were. Can't say I blame you. I am distractingly handsome."

She let out a sharp laugh. "Distracting? Maybe. Handsome? Debatable."

He gasped, clutching his chest in mock horror. "Seraphina, you wound me."

She rolled her eyes, though a traitorous smile tugged at her lips.

They reached the wide marble steps leading outside, and he turned to her.

"Care to join me for a walk?"

She hesitated a moment. "This late?"

"I'm not ready to say goodnight yet," he said softly, offering his arm in a gentlemanly gesture. "Unless you'd rather head back."

Her stomach twisted with nerves, and yet she slipped her hand into the crook of his elbow anyway. "I suppose some fresh air wouldn't hurt."

They descended the steps and left behind the bustle of students for the manicured paths that wove through the university's gardens. Neat rows of moonflowers and twilight roses shimmered under the faint glow of conjured orbs hovering along the walkways.

Aleron's voice broke the hush. "You were incredible in class today. I honestly don't know where you pull that focus from; your responses to the professor's questions about elemental conduits were spot on."

Seraphina felt a blush creeping up her neck. She trained her eyes on the white stones at her feet rather than look at him. "I just study ... a lot. It's no big secret."

He chuckled, kicking at a rock on the path. "You give yourself too little credit."

They strolled along a winding path framed by manicured hedges. Above them, the sky was a deep-blue canvas pricked with stars. Seraphina paused as she caught sight of them, her breath snagging in her throat.

"You alright?" Aleron asked, noticing her sudden stillness.

She tore her gaze away from the constellations. "Yes, of course."

They continued deeper into the gardens, where tall, swaying willow trees encircled a pristine pond. Fireflies flickered above the water, and the faint moonlight painted rippling patterns across the surface. Seraphina paused for a moment as she realized they were utterly alone here, the rest of the university's glow muffled by the veil of leafy branches. Crickets trilled in the undergrowth, a chorus to the slow, sweet hush of water lapping against the pond's edge.

He led her toward a wooden bench beneath a drooping branch. He let go of her arm but only so he could slide a bit closer, turning to face her fully. She felt his stare before she dared to meet it.

"You're quieter than usual," he said softly, resting his forearms on his knees. "Something on your mind?"

She exhaled, fingers twisting in her lap. "I'm just ... nervous. About everything. The classes, the future." Her throat tightened. "You."

Aleron blinked, then slowly, deliberately, pointed to himself. "Me?"

She groaned, dragging a hand over her face. "Forget I said anything."

"Oh, no. Absolutely not. We're unpacking this." He leaned in, his grin wicked. "What is it about me that has you so rattled? My devastating charm? My rakish good looks?"

She smacked his arm. "I'm serious, Aleron."

His grin softened. "So am I." He reached for her hand, his fingers brushing over hers. "What's *really* bothering you?"

She felt hot under his steady regard, like he could see right through her attempts at composure. "I'm worried I'll disappoint you," she admitted, cheeks burning. "And that's not exactly something I've ever cared about before. But with you …" She swallowed. "It's different."

"Seraphina." His voice was rougher now, laden with emotion. "You could never disappoint me. Don't you know by now that I …" He trailed off, drawing in a shaky breath.

Her pulse roared in her ears. "What?" she managed.

He leaned closer, the heat of him wrapping around her like a velvety cloak. "I care about you," he whispered. "I always have."

The words lit her nerves aflame. She dug her nails into the seat of the bench as a flurry of conflicting emotions warred in her chest: surprise, delight, and a persistent whisper of unworthiness. "I'm just me," she stuttered. "You're … you're everything I'm not. Confident, smart, so sure of yourself."

He let out a quiet laugh, shaking his head. "You really think I have it all figured out?" His lips twitched. "That's adorable."

She scowled. "I take it back. You're insufferable." But she couldn't quite keep the smile from tugging at her lips.

"Seraphina," he said, more serious now, voice low and earnest. "You are the most determined, brilliant person I know, but it's more than that." He shifted slightly, brown eyes catching the golden light of the moon. "You see the world like it *could* be. You look at chaos and still manage to find hope. That kind of heart? It's rare. And I admire that more than you realize."

Aleron leaned back, bracing his arms against the bench, his gaze flicking to the night sky once again. "You ever wish on stars?" he mused.

Seraphina quirked a brow. "You mean like a child making a wish on their birthday?"

He shot her an unimpressed look. "I was going for something a little more profound, but sure, let's compare my deep, introspective moment to an eight-year-old wishing for a pet dragon."

She smirked. "That's a solid wish. Who wouldn't want a pet dragon?"

"Good point," he replied, sighing. "Sometimes I just … I get this feeling that if I wish for the right thing, at the right time, the universe will hear me."

Seraphina's chest tightened, a pang echoing in some hidden corner of her soul. His words tugged at something, something she couldn't quite grasp. A memory, distant and blurred, of someone telling her to believe in starlight, to trust it, but just as quickly as the thought surfaced, it slipped away, dissolving into the night air.

She cleared her throat, blinking against the sudden blur of tears. "What do you wish for?"

Aleron turned his head toward her, his dark eyes locking onto hers. "Lately? For the chance to show you, I'm all in. That what I feel is real."

Her heart threatened to burst from her chest. She could scarcely breathe, and yet it felt like all the air in the world had funneled into that intimate space between them. The stars overhead gleamed brighter, as if leaning closer to witness the moment.

Aleron's hand pressed against her cheek, his thumb brushing away a lone tear she hadn't realized she'd shed. "May I?" he asked, voice full of tenderness.

She nodded, words lost in her throat. He leaned in, his lips brushing hers in a gentle question, testing the resolve they'd both been skirting for weeks. She felt the warmth of his breath, smelled the faint hint of spiced cologne, and it broke something inside her, some barrier of fear. Seraphina answered, tangling her fingers in his hair, drawing him closer.

The kiss deepened, slow and sweet at first, then all at once fierce, consuming. He tasted of hope and wild possibility, of something she hadn't even dared to dream of wanting. The world melted away; there was only Aleron, only the press of his lips, the way he breathed her in like she was something worth holding onto.

And stars, she wanted to be held onto.

When they finally broke apart, both were breathing hard, foreheads pressed together. She blinked up at the stars, emboldened by the realization that maybe she wasn't as unworthy as she'd always believed. Because if someone like Aleron, the man who constantly challenged himself and strived to protect and uplift everyone around him, could have feelings for her, then perhaps she truly did have something precious inside her.

A radiant, giddy warmth settled in Seraphina's chest, chasing away the last trace of lingering doubt. Her eyes fluttered back to Aleron, who watched her with a gentle, bright-eyed wonder.

She laced her fingers through his, the new confidence in her voice surprising even her. "Let's make another wish," she whispered, glancing at the stars.

"For what?" he murmured, his lips tilting in a hopeful smile.

She squeezed his hand. "For more nights like this one."

He pressed his forehead to hers once more and brushed his lips to hers in a kiss as soft as starlight.

Chapter 10

INTO THE SHADOWS

FADEYA

In the cool, dim light beneath the university, Hera led Fadeya through a winding maze of hallways. Their footsteps echoed against stone worn smooth by centuries.

"We're in the undercroft now," Hera muttered. "Only select faculty members and students with permission know how to navigate these passages. For now, you'll remain hidden here, away from prying eyes. Any potential bonding should be reported to me immediately. I will give you a map of the university when we get to your quarters."

They rounded a bend into a narrow corridor, its walls adorned with faded tapestries depicting long-forgotten legends and epic feats. The ceiling soared overhead, forcing Fadeya to tilt her head back to see it, a vault of painted stars that made the passage feel as though it touched the very heavens. For a moment, she stretched out her hand as if she could pluck a star from the night sky.

"Bondings?" Fadeya asked, her voice trembling with wonder as they made their way out of the undercroft. "With magical creatures?"

Hera inclined her head. "Precisely. These pairings, between mortal or fae students and their magical counterparts, are vital to keeping the balance of our world. When a creature chooses someone, the two become linked in both power and life force."

They stopped before a wrought iron gate, and Hera pressed her palm against the metal; with a resonant click, the gate swung open to reveal a grand hallway.

For a moment, Hera stood still. Her hand hovered just above her pocket, fingers brushing the fabric as if debating something. Then, with a quiet breath, she reached in and withdrew a slim chain bearing an amulet of polished obsidian.

She held it delicately, the way one might hold a precious item. "Wear this," Hera instructed, voice slightly taut, extending the chain to her. "It harnesses shadows which will cloak you to help you remain unseen. Just place your hand on top of it, and the shadows will appear." She lightly tapped the obsidian; a ripple of dark luminescence danced within. "It will also glow when a surge of magic is near, signaling a potential bond."

Fadeya's fingers trembled as she accepted the amulet, feeling a curious warmth pulse through her skin as she fastened it around her neck. "Thank you," she whispered. *A magic amulet! I've never heard of such a thing.*

"Use it wisely," Hera warned, eyes lingering on the amulet. "We must keep you hidden, and we must keep the bondings safe. Let no one know your true purpose here. If someone happens to see you, they will suspect you are your sister," she added with a thin-lipped smile. "You must avoid being seen by your sister at all costs."

Fadeya's stomach fluttered with nerves, but she nodded. "I understand."

"Go ahead and try it now while we move through the common area," Hera suggested.

Fadeya ran her fingers over the amulet and closed her eyes, willing the shadows to envelop her. *Please work*, she thought.

She opened her eyes to find Hera staring back at her, or rather at the spot she had been standing in.

"Perfect." Hera nodded and gestured for her to follow.

They made their way down the hallway, and the university opened up before them. Fadeya momentarily forgot to breathe as she surveyed the grounds. Ornate statues of winged creatures perched at every landing. Doors with brass handles stood along the walls, each leading to classrooms and offices.

Hera guided her through corridors that grew more crowded with each step. She paused before a massive oak door, laying her hand on the worn brass knob. She whispered to Fadeya, "Stay here a moment while I retrieve the map from Professor Eldwyn." With a nod, Hera slipped inside, leaving her companion alone in the corridor.

Students, human and fae, hurried past, arms laden with books and half-scribbled notes. Some wore long robes embroidered with runes; others, breeches and boots, scabbards clanking at their sides.

Stars, she thought as she observed the students walking past, *I didn't bring anything. Not even a change of clothes.* Her current outfit, simple, practical, and slightly wrinkled from the meadow, stood out among robes stitched with glimmering thread and elegant gowns. *I'll have to ask Professor Hera for some supplies.*

Fadeya's pulse thundered in her ears as she pressed her palm against the amulet, the cool weight of the shadowy stone a steady anchor in the noise of the corridor. She could still sense the slow, thrumming beat of the magic within the gem. A faint draft snaked through the alcove, carrying with it the muted murmur of voices.

Two figures stood there, half hidden in a corner. One was a young fae female with jet-black hair that cascaded down her back. Her eyes were a warm, deep brown, rich as polished mahogany, and framed by thick lashes. Her lips pressed into a line of concern as she leaned closer, her hand draped over the forearm of another fae, a male whose silhouette seemed carved from the shadows.

Fadeya's breath caught at the sight of him.

His face was sharp in all the right places, angled cheekbones, a strong jaw, eyes that gleamed like a starless midnight. And scattered across the bridge of his nose and just beneath his eyes were a dusting of freckles. It was the sort of striking beauty that made her lungs stop working for a moment. He wore an immaculate ensemble in shades of ebony and silver, the fitted sleeves layered with dark trim.

The fae female leaned closer, her voice urgent yet hushed. "You have to find a creature to bond with, Evander. Father expects it to be done soon. He's disappointed you didn't succeed last year. This is your second year; by now, most heirs have forged their bond."

Father, Fadeya thought, inching closer. *They must be siblings.*

The male, Evander, clenched his jaw, his eyes flashing with simmering frustration. "I know, Isadora," he said, each syllable clipped. "I don't need you reminding me of Father's displeasure; he's made it perfectly clear, but I can't compel a magical creature to choose me. The bond must be genuine."

Fadeya's fingers reflexively tightened around her amulet. Despite the distance and the hush of their conversation, she felt the crackle of unspoken tension between them.

Isadora stepped in front of Evander, refusing to let him side-step. She raised her chin, gripping her hands tightly at her sides. "I know you've been keeping something from me," she said, her voice rising with worry. "Why else would you be slipping out at night and sending those long, secret letters to Aranroth?"

Her question hung in the air, broken only by the distant hum of chatter from other students. Evander glanced over his shoulder, searching for eavesdroppers. Even in the shadows, Fadeya could see the tightness in his jaw and the way his shoulders went rigid.

"It's nothing to concern yourself with," Evander replied, trying to sound dismissive, but his voice wavered. "I'm only working on a project Father asked of me."

Isadora snorted, the sound sharp. "Project? Come on! You used to tell me everything. Now you won't even look me in the eye."

Evander lowered his head. "Don't push me on this. It's just … complicated." His tone shifted, holding a note of desperation. "Look, if it were only up to me, I'd—" He cut himself off, throwing another glance down the corridor.

Footsteps echoed from the corner.

"Evander—"

He held up a hand, his expression pinched with urgency. "We can't do this now, not here. If we're late for Professor Flora's class one more time, she'll have us scrubbing cauldrons until sunrise." His brow furrowed as he lowered his voice. "But I promise, Isadora, there's nothing to fear. Just trust me." Evander reached for her arm and steered her gently toward the corridor's end. "Come on," he murmured, a touch of remorse darkening his eyes. "We can talk more after class. I won't keep everything a secret forever."

"You better not," Isadora whispered as she let him pull her along.

Fadeya's chest tightened at the sight of Evander's frustration. Even though she'd only overheard fragments of their conversation, that spark of vulnerability beneath his steely composure drew her in more than it should have.

Hera suddenly appeared, her hand darting out, fingertips brushing Fadeya's wrist in a silent summons. The touch jolted her, not just with surprise, but with the sudden, chilling realization that the shadows cloaking her must have dropped while she lingered too long, too distracted. Without thinking, she ran her fingers quickly over the surface of the amulet at her neck, willing the veil of shadow back into place.

Hera tilted her head and guided her into the swirling current of students. Bodies pressed around them, tunics and cloaks rustling, laughter and chatter echoing off the high-arched ceilings, until the two of them were just another pair swept along by the tide.

They navigated the crowded corridor with unspoken urgency, skirting past chattering classmates. At last, they ducked into a dark room hidden from view. Only then did Hera cast Fadeya a sharp, measured look.

"So," Hera murmured, voice low enough that only Fadeya could hear, "you saw him. Prince Evander."

Fadeya tried, and failed, to keep the heat from blooming across her cheeks. Memories of his dark hair and the quiet thunder in his eyes flared through her mind. She snorted softly, a blend of disbelief and fascination twisting in her chest. "Of course, he's a prince," she said, though her tone held little surprise.

Hera's demeanor changed, her grin changing into a wry, knowing smile. "I've noticed that he's paying close attention to other students' bondings," she said. "I want you to keep an eye on him. His father, King Malveric, has always had his hands too deep in the university's business. I've never trusted him." Her lips pressed thin, as though the admission tasted bitter on her tongue. "Just in case," she added, letting the words hang heavy in the space between them.

Fadeya nodded. She could still feel Evander's shadowy presence lingering at the edges of her thoughts.

They continued up a winding stair, stepping aside as a trio of older students thundered down the steps, nearly colliding with her and Hera. Their excited chatter about an upcoming practical exam trailed behind them like a gust of wind.

As they made it to the bottom of the staircase, a melody caught her attention. A lilting tune drifted through a high-arched doorway, accompanied by the faint strum of stringed instruments. Curious despite herself, she took a step toward the music, leaning into the doorway.

Then she froze.

Silhouetted against the lantern-lit courtyard stood a trio of figures. In the middle, recognizable even in partial shadow, was Seraphina, her twin sister. The shock of it rocked Fadeya to her core, robbing her of breath. It was the first time she had seen Seraphina since arriving, and she hadn't expected to find her so ... at ease.

Aleron, her old friend, touched her sister's arm as he laughed loudly, and Seraphina answered with her own chime of giggles. Cordelia, standing on the other side, twirled her hair around her finger as she watched them both, smiling at some private joke they shared. The small group looked happy, their voices weaving in and out of the gentle music still drifting through the courtyard.

For a moment, Fadeya couldn't look away. Pain passed over her in waves, raw and unexpected. The memory of shared childhood secrets and stolen midnight conversations stabbed at her heart.

She wanted to march into that courtyard, to demand how Seraphina could smile so breezily when she felt as if she balanced on the edge of a blade, but she didn't move; she forced her feet to stay rooted, swallowing the tangled knot of jealousy and betrayal. *Do you even miss me?* she wanted to shout.

Hera stood beside Fadeya, her eyes snapping between the courtyard and the tumult of emotion evident across Fadeya's face.

Her voice, though quiet, carried a resonance. "Now you see how this place can change people," she said. "There's more going on beneath the surface than most care to admit. Bonds can unravel before you even realize what's happening."

Fadeya inhaled slowly, tightening her grip on her father's journal, still clutched in her hands. "I'll manage," she said, forcing the words to sound steady even as her stomach lurched.

Hera's eyes glimmered with understanding that bordered on sympathy. "Come," she said, drawing Fadeya away from the courtyard's view. "Let's secure your quarters. You'll be staying in a smaller wing, near mine, somewhere you can retreat to if you need the space."

Seraphina's laughter rose again, wrapping around Fadeya like a cruel melody. For years, that sound had been home. Now, it only reminded her of everything she had lost. She turned away before the hurt could swallow her whole and followed Hera into the shadows of the corridor.

SERAPHINA

The lecture hall at Astral Unison University was a cavernous space, its painted ceiling enchanted to reflect the evening sky. Seraphina leaned forward in her seat, tapping her fingers against the worn wooden desk as the room hummed with murmured conversations. Beside her, Aleron stretched out lazily, his boots kicked up against the base of the desk in front of him, earning a sharp glare from Cordelia.

It had only been a few days since their kiss in the gardens, but the memory lingered with startling clarity—his breath against hers, the way the world seemed to fall away in that moment. The thought slipped in before she could stop it, and a flush crept up her neck. *Pull yourself together,* she told herself, quickly fixing her gaze on the enchanted ceiling above.

The murmurs died as the great doors at the front of the hall swung open, revealing Professor Eldwyn, and at his side padded a creature of both elegance and power, a great white wolf, its fur like fresh-fallen snow, its eyes brilliantly blue.

Professor Eldwyn's translucent wings shimmered faintly as he moved, folding neatly against his back. He studied the students for a moment, then, in one quick motion, he bowed his head in greeting. The wolf dipped its muzzle in unison.

"Good evening, scholars," he said. "Tonight, we embark on a journey through the annals of history, the essence of magic, and the enigma of human power. This is my bondmate Lunaris." He nodded at the large wolf beside him.

Bondmate! Seraphina thought as her gaze settled on Lunaris. I will never get used to seeing these beautiful creatures.

With a flick of his fingers, Professor Eldwyn sent a ripple of shimmering energy across the room. The ceiling transformed into a living tapestry. Images unfurled like a dream, the primeval forest, where ancient beings, fae, and magical creatures moved with harmonious purpose.

Eldwyn rested a hand on Lunaris's flank. A faint, thrumming bond seemed to connect them, and when the wolf lifted its head, runes glowed briefly along Eldwyn's forearm. "Long before humanity discovered magic, the world was alive with it," Eldryn began. "Fae wove it into the wind and water, dragons into fire and earth. Magic was not learned; it was breathed, felt, lived."

The image shifted, the mist parting to reveal a lone figure standing at the edge of the forest. A human. Then, slowly, the figure reached forward, grasping at a glowing orb of magic.

Eldwyn's voice darkened. "But, then came humans."

A faint prickle ran down Seraphina's spine as she glanced at Cordelia, who was unmoving in her seat.

"Humans were outsiders to magic, and yet, they craved it. Where we fae saw magic as a song to harmonize with, humans saw it as a tool to wield. This divergence shaped the course of history, for better and worse."

A scoff echoed from the back of the room. Seraphina turned to see Emeric slouched against his desk, arms crossed, an insufferable smirk on his face.

"Typical," he muttered. "The fae act as if magic is their birthright."

Beside Seraphina, Cordelia stiffened, her hands curling into fists so tight her knuckles blanched. Isadora, ever composed, merely arched a single brow, but there was something razor-sharp in her eyes.

At the front of the hall, Professor Eldryn moved down the row of chairs. His wings rustled slightly as he turned, his piercing gaze locking onto Emeric. "Do you have a thought to contribute, Mr. Vexley, or are you merely here to provide background noise?"

A ripple of laughter moved through the students. Emeric grinned, unaffected.

"Just seems to me," he drawled, drumming his fingers against the desk, "that history repeats itself, doesn't it?"

Eldryn didn't move, but with a wave of his hand, the enchanted ceiling darkened. The stars above them were snuffed out, swallowed by a tide of red.

Gasps echoed as an image took shape.

Seraphina's eyes widened. This isn't just an image, it's a memory.

Above them, a battlefield unfurled, a scene of chaos rendered in scarlet and ash. It stretched endlessly, a picture from a nightmare, where the earth itself was wounded, blistered by fire, and scarred by fury. Fae warriors lay scattered, their bodies tattered, fragile skin torn open, glowing faintly even in death. Humans, too, lay strewn among the carnage, armor splintered, swords fractured, eyes staring sightlessly at a sky heavy with smoke. Creatures of legend lay broken and humbled in the crimson mud. Clouds rolled restlessly, shuddering with distant echoes, phantom war cries and

129

screams carried like whispers on the wind, trapped in this terrible replay of violence and sorrow.

Seraphina's pulse pounded in her ears. *This was real. This actually happened.*

Each breath the students drew tasted of iron and grief, an overwhelming wave of dread pressing down upon them, suffocating.

Lunaris paced forward, her paw steps soundless on the stone floor, eyes fixed upon the swirling red illusions as if remembering them firsthand.

"The Great Schism," Eldryn said, his voice carrying over the silent hall like a war drum. "A battle that nearly shattered both realms. Humans sought magic's power, not as partners, but as conquerors. They forced bonds where none should exist, tore the balance asunder. And so, the magical realm resisted." His words hung heavy, thick with old wounds that had never truly healed.

"The war waged for centuries," he continued, his voice heavy with sorrow, fingers reaching gently toward the vision suspended above. At his touch, the battlefield dissolved slowly, fragments fading like ink dispersing through water, giving way to a new scene.

Now, standing beneath a bruised and weeping sky, were twelve figures robed in silver and gold. They stood in solemn unity, faces etched with sorrow and resolve. Their eyes shone with the weariness of those who bore the burdens of a world gone wrong. Hands rose, entwined, palms pressed to the heavens as if begging forgiveness for the act they were about to commit.

Magic flowed between them, threads of purest gold intertwined with veins of silver, creating a tapestry of heartbreaking beauty. It rippled outward, delicate as spider silk yet unbreakable as diamond. The students watched, breathless, as this web expanded, shimmering as it stretched across the sky, casting shadows on the faces of the twelve.

"The barrier," Eldryn murmured quietly, his voice echoing with profound sadness. "The strongest enchantment ever woven. An act of mercy, and of loss, sealing magic away from humanity, and humanity away from us."

The vision wavered as it settled into place, golden strands solidifying into a barrier delicate as mist yet immovable as mountains.

Slowly, the image faded, leaving the students gazing upward at the empty air.

Seraphina felt something deep inside her fracture as the vision faded away. Her hands trembled slightly at her sides, and without thinking, she pressed one tightly against her chest, as if trying to ease the pain blooming beneath her ribs. Tears pricked at the corners of her eyes, shimmering in the soft glow that lingered after the memory vanished.

Her brows furrowed deeply, not just in confusion but in genuine anguish. She stood slowly from her seat, her voice thickened by a desperation she hadn't known she carried. "Shouldn't we, shouldn't we be working to bring the realms back together?" she asked, her words strained with urgency, almost pleading. "Magic isn't something to be hidden away, forgotten. It's part of us, too."

Her hand tightened into a fist, nails biting sharply into her palm. She observed the faces around her, searching for understanding, for agreement, for anything that might ease the grief lodged stubbornly in her throat. "There must be another way," she whispered.

Eldwyn watched her in silence, the weight of her words lingering in the space between them. His expression softened, though a flicker of something older—wearier—shadowed his eyes. His jaw tightened, just slightly, like he was holding back more than he dared speak aloud.

Beside him, Lunaris stirred. For a lingering moment, professor and wolf turned toward one another, their eyes meeting in a silent communion, an unspoken conversation flowing between them, filled with careful consideration and mutual understanding.

Above them, the vision flickered once more, changing gently, images fading and re-forming in swirls of silver and gold.

"There are those who still hope for reunification," Eldwyn finally said, his voice cautious. "But we must remember the cost. Magic, in the hands of humanity, has always been unpredictable. The scars of our past bear witness to that painful truth."

Cordelia leaned forward beside her, the movement sharp. Seraphina felt the shift before her friend even spoke, the way the tension rolled off Cordelia like a wave ready to break.

"If we never try," Cordelia said, voice fierce and clear, "how will we ever know? Isn't it possible that humanity has changed? That we've learned?"

A shadow ghosted across Eldryn's face. His eyes darkened, pupils dilating as if he were no longer fully present, as if something ancient and merciless had seized his attention and dragged it backward through time.

Then, slowly, he raised his hand.

Light poured from his palm. It rose in coiling strands, symbols unfurling in the air. "There is a prophecy," Eldryn said. His voice was quieter than a breath.

Eldryn's gaze went glassy, hollow, as if he were watching something far beyond them, something he could not stop. "It speaks of two mortal sisters," he said, "born of the same blood, divided by fate."

The symbols convulsed, shifting faster now, rearranging in jagged, brutal lines. The golden strands warped and twisted into the form of two girls, identical in form but opposite in essence. One bathed in blinding, unyielding light. The other veiled in smoke and shadow, her edges constantly shifting, unable to hold shape.

His fingers clenched, and the vision shattered. His eyes refocused. The weight of reality crashed back in.

"However," Eldryn said, and though his voice was steady, it trembled at the edges, "prophecies are not promises." The words lingered, hanging in the air. He inhaled slowly, wings drawing in tight against his back. "The Council of Twelve fears a repeat of the Great Schism." His eyes swept across the room, methodical and distant, but when it passed over Seraphina, it caught, just for a moment.

"The world beyond the barrier remains wild," he continued. "Unpredictable. Magic is as delicate as it is devastating, and in mortal hands—"

"It's a deadly weapon," Emeric cut in, his voice low and flat. No sharpness this time, no trace of that usual edge. Just a statement, blunt and cold.

Eldryn's eyes narrowed, not in anger, but in something quieter. Sadder.

Beside him, Lunaris pawed at the ground. He let out a low, resonant note, soft and haunting. It shimmered in the air, a chord that echoed Eldryn's tone with eerie precision.

Aleron reached over and gently grasped Seraphina's hand, guiding her back down into her seat. Cordelia sat with a *hrump*, folding her arms and shooting them both a look.

Eldryn nodded to Emeric, then turned his focus back to the room. He clapped his hands once, and a sound cracked through the chamber like lightning, splitting the air. A gust of unseen magic followed, rushing through the space. Across the room, books and scrolls burst into existence on every desk, the pages fluttering open like wings before folding to attention, silent and waiting.

"For tonight's lesson," Eldryn announced, "I want you to examine the Council of Twelve's decision. Were they justified in dividing our worlds? Could there have been another way?" He looked across the room, lingering on Seraphina. "Form groups and discuss."

The hall erupted into movement, though subdued, muffled beneath the weight of what they'd just witnessed. Conversations began, but they were quieter than usual, hesitant. Students drifted into loose clusters, chairs scraping against the stone floor.

Seraphina, Cordelia, and Isadora made their way toward a corner of the hall, the quiet between them thick and uncertain. None of them quite knew what to say. The vision still clung to them—those twelve figures, the barrier, the prophecy.

Then came a loud thud, followed by a very undignified yelp.

Aleron, who had attempted to pull out a chair and sit, had missed the seat entirely. He landed in a heap on the floor, one long leg still tangled awkwardly over the chair's armrest.

Cordelia exhaled through her nose, deadpan. "Why are we friends with him again?"

From the floor, Aleron groaned. "That was a carefully executed fall. Tactical. Keeps my enemies guessing."

Isadora, without lifting her gaze from her book, replied flatly, "You fall even while sitting down."

With great effort and exaggerated drama, Aleron hoisted himself into the chair, correctly this time, and slumped back, draping an arm over his heart. "And yet, I suffer in silence."

Seraphina snorted, but even her laugh felt distant, like it belonged to someone else. She flipped open her book, but the words blurred before her eyes.

Aleron nudged her foot with his. "Speaking of suffering, poor Emeric. Looks like no one's lining up to be on his team."

Cordelia gave a low groan. "Can you blame them?"

Isadora sighed again, turning a page. "He doesn't exactly make himself easy to like."

Across the room, Emeric sat alone at the far end of the hall, flipping through his textbook with a kind of forced casualness that was almost convincing. Almost. His posture was relaxed, his face unreadable, but no one approached him.

No one even tried.

FADEYA

Unbeknownst to them all, in the shadows behind a stone column, a pair of piercing green eyes watched the scene unfold. Fadeya remained hidden, unseen and unnoticed as she watched Emeric, taking in his rigid posture, the way his fingers tapped absentmindedly against the edge of the book, the faint furrow of his brow. She knew what it felt like to be alone. *So, the mask slips,* Fadeya thought, studying him. *He's not all wit and bravado, after all.*

Pity stirred in her chest, unbidden, unwelcome, but beneath it, something deeper flickered; *recognition.*

Chapter 11

THE PRINCIPLES OF MAGICAL BONDING

FADEYA

The worn stone terrace echoed with the sharp click of boots as Fadeya paced outside Professor Hera's office. Light poured over the spires of Astral Unison, setting the enchanted glass windows ablaze. A perfect view of a perfect place, one she should have been part of.

She had seen Seraphina twice more since arriving a little over a week ago, each time worse than the last.

Her fingers curled into fists as she glared up at the university towers. She could picture Seraphina now, breezing through the halls, learning about magic, laughing with her friends, and caring more about living in the moment than the life and family she had left behind. Fadeya's jaw clenched.

With more force than necessary, she rapped on the office door. Everything felt like too much: the swirling of her emotions, the weight of her mother's expectations, the ghostly ache of her father's absence, the jealousy strangling her whenever she thought of Seraphina's success. She needed to spill it all before it drowned her.

"Come in," called a voice from within.

She opened the door to find Professor Hera seated at her desk, lamplight dancing across her silver hair. The pale scar running down her cheek caught the light as she looked up. Offering a smile, she gestured for Fadeya to take a seat in the wingback chair across from her.

"Fadeya." Professor Hera's voice was low. "I'm glad you stopped by."

She sank into the chair, clutching her satchel tightly to her chest, as though it might shield her from the vulnerability bubbling within. She wasn't used to admitting things. Not out loud. Not even to herself. "I hope I'm not intruding," she said hesitantly. "I've been exploring the grounds, trying to get accustomed to the layout of the university."

Hera's gaze softened as understanding crossed her face. "I can imagine how overwhelming it must feel, coming from a non-magical realm to a place so extraordinary." There was a patient, soothing quality to her tone. Reaching out, she placed a reassuring hand over Fadeya's. "There's a sadness in you, I can feel it. You must have longed to be a student here so deeply."

Fadeya blinked hard against the sting in her eyes, her composure slipping. "It's been ... overwhelming," she whispered. "I spent my whole life dreaming of the Starlight Awakening, preparing for it, but when the moment finally came, I wasn't chosen. I wasn't worthy."

Her voice cracked, and she shook her head slightly. "Everything I worked for—it just fell apart."

Hera leaned forward. "Sometimes, the Starlight Awakening can be ... unpredictable. Failing one test isn't the end of your path."

"My mother set the bar so high, I could barely breathe trying to reach it." The words came faster than she meant them to— spilled out like a dam finally cracked open. *You sound like a child,* she thought, but she didn't stop. "She never thought Seraphina had what it took, but now Seraphina's here, thriving, and I'm the one left standing in the wreckage. And I don't know what I'm supposed to do with that."

Professor Hera studied her as she shut the book she had been reading. "Seraphina *did* get in."

"She did," Fadeya said, voice tight as she sat stiffly at the desk across from Hera. Her fingers curled around the edge of the chair, knuckles pale. "And she promised me, *swore*, that she'd write, but nothing. Not a single letter. It's like she's forgotten us now that she's got her new, perfect life."

Hera leaned back in her chair, the leather creaking beneath her. She ran a slow finger along the scar, tracing her cheek, eyes steady on Fadeya. "You know, jealousy often points to what we value most. Maybe instead of letting it weigh you down, you can let it guide you forward."

Fadeya dragged in a breath and pushed back from the desk, the chair legs scraping slightly against the floor. She stood abruptly, crossing the room with tight, restless steps before turning back toward Hera.

"I ... I don't even know where to start," she admitted, wrapping her arms around herself.

"Start by deciding what *you* want," Hera said simply. "Not your mother. Not your sister. *You*." She rested an arm on the desk, tapping a single finger against the polished wood in a steady rhythm.

"You're twins, yes?" A look passed over her face, as if she had already unraveled the tangled knot of emotions inside Fadeya. "That can't be easy, constantly compared to someone who shares your face, your blood."

Fadeya nodded, her throat tight. She remained standing, arms tense at her sides, unable to sink back into the chair. "Yes," she said softly, the word feeling heavier than it should.

Hera rose slowly, the light from the high windows highlighting her hair as she stepped around the desk and approached Fadeya.

She didn't speak at first. Instead, she placed a hand gently on Fadeya's shoulder.

"Fadeya," she said quietly, "we are not always meant to walk the roads others set before us. Even when those roads gleam with tradition and promise, they may not lead where we're meant to go. The Starlight Awakening measures what is seen, but some paths," she glanced out the narrow window, "are forged in the hidden places. In choices no ceremony could ever sanctify." Then, her eyes returned to Fadeya. "Do not let your worth be bound to the expectations of others. Greatness often begins in the quiet defiance of such things."

Hera's gaze drifted past Fadeya, her focus slipping into memory. Her voice softened, almost more to herself than anyone else. "I once had a sister. We were close, like you and Seraphina."

She paused, her throat tightening as she blinked back something unspoken. "But … circumstances pulled us apart."

As the silence settled between them, Hera let her hand fall gently from Fadeya's shoulder, the weight of the moment lingering in its absence.

Fadeya exhaled slowly, her eyes fixed on the worn rug beneath her boots, tracing its faded patterns like they held answers. "I'm sorry," she murmured. "I didn't know."

Hera offered a small, sad smile, her focus returning to Fadeya. "Some losses shape us in ways we never expect," she said. A beat passed, quiet but not empty, before she tilted her head slightly. "Tell me—what else is weighing on your mind?"

Fadeya lowered herself into the chair once more, the wood creaking beneath her. She exhaled slowly, raking a hand through her hair—normally kept neat and precisely in place, but now mussed and tangled, mirroring the storm inside her. "There's something else," she said, her voice steadier than she felt.

Hera didn't return to her chair. She remained at the desk, leaning against its edge with arms loosely crossed. She reached for the teapot and poured herself another cup. "Sometimes," she said, "naming what troubles us is the only way forward. Even when it hurts."

Fadeya hesitated, the words catching on her tongue before she could push them out. "It's my father," she said at last, her voice barely above a whisper. Just saying it made her chest tighten. "He died when I was little."

A tear slipped down her cheek, and she wiped it away with a trembling hand. "He always believed in us—me and Seraphina.

He was the one who told me I could do anything. That I should reach for the stars, no matter how far."

She paused, blinking rapidly, trying to hold herself together. "And I just found out … he went to Astral Unison."

Her eyes flicked up to meet Hera's, but her voice faltered as she added, "His name was Dyaus Elaris."

Then the air shifted.

Hera froze, teacup halfway to her lips. Her fingers tightened around the porcelain so much so that the faintest crack whispered through the room. A sharp breath escaped her, quick and involuntary, her composure fracturing in the silence.

"Dyaus Elaris," she echoed, the name landing like a stone between them. Her eyes fixed on Fadeya with renewed intensity. "I … remember him."

Fadeya's heart stumbled in her chest. She leaned forward slightly. "You … you do?"

Hera nodded slowly. "Yes. He was one of our most gifted students. Talented beyond measure, especially in lunar sorcery." She paused, setting the teacup down on its saucer. "He was bonded to an Alignak."

Fadeya blinked. "A what?"

"An Alignak," Hera said, standing abruptly. She began pacing a short line in front of the window, though her steps lacked direction, as if she needed motion more than clarity. "A creature of the moon. It usually takes the form of a fox, silver-furred, clever, and elusive." She waved a hand as if brushing away fog. "They choose only those with a true connection to lunar magic."

She paused, back still to Fadeya. "Your father could manipulate moonlight," she added. "He wove it into illusions—veils and mirages that could distract, conceal, even soothe. And he could tap into the moon's pull on the tides … and people. Emotions. He could calm anger, ease grief." At last, she turned and moved back to her desk, settling into her chair with a stiffness that hadn't been there before. Her hand trembled slightly as she poured more tea into her cup. The liquid nearly spilled over the rim.

Fadeya watched her in silence, a strange unease crawling along her spine. *Why is she so rattled?*

Her father, so calm, so constant, had once wielded that kind of power? She could hardly reconcile the man who read her bedtime stories with someone who could shift the emotional current of a room.

"What happens to a creature when their bondmate dies?" Fadeya asked, her voice barely above a whisper.

Hera froze for a beat too long. "Most magical creatures live longer than their human counterparts," she said at last, her words carefully measured. "That's one of the many reasons some believe humans shouldn't bond with them."

She took a slow sip of her tea, then set the cup down again, the porcelain clicking faintly against the saucer. "The fae live longer lives, so they often outlive their creature bondmates. In either case ... it's difficult. The one left behind tends to mourn for the rest of their days. Most never bond again." Her gaze dropped to the surface of her tea, but she didn't lift it. She didn't look at Fadeya.

"Why did my mother never tell me?" Fadeya said wistfully.

Hera's fingers lingered on the rim of her cup. "Some truths arrive before we're ready to bear them," she said at last. "Grieving what was kept from you, it's a kind of mourning, too."

Fadeya didn't know if she felt grief. Not exactly. There was no ache in her chest, no sorrow in her bones. Only questions—sharp, jagged things—but what unsettled her most was Hera herself: the slight tilt of her shoulders, the way her spine no longer sat straight, as though even speaking her father's name had called something heavy from the past and laid it across her back.

"You knew him well," Fadeya said, careful now. Watching her. "My father."

A beat of silence.

Hera's lips curved into a forced smile, one that didn't quite reach her eyes. "I knew many promising students."

A deflection.

Hera opened the book she had been reading when Fadeya had arrived. She turned the pages looking for a particular place. "Why don't you rest and join my class this evening? It's time you learned more about bonding."

Fadeya hesitated a moment, sensing the dismissal, then she rose from her chair. She adjusted the strap of her satchel, fingers absently tracing the worn leather, before turning toward the door. Her boots barely made a sound against the polished floor as she crossed the office. She reached for the door handle, fingers curling around the cool brass.

"And don't forget—"

Fadeya stilled mid-motion.

"Use the amulet. Find a place where no one will see you."

She flexed her fingers around the door handle, considering the words. "Thank you ... for everything." She squared her shoulders, tilting her chin up. "Your faith in me, it's given me a renewed sense of purpose." She paused, and then, steadier, bolder: "I promise, I won't let you down."

A slow, knowing smile curved Hera's lips. "I know you won't, Fadeya."

SERAPHINA

The classroom dedicated to Professor Hera's Principles of Magical Bonding class was different from any other place within the university walls. Its ceiling was low, overlapping beams of spell-woven wood that formed the canopy of an enchanted forest.

Tiny fireflies drifted between the branches, illuminating murals that stretched across the walls in shifting scenes of mythical beasts: griffins with sun-struck plumage, wyverns exhaling misty motes of magic, slinking shadow-cats whose eyes followed everyone who passed.

Even the floor was a masterpiece made of drift bone, a pale, salt-scoured wood, and countless gemstones that sloped, just slightly, in a spiral toward the center. At the heart of this spectacle stood Professor Hera. Her turquoise eyes surveyed the class with a penetrating intensity that made Seraphina squirm.

"Welcome," Hera began, "to the Principles of Magical Bonding. In this class, you will learn what it truly means to forge a Celestial Bond with the creatures of our world."

As she spoke, the crystals standing on tall pedestals at the front of the room flared with momentary brilliance. The students sat captivated, aware that this was no ordinary lesson. The Celestial Bond was sacred; its practice had shaped the magical world for centuries.

Seraphina sat ramrod straight. Her dark hair tumbled over one shoulder in an unruly braid, wild strands curling around her face as if they had a mind of their own. No amount of pinning ever managed to tame it—but honestly, it suited her. Each day in the fae realm left her feeling more alive, more like herself. She wore a deep green dress that made her eyes seem brighter, the soft fabric fitted through the bodice and fell into flowing sleeves that brushed her hands. She'd picked it up last week, somewhat reluctantly, when Cordelia dragged her to the village for what she called a "desperately needed wardrobe refresh."

The moment Seraphina touched the fabric, Cordelia had declared, "You have got to be kidding me. That one was *made* for you. Don't argue, don't think, just wear it." And so, she had.

This was the class she looked forward to the most. She had spun so many daydreams of bonding with a magical creature that it was hard to believe it could be a reality.

Beside her, Cordelia practically vibrated with excitement. She reached out, her warm fingers curling around Seraphina's in a brief, comforting squeeze. Seraphina offered a grateful smile to her best friend, relief filling her eyes as she returned the gentle pressure.

Several seats away, Emeric leaned back in his chair, flicking a small, silver coin across his knuckles. His posture exuded an air of disinterest, but his eyes told a different story.

"The bond between us and magical creatures," Hera said, her voice cutting through the room, "is not just a partnership."

She stepped away from the desk, walking slowly across the front of the room, her eyes steady on the students before her.

"It is something far more profound." She paused mid-step in front of Seraphina. "It is a union of souls, a connection forged by trust, respect, and mutual understanding."

As she spoke, the glowing crystals on the pedestals at the front of the room seemed to hum in resonance, their light intensifying briefly before settling back into their rhythmic pattern. A subtle shift in the air prickled along Seraphina's skin, raising the hairs on the back of her neck.

"This bond awakens not only the creature's magic, but your own," Hera said, her voice rising slightly. "Together, you and your bonded become something greater than the sum of your individual parts. You will be partners, protectors, and creators of a shared destiny, but," she added, her tone shifting, "such a bond is not easily earned. It requires more than magic. It requires courage, integrity, and above all, a heart willing to listen."

Seraphina's fingers began to move again as she absorbed the professor's words.

"Are you ready," Hera asked, "to take the first step toward this sacred union?"

Seraphina caught the creak of the door and glanced up to see Aleron slip in.

"I can't believe you let her start without me," he purred in her ear, as he slid into the seat on the other side of her, nearly missing the seat.

Seraphina smirked and gave a slow and silent mocking clap. "You haven't missed much," she replied teasingly. "Just the grand unveiling of why we're all here. Nothing important at all."

"This bond," Hera continued, her voice carrying the weight of reverence, "is sacred and lifelong. It is not a contract, nor a convenience. It is a merging of destinies, a connection that transcends the boundaries of species and magic itself."

Seraphina rested her chin in her hands; the vision before her tugged at something deep inside her—not just awe, but anticipation, a quiet certainty that this was meant for her. She could almost feel it: the warmth of a creature at her side, their breath in sync with hers, their magic coiling together like threads woven into something greater, but which creature would it be?

From the back of the room, Emeric leaned forward, his chair creaking beneath him. "And if the bond fails?" His voice cut through the room.

Professor Hera's eyes snapped to him, cold and unyielding. "Then you weren't strong enough to hold it."

She took a step forward, power coiling around her like a living thing. "The bond is delicate, yes, but it does not break easily. It does not fail from doubt or fear alone. It shatters when the one who holds it lacks the will to endure."

Tendrils of shadow curled around her fingers, twisting like smoke, visible now to every student in the room. Her gaze landed on Seraphina again, piercing, assessing. As if she saw something the others couldn't.

"Trust matters. Respect matters, but so does strength. Some bonds form like a breath of wind, effortless and natural. Others must be fought for, held together by sheer force of will." She closed her eyes for a moment, the weight of her words pressing down on them all. "And if you don't have the resolve to stand firm when the bond resists you, if you aren't strong enough to claim it as yours, then yes, it will fail."

She opened her eyes and turned back to Emeric, her voice softening, but only enough to make the warning cut deeper. "And when it does ... you won't just lose magic. You will lose yourself."

With a sigh, she crossed to the pedestal near the center of the room, where a large, leather-bound book rested. The cover was dark, edges worn from generations of use, embossed with a silver sigil that glinted faintly.

Seraphina watched as Professor Hera's fingers skimmed the cover with care. The book groaned open on its ancient hinges, the sound low and brittle, followed by the delicate rustle of parchment.

144

From the open pages, light bloomed. Soft at first, then brightening into a column that rose toward the ceiling before expanding outward. The air shimmered, and slowly, the far wall of the classroom became a canvas of illusion. Faint lines began to sketch themselves across the wood, forming runes and shifting diagrams. Then, figures emerged, half-real, half-light, like a story being given shape.

The class watched in transfixed silence.

Two figures, drawn in lines of pale light: stag and fae, standing side by side, joined at the chest by a cord of light that pulsed rhythmically, like a heartbeat. Around them, other beasts danced— serpents of flame, birds of water, beasts woven of water and wind. It was harmony rendered in light, a visual symphony of the bond in its purest form.

But then, the images began to change.

The thread between the figures thinned. The creatures sensed it first. They stilled in midair, hovering as if listening for a sound only they could hear. Then, slowly, they peeled away, fading into the margins like smoke dissipating after war.

The fae figure began to glitch. Its arms trembled. Its legs buckled. Cracks formed, deep, splitting ruptures that spread across its entire form.

Seraphina didn't realize she was holding her breath until her chest ached.

The figure convulsed once, then again, its form flickering, struggling to hold. The stag dissolved into nothing, a ripple of light swallowed by shadow.

And then, the fae shattered.

Light splintered in every direction, bursting into a thousand shards that drifted like ash, weightless and silent, before vanishing into the air.

No one in the classroom moved. No one spoke.

The light from the book faded into nothing.

Hera shut the tome with the weight of finality. The sound echoed like the closing of a coffin. She stood still for several seconds, her back to the class, shoulders squared. When she finally turned, her face had changed. Her expression was no longer the cool, composed calm of a professor. It was the face of someone who had seen this play out before. Who had tried to stop it once and failed.

Her hands were clasped so tightly in front of her that the bones had gone pale.

"This," she said, her voice as quiet as it was vicious, "is what happens when arrogance outweighs responsibility. You do not simply lose them," Hera continued. Her voice was flat now. "You lose yourself. You lose *who* you were when you made the bond. And in the aftermath, you have to decide whether the hollow thing you become is worth saving."

She paused.

"And sometimes," she said, softer now. "Sometimes, there's nothing left to save."

The room remained still, the students too awed and too afraid to move. A faint tremor in Hera's hand betrayed the storm simmering beneath her exterior. After a long moment, a voice from the back of the room spoke up. "Professor," a fae female began hesitantly, her voice barely above a whisper, "what creature did *you* bond with?"

The question landed like a blow, and for an instant, Hera's carefully constructed facade cracked. "My bondmate," she said at last, her voice tight, "died many years ago."

Seraphina felt it, how the room shrank around that truth. *How terrible*, she thought.

Hera's fingers drifted to the scar along her cheek, tracing it without thought. "That is a story for another day," she said quietly. Her gaze lingered on the fae female for a moment longer, enough to make her shrink slightly in her seat. "Let us focus on *your* journeys now," she said briskly, the dismissal clear.

Seraphina sat back slowly, trying to shake the chill that had settled in her spine. The remnants of the vision still clung to her skin like cold mist.

Beside her, Aleron leaned in slightly, his voice low. "So …remind me never to ask a personal question in front of the entire class."

Seraphina tried to smile, but it didn't quite reach her eyes. "Do you think it's true? That her bondmate's dead?"

"If it's not, she deserves an award for that performance." They both looked to the front again, where Hera was speaking.

"She's still grieving," Seraphina said softly, more to herself than to Aleron.

"Every weekend, creatures from across the realms come here seeking bonds, just as you do," Hera continued. "They are drawn to the magic of this place and the potential within each of you. But," she said, her gaze sweeping the room with a stern warning, "never, *ever* attempt to bond without my presence. An unstable bond is dangerous, not just for you, but for the creature as well. Such recklessness could harm them irreparably or even destroy you both. Treat this responsibility with the respect it deserves."

Then she picked up her things and gestured toward the massive double doors at the back of the chamber. "Follow me."

Chairs scraped against the floor as the students rose, their emotions a mix of nervous energy and growing anticipation.

Seraphina caught Cordelia's eye as they moved toward the doors. "No pressure, right?" Cordelia whispered, keeping her voice low.

Seraphina huffed a quiet laugh. "You're so lucky you've already bonded."

"Don't I know it! Boyde is incredible." Cordelia beamed, her chest puffing with pride.

They stepped into the twilight-kissed courtyard, the night breeze carrying the scent of something sweet drifting from the dining hall. A path lined with shimmering lanterns wound through the trees, casting soft pools of light on the forest floor.

"No kidding! I hope my bondmate is as incredible as Boyde." Aleron fell into step beside them, buzzing with energy. "I still think about the way she tore through those sirens. Absolutely ruthless."

Seraphina grinned at him. "You just want something big and terrifying so you can look impressive."

"Whatever it takes to get you to go out with me." Aleron retorted, making Seraphina laugh out loud.

Aleron reached for his sword belt, only to knock the hilt into his ribs. "Ow, dammit."

Cordelia arched her brow. "You good?"

"I like to keep things exciting." He chuckled, rubbing his side.

Emeric, walking just behind them, snorted. "Exciting? You're a walking liability."

Aleron shot him a look. "That's just my charm."

"If by charm, you mean complete lack of coordination,"

Hera's attention snapped to them, the weight of it enough to make even Emeric shut up.

"Quiet now," she murmured, her voice low but commanding. "We are nearing sacred ground." They followed her beyond the tree line, where the dense forest opened to reveal a hidden clearing bathed in starlight. At the center stood the Star Shrine, a half-ruined structure of white stone etched with symbols that glimmered under the moon's glow. Vines and silver blossoms crawled across the marble pillars, their blossoms unfurling in the hush of night.

Seraphina's breath hitched as she gazed upon the shrine's archways, which rose toward the sky as if beckoning the stars themselves to descend. "It's beautiful," she whispered, her voice tremulous with wonder.

Hera paused at the threshold, letting the students gather behind her. "This," she said, "is one of the most sacred locations in all our realms. The Star Shrine is ancient, older than any living memory. It is said that the veil between our world and the higher planes thins here, that the starlight carries whispers of destinies and dreams."

Seraphina's pulse raced. She could practically feel those hidden whispers threading through her body. Cordelia sidled up beside her, eyes bright with curiosity. "I've heard rumors that the first of the fae built the Star Shrine after discovering the starlight here was so powerful it allowed them to forge magical bonds with creatures," she whispered.

Professor Hera inclined her head. "Indeed. In the earliest ages, this place was used to sanctify the largest and most powerful bonds. Today, it remains a site where even the faintest star can spark a union between kindred souls. But take heed," she warned softly, her gaze shifting to Emeric, "this is not a place to be taken lightly. The shrine itself can sense your intentions."

Emeric rolled his eyes but said nothing. Aleron, meanwhile, stared at the structure in wide-eyed awe, nearly tripping over a jagged rock as he shuffled forward. "Wow," he breathed, righting himself. "I, uh … didn't realize that I would be able to physically feel the magic."

Seraphina stepped closer to the edge of the shrine, her heart a riot in her chest. The air shimmered, and she swore she could hear the faintest strains of music. "I feel it, too," she murmured, voice tinged with dreamy reverence. "Like the night sky is calling to me."

Isadora pressed a hand to her chest as her eyes swept over the shrine's towering pillars. "Okay," she said, her voice tinged with awe, "even I have to admit, this is a little breathtaking."

Hera led them through the marble archway into a courtyard. She turned to face the students.

"This," she began, her gesture encompassing the vibrant clearing before them, "is where it begins. The place where you may meet the creature destined to become a part of your soul."

The air vibrated with energy as Hera raised a hand, coaxing the mist to swirl and part. Wisps of fog obeyed her magic, revealing the creatures hidden within, beings that felt more like echoes of dreams than flesh and bone.

Luminara stags stood among them, their antlers woven from strands as thin as spiderwebs. Their translucent fur rippled as if stirred by an unseen breeze, and with each step, their hooves pressed faint, glowing impressions into the grass.

They're real, Seraphina thought, as she took it all in. Not just sketches in a storybook.

A sudden flurry of movement drew Seraphina's attention: a knot of umbrin foxes weaving deftly around the stags' legs. Their bodies seemed fashioned from shadow, and their crimson eyes shone with intelligence.

Perched on the lower branches of the surrounding trees sat the iridescent auracats, winged felines whose feathers shone with shifting hues like oil on water. They studied the students as they stretched, their long tails shedding feathers that drifted to the ground.

High above, three gemwing cranes circled with unbroken precision. Their wings, polished facets of gemstone, scattered a cascade of refracted light at each rhythmic beat, shimmering shards that vanished just before they touched the earth.

All around them, smaller creatures moved through the clearing in a silent dance. Tiny glintmoths, pulsing with light, flew through the air, leaving trails of shimmering dust.

One broke from the group, drifting lazily toward Aleron. It hovered in front of him for a moment, then landed softly on his shoulder. His eyes widened, and he stood perfectly still, as if afraid to scare it off. The glintmoth's glow brightened slightly, casting a halo against his neck before lifting off again, vanishing into the swarm like a spark returning to the fire.

Nearby, a school of sky koi hovered as though suspended by an unseen current, their pearlescent scales giving off a gentle glow, fueled by some hidden inner light.

Seraphina gasped when a crystabear trundled past, its crystalline fur gleaming like carved quartz. Its claws, diamonds turned deadly, shown with quiet menace.

Even Emeric, usually too cool to care, looked momentarily taken aback, his mask of indifference slipping in the face of such raw, captivating splendor.

"By the stars," Cordelia breathed, clutching Seraphina's arm. "Nothing could have prepared me for this."

"It's nearly impossible to describe," Seraphina replied, voice trembling. She stood rooted in place, transfixed by the menagerie of creatures.

Professor Hera stepped forward, her very posture commanding despite the unsettling grandeur of the creatures around her. "Each of these beings," she began, "holds a magic woven into their very bones. They have crossed boundaries from faraway realms, drawn here by the spark they sense within you. Remember, they choose you as much as you choose them. Let your hearts speak truth."

A deep stillness settled over the Star Shrine. Every creature turned toward the students with eyes gleaming with watchful appraisal.

Standing at the edge of the group, Emeric surveyed the creatures with a hunger in his eyes. Though he leaned casually against a tree, arms crossed in disinterest, there was no mistaking the calculation in his eyes. Before him, lounged a massive shadowcat, its sleek ebony fur standing out against the twisted roots. The cat regarded him with a lazy, half-lidded stare, amber eyes taking him in.

He let out a low whistle. "I want something big," he muttered, loud enough for those nearby to hear. "Something powerful. Something that'll make anyone who crosses me regret it."

From a few steps away, Cordelia rolled her eyes. She mimicked his stance, folding her arms across her chest, though hers conveyed exasperation rather than arrogance. "You can't just walk up and pick the strongest or the scariest creature," she snapped. "It's not a transaction; you both have to choose each other. There's no forcing it."

He responded with a smug grin that made Seraphina's blood simmer.

"It's not a competition, Emeric," Seraphina said. "This isn't about showing off. It's about showing up, as your true self."

"Oh, spare me. Don't parrot that sentimental drivel." He uncrossed his arms slowly, stepping away from the tree. "Compatibility, mutual respect … please. Unlike what Aleron might've told you, size *does* matter." His gaze settled on her, direct and unflinching. "If I'm going to forge a bond, I'd rather have a partner who can take down a horde without breaking a sweat."

Aleron let out a slow, measured breath, pinching the bridge of his nose before stepping between them. "Stars, Emeric. Do you ever get tired of this?" He dropped his hand and gave the man a flat look. "Strength isn't just about being the biggest thing in the clearing." His eyes landed on a pair of luminara stags gliding past, their glowing antlers scattering shifting light across the mossy ground. He gestured toward the clearing. "But since you're so determined to prove yourself against the biggest, meanest thing out here, there's a crystabear waiting just over there." He folded his arms, voice dry. "Go on, then. We'll wait."

Emeric let out a low chuckle. "Spoken like someone who's never had to lift more than a book." He gave Aleron a once-over, clearly unimpressed. With that, he strode off to the other side of the crowd.

Aleron ran a hand through his hair, letting out a slow breath as he turned to Seraphina. "He doesn't get it," he muttered, shaking his head. "These creatures … they aren't about brute strength or sheer size. Their magic isn't defined by how much damage they can do or how menacing they look. It's about control, precision, knowing when to act and when to wait. A shadowcat, for instance, isn't powerful because it's the biggest predator in the forest. It's powerful because it understands the moment. It strikes only when it chooses, never before."

As if responding to his words, the shadowcat beneath the tree let out a slow, rumbling purr, the sound deep and knowing. It stretched, its muscles rippling with silent power, then settled back down, curling its tail over its paws with ease.

The luminous stags hesitated in their slow, measured steps, one lowering its head to sniff the space near Aleron. Nearby, a cluster of winged felines leapt from their perches, their glowing tails trailing light as they circled Cordelia. She stood motionless, wide-eyed.

Seraphina caught movement in her periphery and turned. Perched on a branch just above her was a sleek, silver-winged feline, its piercing blue eyes locked onto hers. The intensity of its gaze sent an unexpected shiver through her chest. For a heartbeat, nothing else existed; the murmuring forest, the magic, even the others faded away. The creature tilted its head ever so slightly, studying her.

Beside her, Isadora leaned in and whispered, "It's about connection. When the right one chooses you, you'll know. Like they've always been part of you."

Cordelia, still watching the winged felines drift around her, nodded slowly. "That's how it was with Boyde, I didn't have to force it. Didn't have to prove anything. The moment she looked at me, it just ... made sense. Like we'd always been meant to find each other." She glanced down, absently running a hand over her bondmark. "It wasn't about power. It was about trust."

Aleron hummed in quiet agreement, his gaze shifting to where Emeric stood, hands in pockets, staring down the shadowcat as if sheer determination alone could will it into submission. The creature flicked an ear but didn't bother to acknowledge him. Aleron smirked. "He'll probably end up with something like a thunder wyvern. Big, loud, more stubborn than it is smart. The kind of creature that thinks victory is just a matter of hitting hard enough." Aleron crossed his arms. "Which means it's only a matter of time before they knock each other out."

Seraphina barked a laugh, hastily covering her mouth. Emeric's heated glare slid toward them, bristling with annoyance. He looked ready to unleash a scathing comeback, but at that exact moment, a green glow flared on the opposite side of the clearing, shifting his attention.

A female fae named Joelle had quietly stepped forward, her hesitant steps taking her closer to a spellbinding serpentine creature with yellow scales. The serpent swayed in a languid rhythm, its large, curious eyes drinking in Joelle's presence.

"Steady," Professor Hera advised, voice both cautionary and encouraging. "The vyrlith serpent is highly attuned to your intent. Let it approach on its own."

Joelle swallowed, nodding as she extended her hand, palm up. An electric hush fell over the clearing. The serpent lowered its elegant head, pressing its cool snout to her skin. A burst of golden light radiated outward, shimmering in spirals around the pair.

Seraphina's palms grew slick with sweat. She curled her fingers into fists, then forced them open again, willing herself to stay still. *What must that feel like?* she wondered, heart thudding. *To be seen so clearly. To be chosen.*

Beside her, Aleron stood unmoving, his focus on the pair in the center of the Star Shrine. Even Emeric, for all his usual arrogance, had gone still, his usual smirk absent. He stood with his weight slightly forward, drawn in despite himself, watching as the moment unfolded.

Joelle's aura flared, echoing the serpent's golden glow. Tendrils of light wrapped around her arm, forming a sinuous rune. It glimmered fiercely before settling into a faint, steady glow. Professor Hera stepped close, placed a hand over the bondmark, and murmured something that made the mark shimmer briefly and then calm.

"Beautifully done," Professor Hera said to Joelle. "The bond is established."

The vyrlith serpent let out a low, melodic trill, its eyes half-closing in what seemed like contentment. Joelle smiled, her trembling hand reaching out to stroke the creature's scales. "I, I didn't think it would feel like this," she whispered, her voice barely audible. "It's like … it's like I've known him forever."

The clearing remained hushed, the glow of Joelle's bondmark still shimmering faintly, as if the magic itself had yet to settle. The vyrlith serpent coiled loosely around her as Joelle exhaled softly, brushing her fingers over the newly formed bondmark on her skin.

No one rushed to fill the silence. It was a moment to be felt, to be honored. Even the creatures around them seemed to recognize it.

Seraphina swallowed, her eyes lingering on Joelle, the way her body still trembled slightly, as though she were holding something vast and indescribable inside her chest. She understood. They all did. It wasn't just about magic. It wasn't about power. It was about finding something, someone, that had been missing without ever knowing it was gone.

Isadora turned to Cordelia. "Did it feel like that for you?"

Cordelia hesitated, then smiled faintly. "Yes. And no. It was quieter, maybe. Just me and Boyde, but it was the same in the ways that mattered." She looked back at Joelle, her expression unreadable. "You don't realize how incomplete you are until that moment. And then it happens, and suddenly you can't imagine ever being without it."

They all stood in quiet agreement, their gazes drifting back toward Joelle, who was still talking to her serpent, tracing the glowing rune on her arm as if committing it to memory.

FADEYA

From a distance, Fadeya stood cloaked in the shadows of the forest, her presence nearly indistinguishable from the trees around her. The black trousers and fitted shirt she wore, given to her by Professor Hera, had been chosen with purpose, their fabric dull and soundless, designed to help her vanish into the dark.

The faint rustle of leaves overhead provided just enough cover, masking the occasional crunch of twigs beneath her boots. She barely dared to breathe. Her eyes stayed fixed on the scene unfolding at the Star Shrine, every muscle taut with focus.

"It must feel incredible," she said to herself, her voice barely more than a sigh. Her fingers grazed the bark of a tree beside her, grounding her as she tried to temper the longing that swelled in her chest. She continued to watch the serpentine creature as it coiled around the fae student. The creature pressed its snout against her palm, and the connection flared to life in a burst of yellow light.

She could almost feel it herself, the power radiating around the glen, the sense of completeness, the bond that tethered two souls in perfect harmony. For a fleeting moment, she let herself imagine what it would be like to stand there instead, her hand outstretched, a creature choosing her.

The thought curdled in her throat, bitter and sharp. She clenched her jaw, shoving it aside. She wasn't like them, those students who walked so confidently into the clearing, eager to prove themselves, to forge their destinies. She did not belong in their world of magic. The shadows of the university were now her realm, and they felt lonelier with every passing day.

She found Seraphina glowing in the light of the ceremony, as if she had been made for it.

And in that moment, Fadeya felt the distance stretch between them, an aching, widening gulf carved by fate, by choices neither of them had made, by a power that had chosen one sister and left the other in the dark.

A nervous-looking boy stepped forward, his shoulders drawn tight, hands flexing at his sides. The clearing, alive with whispers and the lingering glow of fading magic, seemed to hold its breath as he approached the edge of the clearing where a griffin lurked. The creature moved, its talons pressing soundlessly into the earth. Golden feathers rippled down its spine. Its sharp eyes locked onto the boy, not with immediate acceptance, but with the slow, calculating scrutiny of a creature that did not give its loyalty easily.

The boy hesitated. The griffin did not.

With a single, fluid movement, it strode forward, wings half unfurling in a display of power. The space between them crackled, and the griffin dipped its head, stepping closer.

Magic snapped into place like a thread pulled taut. An explosion of light flared between them, surging outward in a warm, rippling wave. The scent of sunlit fields curled through the air.

Fadeya inhaled sharply, eyes widening as she felt it pass over her, like a tide coming in. The boy staggered, clutching his arm where the bondmark had seared itself into his skin.

Professor Hera was at his side in an instant. Her robes swayed as she reached out, pressing a steadying hand to his arm, her fingers brushing the fresh bondmark. Her expression was interesting; *was that approval? Pride?*

Fadeya's attention shifted as a warning pulse thrummed against her collarbone. *The amulet.* Its vibration was subtle but insistent.

Something was wrong. She swallowed, steadying her breath, willing herself to focus. She scanned the scene before her and noticed a figure moving at the edge of the crowd. Not part of the ceremony. The world narrowed as she spotted him. *Evander, the fae prince.*

He lingered just beyond the gathered students, the look on his face unreadable, his eyes locked on the bonding before him.

Then, as Hera turned her attention back to the surrounding crowd of students, Evander moved.

One hand lifted, pulling the hood of his cloak up over his head, casting his features in shadow. And with a swift turn, he slipped into the trees, vanishing into the darkness as if he had never been there at all. *How strange, she* thought, eyes fixed on the space where he'd stood. *He's definitely hiding something.*

Chapter 12

THE ETHERBLOOM TREE

SERAPHINA

A warm glow bathed the greenhouse as light filtered in through the glass walls, casting reflections across the vines, leaves, and tiled floor.

Seraphina thought the place looked like something out of a legend, a little slice of paradise hidden within the university grounds.

Exotic blossoms unfurled in radiant hues, trickling streams of enchanted water curled around small islands of vibrant foliage, and bridges of twisted roots were cushioned by glowing moss.

At the heart of all this quiet splendor stood Professor Flora, serene like a cypress tree that had stood for centuries, patient, knowing, and just a little out of time. Vines curled near her boots as if drawn to her presence, leaves on the branches above seeming to angle toward her.

To Seraphina, she didn't seem like someone who *taught* magic so much as someone who *had grown* from it, rooted in wild soil, shaped by sunlight and rain.

Beside her was Sylvaris, her bondmate, a tall, willowy plant-being with vines that twisted into limbs and trailing blossoms that released a smell similar to lavender.

"Welcome back, my budding herbalists," Professor Flora said, her voice ringing through the room. "Today, we continue our journey into the tangled roots and blooming branches of magic's vast garden." She placed a hand on Sylvaris, and he responded with a slight bow of his vine-wreathed head.

Cordelia's eyes lingered on Professor Flora and Sylvaris, a mix of fascination and longing in her gaze. She leaned toward Isadora, her voice wistful. "I swear this class gets more enchanting every time we come here."

Isadora caught the look, her expression understanding as she covered Cordelia's hand with her own. "You miss Boyde, don't you?" she asked quietly.

She let out a sigh, her fingers instinctively curling around Isadora's in a brief squeeze. "Every day," she admitted. "It's been too long since I've seen her. I'm heading down to the docks tomorrow to spend some time with her, make sure she's causing just the right amount of trouble." She managed a small smile.

Beside them, Seraphina gently touched a large, moon-white flower. She glanced over at Cordelia and Isadora. "The petals feel warm," she said in a hushed voice. As her fingers lingered, the petals began to shimmer faintly.

Then, the flower began to open. Its petals unfurled slowly, as if unveiling a sacred treasure. From within the bloom, light poured out. Floating up from the heart of the flower came a tiny faerie, radiant and impossibly delicate. Her wings caught the light and refracted it in brilliant halos. Her hair cascaded in flowing waves, trailing behind her like a comet's tail. She hovered in the air before Seraphina.

Then, slowly, the faerie reached out a hand.

Seraphina gasped as the faerie touched her forehead with the lightest brush of her fingers. A brilliant arc of light leapt between them.

The faerie let out a small, melodic sound, part laughter, part song, and drifted away, flitting through the plants nearby.

Professor Flora tilted her head, a smile playing on her lips as if she were listening to something only she could hear. "A starborne faerie," she murmured, her voice drifting like wind through leaves. "She's offering a blessing."

Seraphina watched the shimmering trail of stardust fade in the air, heart still fluttering from the faerie's touch. "What does it mean?" she asked as she moved to take her seat. "Why me?"

Flora's gaze remained on the space where the faerie had hovered. "They don't choose at random," she said. "A blessing from a starborne is a quiet promise, protection, guidance … perhaps even recognition. They see things in us before we see them in ourselves."

Seraphina's lips parted, another question forming, but a sudden rustling snapped the moment in two.

Aleron crashed through the foliage like a baby deer. He muttered something under his breath, swatted a vine from his shoulder, and slid into the empty seat beside her.

"Late again, Aleron?" Seraphina asked, arching a brow.

"Sorry," he replied with a shrug, the corner of his mouth tugging upward. "I overslept. Maybe you shouldn't have kept me up chatting all hours of the night."

He leaned in, voice dropping low enough that only she could hear. "Not that I minded."

Seraphina rolled her eyes, but her cheeks warmed anyway. She turned toward him, her voice edged with amusement. "Well, this time you really did miss something. A starborne faerie *blessed* me."

Aleron arched a brow, interest filling his eyes. "Is that so?"

She nodded, tucking a strand of hair behind her ear. "I couldn't make this up if I tried."

His gaze lingered on her for a beat too long. "Sounds like she saw something extraordinary."

Seraphina's cheeks warmed again, but she held his stare. "Maybe. Or maybe she just felt sorry for me, stuck next to someone who can't manage to show up on time."

He leaned in, close enough for his shoulder to brush hers. "If I'd known faeries were handing out blessings, I definitely would have been here."

She tilted her head, smiling. "You? Show up on time? Now that *would* be magic."

Professor Flora moved through the rows of vibrant greenery, her arms spread wide as she brushed the dew-laden leaves. "You all know of the frost bulb and the harpervine," Flora said, her voice like wind rustling through leaves. She paused beside two raised planters, gesturing first to a blue blossom, its petals faceted like ice. "The frost bulb can reduce fever, numb pain, and, when properly brewed, calm even the most tormented of minds."

She turned to the other—a thick, twisting vine with dark green leaves and vicious-looking thorns that curved like talons. "And this," she said, laying a hand close to the harpervine without touching it, "is a plant of protection and resilience. Its thorns may look dangerous, and they are, but beneath them lies a potent healing sap, capable of sealing wounds and bolstering the body's defenses."

Her gaze swept over the students. "It is vital," she continued, "to understand not only the uses of these plants but the spirits within them. Each living thing here is more than just a tool. Respect them. Speak to them. Work with them, and they will share their gifts freely."

As if to demonstrate, Sylvaris reached out one of her sinuous vine-like limbs toward the harpervine. The moment her essence brushed the plant, its thorny coils shivered, responding to her presence. The vine's tips began to glow a soft, radiant pink, and the menacing thorns slowly withdrew, revealing tiny, glistening droplets of golden sap.

Gasps echoed throughout the greenhouse as the students leaned closer, eyes wide with wonder. Some reached for their notebooks. Others simply stared, transfixed.

Aleron leaned in. "You look captivated," he teased, casting her a sidelong glance that sent a spark skittering down her spine.

Seraphina met his grin with one of her own. "Can you blame me?"

Professor Flora beckoned them forward with a sweep of her arm, guiding the students through the lush undergrowth toward the heart of the greenhouse. In the center stood a magnificent tree, towering far above the other flora, its presence commanding yet peaceful, like a guardian watching over a sacred grove.

Its bark shimmered with silvery-blue lines that wound like constellations carved into wood, casting a faint glow on the mossy floor below. The trunk was impossibly wide, its surface smooth to the touch in some places, gnarled and ancient in others, as if the tree was both old and eternally young. From its branches, long tendrils of translucent leaves hung like silken curtains.

"This," Professor Flora said, her voice reverent as she placed a hand against the bark, "is the etherbloom."

A hushed silence fell over the students.

"Its roots stretch so deep that legends say they reach into the very heart of the earth, tapping into knowledge far older than our oldest spells. It drinks not just from water, but from memory, from energy, from the stories whispered by the stones."

Though no wind touched the air within the greenhouse, the leaves overhead stirred, as if moved by something unseen. A few students lifted their heads, their eyes drawn upward.

"For those who know how to listen," Flora said, eyes half closed as if hearing something far beyond the present, "the etherbloom offers more than knowledge; it offers memory." She placed a hand gently against the bark, her fingers barely brushing the surface. "This tree does not speak with a voice we recognize, but it remembers. It remembers *everything*."

Emeric, positioned off to the side with his arms crossed, let out a snort. "Wisdom from a tree. How riveting."

Seraphina turned a level stare on him, eyes glinting with annoyance. "I'd argue it's more riveting than your snide commentary, Emeric."

He shrugged, a half smile playing on his lips. "Someone has to keep you lot grounded. Don't want us all floating off in a haze of magical reverie." Despite his words, he seemed interested, his eyes lingering on Professor Flora's bondmate, Sylvaris, as the creature wove delicate patterns in the air.

Cordelia shot him a challenging look. "And someone has to teach you how to appreciate beauty. Now hush."

Seemingly unfazed by the exchange, Professor Flora lifted her head with a dreamy look on her face. "Fascination with the natural world is just as important as creating bonds with magical creatures, Emeric," she said. "A healthy balance of both is what keeps this realm functioning." She knelt smoothly, her fingers brushing a cluster of mushrooms at the base of the tree. "There is always more to learn. Even with my bond to Sylvaris, I discover something new every day."

At her side, Sylvaris turned its eyes on Emeric, vines curling upward in a motion that almost seemed curious. Whether it was assessing him for sincerity or merely toying with him in its own plant-like way was unclear. Either way, Emeric shifted uncomfortably under the scrutiny, a faint flush rising to his cheeks as he looked away, mumbling something about nosy plants.

Seraphina admired the lines carved into the trunk of the etherbloom, her eyes narrowed in curiosity. "Professor, do these markings shift in response to people's auras?"

"They do," she confirmed. "The etherbloom recognizes each individual, almost as if reading your intent. The more attuned you are to plant magic, the more it reveals."

Aleron turned back to Seraphina, ideas churning in his mind. He extended a hand. "Shall we see if it likes us?" he asked, voice laced with intrigue.

Seraphina hesitated for only a breath before slipping her hand into Aleron's, fingers curling instinctively around his.

Together, they moved toward the etherbloom's trunk, steps slow and unhurried, as if the world outside had fallen away.

The moment their palms pressed against the bark, golden runes flared to life, brilliant and breathtaking. Magic tingled beneath Seraphina's skin, but it was Aleron's hand in hers that sent a shiver coursing through her.

She glanced up, breath catching at the way the light played over Aleron's face. His breath had quickened, and his brown eyes, usually so steady, were fixed on her with an intensity that made her knees weak.

From behind them, Cordelia's whisper broke the silence. "Look at them, practically shining together. If that's not romantic, I don't know what is."

Isadora smiled back at her. "They're perfect," she agreed.

Seraphina barely heard them, too aware of Aleron's attention and the warmth of his hand wrapped around hers.

"Aleron," she breathed, barely more than a whisper, but his name fell from her lips like a secret.

He looked at her, really looked at her, as if committing every line of her face to memory. "You … you amaze me."

Her chest tightened, words tangling in her throat, but Aleron's fingers only tightened around hers, grounding and steady. Slowly, hesitantly, he lifted their joined hands from the bark, pressing the lightest of kisses to her knuckles. The gesture was soft and careful, nothing more than a brush of his lips, but it sent warmth flooding through her, pooling beneath her skin as the light faded from the tree in front of them.

The subtle moment didn't go unnoticed by Emeric, who rolled his eyes, though he didn't comment again.

They lingered there for a moment longer before Professor Flora's voice rose over the whispers of students. She stood by the etherbloom, her eyes bright and watchful, a faint smile tugging at her lips.

"As I was saying," she began again, "these markings are older than any language you've studied. They tell stories of those who came before, of guardians and sacrifices, of bonds formed and broken. Magic is not just power; it is memory. Every spell, every enchantment, is a story written into the fabric of the world."

She paused, her eyes drifting to Emeric, who had moved closer to the front of the crowd. He was studying the tree with an intensity Seraphina hadn't seen in him before.

"Powerful and royal fae have been known to see visions when they touch the etherbloom. Glimpses of the past, echoes of the ancient guardians, and the first pacts forged in blood and magic. These visions are fragments, whispers of what was, but they carry warnings as well as wisdom."

Seraphina turned her head, her eyes finding Isadora beside her best friend. They had all grown close these past few weeks, close enough that Seraphina hadn't really thought about the fact that Isadora was a fae princess and what that might mean. The title seemed to fall away, leaving only the girl who laughed easily and offered quiet reassurances when nerves frayed.

Isadora stood transfixed, her focus narrowed on Professor Flora. She hesitated only a moment before raising her voice. "Professor," she began, drawing every eye to her. "If the etherbloom can reveal the past, can it also show … what is yet to come? Prophecies or glimpses of the future?"

Aleron's grip on Seraphina's hand tightened, a subtle signal of shared intrigue.

"The etherbloom is bound to time in ways we cannot fully comprehend," Professor Flora replied, choosing her words carefully. "Its visions are rooted in memory, in the echoes of what has been. Occasionally, those echoes may align with what will be, but the future is not as fixed as the past. What it shows are possibilities, not certainties."

Isadora's lips pressed into a thin line; her hands fidgeted uncharacteristically. After a moment, Isadora spoke again, "If someone saw a vision, a glimpse of the future, could it be changed?"

The professor watched her for a moment, assessing. "That depends on the strength of the one who sees and the will of those who act. Magic does not dictate our choices; it merely offers paths. It is up to us to decide which to follow."

Isadora's eyes filled with tears, something dark and uncertain passing through them before her lashes swept down, masking whatever lay beneath. Seraphina bit the inside of her cheek, worry gnawing at her thoughts.

Professor Flora seemed to sense the unease threading through the air. She cleared her throat. "That will be all for today's class," she announced. "Before you go, I'd like each of you to craft an enchantment using ingredients found in the greenhouse, one that can either heal or defend, depending on your intent. Document the process, the properties of each ingredient, and the reason behind your choices. Your completed enchantments and reports are due by the next full moon."

Sylvaris bowed again, the light of the greenhouse reflecting in the glossy leaves crowning his head.

A collective sigh of relief and quiet groans rippled through the students as they gathered their things, the tension easing but not entirely gone. Aleron's hand slipped from Seraphina's, his eyes catching hers with a look that promised they'd discuss this later.

Cordelia was at Seraphina's side, concern written on her face as she watched Isadora linger by the edge of the greenhouse, collecting her things with slow deliberation.

Without hesitation, Cordelia stepped forward, brushing a strand of Isadora's black hair over her shoulder. "Hey," she said softly. "You look like you could use a distraction. How about we go grab some coffee and pastries? Talk about anything but cryptic trees and ominous prophecies."

Her words were teasing, but Seraphina didn't miss the undercurrent of worry beneath them.

"Or about them if you'd like," Cordelia added with a slight shrug. "Your call."

Isadora blinked, as if startled to find them both so close, but then she exhaled, the tension melting from her spine as her lips curved into a small but genuine smile. "That sounds … perfect, actually," she admitted. "I could really use the company."

Cordelia grinned. "Fantastic," she replied, offering her arm to her.

Isadora linked her arm through Cordelia's, and she glanced back at Seraphina and Aleron, her eyes apologetic. "See you both later."

Cordelia shot them a wink over her shoulder as they strolled off, her voice carrying back to them. "Don't do anything I wouldn't do!"

Seraphina chuckled, but the sound caught in her throat when she felt Aleron shift beside her. She turned to find him watching her, one hand rubbing at the back of his neck, a gesture that seemed almost shy, uncharacteristically uncertain.

"So," he started, voice lower than usual, a touch rough at the edges. "I was, um, heading to the library. I thought maybe you'd … want to join me?" His eyes were hopeful. "If you're not busy, I mean."

Seraphina stared for a moment, her words tangling on her tongue. She cleared her throat, forcing herself to sound steadier than she felt. "I … yeah," she managed, a little breathless. "That sounds nice."

Aleron's shoulders relaxed. "Good," he said, relieved. "It's a date, then."

Seraphina's cheeks flamed at the casual ease of it, heat crawling up her neck. His hand ghosted for a moment over the small of her back, a barely there touch that sent a shiver racing down her spine, before he turned toward the path that led to the library. She fell into step beside him. Despite the questions and the uncertainties the last couple of hours had presented, Seraphina couldn't quite fight the heat blooming in her chest, or the way her fingers itched to reach out and tangle with Aleron's again.

Chapter 13

THE HOLLOW ACHE OF LONELLNESS

FADEYA

adeya slipped through the university's grand halls like a whisper of wind, her form half-lost in the play of torchlight along the polished marble floors. In the dusky stillness, every muted footstep felt amplified.

She brushed a strand of brown hair from her watchful green eyes, scanning the corridor carefully before stepping forward. A hush blanketed these corridors at twilight, a silent anticipation that made her skin prickle.

The amulet lay cool against her chest, suspended by a thin silver chain. She felt its magic flare when a bond was occurring, an ever-present reminder of her duties. This week, it had shone more times than she could count.

Each flash of its soft, ethereal light sent Fadeya into motion, hastily fetching Hera so she could guide students through their bonding. What began as an uneasy partnership had grown into a natural rhythm. A glance from Fadeya when the amulet lit, a curt nod from Hera, and they moved like well-practiced dancers.

Their days often ended in Hera's candlelit office, poring over dusty scrolls, sipping tea as they reviewed each freshly formed bond. Though her demeanor remained scholarly and reserved, Professor

Hera's laughter came easily in those late hours, revealing a kindness that made Fadeya's guard slowly slip. Something vulnerable within Fadeya stirred, her walls quietly crumbling, allowing trust to bloom for the first time since she'd lost her father.

"I assume you will be enrolled next year," Hera had said while they had their tea that evening, offhandedly, like it was a fact. "It's been years since I've mentored someone. You have the spirit I've been searching for."

Fadeya hadn't known what to say. She'd tucked the words away instead, like a pressed flower hidden in the pages of her thoughts.

You have the spirit I've been searching for.

The idea stirred something reckless and desperate in her chest—a want for something she could almost touch, but still wasn't sure she deserved.

Yet amid these newly forged bonds and her budding friendship with Hera, a bitter undercurrent tugged at Fadeya whenever she spotted Seraphina. Her sister seemed to glow from the inside out, with her radiant smile and sparkling eyes. Laughter echoed in the courtyards as she bantered with friends or rushed off to another lesson.

Where Fadeya might have once felt pride, she now felt only an unsettling ache. They'd been so close, inseparable, two sisters bound by the same fate. Now, every fleeting glimpse of Seraphina reminded her how they had diverged like opposing tides.

The months had changed them both. Where Seraphina had once flinched from the world, she now seemed to belong in it. And Fadeya, who had always found strength in certainty, in structure, felt unmoored. As if some great wind had blown through the life she'd so carefully constructed and left it in ruins.

She drew a breath to steady herself and drifted through a maze of courtyards near the lecture halls. The moon hung high, its silver light softening the edges of manicured hedges and ornate fountains. Tonight, the amulet lay still against her chest, the remnants of its earlier glow dimming to the faintest ember.

She slowed as she reached the reflection pool, a large willow tree casting ribbons of moonlit shadow across the water. Beneath those drooping branches stood a solitary figure.

She recognized him immediately.

Emeric.

With those broad shoulders and gently curling blond hair. A pang of memory stirred in her chest, recalling their brief but playful flirtation back home, before life had scattered them in different directions.

Uncertain, Fadeya lingered in the shadows and watched him. Arms folded over his chest, Emeric stared into the pool's rippling surface. He looked so alone, weighed down by unseen burdens. A wave of empathy and regret tightened her throat. In that moment, his loneliness mirrored her own, as though they were two halves of a shared sorrow.

Sensing her gaze, Emeric turned, his eyes narrowing as he searched the darkness. Heart pounding, Fadeya pressed herself against the stone arch, torn between stepping forward and fleeing.

After a moment, Emeric let out a slow exhale and returned his attention to the water. He hadn't spotted her, or if he had, he gave no sign.

She inched closer, compelled by a yearning to speak, yet unable to break the silence. The sight of him standing there alone tugged at her deepest fears: that she, too, was nothing more than a solitary figure, caught in a swirl of duties and unfulfilled promises, and that she would never be more.

Her amulet remained cold and silent against her chest, but a quiet instinct, an echo of warning, urged her away. Perhaps tonight wasn't meant for confessions or fragile conversations.

Perhaps some truths were safer left in the shadows.

Fadeya paused, glancing once more toward Emeric's figure beneath the pale wash of moonlight. With a quiet breath, she turned away, footsteps careful on the worn cobblestones as she moved back into the night. Her fingers curled absently around the thin silver chain, the cool metal familiar and reassuring. She whispered a silent plea that the amulet remain dormant, just for tonight, a brief reprieve from the relentless pull of obligation.

Tomorrow she would pick up those burdens once again, but tonight, beneath stars indifferent to duty, she allowed herself the small comfort that she wasn't the only one who felt the hollow ache of loneliness.

Emeric felt it too. And somehow, that small, unspoken understanding was enough.

SERAPHINA

A few days later, a warm breeze carried the scent of midnight roses and freshly cut grass through the university gardens as Seraphina spread out the quilted picnic blanket. Fluffy clouds drifted by in the sky, framing the sun so that pockets of light and shadow danced across the blossoms. A scattering of pastel petals rained down every time the wind rustled the flowering vines. It felt like the garden was celebrating the spring afternoon.

Cordelia breezed in, a woven basket swinging lightly from one hand, the other clutching a wide-brimmed hat like a queen holding her crown. Her gown was a cascade of silk and gossamer lace, dyed the hue of sun-ripened peaches. Around her waist rested a delicate silver belt etched with a floral design.

The skirt fluttered gently at her ankles, revealing leather slippers adorned with tiny moonstones, each stone winking in the sun. She looked stunning, but it was Cordelia's smile, sly and edged with wicked delight, that whispered promises of an afternoon of laughter.

Seraphina smoothed her lavender cotton dress as she knelt, a simple thing with loose sleeves and a scattering of silver-threaded stars embroidered along the hem.

"Hungry?" she asked, her eyebrow arched as she heard Cordelia's stomach growl.

She gave a dramatic sigh. "Always, but also absolutely brimming with excitement." She plopped down beside Seraphina and flung open the basket's lid, unveiling an assortment of pastries, cheeses, fruit tarts, and mini sandwiches. "Just wait until you taste the honey buns I found. You will weep from pure bliss."

Seraphina chuckled, helping herself to a jam-filled pastry. "I have no doubt."

Grinning, Cordelia took a moment to fan herself with a folded napkin. The movement was suspiciously dainty and full of theatrical flair, the sort Cordelia adopted when trying to contain some big secret.

Seraphina narrowed her eyes and tapped her best friend on the arm. "Out with it, Cor. You look like you're about to burst."

Cordelia let out a squeal and grabbed Seraphina's hand. "I asked Isadora to be my girlfriend."

Seraphina gasped, pressing her other hand to her heart in mock astonishment. "*The* Princess Isadora? The fae princess with the starlight eyes and a smile that practically glows in the moonlight?"

At Seraphina's teasing words, Cordelia's cheeks turned a delightful pink. "Yes, the very one."

A bubbly laugh escaped Seraphina. "My, my, that *is* quite the catch. Look at you, Cordelia of the boring human realm, landing yourself a fae princess." She nudged her friend with a playful elbow. "You must teach me your ways."

"Oh, hush." Cordelia tried to sound exasperated, but her eyes danced. "I only asked. It was hardly some heroic feat. We were getting on so well in our study group, and one thing led to another, and … Yes, I might have risked sounding like a lovestruck fool, but I regret nothing."

Seraphina reached for another pastry, effectively concealing the sparkle of pride in her own gaze. "You're smitten."

Cordelia sighed dreamily, leaning back on her elbows. "Smitten is an understatement. Isadora's … everything. She can be as gentle as a warm summer breeze one moment, and then sharper than steel if she's protecting her people. Her magic is so rich it crackles in the air. And the way she laughs, my heart nearly falls out of my chest."

Seraphina studied her friend, noting the sincerity shining in those honey-brown eyes. "Cordelia, you deserve every bit of that happiness."

"Oh, look who's talking," Cordelia teased as she gave Seraphina a playful shove. "You've been sneaking around with Aleron lately. Don't think I haven't noticed those quick escapes from the library or those moonlit walks you try to keep hush-hush."

Seraphina's cheeks warmed. "We've just been … spending time together."

Cordelia scoffed, arching a perfectly groomed brow. "Oh, please. You're beyond spending time." She reached into the basket again, handing Seraphina a fruit tart like it was a bribe. "Spill. Has he finally kissed you? Or are you two still dancing around each other like star-crossed lovers in a ballad?"

Seraphina took the offered tart, toying with its flaky edges. A trace of a smile graced her lips as she remembered Aleron's lips on hers, the warmth of his hands on her waist, and his whispered words that made her heart flutter. "Alright, alright. He kissed me. Just a few days ago."

"Oh, you little tart!" Cordelia gushed, pressing her hands to her cheeks. "I knew it! What was it like?"

Seraphina rolled her eyes fondly. "Magical, I suppose." Her voice softened as she recalled the moment. "It was quick, but … there was something about it that felt like stepping into a new world."

Cordelia sighed wistfully, then pointed a sandwich at her friend. "I knew you were head over heels."

A laugh escaped Seraphina's throat, free and light. "I'm … not sure what I am yet, but we've been seeing more of each other. Walks after class, reading together in the library, sneaking out to explore the university grounds late at night. It's thrilling and comfortable all at once. Like old times."

Cordelia pressed a hand to her heart. "Ugh, that's the dream. Good for you, darling."

They settled into a comfortable silence, nibbling on the array of goodies as birds sang overhead. After a few moments, Cordelia spoke again. "I have been missing Boyde, though."

Seraphina glanced at her, surprise shifting into empathy. "How is your bondmate doing?"

"Oh, she's fine. The last time we worked together on channeling, she nearly knocked me out." Cordelia laughed, but there was fondness in her tone. "I can't wait to see her again. I'm daydreaming about Isadora one second and then longing to train with Boyde the next. My heart feels so full."

Seraphina gave her friend a look. "I'm glad you have found your place in this new world."

Nodding, Cordelia then cleared her throat in a purposeful shift of mood. "Speaking of big events … The Luminous Veil is nearly upon us. Isadora mentioned it to me and said we absolutely must attend. It's a time when the barriers between the magical realm and human realm are thin, and magic just … flows. Isn't that incredible? She claims it's breathtakingly beautiful."

A tug of excitement fluttered in Seraphina's chest. She had been hearing of the Luminous Veil all week. "I've read a few references in the library. It sounds amazing."

"Isadora said the festivities will be grand. Everyone wears beautifully designed gowns and suits, mostly in shimmering fabrics to echo the stars. She's even invited her personal tailor to do the fittings for us. I nearly cried when she asked if we could match." Cordelia laughed, a little breathless.

Seraphina grinned at Cordelia's glee, wholeheartedly happy for her friend. Yet, as the sun edged behind a drifting cloud, the warmth in Seraphina's heart wavered. A shadow seemed to pass over her thoughts. She felt an odd pang within, as if a part of her lay dormant or missing.

"Something wrong?" Cordelia asked, biting into a small lemon tart, not quite aware of the shift in Seraphina's mood.

Seraphina reached for a pastry to occupy her hands. "No, just thinking about all the preparations. You know I hate dress fittings."

"Yes, but I'll be there to make sure you look ravishing."

"Of course you will," Seraphina replied as she mustered a smirk.

Yet even as they launched back into the easy flow of conversation, discussing the color of the ribbons they might use for their hair and which pair of shoes Cordelia would design for the night, Seraphina couldn't banish the lingering emptiness in her chest, the quiet ache whispering that she was incomplete, that there was some deeper truth eluding her.

Chapter 14

THE OTHER SISTER

FADEYA

From her perch in a tree at the edge of the Star Shrine, Fadeya sat and watched another bonding class unfold. She was becoming accustomed to sneaking out and following the class to the Star Shrine. There wasn't a bond every class, but when it did happen, she was filled with awe ... and jealousy.

Fadeya's nails dug into the bark of the tree beside her as she leaned forward. Even from this far away, she could recognize the slight way her twin tilted her head when listening intently.

The bonding class was smaller tonight. Fewer students had been invited this time, though the creatures were no less impressive. It was the firebird that held everyone's attention now.

The phoenix stood at the center of the glade, its feathers catching fire with every movement, brilliant plumes rippling with heatless flame. Its eyes were sun-forged amber, steady and ancient. It did not blink. Did not falter. Its wings flared as if it knew the power it carried and dared anyone to prove worthy of it.

The girl it faced, Aine, one of the few humans in this year, stood with trembling hands and a set jaw. Her long red hair tangled around her shoulders, and her breath came in fast bursts.

There was a flicker between them—a pause in the air. Then the phoenix lifted from the ground with one beat of its wings and landed on her outstretched arm.

A ring of fire burst outward, curling in elegant spirals around Aine, searing a glowing pattern into the grass without burning it. Aine didn't flinch. She lifted her hand, just slightly, and the phoenix bent its head to press its beak to her palm.

Power surged outward, amber and wild. It was done.

Fadeya's throat tightened as students below erupted in cheers. Even Seraphina was smiling, no, beaming, as she clutched Cordelia's hand and turned to Aleron with a wide-eyed look of joy.

That could've been me, Fadeya thought, stomach twisting. Should've been me.

Then her eyes drifted to the dark figure standing apart from it all.

Prince Evander stood at the far edge of the glade, half-shadowed beneath the sprawling boughs of an ash tree. Jaw clenched. One hand resting on the hilt of the curved blade at his hip.

What is he up to? She'd thought it before, but the feeling had only grown stronger over the past few days.

Tonight, as the flames died down and the bonding ceremony concluded, Evander turned, but not toward the path the others followed. He slipped into the woods, instead.

Fadeya's breath caught, her brows knitting in frustration. *Again?*

Without thinking, she slipped from her hiding place, boots silent on the damp earth as she moved through the trees.

Evander moved quickly, his figure blending seamlessly into the shadows of the forest. His steps were deliberate and soundless, like someone intimately familiar with the terrain. Fadeya trailed after him, her eyes straining to keep his silhouette in sight.

The forest thickened with every step, its canopy knitting together so tightly it smothered the sky. Only faint streaks of moonlight sliced through the tangled branches, offering little more than ghostly slivers of illumination. The deeper she went, the heavier the air became, thick, stagnant, charged. No rustling leaves, no distant calls of night creatures. Just silence. A silence so unnatural it pressed against her skin like an unseen hand, amplifying the sound of her own footsteps, the hurried rhythm of her breath.

Everything in her screamed to turn back. Return to the safety of the clearing, but her feet kept moving.

Her thoughts raced as she leapt over a fallen log, trying not to make a sound. *Who was he, truly?*

He was the prince of the realm, yes, but beyond his title, he remained an enigma. She thought of the glimpses she'd caught of him over the last couple of weeks, always watching from the edges, intense and solitary, never engaging unless required.

And of course, he was infuriatingly beautiful.

Don't be foolish, she advised herself. You're here to observe. Not to ogle.

Then, without warning, Evander stopped.

She pressed herself against the trunk of a tree as she tried to still the pounding in her chest. Slowly, she leaned out just enough to catch a glimpse. He stood in a small clearing, barely large enough to let the moonlight pool around him. His hood remained up, but his posture had shifted, less guarded, more purposeful.

Evander reached into his cloak, and something small emerged from the folds of fabric, resting in the center of his palm. Squinting, she tried to make out what he was holding. A faint, silvery glow emitted from the object, casting light across his face, sharpening the high angles of his cheekbones, the strong cut of his jaw.

It was unfair, really, how someone of royalty could be so handsome.

The object in his palm was small, round, almost like a miniature version of the Celestial Orb used in the Starlight Awakening.

Then, without warning, he lifted his head.

Fadeya barely had time to shrink back behind the tree before his gaze swept the forest.

Did he know she was here? She pressed herself against the bark, breath shallow, willing herself into stillness. The silence stretched taut—thick and waiting.

Then his voice broke the stillness. "You've followed me long enough."

The words slithered through the quiet, sending a chill through her veins.

"You might as well come out."

Fadeya's mind raced. Every muscle in her body screamed at her to run, but she forced herself to stay rooted in place. Her lips parted to speak, but no words came out.

Evander's eyes narrowed as he stepped around the tree and came face-to-face with her.

"Seraphina?"

The single word carried an edge of uncertainty. Not suspicion, but something close. His brow furrowed, as if his mind struggled to reconcile what he saw with what he expected.

Fadeya's heart stuttered. He thinks I'm her.

She willed her breathing to steady, forced her shoulders to relax, and met his look with a confidence she didn't feel.

"Yes," she said, slowly, as if weighing the word before offering it.

Evander's eyes lingered on her, doubt lighting his face. He took two slow steps forward, closing the distance between them.

He glanced down, as if only just realizing the small, glowing orb still resting in his palm. He closed his fingers around it and slipped it into the inner pocket of his coat. "What are you doing out here?" he demanded. "Why were you following me?"

Every second he stared at her, doubt gnawed at her resolve, threatening to unravel her composure.

"I was just curious," she answered, her voice barely above a whisper. Her fingers curled around the amulet at her neck.

"Curious?" Evander repeated, his tone flat. He tilted his head slightly, studying her with an intensity that made her stomach twist. "Curious about what exactly?"

The moment stretched taut between them. Fadeya's grip on the amulet tightened. One wrong word, one misstep, and he'd see through her lie. She swallowed hard, willing herself to stay calm.

"I saw you leave the bonding area," she said finally, her words carefully chosen. "It seemed ... I just wanted to see where you were going."

Evander's stare didn't waver. His hand twitched near his dagger; his posture still coiled like a spring ready to snap. "And now that you've seen?" he asked, his voice dangerously soft.

Fadeya didn't answer immediately. Her mind worked furiously, searching for a way to deflect his suspicion, but the way he looked at her ... It was as if he could see every hidden thought, every half-truth she tried to hold back.

"Now I know you're hiding something," she said, surprising herself with the boldness of her words. Her chin lifted slightly, her gaze locking onto his. If she couldn't outmaneuver him, she could at least match his intensity. The moment stretched between them, thick with tension. She had to get away before he started picking apart her lie.

"I just ..." She faltered.

Evander took a step forward, his piercing eyes narrowing.

Panic flared in her like a wildfire. Hera's warning about the amulet echoed in Fadeya's mind now. *This is not a toy, Fadeya. Use it only if you must.*

As her fingers brushed the smooth, cool surface of the amulet, it flared to life with a faint glow. She willed the magic to take hold, her whispered plea barely audible. "Hide me."

The shadows around Fadeya stirred with eerie intent, as if roused from slumber. They slithered across the forest floor, gathering at her feet in inky wisps before rising in slow tendrils. The darkness coiled around her legs, climbing her frame like smoke, cool against her skin. They wrapped around her torso, her arms, her throat, clinging to her like a second skin that shifted, distorting the edges of her form.

Her silhouette rippled, wavering as though she were no longer solid, no longer entirely *there*. The darkness folded inward, enclosing her in a cocoon of shadow that swallowed every hint of light. For a heartbeat, she felt suspended, untethered from flesh and bone. She became part of the forest's hush, more phantom than flesh.

Evander's sharp gasp fractured the stillness. His entire body stiffened, and his eyes, wide with disbelief, scanned the space where she had stood.

"W-what are you?" he breathed, his voice raw with a fear he couldn't disguise.

Fadeya said nothing. Words felt too heavy. Dread prickled across her skin like static, pushing her forward before hesitation could find her. She spun, shadows gripping her like armor, and darted into the forest.

The amulet's magic surged around her, warping the air, silencing the crunch of leaves beneath her feet. Her outline flickered and blurred, a ghost slipping through the trees. Behind her, Evander was still staring into the darkness, searching, too late.

"Wait!" Evander's voice rang out behind her. "Please, wait!"

She didn't stop. She couldn't.

Branches whipped past her, scratching her arms and snagging her cloak. Her lungs burned as she sucked in ragged breaths, her legs aching with the strain of her flight. Still, she pressed on, the shadows coiling and urging her forward, deeper into the forest's embrace.

Fadeya's mind raced, the consequences of her recklessness crashing down on her. *She had used the amulet in front of someone, someone dangerous. Would he tell anyone? Would he come after her?* She couldn't shake the feeling that Evander's gaze was still on her, piercing through the forest like a predator tracking its prey.

Only when the sound of his pursuit faded entirely did she slow, collapsing against a hill of moss. Her chest heaved as she fought to catch her breath, her trembling fingers clutching the amulet. The shadows around her began to recede, peeling away and melting back into the forest floor. She felt exposed without them, as if a protective barrier had been stripped away. She replayed the scene in her mind, her stomach twisting with unease.

"What have I done?" she whispered. The amulet had saved her, but it had also revealed her secret. Evander had seen her vanish, had seen the shadows consume her.

She had to find Hera.

Chapter 15

THE LUMINOUS VEIL

SERAPHINA

The Luminous Veil had finally arrived, an event older than the university itself, a night when the boundaries between the magical and mortal realms thinned to gossamer, inviting celestial energy to touch mortal lives.

Excited voices drifted across the grand courtyard, mingling with the evening breeze. Gowns glittered like captured fireflies, and robes shimmered softly. Small clusters of friends gathered, their laughter mingling with hushed whispers. An electric anticipation hung in the air.

Seraphina stood alone on the raised dais, her eyes lifted to the statue that towered above her.

Aurora, the university's founder, carved with the weight of history. As she studied it, her gaze was drawn not to the sword or the outstretched hand, but to the amulet that rested against the stone folds of the founder's robe. She didn't know why the sight of it stirred her. Only that it did. Like the echo of a name she should know.

The evening air carried the scent of honey cakes and lantern oil, and the hum of conversation from the distant garden barely reached her ears. She should have felt excited, but a prickle of unease crawled along her skin.

A familiar warmth brushed against her senses before she even heard his approach. *Aleron.*

She turned, breath catching as she met his eyes. He stood there, golden-brown under the lantern light, his eyes dark with something she recognized, something that made her stomach flip. In his hand, he held a single lily, delicate and perfect.

"You're daydreaming again," he murmured, a smirk tugging at his lips.

She let out a breathy laugh. "I am not."

His expression shifted as he stepped closer, the space between them narrowing into something more intimate. "You are. I know that look."

She didn't deny it. Instead, she reached for the flower he offered, brushing her fingers against his in the process. A small touch, fleeting, but it sent a ripple through her.

"Tell me what's on your mind," he urged, voice low, coaxing.

She hesitated. She had never been good at sharing her fears, her doubts, but this was *Aleron*.

"I keep thinking I'm forgetting something," she admitted, tightening her grip on the flower. "Something I can't name."

His gaze softened, and he reached for her other hand, intertwining their fingers.

A slow exhale left her lips. The weight of uncertainty didn't disappear, but it felt lighter with him beside her. She lifted the lily to her nose, inhaling the sweet scent before tilting her head up, her eyes meeting his.

"Everything is okay; it'll come to you," he whispered.

His fingers tightened around hers. "Seraphina," he murmured, his free hand cupping her cheek.

Her heart raced as he leaned in, his breath ghosting over her lips, teasing, waiting. The anticipation coiled tight in her chest, and when their lips finally met, it was soft, hesitant yet familiar, like they had been kissing for a lifetime. The sweetness of his mouth sent heat curling through her, a slow burn that only deepened as she pressed closer.

Her fingers slid into his hair, threading through the mass of his black natural curls, twisting around them as he pulled her

184

against him, his hands firm at her waist. The world around them faded into nothing, lost to the press of his body against hers, to the way his lips moved with hungry reverence. His kiss wasn't just a meeting of mouths; it was a claim, a promise, something deeper than either of them could put into words.

Then he faltered, a sharp intake of breath, his grip tightening just a fraction before he caught her bottom lip between his teeth. It was clumsy, eager, *devastating*. A rush of desire shot through her, stealing the breath from her lungs.

She gasped, the lily slipping from her fingers, falling forgotten to the ground, but the sound barely made it past her lips before he swallowed it, his mouth claiming hers again, desperate, insatiable. His hands roamed, sliding down her spine, pressing her closer, like he needed to feel every inch of her against him. Like the space between them was unbearable.

The world beyond them ceased to exist; there was only this, only him, the way his lips moved against hers like he had been starving for her, the way his hands gripped her like he might never let go.

And stars, she didn't want him to.

His breath hitched as she dragged her nails down his back, and a low, ragged groan rumbled from his chest, resonating through her as his fingers roamed her body. Time unraveled, stretched thin between them, until finally, breathless, he pulled back. He rested his forehead against hers, his breath still uneven, lips barely parted as if he were about to steal another kiss.

Seraphina's thoughts spun, caught somewhere between now and the foggy memories of years that stretched out behind them like a shadow. There had been a time, long ago, back when they were students in the human realm, when she used to imagine what it might be like to kiss him, to touch him, but they'd never crossed that line. Never dared. Duty, timing, fear, take your pick.

Whatever it was, it had kept them circling each other like moons caught in separate orbits.

And yet now ... now, here they were, gravity finally winning.

These past few weeks had felt different, softer somehow. Honest. Moments shared without pretense, conversations that were intimate, eyes that met and held just a second longer than they should've. She hadn't realized how much she'd wanted this. Not until it was unfolding beneath her hands.

"Come with me to the Luminous Veil," he murmured, his voice rough with longing.

She laughed, breathless and dizzy, her ears ringing. "Wasn't that implied?"

Aleron chuckled, the sound deep and sinful, vibrating against her lips as she stole another kiss.

His hands traced slow, possessive paths down her arms before sliding to her waist again, his fingers splaying against the curve of her hips. He didn't pull away this time. He lingered, his breath mingling with hers, his thumb grazing the line of her jaw before lifting her chin, forcing her to meet his gaze.

"I just wanted to hear you say it," he replied, his voice low.

His stare stripped her bare, passion unraveling her, threading through her veins like wildfire. She swallowed hard, her fingers dragging up his chest, feeling the steady, powerful rhythm of his heartbeat beneath her touch.

"Yes," she whispered, "I'll go with you."

A ravenous look ignited in his eyes, and his grin was devious in a way that sent a shiver down her spine. He leaned in, his nose brushing hers, his lips just shy of another kiss.

"Good," he murmured. His fingers tightened at her waist, dragging her flush against him. "Because I wasn't planning on giving you a choice."

And then he kissed her again, slow, deep, *devouring*. No hesitation. No teasing. Just raw, burning need, the kind that made her toes curl and her thoughts dissolve.

"Well, that's certainly one way to start the evening."

Seraphina and Aleron jolted at the voice, breathless as they spun toward the interruption, arms still tangled around each other.

A peal of laughter echoed through the courtyard as Cordelia and Isadora swept down the nearby staircase, their matching midnight gowns shifting like galaxies were stitched into every shimmering thread. Cordelia's smirk was downright wicked, her attention bouncing between Seraphina's flushed face and Aleron's slightly disheveled state.

"Oh, please, don't stop on my account," she purred, tilting her head with mock innocence. "Though, Sera, if you're going to be thoroughly compromised, I'd at least suggest a better backdrop. The lighting here is *tragic*."

Seraphina's face burned as she hastily readjusted the fabric of her gown, fingers skimming over the places where Aleron's hands had just been.

Isadora chuckled, gracefully steering Cordelia a few steps forward, closing the distance between them. "Are you excited for tonight?" she asked lightly. "You will never look at the night sky the same after experiencing it. It's truly remarkable."

Seraphina's brows lifted, intrigue sparking in her eyes as she shifted closer. "You've been to the Luminous Veil before?"

"Every year," Isadora replied, her voice tinged with both pride and reverence. "The fae kingdom is my home, after all. Our traditions are woven into who we are, and the Luminous Veil is one of the most sacred and wondrous nights of the year. It's not just a festival, it's a convergence of realms, a celebration of life, magic, and connection. It's unlike anything you've ever seen."

"I hadn't even heard of it until this week," Aleron admitted, running a hand through his hair, attempting to smooth the mess Seraphina had left behind.

Isadora shrugged, taking Cordelia's hand in her own and giving her a smile. "It's not the kind of thing you bring up casually. The fae are ... particular about who they invite. Invitations are rare, and stepping into our home for the Veil means embracing everything it entails."

Cordelia watched her girlfriend, utterly captivated, as if the rest of the world had blurred into nothing.

Aleron chuckled, amusement lacing his voice. "Looks like we're all in for a night we won't forget." He bent down, scooping up the lily Seraphina had dropped, and handed it back to her with a knowing grin. Seraphina accepted it, her smile unfaltering, a quiet thrill curling through her.

She took in the way Cordelia and Isadora glowed beside each other, the instinctive way they fit together. With a teasing sigh, she clasped her hands together. "You two," she declared, voice full of affection, "are the brightest pair in this entire courtyard."

Cordelia shot Seraphina a wink as Isadora pressed a lingering kiss to her temple. "At this rate, we'll outshine the actual stars," she mused, her gaze sweeping over Seraphina's gown.

A slow smile tugged at her lips as she took in the deep sapphire fabric—bold, striking, and completely unexpected on Seraphina. Gold glitter dusted the bodice like stardust, while the fitted waist accentuated every curve before cascading into sheer layers. And then the slit, slicing scandalously high, offering just a whisper of skin beneath the flowing fabric.

Cordelia let out a low whistle. "Okay, I was not ready. That dress looks even better than I imagined. You're making a damn *statement*."

Seraphina arched a brow, smoothing the fabric at her hip with a grin. "Isn't that the point?"

She circled Seraphina once, eyes gleaming. "I mean, obviously, it helps when the genius behind the design is *me*." She gave a mock bow, then flicked an imaginary speck of lint from Seraphina's shoulder. "Custom stitching, fae-threaded silk, that neckline that says *moon goddess, don't mess with me*. You're welcome."

Seraphina gave a little spin. "It's stunning. I almost feel bad for everyone else tonight. Between your talent and my face? Unfair advantage."

Cordelia threw her head back with a delighted laugh. "I've taught you well."

Seraphina twirled the lily between her fingers, casting a glance toward Aleron, whose gaze was decidedly glued to her, his jaw set like he was trying to play it cool and failing spectacularly. "Aleron helped, too," she said, holding up the bloom before tucking it behind her ear. "My favorite flower."

Cordelia clapped a hand to her chest. "Romance. Devotion. A dramatic display of longing. It's almost like you're both—"

"Cordelia," Isadora cut in, shaking her head.

She beamed. "Hopeless."

Aleron huffed a laugh, shaking his head as he slid a hand into Seraphina's. "If that's what we're calling it, I can live with that."

Cordelia walked over to look at the reflecting pool, her fingers tracing gentle arcs through the air. As her palm lifted, a ribbon of water rose from the pool's surface, glinting like crystal under the sunlight. It spun lazily at first, responding to the subtle movements of her hand, before twisting into intricate, intertwining loops. The fluid motion seemed alive, the water obeying her every command. Her focus was absolute, her dark eyes gleaming with delight as she shaped the water into a perfect ring. "There," she said, her grin widening as she admired her work. With a flick of her wrist, she let the water fall back into the pool, the tiny splash sending ripples across the surface.

"Your magic is improving so much, Cordelia!" Seraphina said. Her eyes sparkled with excitement as she moved closer, watching the water ripple with residual energy.

Turning back to Seraphina, Cordelia brushed a stray black braid from her face. "It feels stronger every day," she admitted. Her fingers flexed unconsciously, as though itching to call the water back up and weave it into another creation.

"It's more than just impressive," Aleron said, crossing his arms and nodding toward the reflecting pool. "Water magic takes precision, control. You make it look so easy."

Seraphina stepped closer, her eyes lingering on the rippling surface. "It's not just your control, though," she murmured. "The way you wield it … It's like the water responds to you. Like it's a part of you."

Cordelia's gaze drifted back to the water. "That's how it feels," she said quietly. "Like the water knows me, just as much as I know

it. I don't force it to obey; it's about moving with it, like a dance."
She crouched by the pool once more, fingertips skimming the
surface. Tiny ripples radiated outward from her touch. "Boyde
has taught me so much over these last few weeks."

"That's incredible," Seraphina said, her tone tinged with awe.

Cordelia straightened, brushing her hands on her skirt. "Water
magic is all about adaptability, finding the path of least resistance,
but still holding your ground. Like the way a river carves through
stone, not by brute force, but by persistence."

Isadora chimed in. "That's very fitting for you, Cordelia. You
always seemed so steady, even when everything else is chaos."

Cordelia flushed slightly, her grin turning sheepish. "Well,
someone has to be, with this group," she said, glancing meaningfully at Aleron and Seraphina.

"Hey!" Aleron protested, though his wink betrayed his
amusement.

"Fair point," Seraphina said, nudging Cordelia playfully. "But
seriously, your magic is beautiful. It's … calming. I'm so proud of you."

Cordelia's smile glowed as brightly as her magic. "Thanks. It's
taken a lot of practice, but I think I'm finally starting to understand what it can really do."

The group fell into a comfortable rhythm, their conversation a
mix of teasing and easy laughter as they made their way through
the courtyard. Winged cats prowled among the pillars, their fur
catching the light, while moths the size of a hand flitted lazily
through the air. A faint melody of harps and flutes drifted around
them, weaving through the night air.

And then the wind shifted.

A ripple of magic swept through the courtyard like a current,
sending the moths into a sudden, dazzling spiral. The melody in
the air deepened, and a hush spread through the gathered students as a figure stepped forward, emerging from the shadows
of the archway.

Tall and sharp-featured, Evander carried himself like someone
who had been born to rule. His long, jet-black hair, nearly identical

to Isadora's, cascaded over his shoulders like silk, a striking contrast to the ivory cloak he wore. Silver trim curled along the edges of the fabric, and a scabbard hung at his side. His brown eyes swept over the group with cool calculation, though there was an undeniable warmth when they landed on his sister. Beneath the regal poise, a constellation of freckles dusted his sharp cheekbones and the bridge of his nose—a small, almost human imperfection that only made his beauty more otherworldly. Fae, through and through, breathtaking, untouchable, and powerful.

"I see you haven't gotten into too much trouble," Evander drawled as he nodded to his sister.

Isadora rolled her eyes, though a smirk tugged at her lips. "The night's still young."

Aleron, who had been quietly observing, shot him a grin, eyes full of anticipation. "So, tell me, *Your Highness,* are we trekking to this grand castle of yours, or do the fae have something a little more exciting in store?"

Evander exhaled an amused breath. "Walking? That would hardly be fitting for a night like this." He turned, gesturing toward the open courtyard. "The skyway is waiting."

Seraphina frowned. "The *skyway?*"

As if in response, the air above them warped. The stars seemed to stretch, elongating into ribbons of light that curved downward, forming translucent, glowing pathways that arched across the heavens. They radiated with energy, a bridge of starlight leading toward the distant peaks where the fae castle waited, its towers glowing like frost-kissed ivory.

Cordelia let out a slow, appreciative hum. "Dramatic. I approve."

Evander grinned. "Good. Because I don't do anything halfway."

Without another word, he stepped forward, his boots meeting the starlit path as if it were solid ground. The bridge vibrated beneath him, absorbing his weight, but held firm.

Seraphina exchanged a glance with Aleron, then inhaled sharply and took a step onto the pathway. For a moment, the sensation was like stepping onto water, unsteady, shifting beneath her weight, but then the magic solidified, supporting her. A surge of exhilaration raced through her as she took another step, then another.

Isadora followed, her steps confident, while Cordelia let out a gleeful laugh as she took off in a near-run, twirling in her gown as the magic sent glimmers of light trailing from her footsteps.

Aleron hesitated for only a second before stepping forward. "If I trip and take a nosedive, just know it was fate, not my lack of coordination," he shouted, though his lips twitched with amusement.

"You're assuming we'd believe that," Cordelia shot back.

Aleron huffed but took another step, testing the magic beneath his feet. Soon, they were moving together, their silhouettes illuminated against the vast stretch of night.

The air was thinner, crisp with magic, carrying the faint scent of rain. Below them, the world stretched in a breathtaking panorama, the university grounds, the glowing braziers, the sweeping forests that lined the horizon, all of it bathed in the ethereal glow of the Luminous Veil.

The castle loomed ahead, a marvel of craftsmanship and magic. Its towers, carved from stone, stretched impossibly high, their surfaces threaded with flowering vines that climbed toward the heavens.

As they approached, the pathways of woven light merged into a grand archway, its iridescent shimmer marking the threshold between the skyway and the palace grounds. Beyond it, massive doors of carved oak, inlaid with opal, stood half open, inviting them into the golden-lit grandeur within.

The courtyard stretched wide, its stone pathways laid in intricate designs. Floating lanterns drifted lazily above, casting a warm glow over silken banners embroidered with the sigils of the royal family. The air carried the distant sound of cascading fountains, their waters flowing into basins of jade.

As they ascended the final steps, Aleron reached toward a large, velvety moth that had landed on the front of his coat. The creature twitched its feathery antennae at him but didn't move.

Carefully, he lifted a finger to nudge it away, only for the moth to latch on tighter, its tiny claws catching the fabric. He frowned, trying again, but the moth held firm.

Cordelia grinned. "Looks like you've been chosen. Congratulations, you're a father now."

Aleron sighed, holding his arms out as if unsure of what to do. "Should I poke it?"

Seraphina tilted her head, studying the moth. "I think he likes you!"

"Or," Evander drawled, "it just thinks you're a particularly large and unimpressive tree."

Aleron shot him a flat look before attempting one last time to dislodge the creature. It finally fluttered off, vanishing into the golden haze of the courtyard. He straightened his coat with as much dignity as he could muster. "You're all insufferable."

Cordelia patted his shoulder. "And yet, here we are, bringing so much joy to your life."

At the heart of the palace, a grand staircase spiraled upward, its gleaming steps leading to the figures who awaited just inside. At the forefront, poised and commanding, stood Hadren and Lira Malveric of Avantar, the king and queen of the fae.

The queen was breathtaking. Her silver-white hair had been gathered into an elegant updo, each strand coiled and pinned with meticulous care, crowned with a delicate circlet of crystal. Her brown eyes, rich, dark, and ancient, held the weight of centuries, their wisdom sharpened by the intrigues of countless courts.

Beside her, the king was equally striking. Tall and broad-shouldered, he bore the same effortless authority Evander carried, though his presence was more formidable, more commanding. His long black hair was neatly tied back, framing high cheekbones and a strong jaw, while freckles dusted the bridge of his nose, an echo of his son's, subtle yet unmistakable.

As Evander and Isadora stepped forward, the queen's lips curved into a smile. "You're late."

193

Evander bowed quickly, then responded. "Just trying to make an entrance."

The king's gaze swept over the group as they bowed before him and rose, lingering briefly on Seraphina before settling on Isadora. "And you brought guests."

Isadora straightened. "Yes. We invited some friends."

Amusement softened the regal lines of the queen's face. She exchanged a look with her husband before she turned back to the humans. "Then we welcome you all to the Luminous Veil."

The words felt like a spell settling over them. As the king and queen turned, their robes sweeping behind them, the group began to move forward, drawn by the grandeur of the palace interior, but before Seraphina could take a step, a hand brushed her arm. Evander.

"Seraphina. A word?"

She blinked up at him, confused. "Of course. What's wrong?"

His gaze went briefly to Aleron before he hesitated. Seraphina followed his look, then turned to Aleron with a reassuring smile.

"Would you mind getting us some drinks?" she asked. "I'll be right in."

Aleron studied her for a moment, then Evander, before nodding. "Of course. Don't take too long." He brushed a loose strand of hair behind her ear and then stepped past, disappearing into the golden-lit halls beyond.

She turned to face Evander, and her brow furrowed as she stepped closer, the tension rolling off him like a ripple in the air. "Evander," she said, her voice edged with concern. "Is everything okay?"

He hesitated, his brown eyes searching Seraphina's face. The unwavering assurance in his stance faltered, replaced by a quiet intensity, like he was weighing every word before speaking.

"The other night in the woods," he said finally, his voice low, careful. "I don't understand what happened. Why did you run off after following me?" He paused, his voice lowering. "Do you possess some kind of shadow magic?"

194

Seraphina blinked, caught off guard. "Shadow magic?" She let out a short, incredulous breath, shaking her head. "Evander, I don't know what you're talking about. I wasn't in the woods."

His expression hardened. "You weren't?" His voice held an edge now, not quite accusation, but laced with disbelief.

"No," she said firmly, her brow furrowing. "Perhaps you mistook someone else for me?"

A muscle ticked in Evander's jaw as his expression darkened. The weight of his silence stretched between them. He studied her a moment longer; his stare was enough to make her stomach twist.

"I could have sworn it was you," he murmured, but the certainty in his voice was gone.

Seraphina folded her arms. "I promise you, I wasn't there." She paused, then softened her tone. "Evander, what *exactly* did you see?"

He exhaled sharply, dragging a hand through his hair. "Someone. Something. It looked like you. Moved like you." His eyes narrowed slightly, as if piecing together fragments of a puzzle. "But when I followed … they vanished."

A shiver ghosted down her spine, though she forced a casual shrug. "Well, I hate to disappoint you, but unless I've suddenly developed a talent for being in two places at once, it wasn't me."

Evander didn't immediately respond. He just kept watching her, something lurking behind his gaze.

Finally, he nodded, though his tone was distant. "Perhaps I was mistaken. Forgive me."

Seraphina attempted a smile, though unease still curled at the edges of her mind. "No need to apologize. It's easy to get confused in the dark."

But even as she said the words, she couldn't shake the feeling that whatever Evander had seen, whoever he had followed, it hadn't been a simple trick of the night.

The night of the Luminous Veil was alive at Astral Unison University, and the air buzzed with a quiet, electric anticipation. Students lined the moonlit paths in clusters, their eyes wide with wonder and nerves, whispering excitedly about what the evening might bring. Although most students weren't participating in the fae festivities directly, the campus was filled with celebration. Lights flickered from dormitory windows and common halls where music played, and laughter spilled out into the night.

From Professor Hera's office window, Fadeya could see the distant glow of the Fae Palace. The mere sight filled her chest with a bitter ache, envy tightening its claws around her heart.

Professor Hera moved thoughtfully around the cluttered office, packing a small bag with delicate items—crystals, herbs, and vials that gleamed softly.

"You did the right thing," Hera said. She didn't look up from her task. "With Evander. He's … perceptive and obviously up to no good."

Finally, Hera straightened, meeting Fadeya's gaze with a flicker of genuine concern. "You were wise to get away from him. And wiser still not to tell him anything."

Fadeya hugged her arms around herself, worry tightening in her throat. She nodded and looked back out of the window.

"It's rare, you know," Hera said. "An invitation to the Luminous Veil. Most fae never even set foot near the palace during the event. It's usually reserved for the powerful—royalty, mostly."

Fadeya fingered the amulet hanging cold around her neck, her eyes keen with interest. "Then it's no wonder you were invited, Professor."

Hera chuckled, glancing up from her preparations. "Flattery is beneath you, Fadeya. Though I admit, it is satisfying," she said. "You might be interested to know that your sister, Seraphina, and her companions received invitations, as well. They left for the palace not long ago."

The words struck Fadeya like a sudden gust of wind. A sharp, familiar sting bloomed in her chest, resentment, raw and unshakable. *Seraphina. Always Seraphina.* She turned away slightly, jaw tightening as her hand closed around the amulet at her neck. The metal bit into her skin, grounding her in the swirl of emotion rising beneath her composed exterior. "Of course, she did," she muttered.

Before Hera could respond, footsteps echoed softly outside the office door. Hera's expression darkened instantly. She gestured urgently toward the wardrobe against the far wall. "Quickly, hide yourself."

Fadeya obeyed without question, slipping silently into the darkness of the wardrobe, the scent of cedarwood and old books surrounding her as she peered through the narrow crack.

A sharp knock split the silence, and Hera called, voice steady, "Enter."

The door creaked open, and Emeric stepped inside, all rigid lines and barely contained frustration. Shadows clung to the hard set of his jaw, a storm simmering in his eyes.

Fadeya hated how good he looked, brooding and untouchable.

"Hello, Emeric. To what do I owe this pleasure?" Hera asked, making no effort to mask the annoyance in her voice.

Emeric paced, running an agitated hand over his neck. "Professor. I've been out every night," he confessed bitterly, "to the Star Shrine. *Every single night*, and nothing. No creature will bond with me. It's like they sense something lacking in me."

Hera raised an eyebrow, disapproval etched plainly across her features. "Alone? You know the dangers—"

"I'm aware," Emeric interrupted. "But I must find a bond. I have to. I *need* it."

From the small closet tucked behind the tapestry, Fadeya held her breath. The space was tight, the wooden panel pressing cool against her back. *Emeric* ... Her heart ached a little for him. *I didn't know it had gotten this bad.* She shifted her weight slightly, careful not to make a sound.

"Need." Hera's tone turned almost thoughtful now. "There are those who wait patiently for the right moment, for the bond to come to them." She took a slow step forward. "And there are those who understand that some things must be claimed, seized, when the time is right. The creatures sense desperation, yes, but they also sense will." Her gaze flicked over him with new interest. "Few students possess the ... resolve to do what must be done."

She circled him with unhurried steps, fingers drumming lightly against her folded arms. The faintest glimmer of intrigue sparked behind her eyes. Without a word, she moved to a locked chest hidden beneath a tapestry. Opening it carefully, she withdrew a small, ancient book bound in dark leather.

Fadeya drew a sharp breath, her attention riveted to the book as it seemed to hum faintly, an unsettling energy emanating from its pages.

"This," Hera said, pressing the book into Emeric's trembling hands, "is a key. A gateway to the untapped potential within you. Sometimes, Emeric, the path forward demands defiance, demands reaching for what seems impossible." She tapped the book's cover, her eyes burning into his. "Start here. Perhaps you'll finally find what you seek."

Emeric stared down at the book, uncertainty on his face. "But Professor, I've tried everything already. What could possibly be in a book that will make a creature want to bond?"

Hera nodded, a subtle smile curling her lips as she lightly tapped the book's cover again. "Sometimes, the very thing you need is hidden in the last place you'd think to look. Push beyond your boundaries, defy expectations, Emeric. The answers won't always come willingly; you must seek them out with persistence and courage."

Emeric clutched the book, relief and gratitude washing across his face. "Thank you, Professor. Truly." He turned swiftly and vanished into the hallway, determination brightening his steps toward the library.

Fadeya burst from the wardrobe, questions swirling furiously within her, but Hera silenced her immediately with a raised hand, already moving toward a shimmering portal conjured with a swift, practiced gesture. "I'm late, Fadeya. Be my eyes and ears tonight; I trust you'll remember."

And then she stepped through the gleaming doorway, disappearing into the brilliance of the Luminous Veil. The portal closed, leaving Fadeya alone, the familiar ache of jealousy rekindling.

Curiosity clawed at her, sharp and unrelenting. That book, whatever it was, wasn't ordinary. She'd seen the way Hera's voice had gone quiet, reverent. The way Emeric had held it.

Through the tall window, the night sparkled with celebration, floating lights, distant laughter, music weaving through the air like a spell. Seraphina would be out there, probably glowing beneath the stars, swept up in the beauty of it all. Fadeya swallowed the sharp twist in her chest and turned away.

Let Seraphina have her starlight.

She moved, soundless and sure, slipping into the corridor toward the library and letting the shadows overtake her.

Chapter 16

LYRAE

⌐ SERAPHINA

ordelia, Isadora, and Aleron followed just behind the king and queen as they entered the throne room, their steps echoing softly beneath the sweeping hush that fell over the gathered court. The royal pair glided forward, crowns catching the light. Every eye turned to watch them, and by extension, those who walked in their shadow.

Around the room, the fae stood like living art. Their beauty was otherworldly, ethereal and wild. Some had feathered cloaks, others wore crowns of twisted silver branches or armor that gleamed like lightning. Wings, antlers, horns, even flickering auras of magic adorned them, each displaying a declaration of power, heritage, and magic older than memory. And not a single human among them. Though the fae smiled and bowed, there was intrigue behind their eyes.

Seraphina joined them a breath later, slipping into place beside Aleron as if she'd been there all along. What had passed between her and Evander moments before still clung to her, but she said nothing. Cordelia instantly saw it; her best friend's eyes weren't on the ceiling, the tapestries, or even the fae around them.

"Hey," Aleron murmured. He extended a crystal flute toward her, the pale gold liquid inside fizzing lightly. "You look like you could use this."

Seraphina blinked, as if surfacing from a deep thought. She took the drink, her fingers brushing his. "Thank you."

"You alright?" he said under his breath, his eyes searching her face.

She hesitated, then gave a quick nod. "I've survived worse."

He arched his brow but didn't press.

Cordelia stepped in close, lowering her voice. "You've got that *'I just uncovered a dark secret'* face."

"Something like that," Seraphina replied, barely audible. She sipped her drink slowly, lost in thought.

Evander drifted into place beside them, his expression confused. A quick nod to Aleron, then his gaze lingered on Seraphina for a moment before he turned away, focusing on his parents.

He said he'd seen someone. Something. That looked like her. She didn't know whether to be afraid or furious.

"Mother. Father." Isadora's voice rang out. "Allow me to present my companions from Astral Unison University." The King and Queen turned their attention back to their human guests. "This is Aleron and Seraphina," Isadora said, gesturing toward the couple. "And this," she caught Cordelia's hand, tugging her gently forward, "is Cordelia Hallowmere. My partner."

There was a beat of silence.

Then the queen's eyes lit up, warm and unexpectedly bright. "Oh! How wonderful," she exclaimed, her voice full of affection. She swept Cordelia into an embrace that was far more human than Seraphina expected from fae royalty. "Come, my dear. I must know *everything.*"

Cordelia's eyes widened, but her lips curved in amusement. She shot Seraphina a grin over her shoulder, their fingers brushing one last time before the queen swept her away in a flurry of skirts and questions. Isadora followed, her steps light, almost laughing.

Seraphina's thoughts wouldn't settle. Evander's words echoed through her mind, looping like a thread she couldn't unravel. *It moved like you.* In that moment, the great doors groaned open with a deep, resonant clang.

The room stilled, and then she appeared.

Professor Hera swept into the throne room like a flame, her crimson robes trailing behind her in molten ripples. Embers of enchantment danced in her wake, faint golden sparks that curled in the air before vanishing into nothing. Against the pale shimmer of the palace, she was a striking contradiction: fire in a place built for ice. Fierce, radiant, and utterly unbothered by the sudden hush that fell upon the court, she walked with the ease of someone who feared no judgment.

Whispers stirred the air like a brewing storm.

Seraphina's attention sharpened as King Hadren leaned forward, his brow creasing deeply as his eyes settled upon Professor Hera.

She watched him closely, noting the subtle tension that rippled across his jaw, a reaction he quickly tried to suppress, but not swiftly enough to escape Seraphina's notice. *Why does he look so ... furious?*

There was recognition in his expression, fleeting yet undeniable. King Hadren looked as if he had glimpsed a ghost, a specter from memories buried beneath layers of time and denial. His eyes narrowed slightly, searching Hera's face for clues.

Hera stood unmoving, her attention locked onto the king with calm defiance, steady and unafraid, like a woman returning uninvited to a kingdom she'd once conquered and left in ashes.

Seraphina's gaze flicked between the two fae. *She's challenging him. Here. In front of everyone.*

For a brief instant, Seraphina sensed the whisper of old magic weaving invisibly between them. Hera's expression remained controlled, impassive even, but she noticed the way Hera clutched her hands.

King Hadren's lip curled, his attention moving to his approaching son. "Well. Look who's decided to grace us with her presence."

Evander's shoulders tensed. "It was proper to invite the university faculty. You told me to play politics. This is politics."

"Something is off about her," the king muttered.

Then his eyes landed on Seraphina and didn't move.

A beat. Then another.

"And what was her name again?" he whispered loudly to his son, raising one finger toward her.

Evander hesitated.

Seraphina stepped forward, spine straight, heart hammering. "Seraphina Elaris, Your Majesty."

The king sat back, his expression darkening.

"Elaris ..." He repeated it, tasting the syllables like poison. His eyes narrowed, recognition blooming like a bruise. "Elaris ..."

"Perhaps," Evander cut in, too quickly, "Seraphina would enjoy the dance floor. Aleron?"

"Gladly," Aleron said, stepping between her and the king like a shield. He offered his arm.

Seraphina took it without hesitation, her skin crawling beneath the weight of King Hadren's stare.

As they walked away, Seraphina strained her ears, catching fragments of a tense conversation between father and son. "It's her," the king hissed, his voice edged with agitation. "The *human* girl."

Evander's jaw tightened visibly, his voice low and measured. "You're seeing ghosts."

"No, Evander," the king snapped, the fury in his tone unmistakable. "I remember her face as clearly as if it were yesterday. That girl, she's the one from my vision."

"She's a student. A normal human girl. Let it go."

Seraphina's stomach twisted as she tried to unravel the king's words. *His vision? What does he mean?* She resisted the urge to glance back, focusing instead on Aleron's steady presence as he guided her onto the dance floor.

Aleron spun her into position, his hand warm and reassuring on her waist, though she could feel the slight tension in his fingers. They moved into the rhythm of the music, gliding across the dance floor as if nothing were amiss. Yet beneath his calm demeanor, she caught the unease shadowing his eyes. He leaned closer, his voice a careful whisper against her ear.

"I take it you heard that too?"

Seraphina nodded subtly, barely trusting herself to speak without betraying the storm of uncertainty inside her. "I did."

Aleron's gaze softened, searching her face for answers. "Do you know what he meant? Have you ever met the king before tonight?"

She shook her head, the motion slight enough to remain unnoticed by the dancers around them. "No," she murmured, heart racing again as she echoed her confusion aloud. *It couldn't be a coincidence: first Evander, now the king, both claiming to have seen her …*

Aleron nodded slowly. "Maybe you just remind him of someone. Or maybe he's the type to see omens in tea leaves and candle smoke." His attempt at humor was soft, almost tentative. "It's the Luminous Veil, right? Maybe it makes people see things. Feel things that aren't real."

"I know," she murmured. "But the way he looked at me …"

Aleron's eyes darkened with thought. "I saw it, too. And you're right, there was more to it than mistaken identity. Something deeper." He pulled her in closer and whispered in her ear, "We'll uncover what it means, I promise." He brushed her knuckles with his thumb. "But tonight, let's just focus on the evening. Together."

Seraphina's chest tightened, but this time warmly. She let her hand slide down his arm, squeezing lightly. "You're right," she whispered. "Whatever it is, it can wait."

He smiled then, more fully, spinning her into a turn that sent her dress flaring out. "Exactly. And even if you wake up tomorrow breathing fire, I'll still be standing here, asking the dragon to dance."

She laughed, genuinely. "You're impossible."

"But charming," he said, grinning.

At that moment, Cordelia and Isadora appeared near the edge of the floor, flushed and wide-eyed. "This is incredible," Cordelia said, grabbing Seraphina's arm.

"They say the Veil responds to the magic in the room," Isadora added from behind, "to what's coming."

205

As the music slowed to its final note, applause burst across the hall, bright and scattered. Couples moved from the floor, their chatter and laughter swelling to fill the space the music left behind.

Their small group drifted to the side, standing beneath the arch of a slender balcony that overlooked the great hall.

Cordelia tipped her chin, eyes narrowing across the gathering. *"Who is that?"*

Following her eyes, Seraphina spotted a fae unlike any she had seen tonight. Tall and lithe, her presence was unique among the other fae in the room. Sky-blue hair cascaded down her back. Her gown was beaded in a design of a snake, and around her throat coiled a slender serpent creature that moved slowly in sync with the music.

"She is a *goddess*," Cordelia whispered.

Isadora took her hand. "You're almost right. That is Lady Caelyne Draeven."

Seraphina frowned. "Where have I heard that name?" Her eyes tracked Lady Caelyne's slender fingers, stroking her bondmate's gleaming scales.

"She's one of the Council of Twelve," Isadora replied. "The eldest among them."

Seraphina blinked. "The Council of Twelve still exists?"

Isadora only smiled. "Oh, yes. Nine of the original twelve still walk this earth."

"What exactly do they do?" Aleron asked, folding his arms, eyes scanning the room.

"They are the guardians of our realm's balance," Isadora explained, her voice softening with reverence, "originally chosen to represent each of the great magical domains: Light, Shadow, Flame, Stone, Sea, Air, Mind, Beast, and Star. Over the centuries, their number has shifted, but the original structure holds. The other three seats, Voice, Blade, and Veil, were granted to fae who shaped the binding laws between our realm and others." She nodded toward her parents, who were engrossed in conversation.

"My father holds the Seat of Blade," Isadora continued. "He was chosen for it before he rose to rule. And he still sits among them."

"Are any others here tonight?" Aleron asked, curiosity glinting in his smile.

"Lady Draeven, of course, holds the Seat of Star. Beside her, see the elder with the silver antler circlet? That is Lord Calven Strath, Seat of Beast. And near the pillar, that slender man with the riverstone staff? Lord Ryveth Tal, Seat of Sea."

Seraphina's gaze swept across the indicated figures.

"And the others?" she asked softly.

"Not all are present," Isadora said. "The Seat of Shadow is … vacant. Recently so."

A chill ghosted across Seraphina's skin.

"Lady Merien Vey holds Light. Lord Drekhan of Stone rarely attends these courts, but his sigil was displayed tonight, so one of his envoys must be here. The Seat of Mind is held by Mistress Veylaine; she is reclusive, yet I suspect she watches through more eyes than we can count."

"That's … remarkable," Seraphina whispered.

Isadora looked at her. "They have endured centuries. Through peace and bloodshed. They are why our realm still stands in fragile balance. And perhaps …" Her eyes drifted toward King Hadren. "Perhaps why certain old forces are stirring again."

Above the dance floor, the ceiling began to shift.

It shimmered slowly, then peeled back like petals of a flower, revealing the endless stretch of night beyond. Stars spiraled across the sky in dizzying arcs, constellations unraveling and re-forming. A great lion made of stars roared across the firmament, its mane catching fire as it leapt from one horizon to the next. A serpent of silver light coiled around a moon that hadn't been there a moment before and uncoiled with the beat of a distant drum. A dragon unfurled, so massive it seemed to bridge the realms, wings outstretched in a silent, protective arc.

Gasps echoed around the dance floor, but Seraphina barely heard them.

Light bathed them, casting Seraphina and Aleron in a celestial spotlight, their figures shining.

"Glowing together once again. I'm beginning to see a trend," Cordelia said as she stepped back from the pair toward Isadora.

Before Seraphina could answer, something streaked across the sky, fast and strange. A single glint moth descended from the heavens. Its beating wings released a trail of glittering dust. It drifted downward slowly, spiraling through the open ceiling like a falling star. The entire room fell silent, every head looking upward.

Seraphina's breath hitched as it hovered above them … then dipped. The moth landed gently on Aleron's outstretched hand.

The moment it touched him, magic surged, radiating outward. Beneath its delicate feet, light pooled like water. Its wings stretched, gossamer and translucent.

Cordelia let out a half laugh. "Okay, is it just me, or do the moths really like Aleron?"

Aleron didn't laugh. He stood completely still, his brows drawn together, eyes fixed on the creature perched on his palm. The moth's wings fluttered slowly, steadily. Power flowed from its body, curling around his fingers in strands of magic.

"It's choosing me," Aleron whispered. He lifted his eyes and found Seraphina's, wonder breaking across his face. "It's … choosing *me*."

Gasps rippled across the room. A crowd began to form around the edges of the dance floor, and from the far side of the room, Professor Hera emerged, sensing what was about to happen.

Then came the voice of the queen, carrying across the chamber.

"The glint moth is a sacred creature," Queen Lira declared, her voice humble. "It does not descend for ceremony or spectacle. Only for bonding."

Fae nobles exchanged wide-eyed glances.

Queen Lira continued, a quiet reverence lighting her face as she moved across the room. "It is a symbol of truth, of inner light, and unwavering loyalty. In the old tongue, it is called Lyrae. To be chosen by one is an ancient honor."

The moth, Lyrae, glowed brighter, its light intensifying until Aleron sank slowly to one knee. "I accept," he whispered fiercely.

"Though I do not know why you've chosen me, I embrace this bond with all that I am."

The moth rose gracefully from Aleron's hand, drifting down in a slow, measured spiral toward his chest. As it touched him, it dissolved into delicate ribbons of starlight, weaving around his form, tracing the lines of his arms, circling his back, and embracing his heart.

Magic surged through the room like an unstoppable tide.

An intricate bondmark etched itself onto his forearm, forming the majestic crest of a moth encircled by shimmering constellations.

Then, the magic roared, fierce and overwhelming, unfurling scintillating wings of starlight from Aleron's back, spanning the breadth of the dance floor. They beat once, breathtakingly radiant, then fell away into a cascade of sparkling cosmic dust.

Silence consumed the throne room. Even King Hadren stood motionless, eyes locked upon the young human who'd been chosen by an ancient, sacred power.

"Humans aren't born to this," Aleron said softly, voice rough with truth. "Not to this kind of light. We fight for it; we stumble toward it in the dark. Maybe that's why this bond matters so much to me."

Seraphina's heart burned at the sight of him.

He continued, "You see something in me I've spent a lifetime chasing. Truth. Light. Loyalty. I won't claim to be worthy of it yet, but I will fight to be. Every day."

A faint laugh escaped him, soft, almost breathless. "And maybe that's what makes us human, after all. We fall, but we choose to stand again. And again."

Aleron rose slowly, breathing unevenly. He studied the shimmering bondmark, then lifted his gaze to Seraphina, their eyes meeting as the moth ascended, spiraling upward, leaving a glittering trail behind as it vanished into the stars.

The queen emerged and approached Aleron. "The bond recognized something rare in you—patience, integrity, and the strength to remain true when others might bend. You were not chosen for what you can do, but for who you already are. Hold to that, and you will not lose your way."

Before Aleron could respond, Professor Hera stepped forward, brushing past the queen with polite urgency. "Majesty," she said with a nod, before placing her hand firmly over the still-glowing bondmark on Aleron's arm.

"Let us solidify the bond," Hera coaxed, her fingers dancing through the air, tracing ancient patterns. Threads of light unfurled from her fingertips, sinking gently into Aleron's skin.

Just behind them, Seraphina watched, sharp-eyed and still. She caught it: the smallest flicker, a shift in Hera's focus. Not on Aleron.

On the king.

And the king … he was already watching her.

Hera's expression was composed, but Seraphina didn't miss the tightness at the corners of her mouth, the way her shoulders squared as if bracing for battle.

"Come see me," Hera said quietly to Aleron, "within the next few days, so we can check on your bond." Her gaze returned once more to the king, still watching her, unblinking.

She didn't wait for a reply. With a sweep of her robes, Hera turned and disappeared through the arched doorway at the far end of the hall.

"You wear the bond well," Isadora said as she stepped up to her mother's side. "It chose you for a reason. Don't doubt that."

Aleron blinked, as if words had momentarily abandoned him. He gave her a grateful nod. He turned then, as if drawn by a thread he couldn't ignore, and found Seraphina watching him.

"Would you …" he began, then exhaled, raking a hand through his hair, the beginnings of a smile tugging at his lips. "Would you come outside with me? Just for a moment. I need some air."

She nodded, and together they stepped away from the crowd and into the warmth of the spring night.

Aleron looked at her, his face soft with wonder. "I feel … different," he admitted. "Like I'm not the same person who walked into that room. Like something inside me cracked open and light just poured in."

He paused, took her hands, then leaned in.

His kiss was gentle and sweet. As he pulled back, he said, "I don't know what happens next, but I'm glad you're here with me."

Seraphina's heart clenched. She squeezed his hands. "It's strange ... seeing you like this. Not because you've changed, but because you feel more *you* than ever."

He looked down, a hint of color brushing his cheeks. "Thank you."

Aleron glanced at her again. "Earlier, when Evander pulled you aside ... What was that about?"

Seraphina hesitated. The moment came rushing back.

"He said he saw something," she said slowly, examining the edge of the woods beyond the courtyard. "He said that he saw *me* in the forest. Wielding shadow magic."

Aleron's expression tightened. "You weren't in the woods ... right?"

Seraphina shook her head slowly. "I wasn't, but he seemed so certain." She paused, searching for words.

"Do you think he was lying?"

"No," she said. "I think he believes what he saw. And that might be the most unsettling part."

Seraphina wrapped her arms around herself. "It's been a long evening. I think I'm going to head back."

"You sure you want to leave?"

She nodded once, then caught the concern in his eyes.

"I'll come with you," he said quickly, already stepping into stride beside her. "You shouldn't have to walk back in the dark alone. And honestly ... I think I've had enough excitement for one evening."

The door behind them opened with a creak, and Cordelia slipped through, making a line toward her friends. She threw her arms around Aleron. "I can't believe it. You're officially bonded. With a moth, no less. That's *so* you."

She pulled back, her voice kind. "I'm really proud of you."

Aleron smiled, his face still glowing with that quiet joy. "Thanks, Cordelia. Truly." He glanced at Seraphina, then reached for her hand. "We're heading back to the university, need to breathe for a bit." He gave Cordelia a half grin. "You'd better remember every single detail of tonight so you can tell us everything we missed."

Seraphina nodded, squeezing Aleron's hand. "Especially if anything catches fire or someone starts a duel. I want a full report."

Cordelia laughed, stepping back with a dramatic bow. "You've got it. Go be boring. I'll handle the chaos."

Side by side, they moved toward the skyway, the faint echo of laughter and music fading behind them. And as Seraphina glanced sideways at Aleron, just for a breath, she saw it: the faint outline of wings, shimmering and translucent.

Chapter 17

THE AETHERIC CONDUCTOR

FADEYA

hree days had passed since the Luminous Veil, and the evening had left a mist of magic hanging in the air. Fadeya lounged in one of the high-backed chairs in Hera's study, her legs tucked beneath her as she absentmindedly traced her fingers along the glyphs etched into the desk's surface. Hera sat across from her, a steaming cup of tea in hand. Her typically pristine professor's robes were slightly disheveled. Fadeya couldn't help but notice the tension in the professor's posture, the way Hera's fingers tapped rhythmically against the ceramic cup, betraying her demeanor.

Fadeya studied her. "So," she said at last, breaking the silence, "what happened the other day with Prince Evander?"

Hera didn't answer immediately. She set her teacup down, the clink sounding louder than it should have. Her brows drew together, casting shadows over her eyes.

"There was something about the king's disposition the night of the Luminous Veil," Hera replied. "He's always wanted the crown to hold dominion over the university. It's not a new ambition, but something's changed."

Skepticism crossed Fadeya's face. "You think Evander is acting on that desire?"

"Not exactly." Hera looked out the window to the stretch of sky beyond it. "Evander isn't his father's puppet. He's … different."

"Different how?" Fadeya pressed, her curiosity piqued.

Hera's mouth twisted as she considered her response. "He's brilliant. Far more than he lets on. He masks it behind that cold charm, that carefully curated dispassion, but I've seen the way he watches. He listens more than he speaks. And unlike his father, he's restless."

"Well, it would seem the creatures don't like him, since he hasn't bonded with one yet."

"No," Hera said, her voice clipped. "He claims he's waiting for the right one, but that's not his style. Evander doesn't wait. He calculates. He plots. He's dangerous, Fadeya. Not because he's reckless, but because he's *patient*."

For a moment, neither of them spoke. A tension unfurled in the room, subtle but insistent. And then, A knock. Sharp. Urgent. The door creaked open before Hera could answer. A boy, no older than fifteen, flushed and breathless, stood on the threshold.

"Professor," he gasped. "A bonding. It's happening *now*."

Hera stood smoothing her robes. "Which creature?" she asked.

"The Pegasus," the boy breathed.

A slow smile curved Hera's lips. "Of course. I'll handle it." She started for the door, then glanced over her shoulder and threw a wink at Fadeya. "Seraphina, stay here. I'll return soon."

Fadeya raised an eyebrow but didn't bother replying. The door clicked shut behind her, leaving Fadeya alone with the quiet hum of the study's magic. She stretched her legs, her fingers grazing the edge of the desk once more, when something fluttered to the floor: a folded piece of parchment. Frowning, she bent to pick it up. The note bore Professor Shay's handwriting, neat but hurried. Intrigued, Fadeya unfolded it and began to read:

Hera,

The latest memory adjustment has been completed successfully for the incoming cohort, and we have begun monitoring their integration. However, certain anomalies have emerged among a handful of students. These individuals exhibit signs of partial resistance to the erasure process, a rare but concerning phenomenon.

Will you please inform Quan when he arrives next so he can rework the runes to confirm everything is functioning as it should?

– Prof. Shay

Memory adjustment. Erasure process. The words repeated in her head like a curse. A chill sank into her bones as she read it again, slower this time, trying to make the meaning shift into something less horrifying, but it didn't.

They were altering students' memories.

No, erasing them.

Her stomach flipped as her mind careened to one person.

Seraphina. Had her sister been part of this? Was that why she hadn't written? The parchment trembled in her grip as she folded, her fingers only just steady enough to slide it into the pocket of her robes.

Whatever this was, whatever truth had been buried beneath lies and half answers, Hera had known. *And she hadn't told her.*

The betrayal sliced deeper than she expected. No, she couldn't confront Hera. Not yet. Not without knowing exactly what she was walking into. If this secret had been kept from her, there was a reason. Her trust faltered, wavering like a candle in the wind, but her resolve? That hardened into something unshakable.

She turned toward the door, her amulet warming faintly against her chest, reacting to the Pegasus bonding. Everyone would be there, distracted.

Which meant the library would be nearly empty. And if there was even a sliver of truth to the words on that note, if memory erasure was happening within these halls, then the answers would be hidden there. Fadeya wrapped her fingers around the amulet, drawing strength from its warmth. Then she slipped out of the study and into the corridor beyond.

Her thoughts spun with every stride. *Who was behind the memory adjustments? Why tamper with students' minds?* And most of all, *why did she still remember?*

The stars burned bright, strewn across the velvet sky like glinting fragments of crystal. Around the clearing near the Star Shrine, students gathered, drawn by a bonding taking place. Standing at the center of the clearing, an ebony Pegasus stepped forward. Its coat shimmered, dark as midnight, while silver veins rippled like lightning through its vast wings. Its eyes, a shade of blue Seraphina had never seen before, focused on one individual.

Isadora.

She approached the Pegasus slowly. Her black hair cascaded gently over her shoulders, mirroring the Pegasus's coat perfectly as if they were kin bound by destiny. Strands of power unfurled from her outstretched hand, weaving through the air toward the creature. The Pegasus lowered its head, accepting the bond.

Seraphina glanced at Cordelia, noting the tears gathering silently at the corners of her friend's eyes. *Isadora deserves this bond.*

She thought to herself, her heart swelling as she recalled all the determination and hope that had carried Isadora to this moment.

Professor Hera stepped into the clearing's center. She extended one hand, brushing her fingers against Isadora's forearm to guide the fragile weave of energy. The clearing grew taut with anticipation.

Then Emeric's voice crashed into the stillness, splintering it.

"No! This isn't right!"

The threads of magic jolted violently, their glow fracturing into discordant ripples at his outburst. Emeric stormed forward from the woods, face twisted with raw anguish and defiance, his cloak snapping aggressively behind him. He looked dazed, not like himself. Clutched tightly in one hand was a peculiar instrument, a complex construct of brass gears and glass spheres that shimmered ominously in the moonlight.

"Emeric, what are you doing?" Seraphina cried, her voice edged with fear. She lunged instinctively forward, but a firm hand gripped her arm. Aleron, face stern, eyes fixed on Emeric.

"Stay back," he warned. "That thing looks dangerous."

Emeric ignored them, eyes blazing with desperation as he stalked toward the Pegasus. "This creature was *meant for me!*" he shouted, voice ragged with pent-up frustration. "I've been waiting for my bond, but every creature passes me by! Why does the *princess* get everything? The magic, the power, the bond? What about me?"

Isadora turned slowly, eyes wide. "Emeric, this isn't about deserving or not deserving. You can't force a bond."

"Oh, can't I?" Emeric's lips twisted into a cruel parody of a smile as he raised the strange artifact higher. "This is an aetheric conductor. You have no idea the power it channels. I won't wait any longer. Today, I choose."

The Pegasus reared up suddenly, wings snapping wide in panic. The bond quivered violently, threads dimming, fraying rapidly toward breaking.

"Emeric, stop!" Cordelia cried, stepping forward, desperation vivid in her pleading eyes. "You're terrifying it and disrupting the bond! This is not how it's meant to be!"

Emeric whirled on her, eyes bright with anguish, his voice cracking under the weight of his pain. "What else can I do? Do you know what it's like to live unseen, unchosen? I *will* forge my own fate!"

Seraphina flinched, a forgotten ache stirring deep within her soul, familiar yet hidden in shadow. Professor Hera stood to the side, watchful but unreadable.

"Emeric," Aleron growled, striding forward, rage flaring in his eyes. His hand flew to his sword, nearly missing the hilt in his rush, and he yanked the blade free with an awkward scrape. "Drop the device. Now. Before you do something you'll regret."

Emeric's eyes blazed like twin infernos, wild with something unholy, grief, vengeance, a fury born of loss. He didn't hear the screams behind him, didn't feel the magic thickening the air. With a trembling breath and a twisted snarl, he turned to the Pegasus and activated the device.

The sky ruptured.

A jagged spear of magic, raw and merciless, burst forth, howling as it carved through the night. It struck the Pegasus with a deafening crack, and the creature's scream was a thing of nightmares, shrieking agony that shattered the stillness and pierced the stars.

The bond snapped.

Threads of golden light writhed violently before tearing apart like sinew ripped from bone.

Isadora screamed as the magic recoiled into her, her body convulsing midair as if struck by lightning. She hit the ground with a sickening crunch, her back arching off the soil as pain flooded her. Blood spilled from her nose, her mouth, her ears, as the severed bond ripped through her like wildfire. She tried to scream again, but a broken rasp came out. Her fingers clawed at the earth, desperate for something, anything, to anchor her. Her eyes, wide and unfocused, brimmed with tears that turned to steam against her burning skin.

And still, the Pegasus screamed. It reared in agony, its once-silken coat torn to ribbons, silver blood gushing from the wound carved into its chest. It stumbled, nearly collapsing, its eyes wild and glassy with pain, searching for Isadora, and finding her crumpled and shaking in the dirt.

There was no beauty left at the Star Shrine. Only blood. Only ruin. Only the sound of something sacred, utterly destroyed.

"Isadora!" Cordelia's scream tore through the clearing like shattering glass. She fell to her knees beside her, hands trembling, reaching but not quite touching, afraid that if she did, Isadora would vanish like smoke. "She's alive," she gasped, voice hoarse. "Barely, but she's still here. Stay with me. Please, stay."

Above them, the Pegasus loosed a terrible cry, a sound of grief, of rage, and vanished into the churning dark.

A hush fell, thick and choking. The trees stood still. Even the wind dared not breathe.

Then Aleron's voice cut through the silence, cold as steel drawn across bone.

"What. Did. You. *Do?*"

He moved toward Emeric, sword in hand, fury thrumming just beneath his skin. "You didn't just break the bond. You *shattered* it."

Emeric stood frozen, the aetheric conductor limp in his grip. Its runes, once vibrant, now bled dull red light, flickering like dying embers.

"I didn't mean to," he stammered, his voice cracking. "I just wanted a chance. That's all. Just one chance …"

Aleron stepped closer, each word a blow. "You call this a *chance?*"

Emeric stumbled backward, horror blooming in his eyes. He turned toward Professor Hera, desperate for rescue, for absolution.

She only shook her head, slow and solemn, her gaze colder than the void between stars.

The conductor slipped from his fingers, hitting the earth with a sound like a death knell. Its light died completely. Cold metal. Nothing more.

Emeric turned and ran. Fled into the black trees where the forest waited to swallow him whole.

Hera stooped to pick up the device, brushing dirt from its surface. She studied it with a haunted look. "So," she whispered. "He found it, after all."

Cordelia was still kneeling, her fingers cradling Isadora's bloodless face. "She needs help," she murmured, her voice breaking.

Then Evander burst into the clearing, his face a pale mask of dread.

"No. No, NO! Isadora." He dropped beside her, hands shaking as he touched her face. "I'm here. I'm here, little sister."

Isadora's lips parted, her voice a ghost of itself. "The Pegasus …"

Seraphina moved to her side, her eyes shimmering with unshed tears.

"It's gone," she whispered. "But I'm sure he will recover."

Professor Flora and Professor Shay burst from the trees at a run. Flora dropped to her knees beside Isadora, green light flaring in her palms as she swept over the girl's injuries. Shay halted sharply at her side, blade drawn, one hand weaving a ward of protection. Their bondmate Kymaris's midnight-blue scales glinted faintly as she coiled protectively around Shay, golden eyes locked on the shadows.

"This magic," Flora said, "it's not just physical damage. The bond didn't break clean; it detonated. The backlash is inside her, wild and seething. If we don't act soon, it will kill her."

Evander looked up, face pale, voice hollow. "Tell me what to do."

"We need a plant called blood thorn," Flora said grimly. "It's the only thing that can purge corrupted essence from a broken tether, but it only grows along the northern cliffs." She hesitated.

Professor Shay took a breath and whispered. "Those cliffs …"

"Are deadly," Evander finished.

"I'll go," Cordelia said without pause. Her eyes gleamed with fire and grief. "Tell me what to look for."

"You're not going alone," Seraphina cut in. "I'm coming, too."

Evander stood, tears threatening to spill down his cheeks. "You'll both die without someone who's been there. I know the coast. I'm coming. She's my sister. I won't bury her."

"It is very dangerous," Professor Shay said sharply, stepping to his side. "Perhaps we should send word to your father—"

"There's no time," he cut in, voice firm. "Send the message, but tell him we're already on the move. We leave at first light."

Cordelia turned pleadingly toward Aleron, whose eyes were fixed upon Isadora's pale, quiet face. "Stay with her, please," she whispered. "She can't wake up alone."

Aleron hesitated, then nodded. "I'll stay." He glanced briefly at Seraphina, understanding passing silently between them.

Professor Flora spoke again. "Look for a faint crimson glow, avoid the lower paths, and beware, the waves below are enchanted to drag you under."

Cordelia leaned down, pressing her forehead to Isadora's. Her tears streaked across her cheeks, falling into the hollow between Isadora's collarbones.

"Don't go where I can't follow," she whispered. "I'm coming back. I *swear it*."

220

Seraphina's heart twisted at the thought. *It would break Cor to lose her.* The words rang clear in her mind. *We have to save her.* Resolve hardened in her chest.

Evander leaned in next, gripping his sister's hand with both of his. "Be strong, Isadora," he said, his voice thick with grief. "We'll make this right. I swear it."

Isadora's fingers twitched. A whisper of defiance.

Professor Flora's gaze swept solemnly over each of them. "May the stars guide your way. And your hearts bring you back whole."

Chapter 18

FAILURE

FADEYA

The air in the undercroft was stale, heavy with the scent of rainwater and something else, something raw and human. Regret.

Emeric sat slouched against the far wall, elbows balanced on his knees, fingers tangled in his disheveled blond hair. His usual cocky expression had vanished, replaced by shame. Shadows clung to his face, deepening the lines that hadn't been there before.

Fadeya crept cautiously forward, clutching the stack of library books tight against her chest. She hadn't expected anyone else to be here, least of all Emeric. She'd wanted solitude, a quiet place to dig for answers to the memory-wipe mystery. Her breath caught as her foot brushed a shard of loose stone, sending a faint clatter skittering into the dark.

She went still, heart thudding in the silence.

"Seraphina," Emeric muttered, barely looking up, voice heavy with exhaustion. "Please, just leave."

Fadeya paused, confused by his broken tone, "I'm not Seraphina," she said, stepping closer.

His head lifted slightly, gray eyes dull. "What do you mean?"

"I'm Fadeya," she clarified. "Seraphina's twin."

Confusion lit his face, quickly replaced by suspicion. He stared at her, his eyes raking over her features as if searching for some hidden deceit. "No," he said, shaking his head. "That's not … Seraphina doesn't have a twin."

Fadeya swallowed hard, bracing herself. She'd expected this. "We met back home," she explained, keeping her voice steady. "You probably don't remember because …" She hesitated, the words almost too unbelievable to say. "Because I don't think you're supposed to."

Emeric's body stiffened. "What the *hell* does that mean?"

She took another cautious step forward. His gaze followed, sharp yet guarded. *What happened to him?* she wondered. *He looks … defeated.*

"I think every student at the university is put under some kind of spell," she said, her voice barely above a whisper. "Their memories are being … erased."

He let out a sharp, humorless laugh. "That's ridiculous."

"Is it?" she challenged, her tone sharper now. "You don't remember me, and I know for a fact we've met before. We had conversations. Arguments. You teased me relentlessly, and yet, you look at me now like I'm a stranger."

His expression darkened. "If that's true, why do you remember me?"

She hesitated, glancing away. "I … I don't know. Maybe because I wasn't supposed to be here."

Emeric let out a shaky breath, raking a hand through his hair. "Something's wrong with this place. Something's wrong with *me*. It feels like … like something's crawled into my mind and is pulling the strings."

She studied him. He was unraveling. "Emeric," she said carefully, "what happened?"

His eyes closed, and his shoulders slumped. "I hurt someone," he said hoarsely. "Isadora. I tried to, *stars*, I don't even know why, I tried to steal her bond." He continued, anguish clear on his face. "It felt like something pushed me. Something dark."

Fadeya's stomach knotted, bile creeping up her throat. *He disrupted the fae princess's bond? He was in deep trouble.* She swallowed hard. "Was it an accident?"

His hands trembled, then clenched into fists. "I don't know," he said, voice cracking. "Maybe. Maybe not. I didn't *mean* to hurt anyone, but ..." The words caught in his throat. "No. It wasn't an accident. I—" He swallowed. "I didn't feel completely in control, but I still chose to do it."

There was an obvious battle raging inside him, the guilt, the fear, the unbearable possibility that the darkness might be his own. And in his eyes, she saw it clearly now: a man drowning, not in water, but in the weight of his own regret.

Fadeya knelt beside him, the books slipping from her arms and thudding onto the cold stone. "What do you think the darkness was? Do you think it came from you?"

Emeric's eyes stayed fixed on the floor. "Professor Hera gave me a book." He swallowed hard. "It talked about forced bonds, how magic demanded courage and the strength to take what you desired." His shoulders hunched inward, like he was trying to make himself smaller. "It led me to the forest. To the tool I used. I don't even remember deciding. It was like my mind wasn't fully mine anymore."

Fadeya froze. "The book," she muttered under her breath, recalling the moment Hera gave it to Emeric in her study. "I think Hera might be hiding something," Fadeya said, eyes narrowing in thought. "There's something much bigger going on here."

Emeric buried his face in his hands. "I don't know what I'm going to do. How can I face everyone now? No creature will want to bond with me after this. I've ruined my chances. I'm such a *failure.*"

Fadeya hesitated, then inched closer until their shoulders touched. "You used to call me that," she said quietly. "*Failure.* Like it was some kind of joke."

He lifted his head, blinking. "I did?"

She nodded.

He looked away, guilt flickering across his face.

"I know how it feels, Emeric," she whispered, memories of the past month pressing at the edges of her mind. "I've spent weeks watching from the sidelines while my sister lives the life I thought would be mine." Her voice quivered. "You're not the only one who feels like a failure, but we can move past what we believe is failure … and forge a new path."

Emeric turned his head slightly, his gray eyes locking onto hers. "You make it all sound so easy."

"I sound more confident than I feel," she said quietly, drawing her knees up to her chest and wrapping her arms around them. "I'm not supposed to be here, Emeric. I'm an anomaly."

She glanced sideways at him, then quickly looked away. "I don't know why I'm telling you this. We weren't friends."

"No, I don't suppose we were."

Fadeya turned to look at him again, studying him. "But maybe we could be."

Wariness pulled at his features. "Why are you really here, Fadeya?" he asked, his voice low.

She hesitated. "I'm working with Hera," she admitted. "Secretly. She brought me here to help with bondings."

Emeric's brows rose, surprise flashing across his face. "You? Helping Hera? I find that hard to believe."

"So do I," Fadeya murmured. "Honestly, I'm not even sure why she sought me out. Hera … she's been lying to me. And I think she's somehow connected to the bonding issues that have been happening."

Emeric stilled. His expression shifted to recognition. "You think so?"

"After this?" A chill crept down her spine as she said the words out loud. "I'm almost certain. She wants us to think she's guiding us, but what if she's the one pulling the strings?"

Emeric nodded. "If that is the case, we need to do something to stop her. We will need proof, and we'll need to be careful."

She hesitated, then said softly, "I want to help you, too, Emeric."

He looked wounded, as if she'd offered something he hadn't believed himself worthy of. The light caught on the faint sheen in his eyes, and when he finally nodded, it was with the weight of surrender.

"I need to check on Isadora," he said, voice thick. "See if she's ... if she's going to pull through."

"Is that a good idea?"

"I have to know," he faltered, gasping like it hurt, "if she's still breathing." His voice cracked, breaking. "Or if I need to make things right in a different way."

Fadeya's chest ached. She reached out, laying a hand on his shoulder. "I'm so sorry."

He turned away, his shoulders rigid, head bowed low. "I don't deserve your sympathy."

"Maybe not," she whispered, "but I'm giving it anyway."

A tremor rippled through him, weariness settling deeper across his features. "I'll go tonight," he said, voice flat, stripped of hope. "After curfew. Less chance of being seen."

Fadeya nodded, her throat tight. "Alright. I'm going to dig through these books I found—see if there's anything about restoring memories." She hesitated, then added, "And tomorrow ... we'll meet back here. Whatever we uncover, we share it."

She rose slowly, brushing dust from her skirt, trying to keep her composure intact. "I'll give you your solitude."

Emeric followed, slower. The candlelight carved deep shadows into his face, highlighting the hollows beneath his eyes, the tremble in his hands. "Fadeya," he said quietly, voice rough-edged. "Thank you."

The rawness in his tone struck her. She offered a brittle smile. "Don't thank me yet," she said, tucking a loose curl behind her ear. "You might regret letting me drag you into this."

He let out a low laugh. "I doubt it. Trouble suits me."

She almost smiled, he'd said that to her once before, bold and untouchable, but this time, there was weariness beneath the words, as if *trouble* had cost him more than he'd ever thought it could.

"Well," she murmured, "you've found it."

His gaze lingered on her like he was committing her to memory.

"I should go," she said, her voice unsteady despite her best effort. "We both have things to do."

He nodded. "Be safe, Fadeya."

She stepped toward the door, hand on the iron latch, but paused, her back still to him. "You're sure you'll be alright?" she asked.

Behind her, a faint shift of movement. "I'll manage."

She closed her eyes, just for a moment. Then she opened the door and slipped into the corridor, the shadows swallowing her whole.

And in the dim glow of the dying candle, Emeric sank to his knees. He bowed his head. Shoulders shaking. And for the first time in years, he cried.

Chapter 19

A FAINT CRIMSON GLOW

SERAPHINA

Breath curling like smoke in the brittle dawn air, Seraphina walked between Cordelia and Evander, the three of them slipping beyond the ivy-draped gates of the university just as the first blush of morning lit the cobbled path ahead. Behind them, ancient stone walls loomed, and with every step farther from their sanctuary, a coil of dread tightened in Seraphina's chest.

She tightened her grip on her leather satchel, palm pressed against the modest provisions they had scrounged: enough for a handful of days, if their luck held. Ahead, the path to the northern cliffs rolled out like a harsh summons; each moment they delayed, another breath was stolen from Isadora's fragile life. The memory of Professor Flora's whisper, *Look for a faint crimson glow*, lingered in Seraphina's thoughts, as haunting as the wind that hissed around them.

They had left before sunrise, hoping to wring every bit of daylight from the journey, but the sallow sun offered more pallor than warmth. A frigid gust teased Seraphina's hair free from its braids and tugged at the hood of Cordelia's cloak.

Beneath their boots, the trail hardened into unyielding gravel, sloping upward as the lush grasslands fell behind. Seraphina cast a glance toward Cordelia, whose eyes brimmed with a terror she refused to voice.

Evander walked at the fore, regal poise intact despite the jagged scree underfoot. Each step he took was measured, revealing little of the tension Seraphina glimpsed in the rigid set of his shoulders. There was a time when his distant manner had left her uneasy; now, she could see past it, aware of the quieter kindness he kept so carefully guarded.

They reached the crest of a bluff, wind scouring along its edge. Below stretched a narrow ravine, the path dipping and climbing in an unforgiving arc toward the craggy cliffs. Farther north, a huddle of storm clouds gathered above the sea, purple-black and rumbling like a far-off growl.

"So, how far, exactly, is this patch of blood thorn supposed to be?" Cordelia asked between uneven breaths, one hand bracing her side. "I can't believe I'm winded already. Clearly, I need a more active hobby."

"Another three hours, four at most, if the wind doesn't kick up," Evander answered, his voice carrying over the gale. "My father's cartographers surveyed these coastal lands last season. If their notes are correct, a cove near the highest peak of these cliffs is where we'll find the blood thorn."

"Near the highest point," Cordelia muttered with a grimace. "So, we get to climb higher. Great."

Seraphina squeezed her friend's shoulder. "We'll pace ourselves."

"We'll have to," Evander added, casting his gaze ahead. "Rumor says this coastline is riddled with sinkholes. And the trails aren't exactly known for their stability." He offered a half smile just as a biting gust swept around them. "Though, I suppose I spoke too soon about the wind behaving."

Cordelia snorted, clutching her cloak against the blast. "Thanks for jinxing us, Your Highness."

Concern for Isadora gnawed at each of them. She lay in the infirmary, the healers helpless to halt her decline. Her skin had turned a fragile white, her once-bright voice scarcely more than a whisper.

Seraphina recalled clutching her friend's hand just a few hours before, promising, through trembling lips, that she would find the blood thorn. *I gave my word. I will not falter.* She prayed with every breath that the promise would not ring hollow.

So, they pressed on, one careful footstep after another, across a path that seemed determined to break their spirits. Loose gravel and slick stones conspired beneath their boots, treacherous enough to turn a single misstep into ruin.

Cordelia was the first to trip. Her shoe skidded against wet rock, and with arms flailing wide, she let out a yelp that sliced through the air.

Seraphina lunged and seized her elbow, though the weight nearly dragged both of them down. Evander pivoted with feline quickness, steadying Cordelia's back before disaster could claim them.

"Easy," he cautioned, voice bristling with alarm. "The stone is slick here."

"I noticed," Cordelia muttered, heat flooding her cheeks. "At this rate, maybe I should call Boyde, let her carry us the rest of the way." She managed a breathless laugh to smooth over her embarrassment.

Seraphina gave her a wry look. "Aren't you glad I convinced you to wear something practical?"

Cordelia smirked. "Practicality's never been my strength." Her words were playful, but her look was distant, still tangled somewhere far away. *Isadora,* Seraphina thought.

"I'd welcome Boyde's help," Seraphina admitted. "I only caught a glimpse of her on the ship. I'd love to meet her formally."

Cordelia offered a faint smile but said nothing more.

Time slipped past in fits and starts, moments of focused climbing broken by gusts that forced them to pause and brace against the gale. Seraphina kept her gaze fixed ahead, boots firm on the shifting path.

They reached a cramped ledge by midday, the sky thick with rolling storm clouds. Below, the sea raged against the cliff face, waves hissing upward in great arcs of spray and foam. Their roars swallowed any attempt at conversation, forcing the three to shout or remain silent.

Seraphina took the lead, pressing herself against the cliff wall, edging along the narrow walkway. Every step set her pulse throbbing against her throat. Cordelia followed, grim but steadfast, while Evander brought up the rear, careful in each step.

A piercing cry tore through the roar of the waves, a jolt of terror lancing through Seraphina's veins. She went rigid, salt-laden wind slashing at her cheeks as if daring her to move. Evander muttered something in a language Seraphina didn't understand.

Cordelia inched closer, voice hushed despite the crashing waves. "Please tell me that was just the wind."

The second call that cut the air was harsher. A dark shape soared from the top of a nearby bluff, part woman, part bird, with cruelly curving claws and gleaming black eyes. *A harpy.*

Lore claimed they frequented cliff sides, ambushing anyone foolish enough to tread there. This one's plumage was ash-gray laced with streaks of coppery rust, and the dagger-like gleam of her talons made Seraphina's stomach lurch.

"Bloody harpy," Cordelia hissed through clenched teeth.

Evander's gaze narrowed. "They rarely hunt alone. We should assume more are nearby."

The creature circled overhead, releasing a piercing shriek that sent chills spidering down Seraphina's spine. She clung to the crumbling stone, trying to steady herself. One slip on this ledge, and the sea would devour them whole.

Evander pressed his hand to the rock wall, and a shimmer of magic spilled from his fingertips, unfurling into a curved barrier before them. The wind's wild rush eased inside its protective arc, a hush of momentary safety in the midst of the storm.

The harpy dove in a blur of ragged wings, a shriek of fury echoing off the cliffs. She smashed against Evander's barrier with a flare of light. A harsh, grating sound tore from her beak as she recoiled, sleek black eyes ablaze with hunger, or maybe just fury.

"We need to move," Cordelia bit out. "We have to get down, closer to the water. If we stay exposed here, the harpies have us."

"Incoming!" Seraphina shouted, throat tight with dread.

As if on cue, two more harpies swept into view, leathery wings carrying them in a formation that seemed coordinated. Their talons scraped against Evander's shimmering shield, each impact sending his frame shuddering with the effort to hold it.

Seraphina glanced at his clenched jaw and the sweat filming his forehead. Cordelia slipped on the damp stone, barely catching herself against the crumbling ledge. A triumphant screech rose from the harpies, and Seraphina's pulse spiked in raw panic. If Evander's shield faltered, they were finished.

"Evander! Push them back if you can!" Seraphina's voice sounded thin over the wind and crashing surf.

He winced, casting a glance behind him. "I can try," he said, the strain roughening his words. "But I'll have to drop the shield. Briefly."

"Do it," Cordelia gasped, eyes darting to Seraphina. "We'll hang on!"

Seraphina swallowed the knot in her throat and gave a sharp nod. "Just be quick."

Evander exhaled a steadying breath and let the dome unravel. At once, icy wind and salt spray blasted them.

The harpies lunged, claws poised for the kill. In that breath between heartbeats, Evander thrust out his arms, splaying his fingers. A radiant surge of wrought magic ripped through the air. The nearest harpy screeched and tumbled backward, wings tangling. The second flailed mid-dive, thrown off-balance, while the third twisted in a frantic effort to dodge.

"Go!" Evander roared, turning back toward the ledge, the last embers of magic crackling around his hands. "Down the path, stay low!"

They scrambled along the precipice, each step a struggle to keep from tumbling into the churning sea below. The harpies reeled overhead, screeching in anger and surprise.

Seraphina's limbs ached as she forced herself onward, gripping jagged outcrops and inching down. The switchback path led them closer to the ocean, its roar now a deafening churn of foam and salt against the cliff face.

233

Only when the ledge opened into a weather-worn alcove, where the jagged overhang offered a semblance of cover, did they dare pause.

Evander turned, summoning another burst of power. The harpies dove again, but this time his magic sparked in a brilliant sweep that knocked them back. They shrieked and fluttered away, taking refuge in the swirling storm clouds above.

Seraphina pressed a trembling hand to her chest. "That was far too close."

Cordelia leaned against the rock, breathing raggedly. "The second we're back, I'm signing up for a training regimen. My legs won't stop shaking."

Evander, panting, nodded in agreement. "You're not alone in that," he said, swiping rain from his brow. "I'm spent, but we need to keep moving. The storm's only growing, and if it drives the harpies back or summons something worse …" He let the words hang, ominous and half-formed.

Seraphina set her jaw, forcing determination into her eyes. "For Isadora."

"For Isadora …" Cordelia whispered.

The path wound along the water where the land flattened just enough to give them hope that the rest of the journey would be simple, but the wind rose.

Rain stabbed at them like a thousand tiny knives. Dark clouds coiled overhead, making the whole world tremble with thunder. They scrambled beneath a cliff ledge, the ocean waves lapping at their feet. Lightning tore open the sky, revealing the furious sea beyond.

"We can't keep going in this!" Seraphina yelled. The wind whipped her voice into tatters. "We'll get blown off the ridge!"

"If we turn back, we lose hours," Cordelia snapped, her voice shaking. "Isadora might—" She couldn't finish. The words lodged in her throat, too bleak to speak.

Evander surveyed the churning clouds, each bolt of lightning illuminating his face. Finally, he cleared his throat. "I'll raise the shield again, risky as it is. We can try for the next safe stretch."

Cordelia's teeth chattered. "I think ... it's time I called Boyde. A storm like this might drain us, but she's strong enough to handle crashing waves." She gestured at the torrential downpour, rivulets carving paths into the rock. "She won't mind."

Seraphina hesitated. "A hippocampus might be our best chance at navigating these cliffs without getting swept away."

No more debate was needed. Cordelia slipped out from under the overhang and shut her eyes in silent communion with her bondmate. Below, the sea rumbled as if something large stirred beneath the waves.

Boyde burst through the foaming surface with all the fierceness Seraphina remembered. Part stallion, part sea serpent, she carved through the waves with power, her silver mane streaming like a banner caught in the wind. She let out a high, echoing whinny like crashing surf.

Cordelia's face lit with relief. "Thank the stars. Boyde."

Boyde returned the greeting. Then she peered at Seraphina and Evander, offering a polite snort.

Cordelia moved toward the edge of the cliff, shouting down to her bondmate. "We need to reach a cove higher on the coast where there's a plant called blood thorn. Can you help us find a safer path?"

Boyde flicked her ears, letting out a low rumble in response. She lowered her head, urging them onward.

"She says there's a route along the shoreline," Cordelia explained. "Tide pools and outcroppings, narrow but less exposed to the wind."

Evander grimaced. "Lower might be safer from the gusts, but the waves ..."

Cordelia closed her eyes, as if listening to Boyde's silent reassurance. "She can control enough water to steer the worst currents away. As long as we're careful, it's our best option."

"Then let's trust her," Seraphina said. "We don't have time to waste."

They trudged after Boyde, descending into the storm-lashed shallows. Wind roared at their backs; freezing seawater sloshed around their ankles. Lightning kept ripping across the heavens, casting the towering waves in stark, blinding flashes.

Every step was a desperate dance against slick stone and surging tides. Progress was slow and grueling. Hours bled into one another, exhaustion pooling in every muscle.

At last, the cliff face angled inward, forming a partial rocky canopy beside a waterfall that spilled in ribbons down the stone and into the churning sea below. It was no true refuge, but it offered a sliver of shelter, enough for them to catch their breath.

Cordelia dropped to her knees, burying her face in her hands. Nearby, Seraphina slumped against the damp rock wall, her limbs trembling from the climb. Evander crouched low, elbows braced on his thighs, each breath coming shallow and fast.

For a long moment, none of them spoke. They simply sat there, the roar of the waterfall filling the silence between them.

At last, Evander retrieved a battered flask from his pack and passed it around. They each took a sip, the cool water cutting through the dryness in their throats. Cordelia unwrapped a small bundle of dried fruit and nuts, spreading it between them without a word.

Evander rose slowly, brushing sea spray from his sleeves as if trying to buy himself a few more seconds. When he finally straightened, his eyes flicked between them. "There's something ... you both should know."

Cordelia lifted her head, voice rough. "You're not exactly inspiring confidence with that tone."

Evander exhaled through his nose, running a hand through his damp hair. "Something's not right at the university." He hesitated, then stepped closer, as if afraid the wind might carry his words too far. "My father asked me to look into certain ... disturbances."

Seraphina froze. "Disturbances?"

Evander nodded grimly. "My father believes someone is meddling with the bondings."

Cordelia's hand froze midair, a berry poised halfway to her lips. "So, he asked *you* to investigate?"

"Yes …" Evander said, storm-light flaring across his pale face. He reached into the inner pocket of his coat and drew out a small, glassy orb, no larger than a plum, its surface etched with faint silver runes. The core shimmered with a pale blue light that pulsed softly, like a heartbeat.

"This is called an aether gauge," he explained, holding it out for them to see. "It tests the strength of a bond, measuring the flow of aether between bonded pairs. I've been using it for two years now and keeping detailed records of every bonding ceremony I could observe."

Seraphina leaned closer, eyes narrowing.

Evander's fingers tightened around the aether gauge. "What I've found … is troubling. Bonds have been significantly weaker than those recorded in the generations before us. On average, they're only reaching sixty to seventy percent of the aetheric strength they should. And the pattern is consistent. Too consistent to be natural."

Seraphina's brows drew together. "This has been happening to every student?"

"Not every," Evander said. "But the majority. Enough that the pattern is unmistakable. And the older bonds, those formed before the last few decades, remain unaffected. Something is interfering with new connections."

A gust of wind swept through the alcove, stirring Cordelia's braids. She turned, her eyes drifting out toward the churning sea where a sleek black shape cut through the waves.

Seraphina followed her gaze, a flicker of worry twisting in her chest.

"Can you test mine?" Cordelia whispered.

Evander met her stare, gentleness in his eyes. "If you wish it."

She straightened her shoulders. "I want to know."

Evander nodded and gestured for her to hold out her palm. He pressed the aether gauge into her hand, murmured a brief incantation under his breath, and touched two fingers lightly to her wrist. The orb flickered, then began to glow brighter, its pulse deepening to a low, resonant hum.

After a long moment, the light faded. Evander frowned. "Eighty percent."

Cordelia stared at him. "What?"

"Your bond with Boyde is currently at eighty percent of the expected strength for a full Celestial Bond," Evander said quietly. "Stronger than most I've tested, but still, below what it should be."

Cordelia's breath hitched. She looked once more toward the waves where Boyde swam, her throat working. "But ... we're bonded. I would know if something was wrong."

"Not necessarily," Evander said gently. "The interference affects the flow of aether, not the emotional connection itself. Most don't notice, until cracks begin to show."

Seraphina swallowed hard. *How many others? How many bonds are already failing?* A cold dread settled in her stomach.

"But there's also ... something else." Evander's voice faltered. A bead of sweat slipped down his temple despite the cool air, and he wiped it away with the back of his wrist. "My father, when he was a student at the university, touched the estherbloom tree. It granted him ... a vision. A prophecy, he always called it."

He swallowed and looked out toward the ocean, a distant memory flickering in his eyes. "This vision showed him two humans my father believed would play a pivotal role in bridging our realms, or perhaps in tearing them apart. He never quite understood what he saw. All he knew was the shape of their faces in the glow of that tree. He told me he'd recognize them anywhere, but he never saw either of them again, until recently."

Evander's attention shifted to Seraphina, and her spine prickled under the intensity of his stare. "The other night at the palace, when you were introduced to him ... he recognized *you*, Seraphina. You are the one my father foresaw."

A chill swept through her, sharper even than the storm's bite. "Me?" she managed, voice barely more than a whisper. "But what does that even mean?"

Evander's expression tightened with regret. "I wish I knew. My father spoke only of fragments, half-formed details. He suspects you have a part to play in whatever's happening at the university. And Isadora … she knows more. She told me herself. Just last week, she found old records of that prophecy buried in the restricted archives. She said she wanted to dig deeper, to trace its origins. I was planning to speak to her about it, but then she …" His voice faltered, grief flickering across his features.

"Then she fell ill," Cordelia murmured, her face drawn with worry.

Evander nodded. "She's the one who can tell us more about what my father saw that night he touched the estherbloom tree. If anyone can make sense of why you're at the heart of this, Seraphina, it's her."

Seraphina's mind spun, adrenaline warring with confusion. She drew a shaking breath. "Then we press on. We get the blood thorn, and we help her. After that … after that, I want answers."

When they moved again, it was with a renewed sense of urgency. Evander raised a faint shield around them, and Boyde's magic ebbed and flowed with the raging sea, protecting them from lethal waves. They climbed and crawled up the slick, twisting path, drenched to the bone. Cordelia's limp grew more pronounced. Seraphina's arms shook each time she hauled herself to a new foothold. Evander's mask cracked from exhaustion.

At last, a broad plateau spread before them, overlooking the crashing surf. Lightning illuminated a solitary cluster of twisted stems that gleamed with an uncanny red glow.

Seraphina's heart soared. "I see it!" she yelled.

Cordelia stumbled to her side, followed by Evander, whose eyes sparked with relief. Nestled in a jagged fissure right above them lay the blood thorn, a half dozen coils of barbed, reddish-green stems. A single bud like a ruby heart.

Seraphina sank to a crouch, rummaging for her shears. "Cover me," she told the others.

Evander turned outward, throwing up a shield around them as he scanned the sky for harpies. Cordelia steadied Seraphina's foot on the rock as she stepped up. She snipped the stalks and placed them into a vial designed to preserve their potency. A wave of magic radiated from the plant, as if grateful to be finally harvested.

But even as Seraphina sealed the vial, the wind howled louder. The brunt of the storm had finally reached them, its force no longer a distant threat but a living, battering presence. Air turned sharp with salt and rain, the gale shrieking through cracks in the stone. The very mountain seemed to groan beneath its weight.

Before relief could settle, a monstrous gust slammed into them. Seraphina slid, her cloak whipping like a sail. Cordelia cried out and lunged to catch Seraphina's arm, dragging her back from the ledge.

"I can't maintain this!" Evander shouted, face contorted with effort. The barrier he'd been maintaining waivered, weakening under the sudden onslaught of wind. Raindrops hissed through the failing shield. Every ounce of magic they possessed seemed to be scraping against the storm's raw ferocity.

Boyde let out a resounding call that echoed through wind and rain, summoning her elemental strength. She added her magic to Evander's.

Cordelia closed her eyes, connecting with Boyde, lending her tiny spark of magic, her hope, her desperation, to their joint defense. The three forces twined together into a tapestry of gold and aquamarine, bright enough to defy the storm.

It was enough for them to stagger forward, foot by foot, away from the cliff's deadly drop. Lightning carved open the heavens, and thunder pounded their ears. Still, they managed to climb toward a dark fissure in the rock: a cave mouth.

Once inside, Evander gasped and let the barrier drop. Boyde's magic fizzled to a faint glow around her mane, and Cordelia sank to her knees on the ground.

Drenched and trembling but alive, they collapsed inside the cave as wind shrieked beyond the walls. Seraphina's numb fingers shook while she fumbled with a match, and only after several tense moments did she coax a small flame into being.

Cordelia murmured a farewell to Boyde from the cave entrance, thanking her for the rescue. The hippocampus nodded, then vanished into the storm to rest and recover in deeper waters. Seraphina dropped onto the cave floor, cradling the vial that contained the blood thorn. Hope thrummed through her exhaustion; *Isadora might yet be saved.*

Cordelia pressed her back to the wall, drawing her cloak close. "We should rest here for the night."

"Yes," Evander replied, eyes heavy-lidded as he built up the fire. "At first light, we head back."

Cordelia lay down on the cave floor. "Hang in there just a little longer, baby," she whispered, clinging to the thought that they could brew a medicine from the blood thorn in time.

"We'll save her," Evander vowed, voice shaking with exhaustion as he lay down near the fire.

Seraphina exhaled, every muscle aching with fatigue. Yet as her breathing slowed, a creeping darkness slithered through her veins.

Deep within the uncharted dark, something ancient shifted, a presence older than the stone itself, watchful in the way predators are when they have no need to chase. It didn't lunge or roar. Its awareness slithered into her mind, slow and suffocating, brushing the corners of her half-formed dreams.

Chapter 20

LAST OF THE REALM-BINDERS

FADEYA

Turning the corner fast, boots skidding on uneven stone, Fadeya slammed straight into a wall of warmth and muscle. Her arms flung outward, scrolls flying like startled birds.

"Shit," she hissed, staggering back. "Emeric."

"Hello to you, *failure*." He bent to retrieve a scroll, his movements infuriatingly slow. "Miss me?"

Before she could retort, he'd already snatched half the bundle from her arms, smirking like he owned the hallway. She shoved past him into the undercroft, jaw tight. The door thudded shut behind them, sealing in the thick, iron-rich scent of dried herbs, old parchment, and ink. A long table sprawled at the center, littered with cracked jars and parchment curling at the edges.

Fadeya moved quickly to the other side of the table, breath hitching at the sight of the crooked stack of scrolls and scattered books. Her fingers twitched. *Just a moment.*

She swept her hands across the surface, lining up the scrolls with swift, precise motions, stacking the books so their spines faced outward in an even row. A misplaced inkpot caught her eye, she slid it exactly to the center, exhaling only once everything sat in rigid order.

Only then did she pull a book from the stack, clutching it a little too tightly. "Well," she said, forcing lightness into her voice, "it would seem you are feeling better today."

She could feel his gaze, amused, following her every movement.

"Tonight," Emeric said softly, his voice rough around the edges. He leaned heavily against the table, as if the weight of what he carried had followed him in. "I bring news."

"You sound very dramatic." She didn't look at him, but her fingers paused, just for a moment.

"Seraphina. Evander. Cordelia," he said quietly, a somber weight in his voice. "They've left the university."

She froze, looking up at him in shock. "What do you *mean*, left?"

"They went to the cliffs to search for a plant. The one that might save Isadora." He looked away then, as if ashamed. "I should've gone with them."

The silence between them stretched.

Fadeya's throat tightened. "I read that the cliffs are dangerous," she said quietly. "Especially with the storms coming. I hope ... I hope Seraphina will be safe."

"Evander is with her ..." he said softly. "He's got a decent amount of fae magic, being royal and all." He paused, blinking hard as tears gathered in his eyes. "I just ... I hope they find the plant."

The rough sincerity in his voice struck her like a blow. She blinked, studying him. "You actually care."

He scoffed, rubbing at his eyes. "I'm not a *complete* villain."

"That's debatable."

He forced a smile, crooked and tired. "Just enough to be interesting."

She exhaled slowly, tapping her fingers on the books. "I did find something out, too."

Emeric moved around the table, voice low. "What?"

Without looking at him, she opened the book resting in front of them—*Threads of Aether: A Chronicle of Astral Unison University*. The pages whispered beneath her fingers as she turned to the marked entry. "Why I might be the only one who remembers life before this place. It's the archway."

"The what?" he replied, brows furrowed.

She jabbed a finger at the text. "The entrance everyone walks through. It's enchanted. They added it around twenty years ago to strip the memories of humans coming into the university. That's why you don't remember me."

He blinked. "But you …"

"I came through a portal." Her voice was clipped. "I wasn't invited." *I wasn't supposed to be here.*

Understanding dawned on him. "You didn't walk through the archway, so you remember everything."

She nodded once.

He stepped back, processing. "Why would the fae be scared of humans retaining their memories?"

She pointed at the paragraph toward the bottom of the open page, then began to read out loud.

"Established under the authority of the Second Accord, the Arch of Memory Preservation functions as a critical safeguard within Astral Unison University. Its enchantment is structured not to alter the comprehension of fae knowledge, but to strategically diminish and, where necessary, remove attachments to the human realm. Personal memories relating to family, former relationships, places of origin, and other elements deemed extraneous or disruptive to the stability of inter-realm boundaries are selectively obscured. The process is not a wholesale erasure; rather, it applies precise filters to ensure that students residing within or departing from the fae realm retain only information relevant to their continued presence in, or discreet disengagement from, fae society. This mechanism remains essential to the ongoing protection of the fae realm from inadvertent disclosure or entanglement with human affairs."

"You're telling me," he said slowly, "that they've been doing this to everyone. Without our consent. Without even telling us."

She closed the book, jaw tight. "That's exactly what it says."

"How is this allowed? How can they—" He cut off, shaking his head. "How many people have walked through that arch without knowing what it cost them?"

She swallowed, her throat dry. "All of them. Except me."

He drew back, pacing a tight line behind her chair. "This … this is wrong." His voice cracked on the last word. "It's manipulation. Worse than that, it's theft."

"I spent all this time thinking Seraphina didn't write to me because she didn't care," Fadeya whispered, hanging her head. "She doesn't … *remember me*."

For a long moment, neither of them spoke.

Finally, she looked up at him. "Where do we go from here?"

Emeric swallowed, dragging a hand through his hair, sending blond strands falling messily across his brow. His face darkened. *Haunted.* That was the only word Fadeya could think of. "The aetheric conductor," he said, voice rough. "It's the tool I used to … to disrupt Isadora's bond."

He shook his head once, as if trying to banish the memory. "The book Hera gave me had a map. It led me to a pond in the forest beyond the Star Shrine." He shifted, restless. "The aetheric conductor felt … wrong. Like it wanted to *use* me. There was a pull to it, twisted. The book said it was crafted by Aurora's sister."

Fadeya's breath caught. A thread of cold wove down her spine. "Onyx," she breathed.

His gaze lifted to hers, grim. "The same."

Fadeya stepped back, as if distance could shield her from the weight of that name. "She was consumed," she uttered. "Twisted by shadow."

"That's just it." His voice dropped lower. "The book mentioned another artifact. One crafted by Aurora herself. It's meant to *harness* shadows."

Fadeya's mind spun. "You think it's still there?" she asked as she began to gather the books and scrolls she had borrowed from the library.

"I don't know." His words came out quietly. "But if it is ... I'm not leaving it for someone else to find." His throat bobbed with the force of the words. "I won't let someone else make the same mistake I made."

Her heart thudded hard against her ribs. "You're right," she said, forcing steadiness into her voice even as her blood sang beneath her skin. "We have to see what this artifact is."

He nodded once. "Agreed."

Drawing a long breath through her nose, Fadeya willed the tremor in her fingers to still. "When?"

"Tonight." His mouth tightened. Then, softly, "But first, I need to visit Headmistress Fallyn. It's time I own up to my mistakes." He hesitated. "Meet me at the garden gate in an hour?"

A flicker of wariness shone in his eyes, but beneath it, for the first time since she'd arrived at the university, Fadeya caught a glimpse of something else.

That old glint. The one that had once made her trust him, perhaps too easily.

"I'll meet you there," she whispered.

He held her gaze a beat longer, then drew a deep breath, squared his shoulders, and strode from the undercroft, footsteps fading into the dark.

Fadeya stood alone in the heavy silence, her heart pounding. *Tonight*, she thought.

SERAPHINA

A slow, steady drip echoed through the cavern, each water drop hitting rock like the ticking of an invisible clock. Seraphina stirred from uneasy dreams, groaning as tension thrummed through her limbs. She blinked hard, grappling for any sense of place, until the dying embers jogged her memory.

Her friends lay close by: Cordelia curled in a tight ball by the gutted fire, and Evander sprawled out on the unforgiving stone, one arm draped over his face.

Neither so much as twitched. The sight of them, silent and resting, almost lulled her back into sleep.

But something behind her stirred.

The hairs on the back of her neck rose. Slowly, she propped herself up, pulse thrumming with dread and a strange, aching curiosity. *What is that …?*

At first, she saw only darkness shifting across the cave's recesses. Then an immense presence pressed against the edge of her awareness. Old as the mountains. Vast as the night sky. *Impossible.*

Hello, little one.

The words rumbled through her mind, through her very blood. She slowly turned around, trying not to let terror drown her heart. *Don't panic. Don't panic. Don't panic.*

And there, cloaked in shadows, a dragon stood before her.

For a moment, her mind refused to believe what her eyes saw. A being of legend that belonged more to grand epics and ancient war songs than to the cold reality of her present moment. Not here. Not now. *Not real.*

Yet it was.

Its black scales looked as though they had been hewn from midnight, each facet devouring what meager light filtered into the cave. Faint wisps of steam curled around its nostrils—a subtle reminder of the power coiled in its lungs. Her gaze traveled upward, catching on eyes of molten gold, so bright they seemed a final beacon in a land of nightmares. That look snared her, locked her in place, until she forgot to inhale. *Oh. My. Stars.*

Cordelia jerked awake, eyes wild. "Seraphina, what …" The words withered as she gawked at the massive silhouette.

Across the cave, Evander lurched upright. He thrust out both arms, desperation etched into his face. Pale sparks sputtered at his fingertips, struggling for life, only to fade into nothing. "I can't shield us," he croaked, voice cracking with panic. His magic was exhausted, leaving only a lingering sense of dread in its wake. "Seraphina, Cordelia, run!"

His plea echoed off the cavern walls, slicing through the silence. Yet Seraphina couldn't move, could hardly think.

That dragon's eyes still pinned her, heavy as chain links draped across her shoulders. *Run?* A foolish notion. Instinct whispered what her mind already knew—running would make no difference at all.

Then, that low voice curled through her mind again, more intimate than a whisper: ***Come closer, little one. I mean you no harm ... unless you give me reason.***

Seraphina tore her gaze from the dragon's searing eyes, forcing herself to glance over her shoulder. Cordelia stood like a statue carved from ice, white-knuckled, breath caught somewhere between inhale and scream. Her face had gone slack with terror. And yet ... she wasn't reacting to the voice.

Because she hadn't heard it.

Understanding crashed into her. Before Seraphina could form words, that voice uncoiled through her skull again, deep and hollow-bellied, like stone cracking under the earth.

They do not hear me, child. Not unless I will it. You are the one I've come for.

The statement wasn't laced with malice. The certainty behind it was worse. Unyielding. Absolute. Like history was already written, and she was only now being made aware she'd always been part of it.

Cordelia's hands trembled as she took a step closer to her friend. "Seraphina," she hissed, "what's happening?"

Seraphina swallowed. "He ... he told me to come closer."

Cordelia let out a short, disbelieving laugh. "Yes, of course, he wants you to step right into his jaws."

Across the cavern, Evander strained, desperation written across his face. He tried once more to summon even a flicker of magic, but only faint sparks danced, fading as quickly as they appeared. Cursing under his breath, he shot Seraphina a desperate glance. "See if it will make a bargain," he said. "We can't fight it."

But the dragon only lowered his head further, looking at Seraphina with a calm intensity that belied his monstrous size.

His presence in her mind felt like an ancient tide tugging her forward.

Trust your heart, little one. His voice resonated within her. *You already know why I have come.*

Every fiber in Seraphina's body warned that this was madness. Yet she found herself stepping away from her companions, as if guided by an invisible thread. Her knees quivered, and her heart pounded so fast she thought it might tear free of her chest.

One step. Then another.

"Seraphina," Cordelia choked. But Seraphina couldn't answer. Couldn't explain the pull tightening around her ribs. Her knees trembled. Her breath came fast and shallow. Her heart pounded so fiercely it felt as though it might tear itself from her chest.

"Why?" she asked, voice barely audible.

Amusement radiated through her thoughts, coloring the dragon's tone. *The ember in your soul. It called to me the moment you set foot in these mountains.*

A jolt of heat bloomed in her chest, radiating through her limbs. Magic.

Her vision blurred, edges shimmering with light and shadow both, as if the air itself bent around her.

Behind her, Cordelia called her name again, fear sharpening the edges of it.

The dragon's voice pressed deeper into her mind, a gentle push despite the darkness within its tone: *Show me, little one. Show me the shadows you keep locked away. Let them breathe.*

Her first instinct was to clamp down on the roiling energy, to snuff it out before it devoured her. "I … can't," she managed.

"Seraphina!" Evander yelled, his voice laced with panic. "Whatever's happening, don't give in!"

It was too late. Power sparked down her arms, shadows twisting like ribbons around her wrists. A frantic sob tore from her throat. "What is this?"

The dragon advanced one titanic step. Its presence brushed against her mind. *Your power awakens. Do not fight it.*

A swirl of dread seized her. She felt that same power beckoning from deep within, an echo from an unknown part of her soul. "I'm scared," she admitted, voice cracking.

Behind her, Cordelia threw a rock. It ricocheted off the dragon's back, useless. The dragon didn't even blink. His presence pressed down again.

Be brave, Seraphina.

Then it ripped through her, inky night colliding with a sudden burst of gold, blazing from the dragon's chest like a second sun. The cave erupted in chaos. Power surged through the air, violent and unrestrained, as if two opposing gods had chosen this cavern as their battlefield. The embers at her feet hissed and flared into a brief, furious inferno before vanishing into ash. The walls groaned as dust trickled down from the ceiling.

Cordelia and Evander threw their arms up, silhouettes braced against the maelstrom, their cries lost in the howling, pressure-thick wind. Stone splintered. And in the center of it all stood Seraphina, caught between shadow and light.

Seraphina felt her body lifted from the ground. She hovered there, suspended between searing light and churning shadow, both forces folding around her like twin storms locked in collision.

Her mind cracked under the pressure, splintering, not from pain, but from memories that weren't hers. Ancient visions poured into her: cities carved into mountain tops, dragons weaving through skies thick with stardust, spells etched into the marrow of the world long before language. A lineage of power, of devastation and creation, *of choice.*

And through it all, the dragon's voice, a steady, unwavering current.

Let go of your fear, little one. You are not being broken. You are being forged.

Around her, symbols sparked to life. One by one, they circled her in a halo of burning starlight and devouring dark. Each rune etched itself into her skin, branding her with truths she could neither read nor deny. She was unraveling, and in that unraveling, becoming.

When the final sigil flared into existence, a dragon's eye wreathed in celestial script, seared like a vow into her forearm, it blazed so fiercely that the world vanished in white.

And then silence.

The power drained from the air like breath exhaled. Seraphina collapsed, her limbs no longer hers, her palms pressed to stone still vibrating from the aftershock.

Inside her, something new stirred.

Dazed, she looked up. Slowly, the dragon inclined his head, a gesture of respect.

It is done. You bear my mark, Seraphina.

Seraphina stared at the sigil, dread and awe spiraling inside her. When she touched it, an echo of that power coursed through her fingertips. She swallowed, throat dry as ash, and forced the words past the weight in her chest. "Who *are* you?"

The dragon went still. Not just unmoving, but utterly, terrifyingly still. His eyes narrowed, and the air thickened, suddenly heavy with meaning. When he spoke, it wasn't just sound. It was vibration. It was memory and prophecy braided together in syllables that cracked like thunder.

I am Vyrakthos, he said. Last of the Realm-Binders. And now, your bondmate.

The stone beneath her trembled faintly, groaning as if it, too, remembered that name.

Seraphina's breath hitched. She had no idea what a Realm-Binder was, but her body responded before her mind could catch up, she bowed her head to him.

Vyrakthos moved then, spreading his colossal wings, stirring a torrent of air that made her hair whip across her face. *I will remain close.* His voice had quieted, but it still carried that immutable certainty. *Watching. Waiting. When you stop fearing your path, when you accept what you are becoming, I will return.*

With one powerful sweep, the dragon leapt into the night sky, disappearing into the starlit black. A thunderous roar echoed back, lingering like a benediction.

For a time, the three of them could only breathe in the hush. The tang of scorched magic clung to the air. Seraphina's limbs quivered when she finally attempted to stand, her body still buzzing with aftershocks of power.

Cordelia rushed to her side. She gingerly touched the glowing mark. "Stars ..." she breathed. "Are you ... alright?"

Seraphina shuddered. "I think so. I feel ... I don't even have words for it." She drew a trembling breath, her hand hovering over her chest, where unfamiliar magic now curled like a nest of embers. "It's like something was asleep in me all this time."

Evander lingered behind Cordelia, unable to tear his eyes away from the mark. "I'm not sure if I should be afraid," he admitted. "You look like you were struck by a falling star."

A laugh, too raw to be anything but half sob, broke from her. "Feels like it, too."

Cordelia glanced toward the cave mouth, where the dragon had vanished into the night. "What the hell? Seriously ... What just happened?" Her hand trembled on Seraphina's arm. "Will he come back?"

Seraphina followed her gaze. "He told me he'd return when I was ready, though I have no idea what 'ready' even means." She thought of Isadora, of the promise she'd made. "But that doesn't change why we came here. We still have to save Isadora."

Evander slung his satchel over his shoulder. "Sunrise should be in about an hour. We will leave then."

She studied the runes etched into her skin, the dragon's eye glaring back, encircled by celestial symbols. *Bonded. She was bonded to a fucking dragon!*

She was not the same girl who had crawled into this cavern to escape the storm. Some part of her had been claimed by that black-scaled being.

Despite the tremors of fear snaking through her heart, Seraphina couldn't deny that the tether now weaving between her soul and that ancient being was more than terrifying.

It was exhilarating.

Chapter 21

STARLIGHT BINDS US

FADEYA

Fadeya drew her cloak tighter as she neared the garden gate. The iron arch loomed ahead, half-swallowed by trailing ivy. Her heart pounded faster with each step.

Emeric stood in the shadows beneath it, leaning against the stone wall, arms crossed. His head was bowed, but at the sound of her approach, he looked up.

Relief flickered through his eyes.

"You came," he whispered.

Fadeya stopped just beyond the gate. "Of course, I did."

He pushed the gate open and waited for her to step through. When she did, he fell into step beside her as they began winding down the narrow path beyond the wall.

Fadeya stole a glance at him. He looked … hollowed out. And lonely. She hesitated, then asked gently, "What happened? With Headmistress Fallyn."

Emeric's shoulders drew inward slightly. "I went straight to her after we parted." His hands flexed at his sides, restless. "I told her everything. About the conductor. About disrupting Isadora's bond. About how I let it happen."

He shook his head, his gaze distant. "The artifact had a hold on me. I didn't see it for what it was until it was too late. And even now, I can't explain all of it." His throat worked around the words. "But I know what I did. I know I hurt her."

Fadeya's steps slowed. "Did you tell her that Hera gave you the book? About our suspicions?"

Emeric shook his head. "No. I thought we should do a bit more research before we take that to the faculty. There's too much we don't know yet."

"Probably smart." Her mouth tightened. "I doubt Fallyn would believe you over Hera. Not right now."

"She didn't say I could stay," he said after a moment. "She said the king would decide. When he arrives."

Fadeya's heart clenched. "Ah."

His nod was faint. "I told her I don't deserve to be here. I didn't ask her to defend me. I just … wanted her to know the truth."

Emeric turned to her fully now, his voice rough with sincerity. "I need to make this right, Fadeya. Somehow."

He held her gaze, something unspoken shimmering beneath the regret. "I don't think I could do this if you weren't here." His voice lowered. "I've been alone enough these past few days."

"You're not alone," she said softly. "Not tonight."

Time stretched and folded around them, the forest changing as they went. The silver light of the moon filtered through the canopy in shifting beams, lighting their path in patches. Somewhere far off, a nightbird called once, then fell silent again.

Fadeya glanced up as they passed beneath an arch of vines. Tiny blue butterflies clung to the leaves. With each flutter, a faint trail of sparkling dust followed. She stared, breath caught in her throat. No matter how long she spent in this realm, it still found new ways to astonish her. *Like stepping into a dream.*

It had been nearly half an hour since they left the garden gate. Finally, with a sideways glance at Emeric, she said, "You look like you're about to combust."

He blinked at her, startled.

Her voice held dry amusement now. "Is brooding a full-time occupation, or just something you pick up between disasters?"

Her braid slipped over one shoulder as she stepped over a twisted root.

Emeric's lips twitched. "I call it staying alive. We have no idea what is in the woods."

"I call it thinking yourself in circles," she said, nudging a small fern out of her path. "But if you need the brooding to stay pretty, by all means, carry on."

He huffed a laugh, quiet, but real. "So you *do* think I'm pretty?" he asked, a teasing lilt in his voice.

"Delightful," she shot back without missing a beat, but the heat rising in her cheeks betrayed her.

They continued, pressing deeper until the tangled maze of branches relented, revealing a clearing.

A small, mirror-like lake lay before them, perfectly still, reflecting the scattered constellations above. Fadeya stopped, breath caught in her throat. The sight was … painful. Beautiful in the way old memories were beautiful, sharp-edged and aching.

Her thoughts drifted to her sister. *Seraphina would love this.*

Emeric stood beside her, tension draining slightly from his shoulders as he took in the sight. "I didn't expect such peace here," he murmured, voice thick with unspoken pain.

She didn't look at him. "Even darkness can have its moments of beauty."

They stood in the hush; a breeze stirred the surface of the lake, scattering starlight across the water.

Fadeya sank down onto a moss-covered rock, stretching her legs with a quiet sigh. Emeric remained standing for a moment before settling beside her, arms resting loosely over his knees.

For a while, neither of them spoke. The water lapped gently against the shore. Somewhere across the clearing, a chime rang, crickets or wind or something else entirely. In this realm, it was hard to tell.

Then, quietly, she asked, "How did you find the conductor when you were here before?"

Emeric's attention stayed fixed on the water, but his brows pulled together in thought. "The book Hera gave me had a map," he said. "Roughly drawn, but it led here. To this lake." He paused, frowning. "Only … once I arrived, the map stopped being useful."

Fadeya turned toward him, watching the way his jaw tensed. "What do you mean?"

He shifted, plucking a blade of grass and twirling it between his fingers. "I stood right where you are now, actually. I remember thinking I must've taken a wrong turn. But then … I don't know." His voice lowered. "Something pulled at me. Just this … feeling. Like my feet already knew where to go."

He gestured toward the base of a thistle-choked tree near the far side of the pond. "I walked straight to that spot. There was a small box buried in the weeds. No markings, nothing magical about it from the outside. But when I opened it …" He looked down at his hands. "The aetheric conductor was the only thing inside."

Fadeya blinked. "And you don't know how you knew to go there?"

He shook his head slowly.

They sat in silence again, the lapping of water filling the space between them.

"I was hoping," he said at last, "that if we came back, whatever led me to the conductor would lead us to this other artifact. The one Aurora created."

Fadeya hugged her knees to her chest. "So … what do we know?" she asked, glancing sideways at Emeric. "About the artifact, I mean."

He leaned back on his palms, staring across the water. "Not much. Only what the book said, that it was created by Aurora. It was meant to harness shadows. Counterbalance what Onyx had built."

Fadeya frowned. "Harnessing shadows could mean anything. Is it a weapon? A container? A key?"

He shook his head. "Your guess is as good as mine. Aurora was the one who believed in balance. She didn't create magic to dominate. She believed in tethering things together."

"So maybe it isn't meant to destroy shadow," Fadeya murmured, more to herself now. "Maybe it's meant to *bind* it."

Emeric nodded slowly. "That would make sense. Shadow magic was never the enemy. It was how it was *used* that ruined everything."

They fell quiet again. Wind stirred the surface of the pond, and a few scattered petals drifted from the canopy above, landing gently on the water.

"I keep thinking about the statue," Emeric said suddenly.

Fadeya turned to him. "What statue?"

"The one of Aurora at the university. Outside the east hall. You've seen it, right?"

She nodded, brow furrowed. "Of course."

"I don't know," he muttered, gaze distant. "It always felt strange to me. Like it was ... watching. I've always walked past it and wondered if she'd approve of me being there."

Fadeya tilted her head, her mind tugging at a thread just out of reach. "I passed by it again last week ..." Her voice trailed off as she stared into the trees, half remembering. "I remember thinking the carving was beautiful," she said slowly. "All those tiny details, the sword, the robe embroidered with stars ..." She paused, her brows pinching. "She was wearing ..."

"That necklace," Emeric said, his voice quiet.

Fadeya blinked. "What?"

He nodded toward her hand that was fingering the chain around her neck. "That amulet you're wearing. The statue has the same one." He let out a laugh.

Fadeya looked down. And then—*click.*

"This is it," she breathed. "This *is* the artifact."

Emeric sat up straighter, eyes wide. "Fadeya ..."

"Of course, it is," she said, half laughing, half exasperated. "Of *course,* it is." She surged to her feet, the energy crackling through her suddenly too much to stay still. "I should've realized it."

Emeric followed her with his eyes, still seated, still stunned.

She held the amulet up by its chain, the moonlight gleaming against the iridescent stone. Then she closed her fingers around it, grounding herself. "Watch."

She ran her free hand gently over the face of the amulet and willed the shadows to rise.

The response was instant. A ripple of cold shimmered outward from the stone, and tendrils of shadow curled from the forest floor, drawn to her. They wrapped around her like flowing silk, climbing her arms and shoulders, coiling gently around her torso like a second cloak.

Emeric lurched to his feet. "Fadeya!" His mouth parted in disbelief. "You're wrapped in shadows."

"I know," she whispered.

His brows pulled together. "Why in the name of the stars didn't you mention this *sooner?*"

She gave a short laugh, unspooling some of the tension. "Because the last twenty-four hours have been a disaster?"

"Fair."

They both started laughing, softly at first, then helpless, breathless laughter as the weight of it all seemed to break under the sheer absurdity.

"All that," Emeric said, dropping back onto the moss beside the pond, "and we've been hauling ourselves across this forest for *nothing.*"

She sank down beside him again, the shadows slowly receding as she released her grip on the amulet. Her shoulders dropped for the first time all day.

They sat there in silence for a while, the pond rippling quietly in front of them, a chorus of unseen creatures humming in the night.

Then Fadeya spoke again, her voice softer now. "It was Hera who gave it to me."

Emeric turned his head slowly. "What?"

She nodded. "The day I arrived. She gave it to me to help hide me while I … observed bondings."

His expression darkened slightly, thoughtful. "It still doesn't really make sense that she needed your help for that."

"No. It doesn't," Fadeya said quietly.

He bumped his shoulder gently against hers, and something fluttered low in her stomach. After so many weeks of isolation, the simple presence of another person stirred something she hadn't let herself feel in a long time.

They sat in silence until his voice broke through the stillness.

"Why do you insist on seeing good in me?" he asked, raw vulnerability in his voice.

"I've seen thorns beneath the brightest flowers … and the strongest trees fall to a single storm. You're neither perfect nor broken, Emeric, but you *are* growing."

He frowned. "And what if I never outgrow who I used to be?"

She looked back at the water, her voice a murmur. "Then at least you'll be honest."

Before either of them could speak again, the lake stirred.

A growing light shimmered beneath the surface, and every hair on her body rose. She stood, hand ghosting toward her blade, while Emeric rose, too, slower, entranced.

A creature broke the surface, ethereal and strange. A fish, its scales opalescent, colors shifting with every movement. It hovered near the shore, wrapped in threads of magic.

"Emeric …" she breathed. "Do you *feel* that?"

He nodded, eyes locked on the creature. "It's calling to me."

The fish lifted its head, eyes ancient and knowing.

Emeric's hand trembled slightly as he reached toward the water's surface, fingers hovering just above the shimmering edge. "It's speaking to me," he whispered, voice unsteady.

His eyes had gone distant, like he was listening to something just beyond the veil of sound. "His name is Zeruun. He saw me. He *knows* what has happened."

He turned toward her then, the color drained from his face, pupils dilated with something between awe and fear. "The creatures, they're afraid to bond. They're being silenced."

He pressed a hand to his chest, as if steadying a force inside him. "He speaks for them."

Fadeya's hand tightened on her hilt. "Afraid to bond?"

"Because something is stopping them," Emeric said, voice distant. "*Someone* is stealing the magic."

Emeric stepped forward slowly, his eyes wide, awestruck. "He's choosing me," he said, voice barely above a whisper. "He wants to bond."

He dropped to one knee, reverent, his hand pressed to the earth.

"Zeruun ..." he breathed, his throat tightening. "I'm honored. But I'm not worthy of this bond. I've made mistakes. *Many* mistakes. I've hurt people. I've turned away when I should have stood tall. I've been cruel. Selfish."

Zeruun didn't waver. He rose higher, scales catching the moonlight in waves of blues and silvers, until he hovered eye level with Emeric, as if peering into his soul.

Fadeya stepped back, her breath caught in her throat, watching in silent wonder.

Emeric looked up, his brow furrowed, voice trembling. He pressed a hand to his chest. "He sees *everything*. And he's not turning away." His hand lifted, as if pulled forward by something greater than himself.

Zeruun extended a translucent fin, glowing brighter now, threads of energy spiraling outward like tendrils of light. Between them, a net of magic began to spin, gossamer and radiant, humming with power. Each strand shimmered with memory, pain, hope, and possibility.

Emeric swallowed hard. "Then I accept," he whispered. "All of it. You. Me. Whatever this becomes."

The instant they touched, light exploded.

A brilliant flare engulfed the clearing, blinding and beautiful. Leaves lifted into the air and hovered, suspended in the force of it.

Fadeya shielded her eyes, heat rippling over her skin.

When the light faded, Emeric knelt at the lake's edge, gasping. She dropped beside him. "Emeric, are you okay?" Her hands found his face.

He shook his head, barely. "He saw all of me. And still chose me." Tears rimmed his lashes. Something inside her cracked.

His eyes met hers, wet and shining. "I'm okay, Fadeya. I ..." He exhaled hard. "Zeruun said there's someone. A woman. A human woman, living in the village nearby. He said … she has the answers you've been looking for."

Fadeya helped him to his feet, her thoughts racing. "All I *have* are questions," she murmured.

Emeric turned to Zeruun, awe in every line of him, and bowed his head deeply. The fish dipped once, then disappeared, vanishing beneath the lake with a final burst of light.

He looked at her, a tempest of unspoken hunger swirling in his gray eyes. "Thank you," he uttered, "for not letting me do this alone."

A shaky smile curved her lips; inside, her heart thundered. "Didn't feel like hauling your corpse out of here," she said, the teasing lilt betrayed by the breathlessness in her voice.

His answering grin held a spark of heat, and he moved in closer, as though drawn by an irresistible pull. Gently, he tucked a stray lock of hair behind her ear. The lightest brush of his fingertips ignited a tingling awareness that swept across her skin. She felt him like a current in her blood, each moment more electrifying than the last. He seemed … *different.*

She swallowed hard, her pulse thrumming. Then, acting on pure instinct, she leaned up and kissed him. His mouth tasted of magic and adrenaline, a dizzying mixture that made her heart clench painfully in her chest.

He responded without hesitation, arms sliding around her waist, locking her against him until she felt the planes of his body through the thin barrier of their clothes. The kiss deepened, lips parting to let a rush of heat flow between them, stoking a yearning she hadn't dared to admit was there. A soft, needy moan escaped her, and he swallowed it, returning the sound with a low groan of his own.

Her hands roamed up his chest, past the rapid beat of his heart, and around his neck. She could feel his breath hitch when her fingers tangled in his hair, tugging him closer. Every shift of their bodies, every press of their mouths, sent shock waves of pleasure coursing through her.

Magic flared, heightened by their closeness. Tiny droplets of dew lifted from the lake and twirled around them in a dazzling, starlit dance. An energy surged beneath her skin, in tune with the frantic rhythm of her heart.

He broke away just long enough to exhale her name, voice husky. "I…" His eyes caught on the orb-like droplets of water. "How …?"

"You," she whispered, eyes half-lidded.

He leaned in again, mouth ghosting down the line of her jaw to her throat. A searing awareness bloomed where his lips grazed her skin. She gasped, head tipping back, inviting his exploration. His hands slid over her hips, fingers splaying in an unspoken claim.

She could sense the power of him, the tenderness, too. He wanted her, wanted this. Her hands wandered beneath the edge of his tunic, seeking the warmth of his bare skin. The moment she touched him there, he stiffened with a shuddering breath. His lips found hers again, more urgent this time, as though tasting a forbidden promise.

Around them, the dew droplets soared higher, forming a shimmering halo in the moonlit clearing.

She could barely speak, her voice lost in the fervor of his kiss. "Emeric," she finally managed, clinging to him. Her knees felt weak, as if the ground had turned to air. If not for the iron band of his arm around her waist, she might have crumpled.

Finally, he broke the kiss, their breath mingling hotly in the quiet space between them. "I don't know what happens next."

Her heart clenched, tears pricking at the backs of her eyes. She cupped his cheek, thumb brushing across his parted lips. "We'll face whatever comes, together. *Starlight binds us.*"

SERAPHINA

The storm had passed.

By the time they reached the high cliffs overlooking the valley, the skies had cleared entirely, leaving behind a world washed clean and bright.

Seraphina paused as they crested a rise, her breath catching, not from exhaustion this time, but from wonder.

The cliffs stretched before them in sweeping lines of silver and green, the stone beneath their feet veined with glistening crystal. Far below, winding rivers caught the morning light. Flowers of impossible hues swayed in the breeze, petals shimmering with colors she could not name, colors that did not exist back in the human realm.

Even the air felt different here. Warmer. Wilder. Alive. *How can a place like this exist?*

Beneath it all, in the deepest hollow of her chest, Vyrakthos's power stirred. A steady hum now, a low, constant thrum, as if the dragon's vast heart beat in rhythm with her own.

Cordelia walked ahead, her limp more noticeable today. Her shoulders were tense, her usual stream of commentary long since vanished.

Evander brought up the rear, hood drawn low, steps careful and deliberate. He hadn't said much since the cavern, either.

They're giving me space, Seraphina realized, but they don't know what to do with this.

She wasn't entirely sure what to do with it either.

Still, they were making good time. If they kept this pace, they'd reach Isadora by early evening.

As the sun rose higher, warmth settled into her bones, loosening some of the tension that had been gripping her shoulders since dawn. The path dipped toward a narrow outcropping sheltered by towering ferns and curling moss.

"Let's stop for a bit," Cordelia said at last, her voice hoarse. "I won't be much use if my legs give out before we get there."

No one argued.

They found a flat stretch of stone and unpacked a quick meal of dried fruit, cheese, and coarse bread that tasted like sawdust but filled the ache in her stomach.

Seraphina sat cross-legged, trying to ease the tightness still lingering in her chest. Every so often, her fingers drifted to the mark on her forearm, the dragon's eye still faintly warm beneath her skin.

Cordelia flopped down beside her with a groan, rubbing her thighs. "I'm *never* climbing another cliff in my life," she muttered, though her eyes still held the faint sheen of lingering fear from the night before.

Seraphina managed a small smile. "I think we all earned a few days off."

Evander crouched nearby, rummaging through his satchel. For a moment, she thought he was after more food until he drew out a small object, polished and gleaming in the sunlight.

Seraphina straightened. "Is that—?"

"The aether gauge." Evander's voice was careful, measured.

Her stomach fluttered uneasily. "You want to test my bond."

He nodded. "I'd be lying if I said I wasn't curious. You bonded outside of the university. It's … a unique opportunity."

Cordelia leaned forward, brows raised. "Unique, or reckless?"

Evander flicked her a look. "Both. But we'd be fools not to understand what we're dealing with."

Seraphina hesitated, fingers curling around the edge of her tunic.

But another part of her, sharp and new, rose against the fear. *You were not broken. You were forged.*

Slowly, she nodded. "Alright."

Evander exhaled, as if he'd half expected her to refuse. "Hold it between your hands. Focus on the bond. Don't force it, just let it rise."

Seraphina reached out with trembling fingers. The orb was cool against her skin, light as glass, yet thrumming faintly beneath her palms.

She closed her eyes.

The moment she reached inward, *there he was.*

Vyrakthos's presence surged upward, as if sensing her touch. The steady heartbeat of ancient power unfurled within her, a tide that threatened to pull her under even as it lifted her higher.

The orb flared to life. First a soft glow, then a violent pulse of gold and shadow, twin strands spiraling upward through the clear sphere.

Cordelia let out a strangled gasp. "Stars."

Evander swore under his breath. The glow intensified, surpassing the usual markers etched into the gauge's rim. The threads spun higher, faster, until they burst into a column of searing light.

The orb trembled in Seraphina's grasp. Evander lunged forward, snatching it back before it cracked outright.

For a long moment, none of them spoke.

Evander stared at the gauge, then at her, his face pale, voice low. "I've … I've never seen anything like this."

Seraphina's heart hammered against her ribs. "What does it mean?"

"It's stronger than any bond I've ever recorded," he said faintly. "Stronger than elder bonds. Stronger than royal lineages."

Cordelia whistled low. "No pressure."

Seraphina swallowed hard. A chill raced down her spine. *Stronger than royal bonds?* The thought twisted uneasily in her gut.

"I don't want to hurt anyone," she whispered. "I don't know what this power will do."

Cordelia reached over and put her hand on Seraphina's shoulder. "We've got your back, Sera. Whatever this means."

A knot of tension loosened in her chest. *I am not alone.*

She exhaled shakily, forcing her hands to still. "We should go. We still need to reach Isadora before nightfall."

Evander tucked the aether gauge away, rising fluidly. "Let's go."

Cordelia pushed herself upright with a grunt.

They gathered their things and set off once more, the cliffs now gleaming beneath the high sun.

FADEYA

Fadeya had always believed magic to be beautiful, something delicate and lyrical, but this city, the fae city nestled just beyond the gates of Astral Unison University, was so much more than that. *It was alive.* A symphony of wonder and color, every breath of it humming with enchantment.

Streets curved in arcs, paved with pearlescent stones that shimmered in the afternoon sunlight.

Every corner offered new delights. Strange and dazzling creatures moved through the city, their laughter like music, their clothes spun from silks. Market stalls spilled into the streets, bursting with wares that defied imagination. Emeric walked beside her silently, but not distantly; he seemed more present now, more focused. Since bonding with Zeruun, something had shifted.

He caught her staring and smiled, and she couldn't help but smile back.

"You haven't blinked in five minutes," he teased, brushing his shoulder against hers. "First time out of your gilded cage?" She shivered pleasantly at the touch, remembering the night before, whispers and heated skin, quiet promises shared under the pale glow of moonlight.

"Something like that," she whispered, unable to tear her focus from the kaleidoscope of life around them. "It's so different from what I imagined."

He snorted. "Magic usually is."

They walked in companionable silence for a few moments, fingers occasionally brushing, sending sparks dancing between them. She kept catching herself staring at him, wondering how this brash, reckless boy had suddenly become someone she trusted, someone she *needed*.

She took a steadying breath. "Did Zeruun tell you why we're visiting this woman?"

Emeric's expression darkened slightly. "He said she has answers you've been looking for. Zeruun seemed certain you'd want to speak with her."

She slowed, her brow knitting in thought. "Answers I've been looking for ..." she echoed softly, the words settling uneasily in her chest. "I have so many unanswered questions. About Hera. About why the creatures are so afraid to bond …" She exhaled sharply, frustration curling in her gut.

Emeric gave a slow nod, his jaw tightening. "It explains why there've been fewer bondings this year. Zeruun said the fear runs deep." He paused, his gaze drifting ahead, unfocused. "I hate knowing I might've made it worse. That I'm part of the reason they're afraid."

Fadeya was quiet for a long moment, the sounds of the fae city echoing around them— wind chimes that sang without breeze, the low murmur of voices speaking languages she didn't know, the occasional flutter of wings overhead—but none of it touched the stillness between them. She studied his profile carefully.

"What you did, interrupting that bond, it *was* wrong, Emeric." Her words weren't cruel, but they were honest. "You took something sacred and used it like a weapon. Whether you meant to or not, it hurt someone. It made others afraid."

He didn't respond, but his jaw clenched, his eyes fixed ahead, unable to meet hers.

Fadeya reached for his hand, her fingers curling into his. "But what matters now is that you *see* it. That you're not running from it. You're trying to make it right, and that does mean something."

She drew in a breath, steadying the ache in her chest. "We've all been used, lied to, and manipulated into playing roles we didn't choose. You choosing to step off that path and make your own? That's brave, Emeric. That's the person I trust."

He turned to her slowly, eyes wide. "Did I tell you my brother attended the university, too?" His voice was suddenly heavy with vulnerability. "Rian. He was the prodigy, perfect, charming, and brilliant. Everything my parents ever wanted. After he left for Astral Unison, our home changed completely. No letters, no news. He disappeared, Fadeya. Just vanished."

Her chest tightened painfully. "That's why you came here?"

He nodded slowly. "My parents acted like it never happened, just shoved their grief behind fake smiles. Pretended everything was fine. I came here to find him. I've searched, Fadeya. I've asked questions, and it's like he just disappeared into smoke."

"I understand what that's like," she admitted. "My father went away on a work trip when I was young. He never returned. For years, my mother told me he died in some accident, just another human tragedy." She swallowed past the lump forming in her throat. "But recently I discovered he attended Astral Unison University, too."

Emeric blinked, head tilting slightly as if he'd misheard. "You never knew?"

She shook her head. "Not until Hera found me. So many secrets. Too many coincidences."

He pressed closer, fingers gently brushing her jawline. "Maybe it isn't a coincidence that we found each other, Fadeya."

"Careful, Vexley. Keep talking like that, and I might start to think you like me."

He brushed her hair from her face. "Can't have that, can we?"

But then Emeric stilled.

His brow furrowed, the lines of his expression shifting from warmth to something puzzled. "Wait …"

Fadeya pulled back slightly, sensing the change. "What is it?"

He blinked, almost startled by the thought. "Why do I remember him?"

She frowned. "Your brother?"

He nodded, slowly. "If I crossed through the archway like every other student, then why do I still remember him?"

Fadeya's eyes widened, her mind flipping through the pages of the book she'd found. Her voice came softly, tinged with awe. "The passage said that memories of the human world are erased unless deemed essential by the magic that governs the archway. If your brother is, or was, also in the fae realm, then your memory of him must have been preserved. The magic must have decided it was necessary. That … *he* was necessary."

Emeric stared past her, the weight of it sinking in slowly. "Then maybe … he's still here." His voice cracked slightly. "But what if he doesn't remember *me*?"

The ache in his question was palpable. She reached for his hand, interlacing her fingers with his. "Then we remind him. We don't give up."

Emeric looked down at their joined hands, the smallest of nods forming as if they were the only thing keeping him grounded.

They walked a bit farther, then Emeric inclined his head toward a humble cottage nestled between two large trees, vines creeping along its stone walls. "We're here."

The cottage was simple yet welcoming. Flowers grew in boxes on the windows, and little creatures were painted on the table outside the front door.

They approached quietly, their footsteps muffled by moss-covered stones. Emeric knocked sharply, the sound echoing around them.

The door opened slowly, and a woman appeared, her hair tousled by the breeze drifting through the open windows, the scent of herbs and something warm from the oven clinging to the air around her.

Fadeya's breath caught. The woman's rich brown curls cascaded around a face so familiar it made her heart stutter painfully. Emerald eyes, her own eyes, stared back at her in wide disbelief.

Emeric cleared his throat. "My name is Emeric Vexley, and this is—"

"Fadeya Elaris," she said quickly, unable to look away from those hauntingly familiar features.

At her name, the woman staggered slightly, one hand reaching blindly for the doorframe as if suddenly unmoored. She stared, mouth slightly agape, as if seeing a ghost.

"Fadeya?" the woman breathed, her voice fragile. "Can it be true?"

Fadeya's heart hammered violently. "Do you ... know me?"

The woman moved suddenly, fiercely, pulling her into a crushing embrace. "I thought you lost," she whispered fiercely, voice breaking as tears soaked Fadeya's shoulder.

Finally, the woman stepped back, tears shimmering on her cheeks as she took in Fadeya's stunned expression. "You look so much like him. Your eyes ..." She laughed shakily, wiping tears away hurriedly. "I'm sorry, it's just—"

"Who are you?" Emeric interrupted, protectively stepping closer to Fadeya.

The woman straightened, sorrow and joy warring openly on her features.

"I'm Cora," she said, voice trembling slightly. Her eyes, so painfully like Fadeya's, searched desperately for recognition. "Cora Elaris. Your father's sister."

Chapter 22

SAME SPARK, SAME FIRE

FADEYA

The inside of the cottage was sun-warmed and lived-in, charming in a way that felt quietly intentional. Daylight spilled through crooked windows framed with lace curtains. The plastered walls were slightly uneven, painted a sage green and accented with shelves crowded with books, glass jars filled with herbs and flower petals, and a few trinkets that looked far older than the cottage itself. A kettle whistled on the stove, and somewhere nearby, the scent of fresh bread mingled with lavender and thyme. It wasn't grand or polished, but it was *welcoming*.

A scraping sound pulled Fadeya's attention toward the hearth, where something large and dark shifted into motion. A creature unfolded itself from the corner. It looked like a domestic cat, if you ignored the fact that it was the size of a panther. Its body was lean, all sinew and bone under black fur that seemed to drink in the light. Its ears were long and soft-looking, flopping to the sides like a young puppy. And its tail swished slowly, back and forth, like a pendulum counting down.

Then it made a sound. Low. Rumbling. Not a purr, not a growl, but something in between.

"Oh, hush," Cora said, waving a hand. "They're family, Zareth."

Zareth blinked and padded forward, his footsteps soundless on the wooden floor. He moved toward Fadeya, tail flicking once like a whip, and sniffed the air around her before giving an approving grunt.

"Zareth's my bondmate," Cora said, turning back toward the hearth. "Don't let the dramatics fool you; he's a softie."

"Liar," Zareth muttered in a gravelly voice, low but clear.

Emeric smirked. "I think I like him."

"Of course, you do," Fadeya muttered, shaking her head as she slowly followed Cora toward the kitchen area. Her limbs still trembled slightly from the whirlwind of emotions: shock, disbelief, awe. *She's my aunt ... How did I not know about her?*

Cora moved toward the stove, grabbing herbs and vegetables from hanging bundles. Within minutes, she had a pot boiling over the fire, the scent of savory root stew rising in a comforting wave.

"You've got your father's smile," she said over her shoulder. "Same spark. Same stubborn fire."

Fadeya tried to respond but only managed a nod. Her throat was still tight.

Cora handed her a bowl and nodded toward the table. "Eat. I'm not a chef, but I promise it won't kill you."

Fadeya sat, fingers gripping the warm bowl. She hadn't realized how hungry she was until now. Beside her, Emeric was already spooning stew into his mouth like he hadn't eaten in days.

"So," Cora said, easing into a chair with Zareth curling protectively at her side. "Tell me about your studies. What's your focus at Astral Unison?"

The question landed like a stone in Fadeya's stomach.

Fadeya hesitated, staring down at the steam curling from her bowl. "I ... I'm not actually a student."

Cora's brows drew together. "You're not?"

Fadeya's fingers tightened on her spoon. "My twin sister, Seraphina, is. I came to the university ... under different circumstances."

Emeric looked up at her but said nothing. He knew this was her story to tell.

Cora's voice shifted slightly, spoon frozen in her hand. "What circumstances?"

Fadeya forced herself to look her aunt in the eye. "A professor recruited me. She said I could help her watch for bondings. Report them to her."

The air in the cottage went still.

Cora rose from her seat in a single, smooth motion. "*Hera?*" Her face had gone pale, her expression hard.

Fadeya and Emeric both jerked upright.

"Yes," Fadeya said quickly. "Why?"

"She's *still* at it," Cora hissed as she began pacing. Her hands trembled, not with fear, but fury. Zareth stood, too, his eyes locked on Cora, tail flicking in agitation.

"Still doing her dirty work in the shadows," Zareth growled. "Still pulling strings where no one can see."

"What do you mean?" Emeric asked sharply. Putting his spoon down.

Cora stopped pacing and turned back to face them, her eyes blazing. "She's the reason your father left the magical realm."

Fadeya's breath caught. *What does that mean?*

Cora stepped closer, her voice burning. "Your father was one of the most gifted students of his generation. Brilliant. Relentless. When he graduated, he was offered the most prestigious internship at the university, under Hera. He was honored." She paused, the memory crossing her face like a cloud over the sun.

"But something changed. One term into the internship, and he stopped talking to me. He stopped sending letters. When I finally tracked him down, he told me only one thing: he had discovered something. Something he shouldn't have. And he was leaving."

Fadeya leaned forward, barely able to breathe. "Did he ever tell you what it was?"

"No." Cora's voice was flat. "He said knowing would put me in danger. That he was already marked."

Fadeya blinked hard. "So, he ran?"

Cora looked at her, eyes filled with a pain that had long since scarred over. "He returned to the human world. Said it was the only place he would be safe. A few years passed, and then I got a letter. He'd married and had twins. He said he was happy." Her mouth quivered slightly. "I didn't hear from him again until a decade ago. A short note. Said he was thinking of visiting, but he never made it."

Fadeya slowly lowered her eyes, her thoughts a swirling mess of grief and confusion. "He never told us. Never even mentioned he had a sister."

Cora nodded solemnly. "Travel between the mortal and magical realms is rare. Controlled. You don't just hop over for a visit. I imagine he didn't want to open the door to something that could hurt you. Or maybe he was protecting me. Maybe both."

Fadeya's fingers drifted along the rim of her bowl, her thoughts unraveling. "He said it was just a short work trip …" Her voice faltered, the memory tugging at something she hadn't let herself fully see. "He packed a bag. He … he was going to try. To come see you." The words tumbled out, raw and forming into something she hadn't pieced together until now. Her eyes widened slightly. "Oh." She swallowed. "There was an accident. He died … before he made it *here*."

Cora froze. For a long, aching moment, she said nothing. She just sat there, staring out the window like it could take her back in time. Then she let out a shaky breath, one hand rising to cover her mouth as her eyes filled with tears.

"I always wondered," she whispered, sitting back down in her chair. "For ten years, I've wondered why he never came. I thought maybe … maybe he changed his mind. Or something happened and he couldn't write." She looked up at Fadeya, tears sliding freely down her cheeks. "But he *tried*. He was coming."

Fadeya nodded, her own eyes blurring. "He was. He just … didn't make it."

Cora reached across the table and took Fadeya's hand in both of hers. Her grip was strong, grounding. "Thank you for telling me," she said hoarsely.

Fadeya squeezed her hands and whispered, "You're welcome." She took a moment, composing herself the best she could, given the circumstances, then she picked up her spoon and took a bite.

276

"Will you tell me more about him? What was he like?" she said after a moment.

Cora's expression softened, and Zareth lay down once more at her side, his long tail curling around the leg of her chair.

"Let's see ..." she murmured, rubbing her chin. "There was the time he decided we should build a treehouse."

Fadeya tilted her head, already smiling. "A treehouse?"

"In the middle of winter," Cora said, "he found this old, half-frozen pine in the woods behind our house, split straight down the trunk, barely standing. He swore it was perfect. Said it just needed some love. Typical." She chuckled as she remembered. "We snuck out for days with stolen nails, crooked boards, and a hammer that was probably cursed. The thing looked like it had been assembled by drunken squirrels, but we were so proud of it. Slept in it one night with a sleeping bag and a candle. Froze our asses off."

Fadeya laughed, the sound cracking open something in her chest.

"It collapsed the next morning," Cora said with a wry smile. "We were in trouble for weeks, but that was your father. Always building something, even if it wasn't meant to last. He just wanted to try. Wanted *us* to try."

Fadeya smiled faintly, but her gaze dropped to her hands. "He sounds so much like Seraphina," she murmured. Her chest ached with the sudden, hollow tug of her sister's absence.

Cora poured some more tea in her cup, then her expression grew distant, her voice quieter. "He was funny. Not the kind that told jokes, but the kind that made you laugh without meaning to because he saw the world differently. He could find wonder in anything. A broken tree, a shooting star, or a coin in a fountain. He was a dreamer."

She paused for a moment before taking a sip. "But more than that, he was *kind*. He was the type of person who remembered your favorite color, who noticed when you'd had a hard day, and brought you a stupid flower he picked just to make you smile. He believed people were good, even when they didn't deserve it."

Cora looked at Fadeya, tears welling in her eyes again. "He encouraged everything I did. Every idea, every ambition. Even when they were ridiculous. He made you feel like the impossible was always just a little out of reach, but never too far. And stars help anyone who made you feel small. He'd come for them with fire and fury."

Fadeya didn't realize she was crying until Cora leaned over and began rubbing slow, soothing circles across her back. "That's how I remember him, too," she whispered. "He always encouraged us to dream big."

The room around them seemed suspended in a kind of spell. The fire in the hearth had burned low, its glow turning golden against the crooked walls, while the scent of steeped herbs lingered like incense. Outside, the light shifted inch by inch across the windowpanes, fading from the brightness of late afternoon into the long, honeyed hush of early evening.

They traded stories the way one might pass a favorite book. They laughed, too—not the hollow kind, but the laughter that slips out between sentences, fragile and real. And through it all, Fadeya felt something knitting together in her chest, an ache she hadn't known was there, easing for the first time in months.

Eventually, Emeric stirred and stood, stretching until his spine gave a pop. "We should head back," he said gently, placing his hand on Fadeya's shoulder. "The sun is nearly gone. If the university gates lock before we get in, we'll be sleeping in the forest."

Fadeya nodded, though she didn't move. She wasn't ready. Not yet.

"Wait," Cora said. She crossed the room, her bare feet quiet on the wood floor. She knelt beside a chest tucked beneath the window and flipped the lid open, rummaged for a moment, then pulled something free. A book.

Fadeya's breath caught. The leather cover was weathered, edges curled like leaves in autumn. She knew that journal. Not that one specifically, but one just like it. *Her father's.*

"I found it in the things he left behind," Cora said, brushing a bit of dust from the cover. "He wrote constantly when we were kids. Always had a notebook with him. This one ..." She hesitated. "This one was from right before he left. The last few months he spent here."

She handed it over, and Fadeya took it slowly.

"I tried to read it once," Cora said, rubbing the back of her neck. "Got a few pages in, but I couldn't do it. I didn't have the heart. I thought maybe, one day, I'd have the strength to finish it, but I never did." She looked at Fadeya, hope stirring behind her tired smile. "Maybe you are."

Fadeya turned the journal over in her hands, thumbing the cracked spine, the soft corners. "Thank you," she whispered.

Cora stepped forward and wrapped her in a fierce embrace. "I always hoped I'd meet you someday. And Seraphina, too. Maybe one day I'll have the opportunity to meet her, as well."

Fadeya buried her face in her aunt's shoulder, nodding. "I know she would love that."

They left in silence, the journal tucked safely in Fadeya's satchel.

She turned only once, just before the trees swallowed the cottage from view. Cora was still watching, her silhouette framed by the doorway. Zareth's eyes glowed faintly at her feet like embers that refused to go out.

SERAPHINA

The wind whipped through the university courtyard as Seraphina, Cordelia, and Evander rushed through the massive stone archway, footfalls echoing in frantic haste. It was early evening, the sun dipping beneath the horizon, but the three could see lights blazing in nearly every window of the infirmary wing ahead. Classes had been canceled; rumors about Isadora's dire condition had spread quickly, drawing most of the faculty and half the student body into anxious vigil.

Seraphina's heart hammered in her chest, not only from the sprint, but from adrenaline fueled by something else, something far more powerful. Within her soul, she felt a tug, an ancient presence stirring. She pushed it down, resisting the mental intrusion that clawed at the edges of her mind.

They burst through the oaken doors of the infirmary. At the far end, Professor Flora bent over a table loaded with alchemical equipment. Her eyes flicked up at the newcomers.

"Thank the stars you're here," Professor Flora said, a measure of urgency woven into her normally calm voice.

Cordelia held up the blood thorn, its dark crimson petals exuding a faint glow. "I hope this will be enough. We found it two days ago."

"Has it been two days?" Seraphina whispered. Her voice sounded oddly hollow in her own ears. She tried to keep her tone steady. Aleron stood up from where he had been keeping silent vigil and made his way over to her. Gently taking her hand, he led her to a chair and guided her to sit.

"It still holds potency," the professor said with relief as she examined it. She motioned for Cordelia and Evander to help prepare the instruments. "We have precious little time. Isadora's condition worsened earlier today. She's fighting, but her vitals are getting worse."

Seraphina watched Cordelia's hands shake as she wiped a strand of sweaty hair from Isadora's temple. Evander hovered close, fear etched across his features. Her heart pounded, each beat echoing the silent plea in her chest. *Please. Let this work. Let her live.* She drew the cloak tighter around her shoulders, fingers fidgeting with the frayed edge as if the motion could keep the panic from rising.

"I'll begin the distillation," Professor Flora said as she poured a yellow liquid into a beaker. "Evander, fetch fresh water from the well outside. Cordelia, keep careful watch on the temperature here." She gestured to a thermometer connected to the beaker she was stirring.

Aleron sat close to Seraphina, his arm wrapped tightly around her shoulders. He kept sneaking glances in her direction, worried, searching, but his concern only twisted guilt deeper into her chest. *This moment wasn't about her. It was about Isadora.* So, she mustered her best *I'm-okay* smile, even if it didn't quite reach her eyes, and gave his knee a gentle pat.

She felt her bondmate's magic stir beneath her skin, a quiet thrum, curling just beneath her sleeve like a secret. The connection was there, constant, but now it flared with purpose, reacting to her panic with a silent urgency that matched the frantic rhythm of her heart.

The dragon was awake. His presence pressed against her mind, not with words, but with sensation, a deep echo that rippled through her chest.

Do something, he seemed to whisper.

Seraphina drew in a sharp breath as something shifted in her ribs, low and aching, like her heart was no longer her own. Her feet moved of their own accord as she crossed the room toward Isadora's bedside. There was magic building beneath her skin. She clenched her fists, trying to steady her breath. The fear, the pressure, the unknown, none of it mattered. Not compared to the girl lying before them.

Seraphina's throat tightened, but she didn't look away. Instead, she leaned into the dragon's magic. It wrapped around her like armor. Not something to fear. *Something to wield.* Torrents of energy swept into her mind with the force of a rising tide. It steadied her, giving her strength and clarity.

She drew in a long, trembling breath and closed her eyes. And there it was again, that flicker. That pull. The dragon's magic didn't scream. It *sang*.

Help her, it hummed, almost gently.

Heat bloomed across her palms as she let go of the tight grip she had on herself, magic rising from deep inside her. It wasn't visible, but she could feel it, threading outward, weaving itself into the medicine Professor Flora was mixing like a final, vital ingredient.

Professor Flora worked swiftly, grinding the blood thorn's petals and roots. The mortar released a pungent aroma, sweet yet metallic. When she finally completed the mixture, she poured the dark liquid into a long, narrow vial.

She carried it gently toward Isadora's bed. The girl lay limp, her complexion like parchment. Cordelia sat by her side, anxiety turning her knuckles white.

"Isadora," Cordelia whispered, voice trembling. She took Isadora's hand. "You'll be alright."

Professor Flora tilted Isadora's head and poured the medicine past her lips. Everyone in the room watched in tense silence, clinging to hope. For a long, breathless moment, nothing happened.

Then, Isadora stirred.

A rasping cough escaped her lips; her eyelids fluttered. Professor Flora guided the rest of the infusion, her clinical composure gone and replaced with a look of relief.

Cordelia brought one hand up to her mouth, tears brimming at the corners of her eyes. "She's waking," she breathed.

"Thank the stars," Evander whispered. Then, in a louder, broken tone, "Isadora, can you hear me?"

A faint voice parted Isadora's lips. "E … Evander?" she croaked, eyelids heavy, but open.

Cordelia exhaled a sob, leaning her forehead against Isadora's. Evander let out a trembling laugh. The tension in the room unwound like a loosened spring, relief coursing through everyone present.

She looked impossibly small beneath the blankets, her breath shallow, barely stirring the air. Aleron knelt, his hand settling lightly on Isadora's shoulder.

Evander stood and drew Seraphina into a fierce embrace. "Thank you," he whispered, his voice rough with emotion. He pulled back just enough to look her in the eyes. "Thank you, both of you. I couldn't have done this without you. I'm in your debt."

Seraphina swallowed, forcing a smile. "I'm just glad we could help," she murmured as he turned to Cordelia and hugged her, as well.

Cordelia's face was wet with tears when she looked up, her eyes locking with Seraphina's across the space. That look hit Seraphina like a blow.

They had done it. They had saved Isadora's life. *Did I just wield magic?* The thought pulsed inside her like a heartbeat, sharp and disorienting. Her hands still tingled. Her skin still hummed with heat. No one else had noticed, but *she* had felt it. Rising from the bond, rushing through her veins, altering something fundamental inside her.

Professor Flora offered Seraphina a smile and a squeeze on the arm, a silent thank you. Then she turned her attention fully to Isadora, already checking her vitals, murmuring observations under her breath as color slowly returned to the girl's cheeks.

Seraphina stepped back, letting the whirlwind of celebration rush past her. Relief hung thickly in the air. Laughter rang out in sharp bursts, feet pounded down stone corridors, and voices braided into one another, sharing the news. It should have comforted her. It didn't.

When the commotion had settled, she slipped out and headed back to her dormitory, needing a reprieve from the emotions of the evening and the weight of everyone's gratitude. The door closed behind her with a thud. *What just happened in there?*

She didn't realize how hard she was shaking until her knees gave way. She caught herself on the edge of the bed, breathing hard. Her hand drifted to the place on her arm where the mark hummed under her sleeve.

The dragon's eyes flashed in her mind. Her body still echoed with the sound of his roar, as if it had carved itself into her soul.

A knock. Soft. Tentative.

"Sera?" Aleron said, sounding uncertain. "Are you alright?"

She didn't answer, just moved to the door and opened it.

Aleron stood there scanning her face. Searching. She stepped aside, letting him enter. "Aleron ..." she managed, barely. Her lips quavered. She tried again, but her breath hitched, breaking under the pressure of what she couldn't say.

Then he was there. No hesitation. His arms were around her, anchoring her as she broke down, sobbing into his shoulder. The first real emotion she'd shown all night.

"Hey ... hey. It's okay. Isadora's going to be fine," he said, one hand stroking her back.

"It's not about Isadora," she whispered, wiping her tears with the back of her hand.

His arms tightened, and he guided her to the chaise at the foot of the bed.

"I'm here, Seraphina," he said, kneeling in front of her, like she was something fragile and holy. "Whatever it is, you can tell me."

Seraphina's breath came in ragged gasps, the world narrowing until all that existed was the thundering beat of her heart. Her fingers shook as they curled around the fabric of her sleeve, pulling it up inch by inch, until the bondmark etched into her skin gleamed softly in the candlelight.

"It happened after we found the blood thorn," she murmured. Her eyes darted nervously to Aleron's face, searching for something to ease the chaos inside her mind. "It was a dragon, Aleron. Colossal, ancient ... I didn't mean to, but we were cornered and out of time. I acted purely on instinct, and then—" Her voice broke, words tumbling into silence as dread twisted sharply in her chest. "He bonded to me."

Aleron's eyes widened, shock momentarily robbing him of speech. He reached out instinctively, fingers grazing her arm. "You ... you bonded with a *dragon*?"

Her eyes shimmered with unshed tears, her voice shaking as fiercely as her hands. "I feel him constantly, like he's wrapped around my soul. Watching, waiting. I feel like something feral and devastating has been poured inside me, and now it moves through my veins, rage, power, more than I can contain." She bowed her head, her hair cascading like a curtain around her shoulders. "I don't know if I can bear it."

Aleron's eyes softened, his hand reaching out again, tenderly cupping her cheek and lifting her face to his. "He chose you, Seraphina. He bonded with you because he knows you *can* handle it. Because you're worthy."

She leaned helplessly into his touch, tears slipping silently down her face. "I'm terrified, Aleron. What if I lose myself in it? The power … it feels infinite, unstoppable. Too immense for someone like me."

"This fear that you have, it will pass," he promised, voice deep with understanding. "When Lyrae first bonded with me, I didn't think I was worthy of it. Every day, every moment, it grows clearer, stronger. It will for you, too." He rose fluidly from his knees, settling onto the chaise beside her, his warmth grounding her.

She sniffled, shaking her head in quiet protest. "It's more than feeling unworthy, Aleron. Though stars know, I feel that, too." She sucked in a shaky breath, rubbing angrily at the tears that refused to stop. "I wish I could make you understand; it's like wildfire beneath my skin, threatening to consume me whole. I'm scared I'll burn from the inside out."

Aleron drew her gently into his arms, fingers softly threading through her hair, pushing the damp strands behind her ear. "Oh, Seraphina," he whispered, adoration in his tone that stole her breath. "You are the kindest, strongest person I've ever known. From the moment I met you, I saw greatness burning bright within you. Every day, you inspire me to be better, to be worthy of the light you bring into this world."

His thumb gently brushed across her cheek, wiping away another tear. "You have changed me, opened my eyes and my heart."

His words chased away some of the shadows lurking at the edges of her mind, grounding her in a semblance of calm. Seraphina lifted her face, searching his eyes, and then slowly brushed her lips against his. The world around them faded away as he pulled her closer, his grip tightening, a silent vow passing between them.

Their kiss deepened, passion rising like an unstoppable tide. She felt her fears recede beneath his strength, his touch igniting sparks along her skin.

He pulled away for a moment and looked at her.

"I can't think clearly when you look at me like that." She laughed through her tears. Her fingertips drifted to his chest.

"Then don't think," Aleron whispered. His lips hovered just inches from hers, their breath mingling as he leaned closer, "Just *feel.*"

Heat blossomed within her, spreading like wildfire, replacing all her fears with insatiable need. She slid her arms around his neck, pulling him against her as she lay back on the bed, claiming his lips in a kiss that seared through her body.

Aleron's hands moved with confidence and hunger, sliding beneath her shirt, fingertips tracing teasing circles along her sensitive skin. "You're so beautiful," he whispered, voice rough with longing as he tugged the fabric upward.

"Aleron …," she breathed, lifting her arms, allowing him to slip the fabric free. The candlelight danced over her bare skin, highlighting her curves and the delicate flush spreading from her cheeks down her neck.

His gaze was worshipful as he explored every inch of her with slow, tantalizing touches. His mouth followed his calloused hands, blazing a trail of kisses across her collarbone, her shoulders, down to the swell of her breasts. Seraphina arched beneath him, her fingers gripping his hair, guiding him closer, needing more.

"I want every part of you," Aleron breathed against her skin. She reached for him, quickly undoing the buttons of his shirt, revealing his chest, the rich tone of his skin glistening softly in the candlelight. Her lips brushed against him, tracing the planes of muscle, the steady, fierce beat of his heart matching her own frantic rhythm.

He groaned deeply as she tugged his shirt away, her hands exploring every inch of him. "I need you," she whispered, her voice barely audible but filled with desperation.

Aleron's eyes darkened with intensity. "Seraphina," he rasped, capturing her mouth in another searing kiss, his hands swiftly removing the rest of their clothes. Skin pressed to skin, a carnal fervor ignited between them, an undeniable force driving them closer.

In that moment, she caught sight of something extraordinary: a faint, shimmering outline of wings spread gently from Aleron's back, ephemeral yet breathtakingly beautiful. Her breath caught sharply, heart stuttering as awe mixed deliciously with desire.

They moved together fluidly, passionately, their bodies perfectly attuned to each other's rhythms. Every touch, every kiss, stoked the fire between them.

When they finally joined completely, pleasure surged through her veins, sweeping away every lingering trace of fear and uncertainty. Aleron's name fell from her lips in a broken plea, echoed in his deep, fervent whispers as he followed her into bliss.

Yet even as she clung to him, breathless and safe in his embrace, she felt a distant shadow within, an ever-watchful presence, a reminder that *he* was still waiting

Chapter 23

THE PROPHECY OF THE FRACTURED REALMS

FADEYA

I was told that bonding would make me stronger. What they didn't say is that it would also make me softer. That I would feel everything more deeply, the pain of others, the weight of silence, the joy of small things. That's the price of connection. And the gift."

The words echoed through Fadeya's mind like a haunting refrain, clinging to the edges of her thoughts as she lay beneath the low ceiling of her hidden room. The journal lay open on her chest, her father's scrawl branded into her memory, a scar she hadn't expected to uncover.

He had a sister. A truth so impossible it still didn't feel real.

She blinked up at the wooden beams overhead, her eyes dry and aching. The candle on the floor had long since guttered out, smoke-stained wax pooling like blood on stone. Faint blue light spilled through the slats in the wall, just enough to brush against the golden curls resting beside her.

Emeric's arm lay draped across her waist, heavy with sleep. She turned her head slowly, just enough to watch him in the soft light. The line between his brows, so often etched deep with worry, had vanished. In sleep, he looked younger. Lighter. Like something within him had eased.

His bond was changing him.

Her heart ached at the sight. Her father had been right. This was what bonding could be.

Carefully, Fadeya slipped out from under his arm, moving slowly enough not to disturb him. Her feet touched the cool stone floor, and she reached for her clothes—her familiar black tunic, cinched at the waist with a leather belt, slim-fitting slacks, and her well-worn boots.

She braided her hair quickly, fingers moving out of habit. Last, she fastened Aurora's amulet around her neck, the cool metal settling against her collarbone like a whispered secret.

Does Hera know it was forged by Aurora herself? The thought flickered as her fingertip traced the delicate engraving around the stone.

She glanced back over her shoulder. Emeric hadn't stirred. *Should I wake him?* She hesitated. *No. Let him sleep. He needed it.* The past few days had hollowed him out, sleepless nights, constant worry, the weight of not knowing if Isadora would pull through.

Fadeya could still see the way his shoulders had dropped when they'd finally heard she was going to be okay. That first breath he'd taken, like he'd been drowning and had just broken the surface. He hadn't said much, just wrapped his arms around her and held on, like he didn't trust the world to stay steady without her there beside him.

He deserved this moment of peace.

Slipping the journal into her satchel, Fadeya stepped into the corridor and quietly shut the door. Somewhere far off, a charm chimed with the morning bells, its soft note echoing through the halls like a summons.

Hera would be waiting for their morning tea.

She paused at the door to the professor's study, her hand hovering just shy of the handle. *Had Hera known? About her father's sister? Had she kept it from her deliberately?* She knocked once. And stepped inside.

Fadeya felt the tension hit her like a physical force the moment she crossed into Hera's study. The room was darker than normal, curtains drawn so tightly against the rising sun that the air felt dense and oppressive. A single lamp flickered weakly on Hera's desk, illuminating stacks of notes and scribbled parchments that hinted at the professor's increasingly frantic obsession.

Hera stood behind her desk, shoulders rigid as if braced for battle, turquoise eyes gleaming dangerously in the dim light. A bottle of amber liquid sat uncorked beside a glass, half-full, where her usual teacup might have been. Her typical meticulous appearance was frayed, a carefully crafted facade starting to unravel at the edges. Her hair, always bound in severe discipline, now spilled messily from its pins, strands escaping like cracks in a crumbling wall.

"Close the door," Hera snapped, her voice slicing through the silence. Fadeya felt her pulse quicken as she obeyed, pulling the door shut behind her, trapping them both in the tension-thickened gloom.

Fadeya dipped her chin in a show of deference as she tried to keep her expression neutral. "Professor," she said softly, "good morning."

"Something monumental happened last night. A surge so powerful it nearly shattered the wards." Her voice was full of anger, and beneath it, a hint of fear. The lamplight accentuated the pale scar running down her face.

Fadeya stiffened, the coil of unease tightening in her chest. She resisted the urge to fidget with her amulet. "I'm … not sure I follow," Fadeya ventured. "Could you elaborate?"

Hera's pacing grew more agitated. She ran a hand through her hair, loosening a pin, and a curl slipped free. "A *bonding*," she said, spitting out the last word with rage. "A major bonding, not the trivial ones we sometimes see with lesser creatures. No. This felt ancient. *Significant*." She paused, eyes narrowed on Fadeya. "Enormous, terrifying power. And it's gone unsanctioned."

Fadeya tried to keep her face a mask of polite neutrality. Inside, her mind swirled with questions. *Was it Emeric or someone else?*

"I heard some vague rumors yesterday," Fadeya replied, "about an expedition for a rare medicinal plant. Something about a miraculous recovery in the infirmary." Her eyes drifted thoughtfully. "But I haven't heard anything that suggests a major bonding."

Hera leaned forward again, the corners of her mouth twisting. "Can you imagine how this looks for me? My entire reputation rests on my control over these wards, and that includes the detection of any unlicensed bond forging." She exhaled a long, shuddering breath.

Fadeya took a tentative step closer. The thick rug muffled her movement. "I'm certain you'll uncover the truth, Professor," she said, allowing her tone to sound admiring, if only slightly. Perhaps stroking Hera's ego would temper her wrath. "No one is better equipped than you are to investigate such an occurrence."

Hera snorted again, though the glimmer of vanity did not go unnoticed. "Perhaps," she allowed. "But I can't do it alone. We have nearly a hundred students." Her eyes flashed. "I need your help."

Fadeya paused, steeling herself. "Me?"

"Yes, you," Hera snapped. "Rumors. I want to know the moment you catch even a whisper of who might have forged this bond. And if you discover evidence, you come straight to me."

Fadeya inclined her head. "I will do what you ask, of course."

Hera sank into her chair, pressing her fingers together as if she were a queen hearing a subject's pledge of loyalty. Her lips curved into something resembling a smile, but it was more predatory than friendly. "Good. I will not be undermined, Fadeya. The university's wards, its secrets, *my secrets*, must remain intact. If someone bonded to a powerful creature, it means they've circumvented the university's protocols. That's treasonous in my eyes. We must root it out and handle it accordingly."

Fadeya repressed a shiver, forcing her posture to remain steady as her mind went to Emeric and his bond. "What if the bonding was accidental?" she asked hesitantly. "What if the student didn't realize what they were doing?"

"Ignorance is no excuse for the devastation a misaligned bond could bring. Bonds like this have repercussions far beyond a single person or creature." She shifted in her seat, her stare distant, almost haunted. Then, with a blink, her focus returned. "I want answers."

Fadeya bowed her head, her face an impassive mask. Inside, her thoughts churned like a tempest. "As you wish, Professor," she managed.

A tense silence filled the room. Only the gentle crackle of the lamp's flame broke the stillness.

Finally, Hera dismissed her with a curt nod, picking up a quill and glaring at a stack of parchment as if it had personally offended her.

Fadeya paused at the threshold, turning back just enough to meet Hera's eyes. "I'll keep watch," she said. "You'll know anything I learn."

"See that I do," Hera replied, the shadows under her eyes making her look older. "And Fadeya,"

She halted, the doorknob in her hand. "Yes?"

"Don't fail me," Hera said. The words were calm but carried a threat that coiled through Fadeya's spine.

She inclined her head once more, stepped into the hallway, and shut the door behind her. Only then did she allow her shoulders to sag.

She had no intention of betraying Emeric, or whoever had caused that surge, but to keep suspicions from swirling, she'd have to play the game carefully.

Her steps turned toward the library. Emeric needed sleep, real rest, and she needed distance, space to clear her thoughts. At this hour, the corridors were quiet, the library likely still empty. Exactly what she needed. A place to think. A place to read.

She hadn't finished her father's journal, but the words had already taken root in her mind. It felt like she was circling something important, pieces scattered across the page like a puzzle waiting to be solved.

SERAPHINA

That morning, the library reverberated with magic, its power pressing against Seraphina's senses as she sat at the massive moonstone table in its heart. The bondmark etched upon her forearm glowed faintly, shimmering silver against her pale skin. Around her, floating spheres of light hovered and adjusted themselves, illuminating the texts spread open before her.

She leaned closer, frustration twisting her features into a scowl, her emerald eyes narrowing as they traced the lines of endless, irrelevant words. Each tome was richly bound, filled with stories of Astral Unison University's glorious past, its triumphs immortalized, but nothing spoke of dragons or bonding with them.

Seraphina's sigh echoed softly, swallowed by the cavernous space. The library sensed her restlessness; it shifted, shelves whispering secrets she couldn't quite decipher. Her bondmark flared once more, sending tendrils of fire through her veins, fierce and thrilling.

"This is ridiculous," she muttered, frustration turning her voice sharp as she shut another book with a snap.

The air shifted subtly, charged by the quiet arrival of someone familiar. She lifted her head, heart stuttering slightly as Aleron strode toward her. His dark eyes met hers immediately, concern engraved on his face.

"I've been looking for you everywhere," he said as he leaned in and pressed a kiss against her forehead.

Seraphina offered a half smile, exhaustion dimming its edges. "I needed some answers."

His brow furrowed as he noticed the weary shadows beneath her eyes. "Have you found anything?"

She shook her head slowly, frustration sharpening her voice again. "Nothing useful. Nothing about dragons or bonding. Just endless histories of the university's founder and her legacy."

He reached across the moonstone table, his hand enveloping hers. "Perhaps you're searching in the wrong place."

Her eyes narrowed slightly. "I've been here half the night."

A rustle interrupted her as the shelves shifted subtly, revealing a row of older books she hadn't seen during her many hours of searching. A thin book bound in dark leather, etched with silver runes, seemed to move forward on the shelf, beckoning to her.

"What is that?" Seraphina rose and moved as if drawn by an invisible thread. The moment her fingertips brushed the smooth leather, power jolted through her veins, igniting her bondmark.

"The library must have wanted you to find this one," Aleron said softly, stepping close behind her.

"It would appear so," she whispered, opening the delicate cover. Her voice trembled as she began to read aloud:

The Prophecy of the Fractured Realms

Born beneath the twilight's veil,
Twin fae sisters destined to fail.
Bound together, yet paths divide,
Light and shadow, side by side.
From their choices, the realms shall part,
A tear to break each sister's heart.
Through dragon's fire and starlight's divide,
Their bond shall waver, and love denied.
The realms each shall rend and break,
Humans and magic, two worlds they will make.
Yet, in the fracture, hope takes root,
As mortal stars tread fae's pursuit.
Human twins, flames mirrored true,
May heal the realms where sorrow grew.
Through dragon's bond, and starlight's call
A test of will could bind us all.
Should they falter, shadow reigns,
Darkness binding, hope in chains.
But if the shadows are undone,
The sundered realms shall become one.
Twins of twilight, twins of man,
Fate shall rest within their hands.
To heal, to shatter, the tale unknown,
To forge anew or continue alone.

Seraphina's eyes widened as she read it again. "Darkness binding ..." she murmured, fear lacing her voice.

Aleron's grip on her tightened protectively. "I think we should speak to Professor Eldryn," he suggested. "He knows more about ancient prophecies than anyone else."

Seraphina nodded reluctantly. "You may be right. I'm hesitant to reveal my bond to anyone, but he might be able to tell us more about this passage. Let's go see him."

They moved through the silent corridors, Aleron's presence steady beside her, a quiet lifeline. His hand wrapped gently around hers. Seraphina could feel the pull between them, the unspoken connection that had grown stronger with each passing day. His presence was a comfort, and she couldn't imagine going through this without him. She found herself wanting to say something, anything, but the thought of the prophecy, of everything that had been uncovered, held her words hostage.

He paused just before Eldryn's office, pulling her closer to him, eyes deep with intensity, fingertips gently cupping her cheek.

"You are not alone," he whispered. "Never."

FADEYA

Hidden in the shadows with her father's journal in her hands, Fadeya watched the scene unfold, her heart twisting with a mix of emotions she couldn't quite place. She had been in the library reading when her sister came in. She quickly noticed the difference in her sister, even from her hiding spot. That was a bondmark on her arm, and she had mentioned a dragon.

Had she bonded with a dragon?

The amulet around her neck warmed as if it sensed magic close by.

She followed them as they left the library, sticking to the shadows but trying to stay within earshot of their conversation. Seraphina's bond might be the one Hera was so angry about.

The pair stopped in front of a large office door, and Fadeya's jaw dropped when she witnessed their brief but intimate kiss. Aleron and Seraphina were … *together?*

Her thoughts spun wildly as she slipped unnoticed into the dimly lit study behind them, the shadows coiling obediently around her, shielding her from sight. Aleron and Seraphina sat at a polished round table, their attention fixed on a professor whose voice was too low to hear clearly from afar.

Drawing a deep breath, Fadeya tightened her grip on the amulet around her neck and moved closer.

SERAPHINA

Inside Eldryn's study, the professor listened intently as Seraphina recounted her discovery in the book. His expression grew darker with each passing word, shadows flickering across his aged face.

He has heard this before, Seraphina thought, watching the subtle crease deepen between his brows. She sat stiffly across from him, wrapped in Aleron's coat, the fabric too big in the shoulders but warm and most importantly, covering her bondmark.

"The Fractured Realms," Professor Eldryn finally said, his voice low and grave, "tell the story of fae twins: Onyx and Aurora. Onyx bonded with a dragon and succumbed to darkness, consumed utterly by the allure of unbridled power." He paused. "Aurora, however, chose duty over her own blood, founding this very university to preserve magic and education, though it broke her heart. And now the prophecy foretells the coming of human twins who will mend what was long ago torn asunder."

"Twins?" Seraphina whispered, the word catching uncomfortably in her throat. She felt an inexplicable tightness, as if the word itself tugged at a hidden memory, something important that hovered frustratingly beyond her grasp.

"Are dragons evil?" Seraphina's voice quivered as her mind instinctively reached out for her bondmate, *Vyrakthos.* Even now, she could feel the dragon's presence, listening, waiting patiently, alert, and curious.

Eldryn rubbed his thumb slowly against his lower lip as he considered her question. "Dragons embody primal magic, fierce, untamed. But evil? Not inherently. Yet their power can corrupt. There has only been one recorded bond with a dragon in history."

She tried to appear calm, but her thoughts churned. *One bond in all of history ... until now.*

"Twins," Aleron muttered. "Could one person not mend what is broken?"

Eldryn looked up at him. "Mending requires more than strength. It requires reflection. Unity. The story of Onyx and Aurora is not a tale of light triumphing over darkness. It's a tale of one who *split*, and one who *endured*. To heal what was fractured, both pieces must return."

Aleron glanced at Seraphina and immediately caught the tension in her posture, the way her shoulders had gone stiff.

"Thank you, Professor," he said, rising to his feet. "This has been ... enlightening. But we should let you return to your work."

Eldryn gave a slow nod, his gaze lingering on Seraphina. "The past has a way of resurfacing when you least expect it," he said.

Seraphina stood quickly, offering a faint, polite smile that didn't quite reach her eyes. The moment the door clicked shut behind them, she exhaled, long and shaky.

Aleron walked beside her, quiet for a few steps before speaking. "I'm not sure we actually learned anything new."

"No," Seraphina murmured, her stare fixed on the stone floor ahead. "But something about that felt ... important." She hesitated, then looked up at him. "I need to go and check in with Isadora. And Cordelia. I'm sure they haven't eaten today—I'll take them some breakfast." Her voice was soft, but resolute. "I need to think about all this more. Process it." She took a breath. "I'll meet you later?"

Aleron gave a gentle nod. "Of course. Take care of them. And yourself."

She offered him a small, grateful smile before turning down the corridor. He watched her go, the borrowed coat swaying with each step, until she disappeared around the corner.

FADEYA

Fadeya stood frozen against the wall, breath hitching. The prophecy curled within her mind, unraveling an unbearable truth. Sisters—twins—divided by destiny, one bathed in darkness, the other illuminated by light. Could it be about *them*?

Emeric. She needed Emeric, now.

Chapter 24

PEOPLE WORTH FIGHTING FOR

FADEYA

ldryn's words wouldn't stop repeating in her head. *Twins. Dragons. A fracture that could only be mended by two halves.* They rang through her thoughts with every step she took back toward her room. Her boots hit the floor with an uneven rhythm, faster than usual.

She reached the door and pushed it open. The sound of the door creaking on its hinges was sharper than she expected, startling in the otherwise quiet space.

Emeric was still in bed, half sitting up, bleary-eyed and drowsy in the late-morning light. One hand dragged through his rumpled curls; his other arm braced behind him. The blanket had slipped low around his waist, and warmth clung to his skin like sleep hadn't fully let go.

He looked at her, brows pinching slightly in concern as his gaze focused. "Fadeya?" His voice was thick with sleep. "Is everything alright?"

She hovered in the doorway for half a breath, her chest rising and falling too fast. "I—" Her throat was dry, the words catching. "I need to tell you something. It's important."

That woke him. He sat up straighter, the blanket rustling as he shoved it aside, eyes narrowing as he took in her expression. "What happened?"

Fadeya stepped inside and let the door fall shut behind her, the journal clutched tightly in her arms. She drew a shaky breath, crossing the room slowly, like her legs didn't fully trust the weight of what she carried.

"I finished my father's journal this morning …" she began, her voice raw, almost breaking. She stopped at the edge of the bed. "There's a ritual he describes, one Onyx used during the war. She learned how to siphon magic from the bonded."

She glanced up, meeting his eyes.

"Someone here at the university had learned the same ritual," she continued, her voice tightening. "Someone's been siphoning magic for *years*. That's what's causing the surges. The instability."

Emeric sat back, blinking once, then again, as the implications sank in. He ran a hand down his jaw. "Your father knew about this?"

"Apparently," she whispered. Her fingers were white-knuckled around the edges of the journal now. "Maybe that's why he left the realm."

Her hands trembled slightly as she opened the journal and read him the passage.

I found a fragment of Onyx's notes buried within the restricted archives. She had discovered a way to siphon magic from the bonded—draining power not just from magical beings, but from the threads that connect them. She called it the Mirrorwell Ritual.

It begins with the creation of a shadow tether. Once anchored, the siphoning is slow. Subtle. Most don't realize they're being drained until the symptoms show: fatigue, memory gaps, unstable magic, and emotional dissonance between bondmates. It can go unnoticed for years. Something similar has been happening here at Astral Unison. If someone has resurrected that knowledge … it would explain the arcane instability I've been feeling for months.

The silence between them thickened, heavy with the sudden clarity of danger. Emeric's jaw worked, his expression tight.

"Is there something else?" He already knew her well enough to read her.

The words spilled out in a rush. "Seraphina was in the library this morning. She has bonded with a dragon. I think … I think she's the one who caused the surge Hera was furious about."

The moment the words left her mouth, the room seemed to shift around them.

Emeric's breath caught audibly. "A *dragon*?" he repeated, the word hollowed out with disbelief. "Wait—" he blinked, confusion creeping in, "You spoke with Hera? She knows about this?"

"I went to meet her this morning, so she didn't suspect anything was amiss. She knows someone bonded without her approval," Fadeya said. "I thought it might've been you. Maybe it was *both* of you."

She moved to sit beside him on the edge of the bed, folding her legs slowly beneath her as if she'd finally allowed herself to feel the weight of it all. Her shoulder brushed his, solid and real.

"There's more," she said quickly, barely above a whisper. "Professor Eldryn told Seraphina about a prophecy. About *human twins*. Emeric—" She turned to him, her voice breaking around the words. "What if it's about us?"

She didn't know what answer she expected. Part of her was afraid of hearing one at all. The room felt like it was spinning; it all felt like too much to comprehend.

Emeric didn't speak right away. He simply turned toward her, his movements slow and steady, as if sensing the storm still churning behind her eyes.

"Fadeya," he said, voice quiet but firm, "listen to me. You have nothing to fear."

She stared at him, her breath caught somewhere between panic and relief. The silence stretched, charged with everything unspoken, everything *felt*.

And then she moved. She surged forward and closed the space between them, her lips crashing against his. It was desperate. Wild. A collision of fear and hope, of unspoken truths and aching hearts. Her fingers clutched at his shoulders as if holding on could somehow keep everything from spinning out of control.

Emeric's hands found her waist, steadying her, pulling her closer with quiet certainty. His kiss matched hers, full of questions, full of something deeper than either of them had dared speak aloud.

When they finally broke apart, breathless and shuddering, Emeric moved back just enough to meet her eyes, his thumb tracing soothing circles on the back of her hand. "There's something that's been on my mind this morning," he said, "Professor Flora's lesson a few weeks ago about the etherbloom tree. She said it reveals truths to royal fae who touch it. Maybe it can reveal the truth about who is siphoning magic."

"What exactly are you suggesting?" Fadeya's brows knitted together in uncertainty.

He drew a steadying breath. "We need allies. Prince Evander is our best chance. He might help you use the tree's magic."

She hesitated. "Do you truly think it's wise to bring other people into this?"

Emeric nodded, conviction firm in his voice. "He cares for your sister. He'll want answers, too, and his father has no love for Hera. I just know she has something to do with this."

Fadeya squared her shoulders, determination steeling her spine. "All right, let's go speak with him." She stood and started for the door.

"Wait," Emeric said softly, tugging her hand back. His eyes were troubled now, guilt shadowing their depths. "Perhaps you should go alone."

"Oh," she breathed, uncertainty clouding her courage.

"With Isadora," he began, his voice tight with pain, "after everything, I owe her an apology. It would be better if you spoke with Evander privately. He's less likely to help you if I'm there."

She nodded slowly, compassion mingling with her unease. "Meet me here later?"

Emeric's gaze softened, the tenderness returning. "I'll be here," he promised, squeezing her hand once more before reluctantly releasing her.

She watched him as he tugged on his shirt; she knew him well enough by now to see the tension in his jaw.

Without a word, he crossed the room and opened the door. For a moment, he paused there, his hand on the frame, his body half turned like he wanted to say something, but instead, he glanced over his shoulder, the corner of his mouth lifting in a crooked, familiar grin. He threw her a wink and then slipped out, the door clicking shut behind him.

Fadeya stood still, her chest tight with emotions. Fear. Hope. Guilt. Longing. All of them tangled and pulling her in different directions. She let the silence settle, then drew a slow, steadying breath.

There was no more time to hesitate. *It was time to find the fae prince.*

SERAPHINA

Seraphina pushed the door open with her shoulder, carefully balancing a breakfast tray of warm bread, fruit, and a steaming mug of tea. Flowers surrounded Isadora as she sat upright in bed in the infirmary, the color slowly returning to her cheeks.

Cordelia practically skipped beside her, eyes sparkling with relief and affection.

Seraphina smiled as she approached, the scent of lavender and honey drifting from the tray. "You're awake," she said softly, her voice carrying more emotion than she meant to let show. "And just in time—I brought food."

She set the tray on a table beside the bed. "You look absolutely radiant," Seraphina said, reaching out to squeeze Isadora's hand. "Like you've just woken from a refreshing nap, rather than, you know, recovering from near death."

Isadora chuckled. "Thank you, Sera. The doctor says I can leave the infirmary tonight."

Cordelia leaned forward, brushing a strand of hair tenderly from Isadora's face. "It takes far more than a brush with death to keep you down, my love. You're crafted from stardust and stubbornness."

Isadora grinned broadly, eyes filled with adoration. "It's true. My endurance is legendary."

The three girls shared a laugh that quickly quieted as footsteps echoed from the entrance.

Seraphina stiffened.

All eyes turned to the doorway, where Emeric entered hesitantly, eyes downcast, shifting uncomfortably from foot to foot.

Cordelia's light vanished in an instant, replaced by protective fury as she placed herself between Isadora and the doorway. Her voice was low, edged with steel. "You have some nerve showing your face here."

"I know," he replied quietly, raising both hands in surrender. His gray eyes were rimmed with exhaustion and remorse. "I've come to apologize. Isadora, what I did was incredibly wrong. I betrayed you and disrupted something sacred, and I will never forgive myself."

Cordelia crossed her arms, distrust radiating from her every movement. "Pretty words don't fix shattered bonds, Emeric," she spat.

He nodded solemnly, taking a cautious step forward. "I understand, but I've been doing everything in my power to make amends." He hesitated briefly, then continued, "My new bondmate, Zeruun, has helped me communicate with the Pegasus. I apologized deeply for my actions and … Zeruun facilitated a conversation. The Pegasus is healing and willing, if you still desire it, to give bonding another chance."

A stunned silence filled the room.

Isadora looked first to Cordelia, whose expression remained stormy and protective, then to Seraphina, who simply watched quietly. Finally, Isadora drew a deep breath and nodded slowly.

"I accept your apology, Emeric," Isadora said softly. "Thank you for reaching out to the Pegasus. It means more than you could know."

Cordelia scoffed, unconvinced. "You're far too forgiving. I'm surprised there was a creature willing to bond with him."

Emeric met Cordelia's fierce stare, sincere regret reflected on his face. "I promise, Cordelia, I'll spend whatever time I have left here at the university proving I'm worthy of that forgiveness."

His eyes shifted subtly toward Seraphina and looked at her arm, where she tugged at the sleeve covering her bondmark. She nodded at him, then moved to gather her things.

All morning, an irresistible pull had been drawing her toward her new bondmate. Questions burned inside her, insistent and unanswered. *It was time.*

"I, uh, I need to go," she murmured, stepping back, her bag slung over her shoulder. "I'm glad you're feeling better, Isadora. Cordelia ... Emeric." She offered a forced smile, avoiding Emeric's searching stare as she quickly turned toward the door.

As she stepped into the hall, she closed her eyes, focusing inward. "I'm ready," she whispered mentally, sending the message clearly into the ether.

Immediately, a deep, resonant voice echoed in response. *I will meet you at the Star Shrine.*

FADEYA

Sprawled on a blanket in the courtyard, Evander held a book above his face, shielding his eyes from the sun. Fadeya's steps slowed as she neared him. Doubts whispered at the edges of her mind, tugging at her caution, unsure if placing her trust in him was a mistake.

Evander sensed her presence and looked up, his dark eyes piercing through her uncertainty. A warm smile began to form. "Seraphina! How's Isadora doing?"

Fadeya froze momentarily, her heart tightening in her chest. She took a steadying breath, summoning courage from deep within. *You've come this far,* she reminded herself. "My name is Fadeya," she began softly, her voice barely above a whisper. "I'm Seraphina's twin sister."

Evander's eyes widened in surprise, and he slowly closed his book, confusion on his face. "Fadeya …" he murmured as though testing the name on his lips. "Twin sister?"

"I'm the one you met in the woods," she clarified, watching the realization dawn vividly in his expression.

"You …" His voice trailed off, his body now coiled with tension as he stood. A shadow crossed his face, skepticism sharpening his keen features.

"Yes," she said, sincerity coloring her tone. "I'm sorry I couldn't reveal myself then. I was frightened, confused."

Evander didn't speak, his gaze scanning her face like he was trying to spot a lie.

"The shadows that enveloped you that night," Evander whispered, questioning.

"It's complicated," she sighed, reaching up to reveal the delicate amulet nestled at her throat. "Professor Hera brought me here a couple of months ago. She told me Seraphina and the others were in danger, that she needed me to uncover who was sabotaging bonds. But now," she hesitated, her fingers anxiously tracing the intricate design of the amulet, "now I see it was all deception. She gave me this amulet to help me spy on the students here. It harnesses shadows." Each confession felt like a stone dropped into a pond—circles of dread widening inside her as she spoke.

Evander's expression twisted, visibly disturbed, as he dragged a hand through his dark hair, fingers catching slightly in the strands. "So, my father was right," he muttered, gravely.

How much should I tell him? The question echoed like a drumbeat in her mind. If they were going to survive this, if they truly needed an ally, then maybe the answer was *everything*.

"Hera told me to stay in the shadows," she murmured, letting her gaze search the garden for anyone who might be listening. "Now I understand why—because the archway steals human memories the moment we cross it."

Evander's head snapped up, eyes flaring. "You know about the archway?" The words were half challenge, half wonder. Realization kindled in his stare, and Fadeya's stomach twisted.

"You've known all along," she breathed, anger sparking beneath her shock. "Yet you said nothing to Seraphina. Nothing to Cordelia."

His silence weighed between them. At last, he stepped closer, voice rough. "It wasn't my secret to share. The Council of Twelve guards its truths, and I've learned not to meddle in their designs."

Confusion flickered across her face, but she pressed on, urgency sharpening every syllable. "Evander," Fadeya urged, "I know you have no reason to trust me, but I desperately need your help. You have to touch the etherbloom tree with me."

Intensity flashed in his gaze. "What do *you* know about the etherbloom tree? Where are you getting this information?"

"I know only that it reveals truths to fae royals who touch it," she answered, her voice quivering slightly.

"The prophecy," Evander murmured to himself, his eyes darkening further.

"Please, Evander," Fadeya pleaded. "Seraphina is in danger. She bonded without Hera's permission, and it's only a matter of time before she's discovered." She lowered her voice to keep panic from overcoming her. "She needs your help."

His eyes narrowed with cautious deliberation. "I suppose I shouldn't be surprised that you know about the dragon." He wiped at the sweat forming at the back of his neck. "If I ever need a royal spy, you're hired."

"I'm serious," Fadeya whispered, the words rushing forth. "Hera cannot find out about my sister's bond."

He reached into his pocket and fiddled with something for a moment, thinking. After pausing, he said, "It is true that I've never seen a bond like Seraphina's."

309

He looks almost haunted by it, Fadeya thought as she studied his expression. He looked toward the greenhouse in the distance and continued. "Her bond is powerful. Even more powerful than … than my father's."

Fadeya's mind spun. How could it be more powerful than the fae king's bond?

"If Hera is the person who has been causing disturbances in the bonds, she will stop at nothing to get her hands on Seraphina." Evander released a slow breath, tension easing slightly as he wiped his palms down the sides of his trousers. He nodded decisively, motioning for her to follow. "I suppose I do owe Seraphina a debt for going to find the blood thorn. I'll come with you to the etherbloom tree."

Relief swept through Fadeya, hope flooding her chest as she fell into step beside him. "Thank you," she whispered, gratitude resonating in her voice as they moved swiftly toward the greenhouse.

Warm air thick with floral fragrance enveloped them as they stepped into the greenhouse. Evander moved swiftly, navigating the winding stone paths, the sun filtering through glass panels and dappling his black hair with golden patches of light.

She matched his pace, as doubts swirled through her mind. *Could Evander truly be trusted?* She glanced at him sidelong, noting the determined set of his jaw. Whatever his motivations, his loyalty to Isadora seemed genuine enough.

At the greenhouse's heart stood the etherbloom tree, majestic and ancient. Its bark twisted toward the vaulted glass ceiling. It was more massive than she had thought it would be.

Evander halted abruptly and turned to face her. "Once we touch the tree, truths will be revealed. I can't say what we'll see, and they might not be the answers you're looking for. Are you ready for that?"

Fadeya swallowed hard but nodded firmly. "I have to be. For Seraphina."

He hesitated, searching her face as if trying to see beyond her words, before extending his hand toward her. "Then we do this together."

310

Fadeya placed her hand in his, and an electric charge surged between them, unexpected yet oddly comforting. Evander gave her a questioning look, then guided their joined hands forward, and together they pressed their palms against the etherbloom tree's bark.

Instantly, a wave of power surged from the tree, blinding white light enveloping them both. The world around them vanished, replaced by images that danced vividly in front of their eyes.

The vision rippled, then coalesced sharply into aching clarity. She recognized him instantly—her father, Dyaus, standing tall and defiant, his figure haloed in an eerie glow. He stood shaking, holding a scroll so tightly his knuckles turned white.

"Father ..." Fadeya whispered. Evander clutched her hand tighter.

"You really thought no one would ever discover this?" Dyaus challenged, voice clear, righteous fury echoing through every syllable. "This ends today. No more stealing magic from the bonds, no more hiding who you are."

In response, the shadowed figure across from him remained still, contemptuous silence stretching long enough to freeze the air. Dyaus took a half step back, instinct guiding him to brace himself just as a wave of vicious magic crashed against him. The force knocked him violently to his knees, and his spine arched in agony.

"No," Fadeya whispered, her father's words ringing in her ears.

Slowly, the shadow turned, revealing a woman with a jagged scar running down her face. Her eyes were dark pits gleaming with cold triumph, and her mouth curled into a cruel, satisfied smirk.

"Hera," Fadeya gasped, her voice choking on tears. Pain pierced her chest like a blade; betrayal flared so hot it turned grief into rage. *It was her. But why?*

Hera stepped forward with dreadful calm, her eyes sharp and merciless. "Oh, Dyaus," she said, her voice like poisoned honey. "You had such extraordinary promise, more than most. I truly thought you were destined for greatness."

She circled him slowly, her tone darkening. "Imagine my surprise when you disappeared without a word. *Vanished.* Left behind everyone who believed in you. Left me behind. For so long, I wondered *why*. Why you would flee, why you would abandon your place, your power. But now I see it clearly."

Her lips curled into a cruel smile. "You discovered the truth, didn't you? My secret. And instead of facing it, you ran. Not out of principle, not out of courage, but *fear*. How disappointing. In the end, you're nothing more than a *coward*."

Through the haze of pain, Dyaus fought against the crushing grip of Hera's magic, every muscle straining, breath ragged. He slowly stood once more, knees threatening to buckle, but his eyes, burning with defiance, never left hers.

"Cowardice may have driven me once," he rasped, blood on his teeth, voice low. "But now I have reasons greater than fear. I returned because I found something worth fighting for. *People* worth fighting for."

"Oh, what sweet sentiments," Hera sneered, eyes glittering as she leaned close, fingers curling ominously over his bondmark. The scroll fell from Dyaus's hands, glowing weakly as his bondmark flickered and dimmed.

Fadeya tried to scream, to move, to do anything, but she was frozen in place, helpless as the magic held her still. Her eyes locked on her father, his figure wavering in the shimmer of Hera's cruel spell. His strength was failing, draining away like sand in an hourglass.

He fell to one knee, then the other, sorrow in his eyes, but not for himself. With a trembling breath, he whispered, "My little stars." His voice cracked like a breaking promise.

Then he collapsed, his body crumpling to the ground, lifeless. The light in his eyes snuffed out.

Fadeya's scream finally tore free, a sound of pure heartbreak. Tears blurred her vision, hot and relentless, but they couldn't wash away the image of him lying there. She knew it wasn't happening in that moment. It was a vision of the past, but knowing didn't dull the ache. Knowing didn't stop her heart from fracturing into a thousand pieces, each one screaming the same truth: she was losing him. *Again.*

Evander wrapped his free arm around her, keeping her upright as the scene around them shifted.

Now, King Hadren appeared before them, not as the crowned ruler they knew, but as a young man, no older than Evander. He stood in the very spot they occupied, his expression dazed, as though he, too, had been pulled through time. Confusion flickered across his features as he looked around the greenhouse. Slowly, reverently, he reached out with both hands and placed them on the trunk of the etherbloom tree.

The moment his palms touched the bark, the world around them shifted.

A deep hum vibrated through the earth, and Hadren's eyes flew wide, glowing faintly as the vision took hold. His breath caught, then, suddenly, his thoughts were no longer his own.

Projected before them, the vision unfolded:

Twin humans stood back-to-back at the Star Shrine deep in the woods. The trees around them rose like giants, their branches woven together above to form a canopy. One sister was cloaked in darkness, shadows curling around her like serpents, while the other radiated a soft, golden glow, her hands trembling with restrained power. Their magic surged in opposing currents, colliding where their shoulders touched, light and shadow straining against each other.

Their expressions were tormented, both fierce, both afraid. Tension rippled between them. A voice emerged, layered with age, power, and something older still, the voice of a Star.

"They stand at the edge of all things, the twins of man. Mortal-born yet holding the power to bind or break what even time cannot repair. One carries compassion, the other truth. Together, they bear what the ancients feared most: choice."

The vision twisted again, showing two paths diverging. In one, the twins joined hands, and a wave of healing light surged outward, magic and humanity intertwined, realms rebuilding in harmony. In the other, their bond severed, one falling to shadow, the other consumed by grief, and the world splintered. Fire rained from the sky. Cities crumbled. Magic fled.

"They are not bound by prophecy," the voice continued, rumbling like distant thunder. "They are the fulcrum. Where they lean, the realms will follow. Watch them well … for in their hands lies creation, or ruin."

The vision dissolved like mist, but its weight lingered heavily in the air. Fadeya stood frozen, her body trembling in Evander's arms as though the grief might pull her under. Her fingers clutched at his shirt, needing something solid to hold onto. Her voice, when it came, was hollow.

"What does this mean? I don't understand," she whispered, her voice trembling. "That was me … and my sister."

Evander's gaze remained on the fading glow of the vision, his expression dark with something between awe and dread. He nodded slowly. "My father has spoken of his vision to me before, but I didn't truly believe it … until now."

"Hera …" Fadeya breathed, the name falling from her lips like a curse. Her knees buckled, and she sank to the ground, one hand still clutching Evander's arm. Her eyes were wide, distant, as the pieces fell into place. "She killed my father." The words tasted like ash. "How could she?"

Grief and betrayal twisted through her chest. The woman she had trusted, the one who had given her purpose, had been the very hand that destroyed everything.

Evander sank to his knees and held her tighter, steady and silent for a moment as if trying to anchor them both in reality. Then he pulled back just enough to look into her eyes, his own gaze sharp with purpose.

"This is bigger than us, Fadeya," he said quietly, but with unshakable conviction. "We need my father. He has to be informed. We cannot take this on alone."

Fadeya gave a faint nod, but her movements were slow, distant—like her spirit lagged behind her body. Numb. Disconnected. Evander rose and extended his hand without a word.

She took it.

Her fingers trembled in his grasp as he helped her to her feet, and together they staggered from the greenhouse. The air buzzed with color and noise. Birds chirping. Leaves rustling. Voices echoing faintly in the distance. It all felt wrong, like the world had no right to go on spinning after what they'd just seen.

"Are you alright?" Evander asked, finally letting her hand go.

"No," she said, barely above a whisper. "But that doesn't matter. I have to warn Seraphina."

He nodded. "Go. Find her. I will bring my father and his army back here."

Fadeya hesitated, her heart aching as she looked back toward the greenhouse. Her father's last words still echoed in her chest.

My little stars.

Her grief was a wound, but it was also a torch. She would carry it.

They shared one final look, eyes filled with everything they couldn't say: grief, fear, hope. Then they turned away from each other and ran, each propelled by love and duty.

Chapter 25

BEYOND THE VEIL

SERAPHINA

The woods whispered.

Not in the way wind rustled leaves, or small creatures scurried beneath brush. No, this was something older. Deeper. An energy that thrummed through root and branch, something ancient pressing against Seraphina's skin with each step she took.

The path to the Star Shrine was barely a trail at all, more of a memory the forest hadn't yet forgotten. She stepped over tangled roots, ducked beneath low-hanging moss thick with dew, and let her hand brush the bark of a tree glowing faintly with light.

Something inside her had begun to stir when she'd stepped off the university grounds, a current winding through her chest and spreading through her limbs like flame beneath her skin.

And then, the world darkened.

It wasn't the setting sun, though dusk was quickly approaching. No, this was a shadow, vast and terrible.

A roar split the heavens.

Seraphina shielded her eyes, looking up as the trees trembled around her.

He came down like a meteor: wings unfurled, black as volcanic rock. Gold eyes blazed like twin suns as his massive form crashed into the glade ahead, sending leaves and loose branches flying in every direction.

Vyrakthos, Last of the Realm-Binders.

And her bondmate.

His voice echoed in her mind. ***Hello, little one.***

She could only gape. Her knees threatened to buckle. He was massive. Far larger than she remembered. "You're here," she said, forcing the words out through a throat gone dry.

He lowered his head, smoke curling from his nostrils. ***You summoned me, did you not?*** A chuckle followed, low, rich, and almost … affectionate. Then his body shifted, one massive wing lowering. ***Come. I have something to show you.***

Seraphina hesitated, staring at the wing and the ridged back that shimmered like dark armor.

You're afraid, he said, no judgment in his tone.

"Terrified."

Good. You'd be a fool not to be. He lowered his head to meet her eyes. ***But you'll miss the sunset if you keep dithering.***

She took a step. Then another. Her boots sank slightly into the soft earth, but she barely noticed. All she could see was him, Vyrakthos, as vast and still as a mountain, waiting. Her hand twitched as she reached out. When her fingers touched the sleek black of his side, heat radiated through her palm.

And then, something surged between them. A jolt. A connection. *Their bond.*

She swallowed hard and began to climb. Her muscles screamed in protest, aching with the effort, but she didn't stop. The spaces between his scales offered narrow ridges, just enough for fingers and boots. It was like climbing a cliff face sculpted from scales, alive and breathing. *This is crazy.*

At last, she swung her leg over and settled onto his back. Her thighs gripped the ridge of his spine, hands finding hold on the edges of his plated scales. She was shaking, from effort, from adrenaline, from sheer disbelief. *Thank the stars I wore trousers*, she thought. A dress would've been a disaster.

Vyrakthos stirred beneath her, shifting with a creak like stone cracking in winter. He rumbled, low and deep, a sound that rolled through her body more than her ears.

And then he leapt.

The world dropped as the ground vanished beneath them.

Her scream tore free before she could stop it, whipped away by the wind. Air slammed into her face with brutal force, flattening her against his back, catching her hair in a wild torrent. She clung to him with everything she had. Her fingers curled into the grooves of his scales, arms tight, legs locked. There was no saddle, no reins, no safety. Only trust. *Only him.*

The sky was a blur around them, clouds streaking past like brushstrokes, stars peeking through the fading light. Wind howled past her ears, loud enough to drown out thought, but slowly, breath by breath, her panic ebbed.

And then, the sky opened. *Oh. My. Stars.* Below them, the fae realm unspooled in brilliant color. Rolling fields shimmered in shades of emerald and gold, rippling like silk under the setting sun. Rivers wound like ribbons, glinting where the light kissed their surface. One by one, lights winked to life in the town beyond, casting a glow against the encroaching dusk.

Trees taller than buildings rose from the forest floor, their leaves glowing with bioluminescent hues of violet, teal, and pale blue, painting the treetops like an aurora.

"It's *beautiful*," she breathed.

You sound surprised, Vyrakthos said, his voice a low hum beneath her thoughts.

She shifted her weight, leaning slightly to look down again. The landscape rolled out beneath them like a dream. "I guess I am," she admitted. "I've spent so long thinking the stories were exaggerated. I've been here for months and haven't really seen much of the fae realm. Not like this."

Her eyes were wide as she took it in. "It feels like something out of a storybook."

It's better than the storybooks.

319

He banked left, soaring over a valley lush with vineyards, then over terraced fields where children chased glowing birds between rows of corn and beans. "How does this all exist?" she asked.

Fae magic, he said. And bond magic. Creatures lend them power. They shape it into a life of abundance. Every bonded contributes something. Food, healing, clean water. Even a whisper of foresight.

They flew on, the wind streaming past her in wild currents, the sun now kissing the horizon, setting the world ablaze in hues of amber and rose. Below, life unfolded like a moving tapestry. She saw an artist standing on a floating platform, their brush sweeping across a massive canvas suspended in the air, lit by orbs of hovering light that shifted hue with each stroke.

Farther on, sparks danced from the forges of smiths working deep in the mountains, their hammers ringing like bells.

They passed over cities built into the canopies of colossal trees, their branches interwoven with bridges of woven wood and glass. There, she caught glimpses of lovers spinning in gravity-defying dances, music trailing behind them, laughter rising into the sky.

There is another place you must see, Vyrakthos whispered into her mind, his voice coiling like smoke through her thoughts.

She leaned forward instinctively, gripping his scales. "Where are we going?"

You'll feel it.

And then, she did. The world shifted.

An invisible threshold brushed over her like water slipping up her spine. The air thickened, as if the world had drawn itself inward for a moment.

Her heartbeat stuttered. Every hair on her body lifted. It was like being dipped in the ocean.

"Vyrakthos," she started, but his name caught in her throat.

And then they were through.

Color faded. Light dimmed.

Below them, the human realm stretched out in shades of gray and brown. Forests thinned to dry thickets. Fields were fallow.

Villages were small and weary, and fires flickered low. The rivers ran sluggish, some barely more than muddy scars.

Seraphina leaned forward, one hand gripping a ridge of Vyrakthos' scales. Her mouth opened in disbelief. "But ... we traveled for *weeks* across an ocean to reach the fae realm," she said, her voice barely audible above the wingbeats. "How can the human realm be *so close*?"

The realms exist side by side, he replied. But the veil between them is warded to make humans forget. They can't see it. Can't enter, unless allowed.

Her heart sank like a stone in her chest. "It's so close. And yet, it feels like another world."

It is, he said, no comfort in his tone.

They flew in silence for a moment.

"It's not fair," she said. Her voice cracked.

No, he agreed. *It's never been fair.*

She clenched her jaw. The muscles in her neck tensed. "Humans are suffering. Why don't the fae help them? Why doesn't someone *do* something? I don't remember it being this bad."

She stopped. The words curled into a knot in her throat, a sick realization forming. *Why don't I remember?* Why had it seemed better in her memory? Cleaner. Fuller. Why had the crops been green in her mind? Why did she remember laughter?

Vyrakthos descended lower, his wings stirring the dust from the treetops.

Because change is dangerous, he said. *Change threatens those in power. They don't want you to remember.*

Below them, a village came into view. A crowd huddled around a burning pyre, not in ceremony, but in grief. Someone had died. Maybe many someones.

A thin figure, child or elder, she couldn't tell, clutched a tattered cloth and sobbed, their face turned to the smoke.

Seraphina's stomach clenched, twisting like something alive had curled inside her and was beginning to thrash, but beneath the nausea bloomed something hotter, fiercer. A heat stirred low in her core, snaking up her spine and out through her limbs, licking beneath her skin like a fuse catching flame. She wanted to scream, to tear the sky open and set the barrier ablaze, to burn until something *changed*. Her hands shook, heat pulsing through her fingertips. Fire swelled inside her, wild and insistent, demanding release.

"It's not fair," she whispered again, but this time it was less of a protest and more of a prayer.

This world, *her* world, was broken.

A low vibration rose from his chest as he turned his great head, his eyes locking onto hers. *Good*, he said. *Now you see.*

Seraphina turned toward him, her face flushed, eyes shimmering with heat and disbelief. "You *wanted* me to feel this?"

I needed you to remember it, he said. *Not just with your mind, but with your fire. With the part of you that was born to burn away the old and forge something new.*

"What do I do with this?" she asked. "With all of this fire inside me?"

My first bondmate had power like yours. Fierce. Unrelenting, but her fire was never meant to heal. It was a weapon she turned toward anyone who stood in her way.

He tilted his head slightly, as if remembering her face. *She didn't want unity. She wanted dominion. She saw the brokenness of the world and believed it was hers to conquer, not mend.*

Seraphina began to sweat, the fire inside her churning at his words.

She made a choice, he continued, voice low. *To burn bridges instead of building them. To silence instead of listen. She believed if she held enough power, the world would bend.*

He exhaled, the sound like a gust of wind through a forest. *But power taken without purpose only feeds the dark. And it fed on her until there was nothing left. Just ambition and ash.*

Onyx. Her mind churned. Tears stung at the corners of her eyes, hot and unbidden. "You really think I can do better?"

Vyrakthos turned his head forward, voice steady with quiet certainty.

I wouldn't have chosen you if I didn't.

They circled back, crossing the barrier once more. The air warmed. Color returned. The university rose ahead, its towers lit by evening starlight, but Vyrakthos veered north, gliding toward a high hill beyond the grounds. He landed with grace that belied his size, wings folding.

Seraphina slid off, legs shaky. Her skin tingled with the weight of everything she'd seen.

They stood together, looking down on the glimmering world. Magic sparked in the air between them, a tether drawn tight.

"It feels different," she said. "The bond."

It is. You're awakening. Your power is responding to mine.

She closed her eyes. "It's ... a lot."

Then let it be a lot. Power doesn't wait for your comfort. It simply is.

She looked up at him, suddenly afraid. "What happened? To your last bondmate."

He looked away. *I severed the bond before she could destroy more than herself.*

The air went still.

"You can do that?" she whispered.

Yes.

"Would you ... do it again?"

He turned to her, eyes burning like coals. *Only if I had no choice, but you, little one, are already stronger than she ever was.*

A memory flickered. A voice. *Are you strong enough, Seraphina?*

"What does it mean?" Seraphina asked after a moment, her gaze never leaving the ancient creature before her. "Your name. Vyrakthos, Last of the Realm-Binders."

Once, he said at last, *there were many of us. Fae. Beasts. Humans touched by magic. We believed the realms should never have been severed. That harmony was possible, that the divide was a mistake. However, we were outvoted by the Council, cast as dreamers. Or worse, traitors. One by one, my kind faded or fell. I am the last of our circle. The final voice that remembers what was lost.*

Then Seraphina stepped forward and laid a hand against his scaled leg. Magic coursed through her veins, wild, certain, *hers.* It didn't matter that she couldn't name what had shifted within her. She was not the girl who had arrived at Astral Unison full of questions and doubt. That girl had been remade in fire. And though so much about her had changed, one truth had endured— she still dreamed. Still believed in something better.

Her voice rose, sure and steady. "You are not alone," she said, every word forged in fire and truth. "I will remember. I will fight to save humanity—and to reunite the realms."

A long breath escaped the dragon. He lowered his head, eyes shimmering with something close to awe.

"Then let it be known," he said out loud, his voice echoing like thunder through the wind and sky, *"You are no longer only Seraphina of the human realm."*

His next words burned into her, body and soul. *"You are Seraphina, Realm-Binder. The first of a new age."*

Seraphina bowed her head, her hand pressed to her heart. "Thank you, bondmate," she whispered, the words trembling with fierce gratitude. "I will do everything in my power to be worthy of the name."

They stood there for a long moment in quiet harmony, two beings bound by fate, standing at the edge of something greater than either of them alone. The air around them hummed with unspoken understanding, the weight of the vow settling like stardust across her shoulders.

Then Vyrakthos shifted, the earth groaning beneath him as he slowly unfurled his wings. The great expanse of them shimmered in the moonlight.

There are some things I must attend to, he said in her mind once more.

"You are no longer alone, Vyrakthos," she said, wind tugging at her hair.

And neither are you.

And then he rose, wings slicing through the air, climbing higher and higher until he became a silhouette against the stars.

Seraphina stood there, watching. Magic still curled in her veins, but it no longer felt like a foreign thing. It felt like her own.

She walked back slowly, drawn again to the Star Shrine. The stones shimmered with energy. The wind had gone still.

She knelt at a glowing rune, letting her fingers drift over its carved lines. A small lily bloomed between the stones. White. Fragrant. Fragile. She bent and plucked it.

Then, a voice pierced the quiet. "Seraphina."

She turned.

Aleron stood just beyond the circle of stones, chest rising with uneven breaths, his eyes locked on hers like he wasn't sure she was real.

"I've been looking everywhere for you."

FADEYA

Fadeya's heart pounded, each beat a painful echo of the grief pressing down on her. Through the haze of her tears, she caught sight of Emeric slipping silently from the infirmary, exhaustion carved deep into the lines of his face. Her breath hitched, sorrow tightening in her chest like a vice. But she didn't stop. Desperation surged through her, driving her forward, her footsteps echoing against the stone as she raced down the corridor.

"Emeric!" she cried, her voice breaking as she crashed into him, momentum nearly sending them both sprawling. His arms instinctively wrapped around her, steadying her trembling form, pulling her close. Her fingers twisted desperately into the rough fabric of his tunic, terrified that if she loosened her grip, he would vanish.

"Fadeya?" Emeric's voice was ragged, startled yet instantly protective as he tightened his embrace, sensing the profound pain that racked her body. "What's wrong? What's happened?"

She shook violently, buried her face deeper into his chest, her sobs pouring out uncontrollably, mingling incoherent words with cries of anguish. Her voice cracked, fragmented pieces barely audible. "It's Hera ... she ... she drained my father of his magic. Evander and I saw everything when we touched the etherbloom tree. Hera killed him, Emeric. My father ... She killed him!"

Emeric's eyes widened in shock, swiftly darkening into quiet fury and profound sadness. Tenderly, he cupped her tear-streaked face, wiping the moisture from her cheeks. "Fadeya, slow down. Breathe, please." His voice softened, gentle despite the anger in his gaze. "I'm so sorry. I'm here."

She drew back slightly, clutching his arms, determination igniting through the grief. Her tears were still streaming, but an unyielding fire blazed behind them. "Evander went to summon his father, but we need to find Seraphina. She is in danger."

Without hesitation, he clasped her hand firmly. "I just saw Aleron head into the forest. He was walking toward the Star Shrine. I'm sure he was looking for Seraphina."

"Let's go," Fadeya replied, strength returning to her voice.

Together, they plunged into the depths of the forest, their feet swift on the damp, moss-covered paths. As they moved farther into the dense woods, whispers of magic seemed to brush against their skin, heightening their urgency.

"The etherbloom revealed more than my father's death," Fadeya panted, her voice urgent yet quiet. "When King Hadren attended the university, he touched the tree himself. He had a vision ..." She paused a moment. "His vision was of Seraphina and me."

Emeric stopped and turned to her, intrigue and worry warring on his features. "What else did it show?"

Her voice lowered, carrying an ominous weight. "There was a voice that came from the stars. It said, 'They stand at the edge of all things, the twins of man. Mortal-born yet wielding power to bind or break that which even time cannot mend. One carries compassion, the other truth; together, they bear the thing ancients feared most: choice.'"

"The prophecy Seraphina discovered, it's the same, isn't it?"

"It has to be," she whispered grimly.

Suddenly, Emeric pivoted, his eyes distant and glazed as Zeruun's voice urgently filled his mind. *Emeric, the creatures are restless, the forest trembles. Something unnatural approaches.*

Emeric shuddered visibly, eyes snapping open with newfound intensity. "Zeruun warns us that the forest senses grave danger. Seraphina might already be in trouble."

Panic surged through Fadeya, lending fresh speed to her strides. *What if I'm already too late?* Her thoughts spun with terrible images of Seraphina caught in Hera's trap, alone and unaware, defenseless.

The trees thinned abruptly, giving way to the clearing surrounding the Star Shrine.

And there she was. Seraphina. *Safe.*

Her sister sat beside Aleron at the Shrine's base, her figure cloaked in silver moonlight. They were speaking in low voices, the sound carrying just faintly through the clearing, but the moment Fadeya burst into view, their heads snapped up.

Seraphina sprang to her feet, alarm widening her eyes. Aleron swiftly stepped in front of her, drawing his sword, wings of starlight appearing and flaring out behind him. "Who are you?" he demanded harshly, suspicion threading his tone.

Fadeya raised her arms, palms open. Her breath trembled in her throat, her voice barely holding steady. "My name is Fadeya," she declared. "Seraphina, I'm your sister, your twin."

The silence that followed nearly shattered her.

Seraphina's face drained of color, confusion and disbelief clouding her expression. She didn't speak at first. Just stared, wide-eyed. Then slowly, she shook her head. "No," she whispered. "That's … that's not possible."

Desperation surged through Fadeya's heart. I had hoped, somehow, that she would remember …

She took a shaky step forward, her voice tight with emotion. "You don't remember because of the archway—the one you passed through when you arrived at the university. It's enchanted. It erases memories from the human world … from before."

"The archway?" Seraphina repeated. "I … I remember walking through it, but—" She pressed her hand to her temple. "Why would they do that?"

"I know you're confused," Fadeya said, her voice rising with desperation. "But you have to trust me—you're in danger. We don't have time to explain everything here."

Aleron shifted, his stance tense, blade still raised. The starlit wings behind him beat once. "You expect us to follow a stranger blindly?" he snapped. He shot a wary glance toward Emeric, uncertainty flickering in his expression. "Why should we believe a word you say?"

Emeric stepped forward. "Fadeya is telling the truth, Aleron. Seraphina, trust us, we know about your bond with the dragon."

Seraphina hesitated, bewilderment flickering through her narrowed eyes. "My bond … how do you—"

An icy blast tore violently through the clearing, frosting the ground and seizing the air from their lungs. Shadows twisted and writhed, whispering dark secrets as the chill settled deep into their bones, forewarning imminent danger.

Fadeya's breath caught in her throat. She barely had time to react before Aleron moved.

In one swift motion, he stepped in front of Seraphina, arm outstretched, and then the world lit up.

A barrier of starlight burst from his hand, flaring into existence with a force that pushed the icy magic back. The shield shimmered, crackling with energy that made the hairs on Fadeya's arms stand on end.

She blinked, stunned. *What was that?* Even Aleron looked shaken, staring down at his hand like it had betrayed him.

"I didn't know I could do that," he muttered, more to himself than anyone else.

Fadeya's heart pounded in her chest as Seraphina clutched his arm, her expression mirroring the disbelief now written across Aleron's face.

From the swirling darkness, Hera emerged.

Her crimson cloak snapped fiercely in the biting wind. Her long silver hair, no longer bound in its usual updo, whipped about her shoulders in wild, chaotic tendrils. The jagged scar that sliced down the left side of her cheek seemed to glow faintly. Her gaze, filled with anger, pierced directly through Fadeya. "I should have guessed I'd find you here."

Chapter 26

BETRAYAL

FADEYA

"Fadeya," Hera drawled as she moved across the glen toward her. "Already spinning your webs of deceit?"

Aleron lunged forward, wings flaring with a sharp snap as they caught the wind and lifted him off the ground. He jerked upward awkwardly, shock flashing across his face as he hovered, unbalanced. He clutched his sword clumsily, the weight unfamiliar in midair. "Don't take another step," he growled, trying to keep his voice steady as his wings beat behind him, struggling to hold position.

Hera raised her hands in mock surrender, eyes shimmering with an insincere gentleness. "Come now, no need for theatrics." Her gaze slid, serpent-like, toward Seraphina, pausing at the luminous bondmark on her arm. "Seraphina," she purred, stepping closer, "you've bonded. A powerful creature, indeed. I felt it the moment you returned; extraordinary, isn't it? Allow me to guide you."

Seraphina glanced uncertainly between Fadeya and Hera.

"Don't believe her," Fadeya interrupted, desperation sharpening her tone. "She siphons magic from bonds. You're just another source for her to drain."

Hera laughed, the sound slicing through the night, sharp and cold. "Seraphina, this ... *miscreant* is the monster here." She gestured toward Fadeya, a look of disgust painted on her face. "She is a shapeshifter, an impostor wreaking havoc at the university. I've been hunting her for weeks."

Seraphina's eyes were wide with panic. "Is this true?" she whispered, horror creeping into her voice.

"No!" Fadeya cried, her fingers trembling with fury, eyes wide with anguish. "She is lying. She … she killed our father." Her voice cracked, the truth tearing from her throat. "I saw it with my own eyes when I touched the etherbloom tree. She drained every drop of magic from him, then left him to die."

Her body swayed with the force of her grief, and Emeric stepped forward without hesitation, wrapping an arm around her shoulders to steady her. She leaned into him instinctively, drawing strength from his presence.

Fadeya turned toward Hera, eyes blazing through a veil of unshed tears. "He trusted you. *I* trusted you."

Hera's serene mask splintered, her turquoise eyes storming with fury. Shadows writhed eagerly around her fingertips as her voice dropped to a lethal whisper. "You're as weak as your father was. Foolishly trusting." She turned her anger toward Seraphina. "If you refuse me the bond, Seraphina, I will seize it by force."

A maelstrom erupted, shadows lunging toward Seraphina, suffocating and heavy.

"Seraphina, run!" Fadeya's scream shattered the paralysis.

From above, Aleron roared, a flash of silver and wing as he plunged downward, sword gleaming defiantly in hand, but Hera was quicker.

Laughing darkly, her shadows ripped a fallen log from the earth and hurled it skyward. The impact cracked like thunder, slamming Aleron violently from the sky.

"Aleron!" Seraphina shrieked, sprinting to his fallen form as he skidded across dirt and blood-streaked leaves. He lay motionless, breathing shallowly, but alive. A whir of wings stirred the trees as Lyrae, Aleron's bondmate, emerged from above. Without a sound, she swept down and wrapped her wings around him, weaving a protective cocoon of glowing threads.

Hera's mocking laughter sliced through the air. "Foolish boy. Barely touched magic, much less mastered the sword. Pitiful." Her eyes glittered, merciless as she approached Seraphina. Power surged around her hands. "Come now, *Seraphina*. We wouldn't want anyone else to get hurt. If you won't surrender your bond willingly, I will rip it from your bones."

Magic erupted, fierce and devastating. Shadows leapt toward Seraphina, only to collide with a towering wall of shimmering water.

"Stay away from her!" Emeric commanded, emerging from behind Fadeya like a force of nature, water cascading around him in powerful torrents.

Hera snarled, "Another unsanctioned bond? I would have assumed the creatures would have been warned about *you*." She spit.

Water and shadow collided violently, filling the clearing with steam and fractured starlight. Emeric fought valiantly, each strike precise, waves crashing against shadow-forged blades.

Emeric whispered to her, urgent and pleading. "Fadeya, take Seraphina and *go*."

"No." The word tore from her. "I won't leave you."

"How touching," Hera sneered, wreathed in shadow like a queen draped in rot. "Fadeya, the *failure*, finding solace in the other university castoff. And you—" her eyes flicked to Emeric, disdain curling her lips, "—do you truly believe your pitiful magic stands a chance? You're nothing more than a drop in the ocean, *boy*."

Emeric straightened, defiance flaring within him. "A single drop can still drown you," he growled.

He flung his arms wide, and the ground answered. Water surged up from the earth in roaring waves, spiraling around him in a vortex. It wasn't just magic; it was fury, sorrow, protection, all woven into a torrent that lashed toward Hera. The clearing trembled with its power, trees bowing under the pressure, steam rising in great gusts as water collided with shadow.

For a breathless moment, it looked as if he might overwhelm her.

But Hera only smiled as her shadows slipped beneath his attack, unnoticed until it was too late. They lashed out, slicing clean through his Achilles tendons with a nauseating, wet *snap*.

Emeric crumpled.

"No!" Fadeya screamed, lunging forward as he collapsed to the stone. Blood pooled beneath him.

Hera advanced, shadows swirling around her arms, coalescing into a spear of darkness. Her lips twisted into a cruel, satisfied smile. "It's nothing personal, Emeric. You're simply *in my way*."

"Hera, please!" Fadeya begged, desperation thickening her voice. "Stop this."

Hera paused, the spear hovered in her grasp. She looked at Fadeya, and for a moment, something flickered in her expression. *Was that mercy in her eyes?*

Emeric took that moment.

With a cry, he thrust a blood-slick hand toward Hera. Water rushed from the cracked earth in a desperate, furious tide. Steam hissed where it met shadow; the shock staggered Hera a half step, the spear tipping. It wasn't as strong as before; his power faltered, stretched too thin by pain and blood loss.

Hera's face hardened. "So be it," she whispered.

The spear blurred, a shard of night turned weapon, and time shattered anew. Fadeya saw it all in crystalline detail—the way the darkness rippled, the gasp that tore from Emeric's throat, the sickening thunk as shadow met flesh and bone. The force lifted him from the ground, pinning him to the stone. Blood sprayed in an arc across her cheek, hot and shockingly real.

Black tendrils bled from the wound, curdling through his skin like ink in water. "Stay with me," Fadeya pleaded, voice breaking.

Emeric let out a faint gasp, his strength draining with every heartbeat. His trembling lips moved, and when his eyes met hers, they were filled with a haunting tenderness.

"Fadeya …" he breathed, her name falling from his lips like a prayer.

"Emeric," she choked out through sobs. She reached for his hand, clutching it tightly as if she could anchor him to life.

He closed his eyes, breath rattling. "You're not a failure," he rasped, each word a tremor of pain. "You are … everything." His fingers, warm, then chilling too fast, tightened around hers before slackening.

A final exhale ghosted across her cheek.

Fadeya's anguished scream shattered the night, grief overtaking her as she clung desperately to Emeric's lifeless body.

Seraphina remained frozen beside Aleron, her hand gripping his arm like a lifeline, knuckles white and trembling. Tears clung to her lashes, distorting the world into shimmering fragments. She couldn't breathe, couldn't think, until the ground beneath her boots shifted, a low groan rising from the earth itself. The rumble vibrated through her bones, snapping her out of the fog. Her breath hitched, then spilled out in a shaky exhale. "Thank the stars," she whispered, voice cracking as relief washed over her.

A deafening gust roared down from above, rattling the stones of the Star Shrine and sending spirals of dust curling into the air.

Vyrakthos landed with a thunderous impact, talons gouging deep into the sacred marble. His scales shimmered like obsidian, and fire flickered at the corners of his massive jaws, illuminating the celestial carvings in the stone.

His gaze swept the space before landing on Hera. *"Onyx,"* Vyrakthos growled, *"your betrayal ends now."*

Fear and surprise flickered across Hera's face, hand tracing her darkened bondmark. "Vyrakthos," she breathed, taking a step back. "How are you … I thought you were dead."

The dragon's growl deepened, reverberating through every stone. *"You thought wrong."*

Chapter 27

BOND ONCE BROKEN

SERAPHINA

"Onyx ..." Seraphina's voice trembled, her breath catching on the name as if speaking it summoned something evil. "Onyx, as in *the Onyx*? Aurora's twin sister?" Her words cut through the air. "The one from the prophecy?"

The silence that followed was thick, suffocating. Hera's jaw tensed. She didn't speak at first, but Seraphina saw the way her shoulders squared, a soldier bracing for war.

"You speak of old stories," Hera said at last, though her voice wavered, no longer wrapped in steel. "Prophecies twisted by time. Don't be so naive."

Seraphina's heart slammed against her ribs. Her skin felt too tight, her thoughts careening toward a memory—Professor Eldwyn's tale of the twin sisters born to bridge the fractured realms. Aurora, the light. Onyx, the shadow. She turned to the dragon beside her, her bondmate, the creature who had given her power, trust. *Hope.*

"I need answers," she whispered, her eyes pleading. "You told me of a bond you once had that was broken. *Was it her?*"

The dragon's massive head dipped once.

"Three hundred and eighty years ago," he replied out loud, *"I was bonded to Onyx. She and Aurora were destined to unite the realms. To bring harmony between fae, mortals, and magical creatures. But*

Onyx ... " He turned his head, meeting Hera's eye. *"She let ambition consume her. She twisted our bond. Took my power, turned it into a weapon, and used me to strike down my own kin."*

Fadeya's tears had slowed, and she lifted her head, her attention fastened to the dragon. Only Hera, no, *Onyx*, remained untouched, her face an impassive mask.

"Is that why you broke the bond?" Seraphina asked, voice trembling.

Vyrakthos's golden eyes turned to her. *"I had no choice. She would have razed both realms to ash in her pursuit of power. Severing the bond was the only way to stop her. I let her believe I perished."*

Onyx's fists clenched. "And how many centuries have you spent hiding while the realms tore themselves apart?" she shouted, voice full of bitter fire. "The prophecy called us to unify the world, not forsake it."

He snarled, teeth bared in rage. *"You forget the prophecy demanded balance. Aurora understood that. You wanted to cleanse the realms, decide who was worthy. You wanted to force bonds. You betrayed your sister. You betrayed us all."*

Seraphina's blood went cold. The dragon's heat radiated at her side, but the air felt thin, suffocating. "But ... didn't Aurora decide to keep the realms separate?" she asked, voice barely audible.

"She did," Vyrakthos said. *"Without Onyx's support, she lacked the strength to unite them. She died protecting what knowledge remained."*

Onyx's eyes flashed with fury. "She *died* because her bondmate couldn't regulate the power she was giving her. She didn't know how to channel it properly. And you," she thrust a finger at the dragon, *"you* let it happen."

Fadeya's voice broke like shattering glass. "You don't deserve another chance at life. It should be *you* who's dead."

"You've lived in shadows," Seraphina murmured, horror twisting through her. "Hiding behind illusions, stealing power from new bonds. Why?"

Onyx tilted her head, lips curling in a smile that didn't reach her eyes. "To finish what we began. Aurora's gone, but the prophecy lives on. The realms *rot*. Mortals crave power, and magical creatures retreat into myth. I planned to rise again, this time, alone. Unchallenged. No twin to betray me. No *dragon* to turn against me."

"The prophecy is clear," Seraphina said, voice steady despite the tremor running through her bones. "'Two *human* twins, flames mirrored true, may heal the realms where sorrow grew.' *We* are the fulcrum, not you."

Onyx barked a laugh. "Humans?" She swept a mocking glance over Seraphina and then to Fadeya, who still sat draped over Emeric's lifeless body. "You soft-skinned things topple kingdoms with your greed, burn forests for kindling, poison rivers for coin. And you think you're destined to fix what you broke?" Her eyes gleamed. "Please."

Fadeya stood slowly; a drop of blood dripped off her chin. "Then why seek me out at all?" Her voice cracked, the memory of their father's lifeless body flickering behind her eyes. "Was it because of our father? Because he stood up to you? Rejected you?"

Onyx's expression shifted to impatience. "Your father was collateral," she said, almost bored. "He learned too many secrets. It seems that may run in the family." She pivoted, looking back at Seraphina. "When you told me you had a twin in the human realm, I knew the clock had struck. Prophecies circle in cycles, and timing is everything."

She took a slow step toward Fadeya, head cocked as though examining a curious insect. "I felt Seraphina's potential the moment she arrived in this realm, so I crossed the veil, eager to see whether her mirror carried the same spark." Her eyes raked over Fadeya from boots to braids, then flicked away with casual disdain. "You don't."

Fadeya's jaw tightened, fury burning in her eyes, but before she could speak, Vyrakthos's growl rumbled through the air. *"You cannot outrun the ruin you caused, Onyx."*

A tremor passed through Onyx, so faint that Seraphina almost missed it. She watched as her gaze shifted, drawn to Emeric's body sprawled across the stone. The blood beneath him still glistened.

"You don't know what it was like," Hera said hoarsely. "The endless hiding. The hunger. The isolation. All because *you* left me."

Fadeya let out a sound of anguish. The echo of her grief reverberated through the trees. Seraphina moved to her side, murmuring comfort even as her own thoughts unraveled.

My sister ... my twin. The words felt foreign, impossible. Yet her soul *knew* it was true.

Then her bondmate moved, the scrape of scale on stone dragging Seraphina back. He unfurled to his full height, his wings brushing the trees, eyes locked on Onyx. ***"You dare face me again? After all the destruction you wrought?"***

She bared her teeth. "I had hoped the world would move on. That I could return and lead it again, but the prophecy ... the prophecy is still mine to fulfill."

She turned to Seraphina, eyes full of disdain. "You think *you* can carry the weight of the realms? You're a child fumbling in the dark."

Seraphina's bond echoed with Vyrakthos's anger. She didn't understand, not fully, but she knew. *Onyx must be dealt with.* With one last squeeze of Fadeya's shoulder, Seraphina turned toward the dragon.

Vyrakthos lowered his massive head, fire smoldering in his eyes, and Seraphina climbed onto his back.

"You haven't the stomach for what must be done," Onyx hissed. She took a step back as Seraphina mounted.

A vortex of darkness rose, swallowing starlight, twisting treetops into silhouettes.

Cold sank its claws into Seraphina's skin. Still, she kept her gaze on Onyx. "You mistake power for strength," she said, voice ringing out clear and fierce above the gathering storm. "But true strength isn't dominance; it's doing what's right, protecting those who cannot protect themselves. It's compassion, even when it costs you *everything*."

"You naive child," Onyx spat. Shadows coalesced at her fingertips, forming a jagged arrow aimed straight at Seraphina's heart.

"You imagine uniting the realms will usher in some glorious peace? Humans are built to betray, to fail. *You* will fail, Seraphina. And when you do, your caring heart will *break* you."

Seraphina lifted her chin. "Only someone who abandoned love long ago could see compassion as weakness." She took a breath, feeling the blazing strength of Vyrakthos surge through her veins. "This ends *now*."

The dragon roared, an earth-shattering sound that sent birds screaming from the tree line. Flame erupted along his wings, meeting Onyx's torrent of darkness midair.

Onyx's eyes widened, just a fraction, as the flare of Seraphina's power held steady, refusing to buckle. But then, her lips twisted into a cold smirk, and her voice rose, slicing the night with a chilling incantation. Shadows exploded from her in great twisting waves, blotting out the moon and ripping open the sky in a maelstrom of violet and ebony.

"Stop!" Seraphina cried, thrusting her palm forward. Light flared, fierce and desperate, but shattered uselessly against an unseen barrier.

Onyx regarded her, amusement glittering in her eyes. "Our paths will cross *again ... twins*." Her eyes drifted slowly to Fadeya, lingering on the tears streaking her cheeks, the blood coating her shaking hands. A mocking smile curled her lips. "You're just like your father—brave and *foolish* to the bitter end." Then she stepped back, shadows folding around her like a shroud, until she was nothing but darkness.

Vyrakthos lunged, flame surging from his throat, but she was already gone. The portal snapped shut. The wind vanished, and silence fell like a hammer.

Fadeya's whisper shattered it. "What have I done?"

Aleron stirred with a low groan, shifting against the ground. Seraphina immediately slid from her bondmate's back, rushing to his side and kneeling beside him. Nearby, Lyre released the shimmering shield she'd woven, wings fluttering softly as she drifted toward the treetops.

Aleron moaned again, fingers brushing gingerly against his temple. Blinking through the haze, his gaze moved past Seraphina, widening as it fell upon the towering form of the dragon looming protectively behind her.

"So," he whispered, awe threading through his voice, "this is him."

Seraphina nodded, her throat aching and too tight to speak.

Vyrakthos stepped closer, lowering his massive head toward her. Warmth radiated from his scales as she laid a hand upon his chin, yet beneath that comforting heat, something darker stirred.

She knows now that I live, his deep voice echoed in her mind. *She will come for us. And for our bond.*

Seraphina's spine went rigid. She swallowed thickly and managed another small nod.

"I must warn the Council of what has transpired here," Vyrakthos said aloud, his voice rumbling through the clearing. *"I shall return."*

Her fingertips lingered on his scales for just another moment before slipping away. The dragon unfurled his great wings, surged upward, and vanished into the dark canopy above.

Behind her, Aleron rubbed his face, pushing himself into a sitting position. His eyes fixed numbly on Emeric's still form. "Emeric ... is he—?"

"Yes," Seraphina whispered, helping him shakily to his feet. Pain tightened her voice, sharpening each word. "Hera—Onyx took him from us." She glanced over at her sister.

Fadeya stood frozen nearby, dazed, her tears unchecked, streaming silently down her cheeks. Her breathing came in shallow, shuddering gasps.

"What do we do now?" Aleron asked, his voice hoarse, unable to tear his gaze from Emeric's lifeless body.

Seraphina turned slowly to face Emeric's body, the grief within her heart tangling fiercely with fury. "We make sure Emeric's death wasn't in vain."

The bond pulsed in response, the dragon's approval tingling through her blood.

Aleron made his way over to Fadeya and rested a hand on her shoulder. "We should take him home."

"Yes…" she mumbled. "Back to the university."

Together, they lifted Emeric's remains from the bloodstained ground. And as they moved, the forest around them erupted into mourning.

Beasts howled, wolves and stags cried out in unison, their voices rising to an aching crescendo. From the lake in the woods, a wail shattered the darkness, a sound so piercing, so utterly heartbroken, it seemed to split the air.

"Zeruun," Fadeya whispered.

Every step up the winding path felt heavier than the last; the very earth beneath their feet seemed to tremble with loss.

They emerged into a moonlit courtyard. The stars blazed overhead, indifferent, eternal. Seraphina looked up, breath catching at their beauty, at their *apathy*.

They slowly lowered Emeric's body to the ground, and Fadeya collapsed beside him, her strength finally giving out as grief overtook her.

Seraphina dropped to her knees beside her and wrapped her arms around Fadeya, pulling her close. The warmth of her sister's body was the only anchor she had as the world seemed to tilt into sorrow.

A few paces away, Aleron stood motionless. His hands trembled at his sides, stained with blood and dirt, his chest rising in shallow, uneven breaths. "We need to tell someone what has happened," he said, voice thick. "We need to find Professor Shay."

Fadeya reached out and brushed her hand along Emeric's cheek. "Find Evander," she choked out. "He's already sent word to the king."

Gooseflesh prickled along Seraphina's arms as power surged in her veins. The remnants of Vyrakthos's magic stirred within her.

She felt the pull of her calling, the unyielding weight of the prophecy urging her forward, begging her to unite the shattered realms. But reality dug deeper, sharper than any destiny: Onyx was still alive. Emeric was dead. And Seraphina stood at the breaking point, caught between destiny and devastation.

Chapter 28

THE WEIGHT OF REMEMBERING

SERAPHINA

The grand hall surrounded them, vast and solemn, its pillars rising until they vanished into the dim rafters above. A faint draft from the open windows stirred the banners hanging on the wall. Seraphina stood tense, the air heavy with unsaid words. Beside her were Aleron, Fadeya, Cordelia, and Evander, each of them marked by exhaustion and grief.

Guards in the king's livery lined the walls in perfect discipline, polished breastplates gleaming in the flickering torchlight.

At the far end of the hall stood King Hadren, tall, broad-shouldered, and tired in a way that no crown could conceal. Beside him, swathed in a deep hood, was Isadora, her skin pale, her eyes shadowed from the ordeal she'd only narrowly survived.

Seraphina braced herself. The bond with Vyrakthos rested within her, awake and watchful. She could feel the dragon, his presence a constant undercurrent of strength. But even now, *he was unsettled. She could sense it.*

At last, the king's voice broke the silence. "Seraphina. Aleron. Cordelia. Step forward."

His eyes swept across them, lingering on Seraphina as if trying to read the future in her face. Then he turned toward Isadora.

"Father," Isadora said, inclining her head.

The king returned the gesture, a mark of respect rarely offered. "I have been told of Professor Hera's true identity. Of *you*," he said, looking directly at Fadeya, "and the part you played in these events."

Fadeya stiffened, eyes cast down. Seraphina instinctively moved half a step closer to her.

"And of the bravery," the king continued, voice hardening, "with which you all fought to protect my daughter."

A murmur stirred among the guards. The king's gratitude was not something given lightly.

"I owe them my life," Isadora said, her voice brittle but clear. "Without them, I would have died."

Aleron stepped forward first, his fist to his chest in salute. "We did only what was right, Your Majesty."

Seraphina caught the way his fingers flexed at his sides.

The king's attention moved to Isadora and Evander. Isadora squared her shoulders; Evander's usually bright eyes were somber. "You have all protected not just my bloodline," the king continued, placing a hand on his son's shoulder, "but the stability of the realm."

King Hadren nodded, and then a guard came forward carrying a large box. He set it on the ground, and the king bent down, pulling from it a smooth, glowing orb.

Seraphina sucked in a breath. *No. It can't be—*

The orb of the Starlight Awakening.

Fadeya went rigid beside her, and Seraphina saw the recognition in her sister's eyes.

"This artifact," King Hadren said, raising the orb slightly, "was used to determine your worth before you came to the university, but it can also restore what was taken. Memories ... sealed at my command. For the safety of the realm."

Gasps echoed around the chamber.

"Our memories?" Seraphina whispered. Her voice felt distant in her own ears.

"Yes," he said simply. "If you choose, you may reclaim them."
He turned back to Seraphina. "Do you wish to reclaim what was
taken from you?"

Seraphina hesitated. What had they taken from her? And why
had it been necessary to forget in the first place?

The bond within her stirred uneasily. Vyrakthos did not like
this orb, but she needed answers.

"I do," she whispered, stepping forward.

The King held out the orb. "Touch it, and speak your name."

Seraphina reached out. The orb dimmed when her fingers
grazed its surface. "Seraphina Elaris," she said, voice trembling.
"I want my memories back."

A burst of golden light flowed outward, flooding the hall. She
staggered as images surged through her.

She saw a younger version of herself running through orchard
rows with Fadeya, giggling over some stolen pastry. She saw her
father pointing out constellations in the night sky, and she remembered the feeling of disappointment that seemed to always hover over
her mother. Faces, voices, entire fragments of her life came flooding
back, hitting her like a wave of bittersweet nostalgia. And through
it all, she felt her bond with Vyrakthos react, ringing as if in protest.
A feeling of darkness prickled along her spine. When the light sub-
sided, she almost collapsed, dizziness claiming her for a heartbeat.

Aleron caught her just in time, pulling her into his arms.
"Seraphina, hey, look at me," he said, voice firm.

She blinked, breath ragged. "I remember," she whispered, tears
spilling. "I remember everything."

A cough broke the hush. King Hadren gestured to Cordelia,
who watched them with glistening eyes of her own, and to Aleron,
who still held Seraphina.

"Step forward," the king commanded. "You, too, have proven your
dedication to the kingdom. You have the choice to reclaim what is lost."

Cordelia and Isadora exchanged a glance. Cordelia's mouth
trembled slightly, but she nodded. "Yes, Your Majesty," she said.
"I will accept what was lost."

"And I," Aleron added, carefully easing Seraphina onto her feet before stepping away.

One by one, they touched the orb. Each time, the light flared, memories cascading back into place. Cordelia gasped, tears welling instantly in her eyes. Beside her, Aleron's eyes closed with quiet devastation, his jaw tightening as his lips parted in a grimace of pain. *His sister...* Seraphina thought as the memory of her death resurfaced in her mind.

They stepped back in unison as the king's voice cut through the stillness.

"We used this artifact to confirm your worthiness for the university's teachings." He brushed his fingers over the orb, its inner light flickering like stars caught in glass. "Now, I would see that same test applied to you once more, Fadeya."

The silence that followed was sharp. Then, Fadeya stepped forward, trembling. "Your Majesty ..." Her voice was soft, splintered. "I don't know if I deserve that choice. I helped Onyx. I trusted her. I dragged Emeric into this. And now ..." Her voice broke, tears threatening. "He's dead. Because of me."

Seraphina's heart clenched. No. Her fingers twitched at her sides. No, Fadeya, that isn't true. You loved him. You tried to save him.

The king's expression shifted. "We were all deceived," he said. "You are not the only one who bears that weight. Redemption is not given freely; it is earned through choice. And now, you have a chance to choose differently. Will you pledge yourself to the university's cause? Will you master your gifts and honor Emeric's memory?"

Fadeya lifted her reddened eyes to meet the king's. "I will," she whispered. She took a deep breath and reached out her hand.

This time, it erupted with a brilliance so intense it was nearly blinding. Shocked exclamations broke from the guards. Even the king's composure cracked, surprise moving across his face. The orb shone in a tapestry of gleaming light, swirling around Fadeya's hand like a flame. The glow bathed her face in ethereal beauty, and for a moment, Seraphina glimpsed what her sister might become: powerful, bonded, *someone who could unite us.*

Then the radiance waned, and the orb returned to its neutral demeanor. Fadeya's mouth hung open, awe warring with sorrow in her eyes. "Thank you," she said quietly. "I promise, I will not fail."

The king bowed his head. "You are worthy, Fadeya Elaris. And the realms are watching. All of you have proven yourselves. I only hope we can unite in time to face the threat Onyx poses. War is coming, and we will need to be united as one to win."

At that, Cordelia sank into a courteous bow. "We will do everything in our power, Your Majesty." King Hadren inhaled as if steeling himself for another wave of responsibilities.

FADEYA

Evander's hand came down gently on Fadeya's shoulder, the contact grounding her in a moment that felt as if it might shatter with a single breath. She looked steadier now, different, somehow—her spine straighter, her gaze clear. *The orb had chosen her.*

"Thank you," Fadeya whispered, lifting her eyes to Evander. Her cheeks colored slightly, but she didn't look away.

Evander gave a half smile, one so unguarded, so heartbreakingly tender, that Fadeya barely recognized him.

"We should speak with my father," he murmured, low enough for only Fadeya to hear.

She nodded once. Speak. Yes. As if words could somehow undo what had been done. As if a crown or a prophecy could ease the ache hollowed out in her chest.

Evander turned, his head tilted in a subtle gesture toward the king. A silent request. A word?

Cordelia stepped back, offering a graceful bow. Aleron followed, his movements stiff with tension.

349

Seraphina lingered a heartbeat longer, dipping her head even as her heart pounded against her ribs. The king's words echoed in her mind as she followed them out. *A war is coming.*

As the doors creaked closed behind the others, the room shifted. King Hadren turned toward Evander and Fadeya, one brow lifted in question.

"Father," Evander began, but his words faltered. He glanced at Fadeya.

She stepped forward, voice firm. "Your Majesty, we've touched the etherbloom tree."

The king's posture stiffened, not in anger, but in stunned disbelief. "You did *what?*"

"We saw the vision," Fadeya said. "The same vision you saw when you touched the tree."

Silence. Then, sharp and clear, "Leave us."

The guards didn't hesitate. In perfect synchronicity, they filed out, the heavy doors groaning shut behind them.

King Hadren reached up and removed his crown. Not piously, but with a weariness so heavy, he seemed to age a decade in that single movement.

He poured himself a glass of water from the decanter near the window, then sat at the long table. With a sigh, he motioned for them to join him.

They obeyed, pulling out chairs and settling across from him.

"I suppose you have questions," Hadren began, his voice thinner now—more human.

Fadeya nodded, her hands clenched tightly in her lap. "Why were we in your vision?" she asked. Her voice cracked around the edges. Her eyes, puffy from hours of weeping, searched his face for answers.

The king looked out the window, across the misty university grounds. He didn't speak for a long moment.

"I wish there was an easy answer," he said at last. "When the Great Schism ended, I was just a boy. The Council of Twelve decided the realms must remain separate, that the merging of the fae and human realms was too dangerous, that the bonds were a threat. I believed them." He paused, his fingers tightening around his glass.

"I met Aurora once. Onyx's sister. She spoke of a dream, of two sisters born in a new age who might succeed where she and her sister had failed. I thought little of it at the time." He turned to look directly at Fadeya. "Until I touched the etherbloom tree years later."

Evander let out a long breath beside her.

"The vision I saw … it stayed with me. Burned itself into my soul." The king's voice dropped. "You were bathed in light. Not Seraphina. *You.*"

Fadeya blinked, shaking her head. "No. That's not possible. The orb didn't even find me worthy last year. Seraphina's the one bonded to Vyrakthos. Not me."

"The orb is powerful," the king said gently, "but it is not perfect. Magic never is. Prophecy, even less so. Destiny bends. It adapts. And sometimes, it hides the truth until the right moment." He reached out, laying his weathered hand atop hers. "You are right where you're meant to be, Fadeya."

She dragged in a shaky breath, the words slipping out before she could stop them. "Then what does that mean for Seraphina?"

King Hadren leaned back in his chair, his brow furrowed in thought as he reached for his glass and took another sip of water. "I can't say," he admitted. "Perhaps she is the sword, and you the shield. Perhaps one of you must lead, while the other ensures the path is safe. I only know this: there is an eclipse coming. Thirty-eight days from now. The Oracle of Dusk will awaken. It sees all futures. All paths. I give you permission," he looked at Fadeya, and then at Evander, "to seek it together. It's time we begin to mend what was broken long ago."

Evander straightened, pride and duty radiating from every line of his body. "Thank you, Father. We will not fail."

The king rose slowly. He returned to the window where his crown waited. "With every passing year," he murmured, "this crown grows heavier." He looked back at his son. "I hope to pass it on to you with a lighter burden."

He placed it atop his head and strode from the chamber, leaving Evander and Fadeya behind.

They sat there for a long time, silent. *One human. One fae. One fate.*

Chapter 29

MAKE A WISH

SERAPHINA

I keep dreaming of stars falling into the sea. Each time, my creature dives after them, returning soaked in light. I think it's a message—about loss, or maybe about hope. That some things can fall and still be found."

The clearing was hushed, heavy with a reverence so profound it felt as though even the ancient pines were bowing in quiet contemplation. Each whisper of the wind seemed laden with secrets, brushing against Seraphina's skin like ghostly fingertips.

She sat with her shoulder braced against the trunk of a tree, the bark rough against her palm as she worked to steady the frantic beat of her heart. Just within arm's reach sat her twin sister, Fadeya, arms wrapped around herself as though she could shield her soul from the lingering chill of regret. Together, they formed a quiet tableau in the lantern light, two silhouettes etched against the darkness.

Between them lay their father's journal, its weathered pages fluttering in the cool night breeze, a quiet echo of the man they'd barely known. A man whose mysteries, whose hidden truths, had reshaped everything they understood about themselves and their fate.

They lingered there, silent, drawing in the night air. Seraphina could almost pretend they were children again, lost in the forest, waiting for their father's call to guide them home, but the memories that now flooded her mind would not allow such simplicity. The orb had returned everything she'd lost, every recollection she had that slipped away. Warm laughter, tearful confessions, whispered tales under starlight—they rushed back in an endless cascade.

"I remember it all," Seraphina said, voice a mixture of wonder and guilt. Her eyes glistened as she looked at Fadeya. "The wishing well in the courtyard, that time you cut your foot on that rock in the creek, mother's rose perfume. Every story Dad ever told us about legendary beasts and forgotten realms. It's as if someone tore down a wall in my mind."

Fadeya turned her head slowly, meeting Seraphina's stare. Her own eyes shone with subdued pain. "I'm glad to have you back."

Seraphina inhaled shakily, letting her hand glide across the page of the journal. "I never realized Dad was so … layered."

Fadeya traced the faded lines of their father's drawings. She paused on a sketch; two figures entwined in strands of luminescent magic. Her voice shook as she whispered, "Fractured Realms, bearers of unity, or bearers of destruction. That's us, Seraphina. Exactly like Onyx and Aurora."

Seraphina felt a shiver ripple down her spine, her fists clenching involuntarily. "We're not doomed to repeat their mistakes. Our path isn't written yet."

Fadeya's voice shook, bitterness lacing her words. "I let Onyx manipulate me. Emeric died because I was weak, because I listened to her promises of power and belonging. How do I escape that?"

"Fadeya," Seraphina reached out and placed a hand on her sister's back. "You're not at fault for any of that. We've both made mistakes, but we can't keep punishing ourselves."

Fadeya nodded, though her shoulders remained tense.

For a moment, Seraphina found herself at a loss. She understood all too well. "I feel the weight of all of this, too." She sighed, dropping her hand and picking up the journal. "Vyrakthos's presence is always there, like a second heartbeat in my chest. Sometimes it's comforting, but other times …" She hesitated, remembering the fierce pulse of draconic hunger that had surged through her the night Emeric died. "Sometimes I catch myself craving power, wanting more, wanting everything. I'm worried Mother was right. I'm not strong enough."

Fadeya's eyes widened in alarm. She reached out and clasped Seraphina's free hand. "We are strong together! You are right. Our path isn't written yet."

Seraphina took a steadying breath, allowing herself to feel the warmth of Fadeya's grip. "We have something Onyx never truly possessed. We have each other."

The clearing fell silent again, broken only by the rustle of leaves overhead. A soft glow pulled Seraphina's attention downward. Fadeya's amulet, hidden beneath her cloak, had begun to shimmer. The metal's faint red glow flickered like an ember on the verge of ignition.

Fadeya gasped, pressing a trembling hand over the amulet. "It's hot," she whispered, face paling.

A surge of alarm coursed through Seraphina, and the mental tether linking her to Vyrakthos surged in response, crackling like static. She felt the dragon's awareness sharpen in her mind, a protective snarl forming at the edges of her consciousness. *Everything is well, little one,* Vyrakthos whispered in her mind.

Seraphina stretched out her hand, feeling the threads of power vibrating from the amulet. Above them, the sky seemed to answer, sending a brilliant arc of starlight streaking across the heavens, burning brightly before fading into oblivion. Her heart clenched with nostalgia, memories of countless childhood wishes flooding her soul.

"Make a wish," Fadeya breathed, the plea like a fragile prayer.

Seraphina closed her eyes, desperation and hope intertwining in her chest. She wished fiercely, fervently. "Let us find our own path. Let us choose the light, together."

When she opened her eyes, she found Fadeya's gaze locked onto hers, tears streaming silently down her sister's cheeks. "I wished the same," Fadeya confessed softly, "Never to be torn apart again."

Seraphina squeezed her sister's hand, feeling strength surge between them, a binding promise. "Then that's exactly what we'll do."

A distant roar shattered the quiet, Vyrakthos's call rippling through her, both warning and reassurance. Their destinies were irrevocably woven.

"We'll face whatever darkness awaits," Seraphina murmured, fire igniting in her soul.

Fadeya drew herself upright, shoulders squared, chin lifted proudly. Her eyes shone with defiance and hope, fierce and unyielding. "Together," she vowed.

They stood that way for a long moment, gathering courage beneath the watchful sky. Then the sisters stood and stepped forward, lifting the lantern from the forest floor. Its flame danced with their every move, illuminating not just the faded journal at their feet, but also the path that stretched into the unknown.

And in the distance, where the stars seemed to cluster in an endless tapestry, another streak of light arced across the heavens, silent, brilliant, and fleeting.

As Seraphina and Fadeya watched it fade, they both felt a stirring in their chests: a shared spark of resolution, promising that whatever end the prophecy threatened, they would not face it alone.

EPILOGUE

She woke to the sound of a distant hum. A soft, shimmering vibration of magic that pulled through her veins like a long-forgotten melody. Her lashes fluttered against the dust that clung to her cheeks, and the cool darkness around her began to blur into the outline of jagged stone and twisted ivy.

Every muscle protested as she moved, her limbs heavy with the weight of centuries spent in an enchanted slumber. She rose gingerly, steadying herself against the cold, damp wall. Her long silver hair cascaded down her shoulders like starlight, gleaming against the dark.

Gritting her teeth, she took a tentative step forward, every movement echoing in her bones with memories, sharp fragments of a past that refused to coalesce. A throne bathed in moonlight, spiraling runes etched by the stars, a pair of turquoise eyes mirrored by her own.

She took a breath, letting the foreign stillness of the chamber settle into her bones, then gently pushed open the moss-covered stone door. Pale light spilled in, illuminating the wild tangle of greenery encasing her hidden sanctuary. As she stepped into the forest, leaves rustling at her ankles, her senses sharpened. Faint threads of magic rippled through the night air, beckoning her forward.

She closed her eyes, surrendering to the call. The hush of the night answered, twining around her heart until realization sank into her very soul. The murmur of that distant magic wasn't just any power; it was hers. Or rather, it was bound to someone who shared her blood, her lineage … *her past.*

When she opened her eyes, a quiet fierceness burned there, the glimmer of determination reigniting after too many lost years. She tipped her head back, let the moonlight caress her face, and whispered,

"My sister is alive."

A breeze stirred, carrying the echo of her words into the darkness, as though the entire wood awoke to hear them. The corner of her mouth curved into a faint smile, one that spoke of relief, hope, and a thousand questions that only reunion could answer.

With one last glance at the crumbling doorway behind her, she turned toward the path ahead, toward the unknown. Toward the bond that called to her with ancient, unyielding power.

She would find Onyx—and she would make it right.

ABOUT THE AUTHORS

Cammy (r) and Aly (l) Crady

⌐ CAMMY

Cammy has been in love with stories for as long as she can remember. She's the kind of person who packs way too many books for a weekend trip and then still ends up buying another one on the way. When she's not writing, she's usually behind her camera, trying to catch a bit of magic in everyday life, or getting lost on winding streets in other countries and calling it "research."

Home is in Florida, where she shares life with her partner, Alex, her daughter, Imani, Alex's son, Benny, their dog, Fox, and two cats who are certain they're running the show. Between road trips that rarely go as planned, bedtime stories that spiral into giggles, and the daily comedy act that is family life, she has no shortage of inspiration.

At the end of the day, she just loves telling stories, whether it's on the page, through a lens, or in the middle of her perfectly ordinary, perfectly chaotic life. Growing up as a twin gave her a built-in co-writer and rival all in one—though writing this book together has proven they're better at finishing chapters than finishing each other's sentences.

ALY

Aly Crady is a reader, artist, and book binder based in Maryland. By day, she works in hospitality, a job that puts her right in the middle of people's lives and stories. She's come to believe that everyone has a story worth telling, and she carries that perspective with her into her own creative work.

At home, storytelling takes on all kinds of forms. Sometimes it's through the books she binds by hand, other times it's in the worlds she escapes to when she's writing, reading, or gaming late into the night. Aly spends a lot of time with her online community too, where friendships, laughter, and shared adventures give her the kind of inspiration you can't plan for. She jokes that her best ideas show up after midnight, though her family suspects it has more to do with caffeine than creativity.

She and her twin wrote this book together, which gave them a chance to explore the bond, rivalry, and shared dreams that inspired Seraphina and Fadeya, capturing all that comes with being a twin.

www.ingramcontent.com/pod-product-compliance
Lightning Source LLC
Chambersburg PA
CBHW020656110726
47901CB00001B/209